HOLLY

By Stephen King and published by Hodder & Stoughton

STEPHEN KING

HOLLY

A NOVEL

HODDER &
STOUGHTON

First published in Great Britain in in 2023 by Hodder & Stoughton
An Hachette UK company

1

A CIP catalogue record for this title is available from the British Library

Hardback ISBN 978 1 399 71291 0
Trade Paperback ISBN 978 1 399 71292 7
eBook ISBN 978 1 444 73172 9

Typeset in Bembo by Palimpsest Book Production Ltd, Falkirk, Stirlingshire

Printed and bound in Great Britain by Clays Ltd, Elcograf S.p.A.

Hodder & Stoughton policy is to use papers that are natural, renewable
and recyclable products and made from wood grown in sustainable forests.
The logging and manufacturing processes are expected to conform to
the environmental regulations of the country of origin.

Hodder & Stoughton Ltd
Carmelite House
50 Victoria Embankment
London EC4Y 0DZ

www.hodder.co.uk

This is for Chuck Verrill:
Editor, agent, and most of all, friend.
1951–2022
Thanks, Chuck.

'Sometimes the universe throws you a rope.'
— Bill Hodges

HOLLY

October 17, 2012

1

It's an old city, and no longer in very good shape, nor is the lake beside which it has been built, but there are parts of it that are still pretty nice. Longtime residents would probably agree that the nicest section is Sugar Heights, and the nicest street running through it is Ridge Road, which makes a gentle downhill curve from Bell College of Arts and Sciences to Deerfield Park, two miles below. On its way, Ridge Road passes many fine houses, some of which belong to college faculty and some to the city's more successful businesspeople – doctors, lawyers, bankers, and top-of-the-pyramid business executives. Most of these homes are Victorians, with impeccable paintjobs, bow windows, and lots of gingerbread trim.

The park where Ridge Road terminates isn't as big as the one that sits splat in the middle of Manhattan, but close. Deerfield is the city's pride, and a platoon of gardeners keep it looking fabulous. Oh, there's the unkempt west side near Red Bank Avenue, known as the Thickets, where those seeking or selling drugs can sometimes be found after dark, and where there's the occasional mugging, but the Thickets is only three acres of 740. The rest are grassy, flowery, and threaded with paths where lovers stroll and benches where old men read newspapers (more and more often on electronic devices these days) and women chat, sometimes while rocking their babies back and forth in expensive prams. There are two ponds, and sometimes you'll see men or boys sailing remote-controlled boats on one of them. In the other, swans and ducks glide back and forth. There's a playground for the kiddies, too. Everything, in fact, except a public pool; every now and then the city council discusses the idea, but it keeps getting tabled. The expense, you know.

This night in October is warm for the time of year, but a fine drizzle has kept all but a single dedicated runner inside. That would be Jorge Castro, who has a gig teaching creative writing and Latin American Lit at the college. Despite his specialty, he's American born and bred; Jorge likes to tell people he's as American as *pie de manzana*.

He turned forty in July and can no longer kid himself that he is still the young lion who had momentary bestseller success with his first novel. Forty is when you have to stop kidding yourself that you're still a young anything. If you don't – if you subscribe to such self-actualizing bullshit as 'forty is the new twenty-five' – you're going to find yourself starting to slide. Just a little at first, but then a little more, and all at once you're fifty with a belly poking out your belt buckle and choles-terol-busters in the medicine cabinet. At twenty, the body forgives. At forty, forgiveness is provisional at best. Jorge Castro doesn't want to turn fifty and discover he's become just another American manslob.

You have to start taking care of yourself when you're forty. You have to maintain the machinery, because there's no trade-in option. So Jorge drinks orange juice in the morning (potassium) followed most days by oatmeal (antioxidants), and keeps red meat to once a week. When he wants a snack, he's apt to open a can of sardines. They're rich in Omega 3s. (Also tasty!) He does simple exercises in the morning and runs in the evening, not overdoing it but aerating those forty-year-old lungs and giving his forty-year-old heart a chance to strut its stuff (resting heart rate: 63). Jorge wants to look and feel forty when he gets to fifty, but fate is a joker. Jorge Castro isn't even going to see forty-one.

2

His routine, which holds even on a night of fine drizzle, is to run from the house he shares with Freddy (theirs, at least, for as long as the writer-in-residence gig lasts), half a mile down from the college, to the park. There he'll stretch his back, drink some of the Vitaminwater stored in his fanny pack, and jog back home. The drizzle is actually invigorating, and there are no other runners, walkers, or bicyclists to

weave his way through. The bicyclists are the worst, with their insist-
ence that they have every right to ride on the sidewalk instead of in
the street, even though there's a bike lane. This evening he has the
sidewalk all to himself. He doesn't even have to wave to people who
might be taking the night air on their grand old shaded porches; the
weather has kept them inside.

All but one: the old poet. She's bundled up in a parka even though
it's still in the mid-fifties at eight o'clock, because she's down to a
hundred and ten pounds (her doctor routinely scolds her about her
weight) and she feels the cold. Even more than the cold, she feels
the damp. Yet she stays, because there's a poem to be had tonight, if
she can just get her fingers under its lid and open it up. She hasn't
written one since midsummer and she needs to get something going
before the rust sets in. She needs to *represent*, as her students sometimes say. More importantly, this could be a *good* poem. Maybe even
a *necessary* poem.

It needs to begin with the way the mist revolves around the street-
lights across from her and then progress to what she thinks of as *the
mystery*. Which is everything. The mist makes slowly moving halos,
silvery and beautiful. She doesn't want to use *halos*, because that's the
expected word, the lazy word. Almost a cliché. *Silvery*, though . . . or
maybe just silver . . .

Her train of thought derails long enough to observe a young man
(at eighty-nine, forty seems very young) go slap-slapping by on the
other side of the road. She knows who he is; the resident writer who
thinks Gabriel García Márquez hung the moon. With his long dark
hair and little pussy-tickler of a mustache, he reminds the old poet of
a charming character in *The Princess Bride*: 'My name is Inigo Montoya,
you killed my father, prepare to die.' He's wearing a yellow jacket with
a reflective stripe running down the back and ridiculously tight running
pants. He's going like a house afire, the old poet's mother might have
said. Or like the clappers.

Clappers makes her think of bells, and her gaze returns to the
streetlight directly across from her. She thinks, *The runner doesn't hear
silver above him / These bells don't ring.*

It's wrong because it's prosy, but it's a start. She has managed to get
her fingers under the lid of the poem. She needs to go inside, get her

notebook, and start scratching. She sits a few moments longer, though, watching the silver circles revolve around the streetlights. *Halos*, she thinks. *I can't use that word, but that's what they look like, goddammit.*

There is a final glimpse of the runner's yellow jacket, then he's gone into the dark. The old poet struggles to her feet, wincing at the pain in her hips, and shuffles into her house.

3

Jorge Castro kicks it up a bit. He's got his second wind now, lungs taking in more air, endorphins lit up. Just ahead is the park, scattered with old-fashioned lamps that give off a mystic yellow glow. There's a small parking lot in front of the deserted playground, now empty except for a passenger van with its side door open and a ramp sticking out onto the wet asphalt. Near its foot is an elderly man in a wheelchair and an elderly woman down on one knee, fussing with it.

Jorge pulls up for a moment, bending over, hands grasping his legs just above the knees, getting his breath back and checking out the van. The blue and white license plate on the back has a wheelchair logo on it.

The woman, who is wearing a quilted coat and a kerchief, looks over at him. At first Jorge isn't sure he knows her – the light in this small auxiliary parking lot isn't that good. 'Hello! Got a problem?'

She stands up. The old guy in the wheelchair, dressed in a button-up sweater and flat cap, gives a feeble wave.

'The battery died,' the woman says. 'It's Mr Castro, isn't it? Jorge?'

Now he recognizes her. It's Professor Emily Harris, who teaches English literature . . . or did; she might now be emerita. And that's her husband, also a teacher. He didn't realize Harris was disabled, hasn't seen him around campus much, different department in a different building, but believes the last time he did, the old guy was walking. Jorge sees her quite often at various faculty get-togethers and culture-vulture events. Jorge has an idea he's not one of her favorite people, especially after the departmental meeting about the now-defunct Poetry Workshop. That one got a little contentious.

'Yes, it's me,' he says. 'I'm assuming you two would like to get home and dry off.'

'That would be nice,' Mr Harris says. Or maybe he's also a professor. His sweater is thin and he's shivering a little. 'Think you could push me up that ramp, kiddo?' He coughs, clears his throat, coughs again. His wife, so crisp and authoritative in department meetings, looks a bit lost and bedraggled. Forlorn. Jorge wonders how long they've been out here, and why she didn't call someone for help. *Maybe she doesn't have a phone*, he thinks. *Or left it at home. Old people can be forgetful about such things.* Although she can't be much more than seventy. Her husband in the wheelchair looks older.

'I think I can help with that. Brake off?'

'Yes, certainly,' Emily Harris says, and stands back when Jorge grabs the handles and swings the wheelchair around so it faces the ramp. He rolls it back ten feet, wanting to get a running start. Motorized wheelchairs can be heavy. The last thing he wants is to get it halfway up only to lose momentum and have it roll back. Or, God forbid, tip over the side and spill the old guy on the pavement.

'Here we go, Mr Harris. Hang on, there may be a bump.'

Harris grasps the side-rails, and Jorge notices how broad his shoulders are. They look muscular beneath the sweater. He guesses that people who lose the use of their legs compensate in other ways. Jorge speeds at the ramp.

'Hi-yo Silver!' Mr Harris cries cheerfully.

The first half of the ramp is easy, but then the chair starts to lose momentum. Jorge bends, puts his back into it, and keeps it rolling. As he does this neighborly chore, an odd thought comes to him: this state's license plates are red and white, and although the Harrises live on Ridge Road just like he does (he often sees Emily Harris out in her garden), the plates on their van are *blue* and white, like those of the neighboring state to the west. Something else that's strange: he can't remember ever seeing this van on the street before, although he's seen Emily sitting ramrod straight behind the wheel of a trim little Subaru with an Obama sticker on the back bum—

As he reaches the top of the ramp, bent almost horizontal now, arms outstretched and running shoes flexed, a bug stings the back of his neck. Feels like a big one from the way heat is spreading out from the source, maybe a wasp, and he's having a reaction. Never had one before but there's a first time for everything and all at once his vision is blurring and the strength is going out of his arms. His shoes slip on the wet ramp and he goes to one knee.

Wheelchair's going to backroll right on top of me—

But it doesn't. Rodney Harris flips a switch and the wheelchair rolls inside with a contented hum. Harris hops out, steps spryly around it, and looks down at the man kneeling on the ramp with his hair plastered to his forehead and drizzle wetting his cheeks like sweat. Then Jorge collapses on his face.

'Look at that!' Emily cries softly. 'Perfect!'

'Help me,' Rodney says.

His wife, wearing her own running shoes, takes Jorge's ankles. Her husband takes his arms. They haul him inside. The ramp retracts. Rodney (who really is also Professor Harris, as it happens) slides into the leftside captain's chair. Emily kneels and zip-ties Jorge's wrists together, although this is probably a needless precaution. Jorge is out like a light (a simile of which the old poet would surely disapprove) and snoring heavily.

'All good?' asks Rodney Harris, he of the Bell College Life Sciences Department.

'All good!' Emily's voice is cracking with excitement. 'We did it, Roddy! We caught the son of a bitch!'

'Language, dear,' Rodney says. Then he smiles. 'But yes. Indeed we did.' He pulls out of the parking lot and starts up the hill.

The old poet looks up from her work notebook, which has a picture of a tiny red wheelbarrow on the front, sees the van pass, and bends back to her poem.

The van turns in at 93 Ridge Road, home of the Harrises for almost twenty-five years. It belongs to them, not the college. One of the two garage doors goes up; the van enters the bay on the left; the garage door closes; all is once more still on Ridge Road. Mist revolves around the streetlights.

Like halos.

4

Jorge regains consciousness by slow degrees. His head is splitting, his mouth is dry, his stomach is sudsing. He has no idea how much he drank, but it must have been plenty to have a hangover this horrible. And where did he drink it? A faculty party? A writing seminar get-together where he unwisely decided to imbibe like the student he once was? Did he get drunk after the latest argument with Freddy? None of those things seem right.

He opens his eyes, ready for morning glare that will send another blast of pain through his poor abused head, but the light is soft. Kind light, considering his current state of distress. He seems to be lying on a futon or yoga mat. There's a bucket beside it, a plastic floorbucket that could have come from Walmart or Dollar Tree. He knows what it's there for, and all at once he also knows what Pavlov's dogs must have felt like when the bell rang, because he only has to look at that bucket for his belly to go into spasm. He gets on his knees and throws up violently. There's a pause, long enough to take a couple of breaths, and then he does it again.

His stomach settles, but for a moment his head aches so fiercely he thinks it will split open and fall in two pieces to the floor. He closes his watering eyes and waits for the pain to subside. Eventually it does, but the taste of vomit in his mouth and nose is rancid. Eyes still closed, he fumbles for the bucket and spits into it until his mouth is at least partially clear.

He opens his eyes again, raises his head (cautiously), and sees bars. He's in a cage. It's roomy, but it's a cage, all right. Beyond it is a long room. The overhead lights must be on a rheostat, because the room is dim. He sees a concrete floor that looks clean enough to eat off of − not that he feels like eating. The half of the room in front of the cage is empty. In the middle is a flight of stairs. There's a push broom leaning against them. Beyond the stairs is a well-equipped workshop with tools hung on pegs and a bandsaw table. There's also a compound miter saw − nice tool, not cheap. Several hedge trimmers and clippers. An array of wrenches, carefully hung from biggest to smallest. A line of chrome sockets on a worktable beside a door going . . . somewhere. All the usual home handyman shit, and everything looking well-maintained.

There's no sawdust under the bandsaw table. Beyond it is a piece of machinery he's never seen before: big and yellow and boxy, almost the size of an industrial HVAC unit. Jorge decides that's what it must be, because there's a rubber hose going through one paneled wall, but he's never seen one like it. If there's a brand name, it's on the side he can't see.

He looks around the cage, and what he sees scares him. It isn't so much the bottles of Dasani water standing on an orange crate serving as a table. It's the blue plastic box squatting in the corner, beneath the sloping ceiling. That's a Porta-John, the kind invalids use when they can still get out of bed but aren't able to make it all the way to the nearest bathroom.

Jorge doesn't feel capable of standing yet, so he crawls to it and lifts the lid. He sees blue water in the bowl and gets a whiff of disinfectant strong enough to make his eyes start watering again. He closes it and knee-walks back to the futon. Even in his current fucked-up state, he knows what the Porta-John means: someone intends for him to be here awhile. He has been kidnapped. Not by one of the cartels, as in his novel, *Catalepsy*, and not in Mexico or Colombia, either. Crazy as it seems, he has been kidnapped by a couple of elderly professors, one of them a colleague. And if this is their basement, he's not far from his own house, where Freddy would be reading in the living room and having a cup of—

But no. Freddy is gone, at least for now. Left after the latest argument, in his usual huff.

He examines the crisscrossed bars. They are steel, and neatly welded. It must be a job done in this very workshop – there's certainly no Jail Cells R Us that such an item could be ordered from – but the bars look solid enough. He grabs one in both hands and shakes it. No give.

He looks at the ceiling and sees white panels drilled with small holes. Soundproofing. He sees something else, too: a glass eye peering down. Jorge turns his face up to it.

'Are you there? What do you want?'

Nothing. He considers shouting to be let out, but what would that accomplish? Do you put someone in a basement cage (it must be the basement) with a puke bucket and a Porta-John if you mean to come running down the stairs at the first shout, saying *Sorry, sorry, big mistake*?

He needs to pee – his back teeth are floating. He gets to his feet, helping his legs by holding onto the bars. Another bolt of pain goes through his head, but not quite as bad as the ones he felt when he swam back to consciousness. He shuffles to the Porta-John, lifts the lid, unzips, and tries to go. At first he can't, no matter how bad the need. Jorge has always been private about his bathroom functions, avoids herd urinals when he goes to the ballpark, and he keeps thinking of that glass eye staring at him. His back is turned, and that helps a little but not enough. He counts how many days are left in this month, then how many days until Christmas, good old *feliz navidad*, and that does the trick. He pisses for almost a full minute, then grabs one of the Dasani bottles. He swirls the first mouthful around and spits it into the disinfected water, then gulps the rest.

He goes back to the bars and looks across the long room: the vacant half just beyond the cage, the stairs, then the workshop. It's the bandsaw and the miter saw his eyes keep coming back to. Maybe not nice tools for a caged man to be contemplating, but hard not to look at them. Hard not to think of the high whine a bandsaw like that makes when it's chewing through pine or cedar: *YRRRROWWWWW.*

He remembers his run through the misty drizzle. He remembers Emily and her husband. He remembers how they deked him and then shot him up with something. After that there's nothing but a swatch of black until he woke up here.

Why? Why would they do a thing like that?

'Do you want to talk?' he calls to the glass eye. 'I'm ready when you are. Just tell me what you want!'

Nothing. The room is dead silent except for the shuffle of his feet and the *tink-tink* of the wedding ring he wears against one of the bars. Not his ring; he and Freddy aren't married. At least not yet, and maybe never, the way things are going. Jorge slipped the ring off his father's finger in the hospital, minutes after Papi died. He has worn it ever since.

How long has he been here? He looks at his watch, but that's no good; it's a wind-up, another remembrance he took when his father died, and it has stopped at one fifteen. AM or PM, he doesn't know. And he can't remember the last time he wound it.

The Harrises. Emily and Ronald. Or is it Robert? He knows who they are, and that's kind of ominous, isn't it?

It might *be ominous*, he tells himself.

Since there's no sense shouting or screaming in a soundproof room – and it would bring his headache back, raving – he sits down on the futon and waits for something to happen. For someone to come and explain what the fuck.

5

The stuff they shot him up with must still be floating around in his head because Jorge falls into a doze, head down and spittle slipping from one corner of his mouth. Sometime later – still one fifteen according to his Papi's watch – a door opens up above and someone starts down the stairs. Jorge raises his head (another bolt of pain, but not so bad) and sees black lowtop sneakers, ankle socks, trim brown pants, then a flowered apron. It's Emily Harris. With a tray.

Jorge stands up. 'What is going on here?'

She doesn't answer, only sets the tray down about two feet from the cage. On it is a bulgy brown envelope stuck into the top of a big plastic go-cup, the kind you fill with coffee for a long drive. Next to it is a plate with something nasty on it: a slab of dark red meat floating in even darker red liquid. Just looking at it makes Jorge feel like vomiting again.

'If you think I'm going to eat that, Emily, think again.'

She makes no reply, only takes the broom and pushes the tray along the concrete. There's a hinged flap in the bottom of the cage (*they've been planning this*, Jorge thinks). The go-cup falls over when it hits the top of the flap, which is only four inches or so high, then the tray goes through. The flap claps shut when she pulls the broom back. The meat swimming in the puddle of blood looks to be uncooked liver. Emily Harris straightens up, puts the broom back, turns . . . and gives him a smile. As if they are at a fucking cocktail party, or something.

'I'm not going to eat that,' Jorge repeats.

'You will,' she says.

With that she goes back up the stairs. He hears a door close, followed by a snapping sound that's probably a bolt being run.

Looking at the raw liver makes Jorge feel like yurking some more, but he takes the envelope out of the go-cup. It's something called

Ka'Chava. According to the label, the powder inside makes 'a nutri-ent-dense drink that fuels your adventures.'

Jorge feels he's had enough adventures in the last however-long to last a lifetime. He puts the packet back in the go-cup and sits on the futon. He pushes the tray to one side without looking at it. He closes his eyes.

6

He dozes, wakes, dozes again, then wakes for real. The headache is almost gone and his stomach has settled. He winds Papi's watch and sets it for noon. Or maybe for midnight. Doesn't matter; at least he can keep track of how long he's here. Eventually, someone — maybe the male half of this crazy professor combo — will tell him *why* he's here and what he has to do to get out. Jorge guesses it won't make a whole lot of sense, because these two are obviously loco. *Lots* of professors are loco, he's been in enough schools on the writer-in-residence circuit to know that — but the Harrises take it to a whole other level.

Eventually he plucks the packet of Ka'Chava from the go-cup, which is obviously meant for mixing the stuff up with the remaining bottle of Dasani. The cup is from Dillon's, a truck stop in Redlund where Jorge and Freddy sometimes have breakfast. He would like to be there now. He'd like to be in Ayers Chapel, listening to one of Reverend Gallatin's boring-ass sermons. He'd like to be in a doctor's office, waiting for a proctological exam. He would like to be anywhere but here.

He has no reason to trust anything the crazy Harrises give him, but now that the nausea's worn off, he's hungry. He always eats light before running, saving a heavier caloric intake for when he comes back. The envelope is sealed, which means it's probably okay, but he looks it over carefully for pinpricks (*hypo* pricks) before tearing it open and pouring it into the go-cup. He adds water, closes the lid, and shakes well, as the instructions say. He tastes, then chugs. He doubts very much if it has been inspired by 'ancient wisdom,' as the label says, but it's fairly tasty. Chocolate. Like a frappé, if frappés were plant-based.

When it's gone, he looks at the raw liver again. He tries pushing the tray back out through the flap, but at first he can't, because the flap only swings in. He works his fingernails under the bottom and pulls it up. He shoves the tray out.

'Hey!' he shouts at the glass eye peering down at him. 'Hey, what do you want? Let's talk! Let's work this out!'

Nothing.

7

Six hours pass.

This time it's the male Harris who descends the stairs. He's in pajamas and slippers. His shoulders are broad but he's skinny the rest of the way down, and the pajamas – decorated with firetrucks, like a child's – flap on him. Just looking at this old dude gives Jorge Castro a sense of unreality – can this really be happening?

'What do you want?'

Harris makes no reply, only looks at the rejected tray on the concrete floor. He looks at the flap, then back to the tray. A couple more times for good measure: tray, flap, flap, tray. Then he goes to the broom and pushes it back in.

Jorge has had enough. He holds the flap and shoves the tray back out. The blood-puddle splashes one cuff of Harris's PJ bottoms. Harris lowers the broom to push it back, then decides that would be a zero-sum game. He leans the broom against the side of the stairs again and prepares to mount them. There's not much to him below those broad shoulders, but the deceitful motherfucker looks agile enough.

'Come back,' Jorge says. 'Let's talk about this man to man.'

Harris looks at him and gives the sigh of a longsuffering parent dealing with a recalcitrant toddler. 'You can get the tray when you want it,' he says. 'I believe we've established that.'

'I'm not eating it, I already told your wife. Besides being raw, it's been sitting at room temperature for . . .' He looks at Papi's watch. 'Over six hours.'

The crazy professor makes no reply to this, only climbs the stairs. The door shuts. The bolt runs. *Snap.*

8

It's ten o'clock by Papi's watch when Emily comes down. She's swapped the trim brown pants for a floral wrapper and her own pair of slippers. *Can it be the next night?* Jorge thinks. *Is that possible? How long did that shot put me out?* Somehow the loss of time is even more upsetting than looking at that congealing glob of meat. Losing time is hard to get used to. But there's something else he can't get used to.

She looks at the tray. Looks at him. Smiles. Turns to go.

'Hey,' he says. 'Emily.'

She doesn't turn around, but she stops at the foot of the stairs, listening.

'I need some more water. I drank one bottle and used the other to mix that shake with. It was pretty good, by the way.'

'No more water until you eat your dinner,' she says, and climbs the stairs.

9

Time passes. Four hours. His thirst is becoming very bad. He's not dying of it or anything, but there's no doubt he's dehydrated from vomiting, and that shake . . . he can feel it coating the sides of his throat. A drink of water would wash that away. Even just a sip or two.

He looks at the Porta-John, but he's a long way from trying to drink disinfected water. *Which I have now pissed in twice*, he thinks.

He looks up at the lens. 'Let's talk, okay? Please.' He hesitates, then says, 'I'm begging you.' He hears a crack in his voice. A *dry* crack.

Nothing.

10

Two more hours.

Now the thirst is all he can think about. He's read stories about how men adrift on the ocean finally start drinking what they're floating on, even though drinking seawater is a quick trip to madness. That's the story, anyway, and whether it's true or false doesn't matter in his current situation because there's no ocean for almost a thousand miles. There's nothing here but the poison in the Porta-John.

At last Jorge gives in. He works his fingers under the flap, props himself on one arm, and reaches for the tray. At first he can't quite grasp it because the edge is slippery with juice. Instead of pulling it toward him, he only succeeds in pushing it a little further out on the concrete. He strains and finally pinches a grip. He pulls the tray through the flap. He looks at the meat, as red as raw muscle, then closes his eyes and picks it up. It flops against his wrists, cold. Eyes still closed, he takes a bite. His gorge starts to spasm.

Don't think about it, he tells himself. *Just chew and swallow.*

It goes down like a raw oyster. Or a mouthful of phlegm. He opens his eyes and looks up at the glass lens. It's blurry because he's crying. 'Is that enough?'

Nothing. And it really wasn't a bite, only a nibble. There's so much left.

'*Why?*' he shouts. 'Why would you? What *purpose?*'

Nothing. Maybe there's no speaker, but Jorge doesn't believe that. He thinks they can hear him as well as see him, and if they can hear him, they can reply.

'I can't,' he says, crying harder. 'I would if I could, but I fucking *can't.*'

Yet he discovers that he can. Bite by bite, he eats the raw liver. The gag reflex is bad at first, but eventually it goes away.

Only that's not right, Jorge thinks as he looks at the puddle of congealing red jelly on the otherwise empty plate. *It didn't go away, I beat it into submission.*

He holds the plate up to the glass eye. At first there's more nothing, then the door to the upstairs world opens and the woman descends. Her hair is in rollers. There's some sort of night cream on her face. In one hand she holds a bottle of Dasani water. She puts it down on the concrete, out of Jorge's reach, then grabs the broom.

'Drink the juice,' she says.

'Please,' Jorge whispers. 'Please don't. Please stop.'

Professor Emily Harris of the English Department – perhaps now emerita, just teaching the occasional class or seminar as well as attending departmental meetings – says nothing. The calm in her eyes is, for

Jorge, the convincer. It's like the old blues song says: *cryin and pleadin don't do no good.*

He tilts the plate and slides the jellied juice into his mouth. A few drops splash onto his shirt, but most of the blood goes down his throat. It's salty and makes his thirst worse. He shows her the plate, empty except for a few red smears. He expects her to tell him to eat that, too – to scoop it up with his finger and suck it like a clot lollipop – but she doesn't. She tips the bottle of Dasani on its side and uses the push broom to roll it to the flap and through. Jorge seizes it, twists the cap, and drinks half in a series of gulps.

Ecstasy!

She leans the broom back against the side of the stairs and starts up.

'What do you want? Tell me what you want and I'll do it! Swear to God!'

She pauses for a moment, long enough to say a single word: '*Maricon*.' Then she continues up the stairs. The door shuts. The lock snaps.

July 22, 2021

1

Zoom has gotten sophisticated since the advent of Covid-19. When Holly started using it – in February of 2020, which seems much longer than seventeen months ago – it was apt to drop the connection if you so much as looked at it crosseyed. Sometimes you could see your fellow Zoomers; sometimes you couldn't; sometimes they flickered back and forth in a headache-inducing frenzy.

Quite the movie fan is Holly Gibney (although she hasn't been in an actual theater since the previous spring), and she enjoys Hollywood tentpole movies every bit as much as art films. One of her faves from the eighties is *Conan the Barbarian*, and her favorite line from that film is spoken by a minor character. 'Two or three years ago,' the peddler says of Set and his followers, 'they were just another snake cult. Now they're everywhere.'

Zoom is sort of like that. In 2019 it was just another app, struggling for breathing room with competitors like FaceTime and GoTo Meeting. Now, thanks to Covid, Zoom is as ubiquitous as the Snake Cult of Set. It's not just the tech that's improved, either. Production values have, as well. The Zoom funeral Holly is attending could almost be a scene in a TV drama. The focus is on each speaker eulogizing the dear departed, of course, but there are also occasional cuts to various grieving mourners in their homes.

Not to Holly, though. She's blocked her video. She's a better, stronger person than she once was, but she's still a deeply private person. She knows it's okay for people to be sad at funerals, to cry and choke up, but she doesn't want anyone to see her that way, especially not her business partner or her friends. She doesn't want them to see her red eyes, her tangled hair, or her shaking hands as she reads her own eulogy, which is both short and as honest as she could make it. Most of all she doesn't want them to see her smoking a cigarette — after seventeen months of Covid, she's fallen off the wagon.

Now, at the end of the service, her screen begins showing a kinescope featuring the dear departed in various poses at various locations while Frank Sinatra sings 'Thanks for the Memory.' Holly can't stand it and clicks LEAVE. She takes one more drag on her cigarette, and as she's butting it out, her phone rings.

She doesn't want to talk to anyone, but it's Barbara Robinson, and that's a call she has to take.

'You left,' Barbara says. 'Not even a black square with your name on it.'

'I've never cared for that particular song. And it was over, anyway.'

'But you're okay, right?'

'Yes.' Not exactly true; Holly doesn't know if she's okay or not. 'But right now, I need to . . .' What's the word that Barbara will accept? That will enable Holly to end this call before she breaks down? 'I need to process.'

'Understood,' Barbara says. 'I'll come over in a heartbeat if you want, lockdown or no lockdown.'

It's a *de facto* lockdown instead of a real one, and they both know it; their governor is determined to protect individual freedoms no matter how many thousands have to sicken or die to support the idea. Most people are taking precautions anyway, thank God.

'No need for that.'

'Okay. I know this is bad, Hols — a bad time — but hang in there. We've been through worse.' Maybe — almost certainly — thinking about Chet Ondowsky, who took a short and lethal trip down an elevator shaft late last year. 'And booster vaccines are coming. First for people with bad immune systems and people over sixty-five, but I'm hearing at school that by fall it'll be everyone.'

'That sounds right,' Holly says.

'And bonus! Trump's gone.'

Leaving behind a country at war with itself, Holly thinks. And who's to say he won't reappear in 2024? She thinks of Arnie's promise from *The Terminator*: 'I'll be back.'

'Hols? You there?'

'I am. Just thinking.' Thinking about another cigarette, as it happens. Now that she's started again she can't seem to get enough of them.

'Okay. I love you, and I understand you need your space, but if you don't call back tonight or tomorrow I'll call you again. Fair warning.'

'Roger that,' Holly says, and ends the call.

She reaches for her cigarettes, then pushes them away and puts her head down on her crossed arms and begins to cry. She's cried so much lately. Tears of relief after Biden won the election. Tears of horror and belated reaction after Chet Ondowsky, a monster pretending to be human, went down the elevator shaft. She cried during and after the Capitol riot – those were tears of rage. Today, tears of grief and loss. Except they are also tears of relief. That's awful, but she supposes it's also human.

In March of 2020, Covid swept through almost all of the nursing homes in the state where Holly grew up and can't seem to leave. That wasn't a problem for Holly's Uncle Henry, because at that time he was still living with Holly's mother in Meadowbrook Estates. Even then Uncle Henry had been losing his marbles, a fact of which Holly had been blissfully unaware. He'd seemed pretty much okay on her occasional visits, and Charlotte Gibney kept her own concerns about her brother strictly to herself, following one of the great unspoken rules of that lady's life: if you don't talk about something, if you don't acknowledge it, it isn't there. Holly supposes that's why her mother never sat her down and had The Conversation with her when she was thirteen and started to develop breasts.

By December of last year Charlotte was no longer able to ignore the elephant in the room, which was no elephant but her gaga older brother. Around the time Holly was beginning to suspect Chet Ondowsky might be something more than a local TV reporter, Charlotte enlisted her daughter and her daughter's friend Jerome to help her transport Uncle Henry to the Rolling Hills Elder Care facility. This was around the time the first cases of the so-called Delta variant began to appear in the United States.

A Rolling Hills orderly tested positive for this new and more communicable version of Covid. The orderly had refused the vaccinations, claiming they contained bits of fetal tissue from aborted babies – he had read this on the Internet. He was sent home, but the damage was done. Delta was loose in Rolling Hills, and soon over forty of the oldies were suffering various degrees of the illness. A dozen died. Holly's Uncle Henry wasn't one of them. He didn't even get sick. He had been double-vaxxed – Charlotte protested but Holly insisted – and although he tested positive, he never got so much as the sniffles.

It was Charlotte who died.

An avid Trump supporter – a fact she *trump*eted to her daughter at every opportunity – she refused to get the vaccinations or even to wear a mask. (Except, that was, at Kroger and her local bank branch, where they were required. The one Charlotte kept for those occasions was a bright red, with MAGA stamped on it.)

On July 4th, Charlotte attended an anti-mask rally in the state capital, waving a sign reading MY BODY MY CHOICE (a sentiment that did not keep her from being adamantly anti-abortion). On July 7th, she lost her sense of smell and gained a cough. On the 10th, she was admitted to Mercy Hospital, nine short blocks from Rolling Hills Elder Care, where her brother was doing fine . . . physically, at least. On the 15th, she was placed on a ventilator.

During Charlotte's final, brutally short illness, Holly visited via Zoom. To the very end Charlotte continued to claim that the Coronavirus was a hoax, and she just had a bad case of the flu. She died on the 20th, and only strings pulled by Holly's partner, Pete Huntley, prevented her body being stored in the refrigerated truck that was serving as an adjunct to the morgue. She was taken to the Crossman Funeral Home instead, where the funeral director had quickly arranged the Zoom funeral. A year and a half into the pandemic, he had plenty of ex-perience in such televised final rites.

Holly finally cries herself out. She thinks about watching a movie, but the idea has no appeal, which is a rarity. She thinks about lying down, but she's slept a lot since Charlotte died. She supposes that's how her mind is dealing with grief. She doesn't want to read a book, either. She doubts if she could keep track of the words.

There's a hole where her mother used to be, it's as simple as that. The two of them had a difficult relationship which only got worse when Holly started to pull away. Her success in doing that was largely down to Bill Hodges. Holly's grief was bad when Bill passed – pancreatic cancer – but the grief she feels now is somehow deeper, more complicated, because Charlotte Gibney was, tell the truth and shame the devil, a woman who specialized in smotherlove. At least when it came to her daughter. Their estrangement only got worse with Charlotte's wholehearted embrace of the ex-president. There had been few face-to-face visits in the last two years, the final one on the previous Christmas, when Charlotte cooked all of what she imagined were Holly's favorite foods, every one of which reminded Holly of her unhappy, lonely childhood.

She has two phones on her desk, her personal and her business. Finders Keepers has been busy during the time of the pandemic, although investigations have become rather tricky. The firm is shut down now, with messages on her office phone and Pete Huntley's saying the agency will be closed until August 1st. She considered adding 'because of a death in the family' and decided that was no one's business. When she checks the office phone now, it's only because she's on autopilot for the time being.

She sees she's gotten four calls during the forty minutes while she was attending her mother's funeral. All from the same number. The caller has also left four voicemails. Holly thinks briefly of simply erasing them, she has no more desire to take on a case than she has to watch a movie or read a book, but she can't do that any more than she can leave a picture hanging crooked or her bed unmade.

Listening doesn't render an obligation to call back, she tells herself, and pushes play for the first VM. It came in at 1:02 PM, just about the time the last Charlotte Gibney Show got going.

'Hello, this is Penelope Dahl. I know you're closed, but this is very important. An emergency, in fact. I hope you'll call me back as soon as possible. Your agency was suggested to me by Detective Isabelle Jaynes—'

That's where the message ends. Of course Holly knows who Izzy Jaynes is, she used to be Pete's partner when Pete was still on the cops, but that isn't what strikes her about the message. What hits, and hard, is how much Penelope Dahl sounds like Holly's late mother. It's not so much the voice as the palpable anxiety in the voice. Charlotte was almost always anxious about something, and she passed on that constant gnawing to her daughter like a virus. Like Covid, in fact.

Holly decides not to listen to the rest of Anxious Penelope's messages. The lady will have to wait. Pete sure isn't going to be doing any legwork for awhile; he tested positive for Covid a week before Charlotte died. He was double-vaxxed and isn't too sick – says it's more like a heavy cold than the flu – but he's quarantining and will be for some time to come.

Holly stands at the living room window of her tidy little apartment, looking down at the street and remembering that last meal with her mother. *An authentic Christmas dinner, just like in the old days!* Charlotte had said, cheery and excited on top but with that constant anxiety pulsing away underneath. The authentic Christmas dinner had consisted of dry turkey, lumpy mashed potatoes, and flabby spears of asparagus. Oh, and thimble glasses of Mogen David wine to toast with. How terrible that meal had been, and how terrible that it had been their last. Did Holly say *I love you, Mom* before she drove away the next morning? She thinks so but can't remember for sure. All she can remember for sure is the relief she felt when she turned the first corner and her mother's house was no longer in the rearview mirror.

2

Holly has left her cigarettes by her desktop computer. She goes back to get them, shakes one out, lights it, looks at the office phone in its charging cradle, sighs, and listens to Penelope Dahl's second message. It starts on a note of disapproval.

'This is a very short space for messages, Ms Gibney. I'd like to talk to you, or Mr Huntley, or both of you, about my daughter Bonnie. She disappeared three weeks ago, on the first of July. The police investigation was *very* superficial. I told Detective Jaynes that, right to her—'

End of message. 'Told Izzy right to her face,' Holly says, and jets smoke from her nostrils. Men are often captivated by Izzy's red hair (salon-enhanced these days, no doubt) and her misty gray eyes, women less frequently. But she's a good detective. Holly has decided that if Pete retires, as he keeps threatening to do, she'll try to lure Isabelle away from the cops and over to the dark side.

There's no hesitation about going to the third message. Holly has to see how the story ends. Although she can guess. Chances are good that Bonnie Dahl is a runaway, and her mother can't accept that. Penelope Dahl's voice returns.

'Bonnie is an assistant librarian on the Bell campus. At the Reynolds? It opened again in June for the summer students, although of course you have to wear a mask to enter, and I suppose soon you'll have to show a vaccination card as well, although so far they haven't—'

Message ends. *Would you get to the point, lady?* Holly thinks, and punches up the last one. Penelope talks faster, almost speed-rapping.

'She rides her bike to and from her job. I've told her how unsafe that is, but she says she wears her helmet, as if *that* would save her from a bad crash or getting hit by a car. She stopped at the Jet Mart for a soda and that's the last . . .' Penelope begins to cry. It's hard to listen to. Holly takes a monster drag on her cigarette, then mashes it out. 'The last time she was seen. Please help—'

Message ends.

Holly has been standing, holding the office phone in her hand, listening on speaker. Now she sits and slots the phone back in its cradle. For the first time since Charlotte got sick – no, since the time when Holly realized she wasn't going to get better – Holly's grief takes a back seat to these bite-sized messages. She'd like to hear the whole story, or as much of it as Anxious Penelope knows. Pete probably doesn't know, either, but she decides to give him a call. What else does she have to do, except think about her last few video visits with her mother, and how frightened Charlotte's eyes were as the ventilator helped her breathe?

Pete answers on the first ring, his voice raspy. 'Hey, Holly. So sorry about your mom.'

'Thank you.'

'You gave a great eulogy. Short but sweet. I only wish I could have . . .' He breaks off as a coughing fit strikes. '. . . only wish I could have seen you. What was it, some kind of computer glitch?'

Holly could say it was, but she makes it a habit to tell the truth except on those rare occasions when she feels she absolutely can't. 'No glitch, I just turned off the video. I'm kind of a mess. How are you feeling, Pete?'

She can hear the rattle of phlegm as he sighs. 'Not terrible, but I was better yesterday. Jesus, I hope I'm not going to be one of those long haulers.'

'Have you called your doctor?'

He gives a hoarse laugh. 'I might as well try to call Pope Francis. You know how many new cases there were in the city yesterday? Thirty-four hundred. It's going up exponentially.' There's another coughing fit.

'Maybe the ER?'

'I'll stick with juice and Tylenol. The worst part of it is how fucking *tired* I am all the time. Every trip to the kitchen is a trek. When I go to the bathroom, I have to sit down and pee like a girl. If that's too much information, I apologize.'

It is, but Holly doesn't say so. She didn't think she had to worry about Pete, breakthrough cases usually aren't serious, but maybe she *does* have to worry.

'Did you call just to bat the breeze, or did you want something?'

'I don't want to bother you if—'

'Go ahead, bother me. Give me something to think about besides myself. Please. Are *you* okay? Not sick?'

'I'm fine. Did you get a call from a woman named—'

'Penny Dahl. Right? She's left four messages on my company voice-mail so far.'

'Four on mine, too. You didn't get back to her?'

Holly knows he didn't. What she knows is this: Anxious Penelope looked on the Finders Keepers website, or maybe Facebook, and found two office numbers for two partners, one male and one female. Anxious Penelope called the male, because when you've got a problem – an emergency, she termed it – you don't ask for help from the mare, at least not at first. You call the stallion. Calling the mare is your fallback position. Holly is used to being the mare in the Finders Keepers stable.

Pete sighs again, producing that disturbing rattle. 'In case you forgot, we're closed, Hols. And feeling like shit, as I currently do, I didn't think talking to a weepy-ass divorced mom would make me feel any better. Having just lost your own mom, I don't think it would make you feel any better, either. Wait until August, that's my advice. My strong advice. By then the girl may have called Momzie from Fort

Wayne or Phoenix or San Fran.' He coughs some more, then adds: 'Or the cops will have found her body.'

'You sound like you know *something*, even if you didn't talk to the mother. Was it in the paper?'

'Oh yeah, it was a big story. Stop the presses, extra, extra, read all about it. Two lines in the Police Beat between a naked man passed out on Cumberland Avenue and a rabid fox wandering around in the City Center parking lot. There's nothing else in the paper these days except Covid and people arguing about masks. Which is like people standing out in the rain and arguing about whether or not they're getting wet.' He pauses, then adds rather reluctantly, 'The lady's voice-mail said Izzy caught the squeal, so I gave her a call.'

Smiles have been in short supply for Holly this summer, but she feels one on her face now. It's nice to know that she's not the only one addicted to the job.

It's as if Pete can see her, even though they're not Zooming. 'Don't make a big deal of it, okay? I needed to catch up with Iz anyway, see how she's doing.'

'And?'

'Covid-wise she's fine. Shitcanned her latest boyfriend is all, and I got a fair amount of wah-wah-wah about that. I asked her about this Bonnie Dahl. Izzy says they're treating it as a missing persons case. There are some good reasons for that. Neighbors say Dahl and her mother argued a lot, some real blow-outs, and there was a buh-bye note taped to the seat of Dahl's ten-speed. But the note struck the mom as ominous, and Izzy as ambiguous.'

'What did it say?'

'Just three words. *I've had enough*. Which could mean she left town, or—'

'Or that she committed suicide. What do her friends say about her state of mind? Or the people she works with at the library?'

'No idea,' Pete says, and starts coughing again. 'That's where I left it and it's where you should leave it, at least for now. Either the case will still be there on August first, or it will have solved itself.'

'One way or the other,' Holly says.

'Right. One way or the other.'

'Where was the bike found? Ms Dahl said her daughter got a soda at Jet Mart the night she disappeared. Was it there?' Holly can think of at least three Jet Mart convenience stores in the city, and there are probably more.

'Again, I have no idea. I'm going to lie down for awhile. And again, I'm sorry your mother passed.'

'Thanks. If you don't start to improve, I want you to seek medical attention. Promise me.'

'You're nagging, Holly.'

'Yes.' Another smile. 'I'm good at it, aren't I? Learned at my mother's knee. Now promise.'

'Okay.' He's probably lying. 'One other thing.'

'What?' She thinks it will be something about the case (that's already how she's thinking of it), but it's not.

'You'll never convince me that this Covid shit happened naturally, jumping to people from bats or baby crocodiles or whatever in some Chinese wet market. I don't know if it escaped from a research facility where they were brewing it up or if it got released on purpose, but as my grandfather would have said, t'aint natcherl.'

'Sounding kind of paranoid there, Pete.'

'You think? Listen, viruses mutate. It's their big survival skill. But they're just as apt to mutate into a less dangerous strain as one that's more dangerous. That's what happened with the Bird Flu. But this one just keeps getting worse. Delta infects people who've been double-vaxxed – I'm a case in point. And people who don't get really sick from Delta carry four times the viral load as the original version, which means they can pass it on even more easily. Does that sound random to you?'

'Hard to tell,' Holly says. What's easy to tell is when someone is riding a hobby horse. Pete is currently aboard his. 'Maybe the Delta variant will mutate into something weaker.'

'We'll find out, won't we? When the next one comes along. Which it will. In the meantime, shelve Penny Dahl and find something to watch on Netflix. It's what I'm going to do.'

'Probably good advice. Take care, Pete.' With that she ends the call.

She doesn't want to watch anything on Netflix (Holly thinks most of their movies, even those with big budgets, are weirdly mediocre) but her stomach is making tiny, tentative growls and she decides to pay attention. Something comforting. Maybe tomato soup and a grilled cheese sandwich. Pete's ideas about viruses are probably Internet bull-poop, but his advice about leaving Penelope 'Penny' Dahl alone is undoubtedly good.

She heats the soup, she makes the grilled cheese with plenty of mustard and just a dab of relish, the way she likes it, and she doesn't call Penelope Dahl.

3

At least not until seven that night. What keeps gnawing at her is the note taped to the seat of Bonnie Dahl's bicycle: *I've had enough.* There were lots of times when Holly thought of leaving a similar note and getting out of Dodge, but she never did. And there were times when she thought of ending it all – *pulling the pin*, Bill would have said – but she never thought of it seriously.

Well . . . maybe once or twice.

She calls Ms Dahl from her study, and the woman answers on the first ring. Eager and a little out of breath. 'Hello? Is this Finders Keepers?'

'Yes. Holly Gibney. How can I help, Ms Dahl?'

'Thank God you called. I thought you and Mr Huntley must be on vacation or something.'

As if, Holly thinks. 'Can you come to my office tomorrow, Ms Dahl? It's in—'

'The Frederick Building, I know. Of course. The police have been no help at all. Not at *all*. What time?'

'Would nine o'clock suit you?'

'Perfect. Thank you so much. My daughter was last seen at four minutes past eight on July first. There's video of her in a store where she—'

'We'll discuss all that tomorrow,' Holly says. 'But no guarantees, Ms Dahl. It's just me, I'm afraid. My partner is ill.'

'Oh my God, not Covid?'

'Yes, but a mild case.' Holly hopes it's mild. 'I only have a few questions for you now. You said on your message that Bonnie was last seen at a Jet Mart. There are quite a few of them around the city. Which of them was it?'

'The one near the park. On Red Bank Avenue. Do you know that area?'

'I do.' Holly has even gotten gas at that Jet Mart a time or two. 'And was that where her bike was found?'

'No, further down Red Bank. There's an empty building – well, there's a lot of empty buildings on that side of the park – but this one used to be a car repair shop, or something. Her bike was on its kick-stand, out in front.'

'No attempt to hide it?'

'No, no, nothing like that. The police detective I talked to, the Jaynes woman, said Bonnie might have wanted it found. She also said the bus and train depot is only a mile further along, right about where you get into downtown? But I said Bonnie wouldn't leave her bike and then walk the rest of the way, why would she? I mean it stands to *reason*.'

She's ramping up, getting into a hysterical rhythm Holly knows well. If she doesn't stop the woman now, Holly will be on the phone for an hour or more.

'Let me stop you right there, Ms Dahl—'

'Penny. Call me Penny.'

'Okay, Penny. We'll get into it tomorrow. Our rates are four hundred dollars a day, three-day minimum, plus expenses. Which I will itemize. I can take Master or Visa or your personal check. No Amex, they're—' *Poopy* is the word that comes naturally to Holly's mind. 'They're diffi-cult to deal with. Are you willing to proceed on that basis?'

'Yes, absolutely.' No hesitation at all. 'The Jaynes woman asked if Bonnie was feeling depressed, I know what she was thinking about, suicide is what she was thinking about, but Bonnie is a cheerful soul, even after her breakup with that dope she was so crazy about she got back on the sunny side after the first two or three weeks, well, maybe it was more like a month, but—'

'We'll talk tomorrow,' Holly repeats. 'You can tell me all about it. Fifth floor. And Penny?'

'Yes?'

'Wear a mask. An N95, if you have one. I can't help you if I get sick.'

'I will, I absolutely will. May I call you Holly?'

Holly tells Penny that would be fine and finally extracts herself from the call.

4

Mindful of Pete's suggestion, Holly tries a Netflix movie called *Blood Red Sky*, but when the scary stuff starts she turns it off. She has followed all the bloody exploits of Jason and Michael and Freddy, she can tell you the names of every movie in which Christopher Lee played the sanguinary Count, but after Brady Hartsfield and Chet Ondowsky – especially Ondowsky – she thinks she may have lost her taste for horror films.

She goes to the window and stands there looking out at the latening day, ashtray in one hand, cigarette in the other. What a nasty habit it is! She's already thinking about how much she'll want one during her meeting with Penny Dahl, because meeting new clients is always stressful for her. She's a good detective, has decided it's what she was born to do, her *calling*, but she leaves the initial meet-and-greets to Pete whenever possible. No way she can do that tomorrow. She thinks about asking Jerome Robinson to be there, but he's working on the editor's draft of a book about his great-grandfather, who was quite a character. Jerome would come if she asked, but she won't interrupt him. Time to suck it up.

No smoking in the building, either. I'll have to go out to the alley on the side once the Dahl woman's gone.

Holly knows this is how addicts think and behave: they rearrange the furniture of their lives to make room for their bad habits. Smoking is rotten and dangerous . . . but there's nothing more comforting than one of these deadly little tubes of paper and tobacco.

If the girl took the train, there'll be a record even if she paid cash. Same with Greyhound, Peter Pan, Magic Carpet, and Lux. But there are two fly-by-nighters on the next block that specialize in transient travel. Tri-State, and what's the other one?

She can't remember and she doesn't want to do an Internet search tonight. Plus who's to say that Bonnie Dahl left on a bus or Amtrak? She could have hitchhiked. Holly thinks of *It Happened One Night*, and how Claudette Colbert gets a ride for her and Clark Gable by hiking

up her skirt and adjusting a stocking. Things don't change that much
. . . only Bonnie Dahl didn't have a big strong man to protect her.
Unless, of course, she'd reconnected with the old boyfriend her mom
had mentioned.

No point picking at this now. There will probably be plenty to pick
at tomorrow. She hopes so, anyway. Penny Dahl's problem will give
her something to think about besides her mother's pointless, politics-
driven death.

I have Holly hope, she thinks, and goes into the bedroom to put on
her pajamas and say her prayers.

September 10, 2015

Cary Dressler is young, unattached, not bad-looking, cheerful, rarely prone to worrying about the future. He's currently sitting on a rocky outcrop covered with initials, high on good grass and sipping a P-Co' while he watches *Raiders of the Lost Ark*. On a weekend, this outcrop – known as Drive-In Rock – would be crowded with kids drinking beer, smoking weed, and grab-assing around, but this is a Thursday night and he has it all to himself. Which is how he likes it.

The Rock is on the west side of Deerfield Park, near the edge of the Thickets. This area is a tangle of trees and undergrowth. From most locations therein it would be impossible to see Red Bank Avenue, let alone the Magic City Drive-In screen, but here a ragged cut runs down to the street, maybe caused by flooding or a long-ago rockslide.

Magic City is barely hanging on these days, nobody wants to swat bugs and listen to the soundtrack on AM radio when there are three cineplexes spotted around the city, all with Dolby sound and one even with IMAX, which is kickin'. But you can't smoke weed in a cineplex. On Drive-In Rock, you can smoke all you want. And after an eight-hour shift at Strike Em Out Lanes, Cary wants. There's no sound, of course, but Cary doesn't need it. Magic City shows strictly second-, third-, and fourth-run movies these days, and he's seen *Raiders* at least ten times. He knows the dialogue and murmurs a snatch now, between tokes.

'Snakes! Why did it have to be snakes?'

Raiders will be followed by *Last Crusade*, which Cary has also seen many times – not as many as *Raiders*, but at least four. He won't stay for that one. He'll finish his P-Co', get on his moped (now stashed in the bushes near the park entrance closest to Drive-In Rock), and ride home. Very carefully.

His current joint is down to a nubbin. He butts it on the outcrop between BD+GL and MANDY SUCKS. He stores the roach, inspects the contents of his fanny pack, and debates between a skinny jay and a fatty. He decides on the jay. He'll smoke half of it, eat the Kit Kat bar also stashed in his fanny pack, then putt-putt his way back to his apartment.

He gets lost in the bright images playing out a quarter of a mile away and ends up smoking almost all of it. He hears the John Williams music in his head and vocalizes, keeping it on the down-low in case anyone else is nearby – unlikely at ten PM on a Thursday night, but not impossible.

'Zum-de-dum-dum, zum-de-DAH, zum-de-bum-zum, zum de—'

Cary stops abruptly. He just heard a voice . . . didn't he? He cocks his head to one side, listening. Maybe it was his imagination. Dope doesn't ordinarily make him paranoid, only mellow, but on occasion . . .

He's about decided it was nothing when the voice speaks up again. Not close, but not all that far away, either. 'It's the battery, hon. I think it's dead.'

There's nothing wrong with Cary's eyesight, and from his vantage point he quickly spots the location of that voice. Red Bank Avenue will never be in the running as one of the nicest streets in the city. There are the Thickets on one side, crowding the few paths and pushing through the wrought-iron fence. On the other are warehouses, a U-Store-It outfit, a defunct auto repair shop, and a couple of vacant lots. One of those was home to a bedraggled little carnival that picked up stakes after Labor Day. In the other, next to a long-deserted convenience store, is a van with the side door open and a ramp sticking out. There's a wheelchair next to the ramp with someone in it.

'I can't stay here all night,' the wheelchair occupant says. She sounds old and wavery, a little irritated and a little scared. 'Call for help.'

'I would,' says the man with her, 'but my phone is dead. I forgot to charge it. Do you have yours?'

'I left it home. What are we going to do?'

It won't occur to Cary until later – too late to do any good – that the woman in the wheelchair and the man with her are projecting their voices. Not much, not yelling or anything, but the way actors onstage project for the audience. Later he'll realize that *he* was the audience they were playing to, the guy sitting on Drive-In Rock with the joint winking on and off like a locator beacon. Later he'll realize how often he stops off here for awhile on his way home from the bowling alley, smoking a doob and watching the movie across the way.

He decides he can't just sit there while the old guy goes off looking for help, leaving the woman alone. Cary is your basic good person, more than happy to do the occasional good deed.

He makes his way down the slope, holding onto branches to keep from going on his ass. He gives his moped – faithful pony! – a little pat as he passes it. When he reaches one of the Red Bank Avenue gates out of the park, he walks down the sidewalk until he's opposite the van. He calls, 'Need a little help?'

It won't occur to him until later, in the cage, to wonder why they picked that particular place to park; an abandoned Quik-Pik store is hardly a beauty spot.

'Who's there?' the man calls, sounding worried.

'Name's Cary Dressler. Can I—?'

'Cary? My goodness, hon, it's Cary!'

Cary steps into the street, peering. 'Small Ball? Is that you?'

The man laughs. 'It's me, all right. Listen, Cary, the battery in my wife's wheelchair died. I don't suppose you could push it up the ramp, could you?'

'I think I can manage that,' Cary says, crossing the street. 'Indy Jones to the rescue.'

The old lady laughs. 'I saw that movie at the old Bijou. Thank you so much, young man. You're a lifesaver.'

Roddy Harris is telling his wife how he and their rescuer know each other. Cary grabs the wheelchair handgrips and aims the chair for the ramp. Small Ball stands back to give him room, one hand in the pocket of his tweed jacket. Cary is so high that he doesn't even feel the needle when it goes into the back of his neck.

July 23, 2021

1

Holly arrives at the Fourth Street municipal parking lot half a block from the Frederick Building and swipes her card. The barrier goes up and she drives in. It's 8:35 AM, almost half an hour before the appointed time for her meeting with Penny Dahl, but the Dahl woman is also early. There's no mistaking her Volvo. It has large photos of her daughter taped to both sides and the back. Printed across the rear window (probably a moving violation, Holly thinks) is HAVE YOU SEEN MY DAUGHTER and BONNIE RAE DAHL and CALL 216-555-0019.

Holly parks her Prius next to it, which isn't a problem. There's no shortage of spaces in the lot; it used to be packed by nine, with the SORRY FULL sign out front, but that was before the pandemic. Now large numbers of people are working from home, assuming they still have jobs to work at. Also assuming they are not too sick to work. The hospitals emptied out for awhile, but then Delta arrived with its new bag of tricks. They aren't at capacity yet, but they're getting there. By August, patients may be bedding down in the halls and snack stations again.

Because Ms Dahl is nowhere in sight and Holly is early, she lights a cigarette and walks around the Volvo, studying the pictures. Bonnie Dahl is both pretty and older than Holly expected. Mid-twenties, give or take. She guesses it was partly the thing about Dahl riding her bike to and from the Reynolds Library that made Holly expect a younger woman. The rest was how much Penny Dahl's voice reminded Holly of her late mother. She supposes she thought Bonnie would look sort of like Holly had at nineteen or twenty: pinched Emily Dickinson face, hair pulled back in a bun or ponytail, fake smile (Holly had hated having her picture taken, still does), clothes designed not just to min-imize her figure but to make it disappear.

This girl's face is open to the world, her smile wide and sunny. Her blond hair is short, cut off in front in a shaggy, sun-streaked fringe. The pictures on the sides of the car are full-face portraits, but the one on the back shows Bonnie astride her bike, wearing white shorts with V-cuts on the sides and a strappy top. No body consciousness there.

Holly finishes her cigarette, bends, scrapes it out on the pavement. She touches the blackened tip to make sure it's cold, then places it in the litter basket outside the swing gate. She pops a Life Saver into her mouth, puts on her mask, and walks down to her building.

2

Penny Dahl is waiting in the lobby, and even with the mask Holly sees the resemblance to her daughter. Holly puts her age at sixty or there-abouts. Her hair might be pretty with a touch-up, but now it's rat-fur gray. *Neatly kept, though*, Holly adds to this first assessment. She always tries to be kind. Ms Dahl's clothes are clean but slapdash. Holly is no fashionista, far from it, but she would never put that blouse with those slacks. Here is a woman for whom personal appearance has taken a back seat. Across the requested N95, in bright red letters, is her daugh-ter's first name.

'Hello, Ms Dahl,' she says. 'Holly Gibney.'

Holly has never liked shaking hands, but she offers an elbow will-ingly. Penny Dahl bumps it with her own. 'Thank you so much for seeing me. Thank you so very, very much.'

'Let's go upstairs.' The lobby is empty and they don't have to wait for the elevator. Holly pushes for the fifth floor. To Penny she says, 'We had some trouble with this darn thing last year, but it's fixed now.'

3

Without Pete or Barbara Robinson helping out (or just hanging out), the reception area feels like a held breath. Holly starts the coffee maker.

'I brought pictures of Bonnie, a dozen, all taken within a year or two of when she disappeared. I've got tons more, but from when she was younger, and that's not the girl you'll be looking for, is it? I can send them to your phone if you give me your email address.' Her delivery is staccato and she keeps touching her mask to be sure it's in place. 'I can take this off, you know. I'm double-vaxxed and Covid negative. I took the home test just last night.'

'Why don't we wear them out here? We'll take them off in my office and have some coffee. I have cookies, if Barbara — the young lady who sometimes helps out — hasn't eaten them all.'

'No thank you.'

Holly doesn't have to look to know they're all gone, anyway. Barbara can't keep her hands off the vanilla wafers. 'I saw the pictures of Bonnie on your car, by the way. She's very attractive.'

Penny's eyes crinkle as she smiles behind her mask. 'I think so. Of course I'm her mother, so what else would I say? No Miss America, but she was a prom queen back in high school. And nobody dumped a bucket of blood on her, either.' She laughs, the sound as sharp as her delivery. Holly hopes she isn't going to get all hysterical. After three weeks the woman should be beyond that, but maybe not. Holly has never lost a daughter, so she doesn't know. But she does know how she felt when she thought she might have lost Jerome and Barbara — like she was going out of her mind.

Holly writes her email address on a Post-it. 'Are you married, Ms Dahl?'

Dahl pastes the note inside the cover of her phone. 'If you don't start calling me Penny, I may scream.'

'Penny it is,' Holly says, partly because she thinks her new client actually might.

'Divorced. Herbert and I dissolved our partnership three years ago. Political differences were part of it — he was all in on Trump — but there were plenty of other reasons, as well.'

'How did Bonnie feel about that?'

'Handled it in very adult fashion. And why not? She *was* an adult. Twenty-one. Besides, the first time Herbie came home wearing a MAGA hat, she actually laughed at him. He was . . . mmm . . . displeased.'

Here is another relationship chilled by the fast-talking man in the red tie. It's not fate and not coincidence.

Meanwhile, the coffee is ready. 'How do you like it, Penny? Or I have tea, and there might be a Poland Water unless Pete or Barbara—'

'Coffee's fine. No cream, just a little sugar.'

'I'll let you add that yourself.' Holly pours into two of the Finders Keepers mugs, which Pete insisted on ordering. Without looking up, she says: 'Let's cross one *t* right away, Penny. Is there any chance your ex-husband might have something to do with Bonnie's disappearance?'

The jagged laugh comes again – nerves rather than amusement. 'He's in Alaska. Left for a white-collar job in a shipping plant about six months after the divorce. *And* he has Covid. His idol refused to wear a mask, so Herb refused to wear one. You know, Trumper see, Trumper do. If you're asking if he abducted his twenty-four-year-old daughter, or tempted her into moving to Juneau to live with him, the answer is no. He says he's getting better . . .'

This makes Holly think of Pete.

'. . . but when I FaceTime him it's all cough-cough-cough, wheeze-wheeze-wheeze.' Penny says this with unmistakable satisfaction.

4

In Holly's office, they take off their masks. The client's chair probably isn't a full six feet away, but it's close. *Besides*, Holly tells herself, *perfect is the enemy of good.* She opens her iPad to the note function and types *Bonnie Rae Dahl* and *24 yo* and *Disappeared on the night of July 1.* It's a start.

'Tell me about when she was last seen, let's start with that. You said it was at a Jet Mart convenience store?'

'Yes, on Red Bank Ave. Bonnie has an apartment in one of those new Lake View condos, you know where the old docks used to be?'

Holly nods. There are several condominium clusters down there now, and more under construction. Soon you won't be able to see the lake at all unless you own one.

'The Jet Mart is at the halfway point of her ride home. A mile and a half from the library, a mile and a half from her place. The clerk knows her there. She came in on July first at four minutes past eight.'

Jet Mart regular stop, Holly types. She hits the keys without looking, keeping her eyes on Penny.

'I have the security camera video. I'll send that to you, too, but do you want to see it now?'

'Really? How did you get that?'

'Detective Jaynes shared it with me.'

'At your lawyer's request?'

Penny looks perplexed. 'I don't have a lawyer. I used one when I bought my house in Upriver, but not since. She gave it to me when I asked.'

Good for Izzy, Holly thinks.

'*Should* I have a lawyer?'

'That's up to you, but I don't think you need one right now. Let's look at the video.'

Penny gets up and starts to come around the desk.

'No, just hand it to me.'

Double-vaxxed or not, home-tested last night or not, Holly doesn't want the woman looking over her shoulder and breathing on the side of her face. It's not just Covid. Even before the virus she didn't like strangers in her personal space, and that's what this woman still is.

Penny opens the video and hands her phone to Holly. 'Just hit play.'

5

The security camera is looking down from a high angle, and it's far from crystal clear; no one has cleaned the lens in a long time, if ever. It shows the so-called Beer Cave, the clerk, the front door, the miserly parking area, and a slice of Red Bank Avenue. The time-stamp in the lower lefthand corner reads 8:04 PM. The date-stamp in the righthand corner reads 7/1/21. It's not dark yet, but – as Bob Dylan says – it's getting there. Plenty of light still left in the sky, enough for Holly to see Bonnie pull up on her bike, take off her helmet, and shake out her hair, which was probably sweaty. The last week of June and the first week of July were very hot. *Poopy* hot, in fact.

She puts her helmet on the seat of her bike but enters the store still wearing her backpack. She's in tan slacks and a polo shirt with **Bell College** above the left breast, and the bell tower logo above the words. The clip is soundless, of course. Holly looks at the little movie with the fascination she supposes anyone feels when looking at someone who went from a clean, well-lighted place into the unknown.

Bonnie Rae goes to the back cooler and gets a bottle of soda, looks like a Coke or Pepsi. On her way to the cash register she stops to inspect the snack rack. She picks up a package. Might be Ho Hos, might be Yodels, doesn't matter because she puts it back, and in Holly's mind she hears Charlotte Gibney say, *I must maintain my girlish figger.*

At the register she has a brief conversation with the clerk (middle-aged, balding, Hispanic). It must be something funny because they both laugh. Bonnie rests her pack on the counter, unbuckles the flap, and puts her bottle of soda inside. It's big enough for the shoes she wears at work, maybe, plus her phone and a book or two. She slides the straps back over her shoulders and says something else to the clerk. He gives her some change and a thumbs-up. She leaves. Puts on her helmet. Mounts her bike. Pedals away to . . . wherever.

When Holly looks up and hands back the phone, Penny Dahl is crying.

Tears are hard for Holly to handle. There's a box of tissues beside her mousepad. She pushes it toward Penny without making eye contact, nibbling at her lower lip and wishing for a cigarette. 'I'm sorry. I know how hard this is for you.'

Penny looks at her over a bouquet of Kleenex. 'Do you?' It's almost a challenge.

Holly sighs. 'No, probably not.'

There's a moment of silence between them. Holly thinks of telling Penny she recently lost her mother, but it's not the same. She knows where her mother is, after all: under dirt and sod at Eternal Rest. Penny Dahl only knows there's a hole in her life where her daughter is supposed to be.

'I'm curious about your daughter's helmet. Was it with her bike when it was found?'

Penny's mouth falls open. 'No, just the bike. You know what, Detective Jaynes never asked about that and I never thought of it.'

Penny gets a pass, but Izzy Jaynes sinks a bit in Holly's estimation. 'What about her pack?'

'Gone, but you'd expect that, wouldn't you? You might wear a pack after you got off your bike, she wore it into the store, but you'd hardly keep wearing your helmet, would you?'

Holly doesn't answer, because this isn't a conversation, it's an interrogation. It will be as gentle as she can make it, but an interrogation is what it is.

'Catch me up, Penny. Tell me everything you know. Start with what Bonnie does at the Reynolds Library and when she left that evening.'

6

There are four assistant librarians at the Reynolds Library on the Bell College of Arts and Sciences campus. During the summer, the library closes at seven. The head librarian, Matt Conroy, sometimes stays until closing, but that night he didn't. Margaret Brenner, Edith Brookings, Lakeisha Stone, and Bonnie Dahl saw out the last few visitors by five past. Before locking they split up and took a quick sweep through the stacks for anyone who either didn't hear the closing bell or chose to ignore it while reading one more page or taking one more note. Bonnie had told her mother that sometimes they found people fast asleep in the reading room or the stacks, and on a few occasions they came across couples who had been overcome with passion. *In flagrant delicious*, she called it. They also checked the restrooms on the main level and on the third floor. That night all the customers were gone.

The four gabbed for a bit in the break room, discussing weekend plans, then turned out the lights. Lakeisha got into her Smart car and drove away. Bonnie got on her bike and headed for her efficiency apartment, where she never arrived. Penny hadn't been very concerned when she called Bonnie the next morning and got voicemail on the first ring.

'I wanted to ask if she'd like to come over on Friday or Saturday night and watch something on Netflix or Hulu,' Penny says, then adds, 'I was going to make popcorn.'

'Is that all?' Holly's nose for a lie isn't as strong as Bill Hodges's was, but she's good at knowing when someone's shading the truth.

Penny colors. 'Well . . . we'd had an argument a couple of nights before. It got a little heated. Mothers and daughters, you know. Movies are how we make up. We both love the movies, and now there's so much to watch, isn't there?'

'Yes,' Holly says.

'I assumed she was on the phone with someone else and she'd call back.'

But there was no callback. Penny tried again at ten, then at eleven, with the same result: one ring and then voicemail. She called Lakeisha Stone, Bonnie's best bud on the library staff, to ask if Bonnie was still mad at her. Lakeisha said she didn't know. Bonnie hadn't come in that morning. That was when Penny began to get worried. She had a key to her daughter's condo apartment and drove there.

'What time was this?'

'I was worried and not checking the time. I think around noon. I wasn't afraid she'd gotten sick with Covid or something else — she always takes precautions, and she's always been healthy — but I kept thinking about an accident. Like a slip in the shower, or something.'

Holly nods but is remembering the security video. Bonnie Rae wasn't wearing a mask when she went into the store and neither was the guy at the register. So much for always taking precautions.

'She wasn't at her apartment and everything looked normal so I drove to the library, really getting worried now, but she still wasn't there and hadn't called in. I called the police and tried to file a missing persons report, but the man I talked to — after being on hold for twenty minutes — told me that it had to be at least forty-eight hours for a "teen minor" or seventy-two hours for a legal adult. I told him how she wasn't answering her phone, like it was turned off, but he didn't seem interested. I asked to speak with a detective and he said they were all busy.'

At six that evening, back home, Penny got a call from Bonnie's friend, Lakeisha. A man had arrived at the Reynolds with a blue and white Beaumont City ten-speed in the back of his pickup. That kind of bike has a package carrier, to which Bonnie had pasted a bumper sticker reading **I ♥ REYNOLDS LIBRARY**. The man, Marvin Brown, wanted to know if it belonged to someone who worked at the library, or maybe someone who used the library a lot. Otherwise, he said, he guessed he probably should take it to the police station. Because of the note on the seat.

'The note saying *I've had enough*,' Holly says.

'Yes.' Penny's eyes have filled with tears again.

'But you wouldn't call your daughter suicidal?'

'God, no!' Penny jerks back as if Holly has slapped her. A tear spills down her cheek. '*God*, no! I told Detective Jaynes the same thing!'

'Go on.'

The staff all recognized the bike. Matt Conroy, the head librarian, called the police; Lakeisha called Penny.

'I kind of broke down,' Penny says. 'Every psycho stalker movie I ever saw flashed in front of my eyes.'

'Where did Mr Brown find the bike?'

'Less than three blocks down Red Bank from the Jet Mart. There's an auto repair shop for sale across from the park. Mr Brown has a repair shop on the other side of town and I guess he's interested in expanding. A real estate agent met him there. They examined the bike together.' Penny swallows. 'Neither of them liked that note on the seat.'

'Did you talk to Mr Brown?'

'No, Detective Jaynes did. She called him.'

No personal interview, Holly types, still keeping her eyes on Penny, who is wiping away more tears. She thinks Marvin Brown may be her first contact.

'Mr Brown and the real estate man discussed what to do with the bike and Mr Brown said well, why don't I run it up to the library in my pickup, and after they looked the place over — the repair shop, I mean — that's what he did.'

'Who was there first? Brown or the real estate agent?'

'I don't know. It didn't seem important.'

It may not be, but Holly intends to find out. Because sometimes killers 'find' the bodies of their victims, and sometimes arsonists call the fire department. It gives them a thrill.

'Any further developments since then?'

'Nothing,' Penny says. She wipes her eyes. 'Her voicemail is full but sometimes I call anyway. To hear her voice, you know.'

Holly winces. Pete says she'll get used to clients' tales of woe eventually, that her heart will grow calluses, but it hasn't happened yet, and Holly hopes it never does. Pete may have those calluses, and Izzy Jaynes, but Bill never did. He always cared. He said he couldn't help it.

'What about the hospitals? I assume they were checked?'

Penny laughs. There's no humor in it. 'I asked the policeman who answered the phone — the one who told me all the detectives were busy – if he would do that, or if I should. He said I should. You know, your runaway daughter, your job. It was pretty clear that's what he thought she was, a runaway. I called Mercy, I called St Joe's, I called Kiner Memorial. Do you know what they told me?'

Holly is sure she does, but lets Penny say it.

'*They said they didn't know*. How's that for incompetency?'

This woman is distraught, so Holly won't point out what would have been obvious to her if her focus hadn't narrowed to exclude everything but her missing daughter: the hospitals here and all over the Midwest are overwhelmed. The staff has been inundated with Covid patients – not just the doctors and nurses, everyone. On the front page of yesterday's paper there was a picture of a masked janitor wheeling a patient into the Mercy Hospital ICU. If not for the computerized record-keeping systems, the city's hospitals might have no idea of even how many patients they have in care. As it is, the information must be lagging well behind the flood of sick people.

When this is over, Holly thinks, *no one will believe it really happened. Or if they do, they won't understand* how *it happened.*

'And since then, has Detective Jaynes been in touch?'

'Twice in three weeks,' Penny says. She sounds bitter, and Holly thinks she has a right to be. 'Once she came to my house – for ten minutes – the other time she called. She has Bonnie's picture and said she'd put it on NamUs, which is a nationwide missing persons database, also on NCMEC, that's—'

'The National Center for Missing and Exploited Children,' Holly says, thinking that was a good call on Izzy's part even though Bonnie Rae Dahl isn't a child. Cops often post there if the missing person is young and female. Young females are by far the most common abductees. Of course, they are also the most common runaways.

But, she thinks, *if a twenty-four-year-old woman decides to up stakes and start over somewhere else, you can't call her a runaway.*

Penny pulls in a shuddering breath. 'No help from the police. Zero. Jaynes says sure, she might have been abducted, but the note suggests she just left. Only why would she? *Why?* She has a good job! She's in line for a promotion! She's good pals with Lakeisha! And she finally dumped that loser of a boyfriend!'

'What's the name of the loser boyfriend?'

'Tom Higgins.' She wrinkles her nose. 'He worked at the shoe store out at the Airport Mall. Then the mall closed down during the first Covid wave. He tried to move in with Bonnie to save on the rent, but she wouldn't let him. They had a big fight about it. Bon told him they were done. He laughed and said she couldn't fire him, he quit. Like it was original, you know. Probably he thought it was.'

'Do you think he had anything to do with Bonnie's disappearance?'

'No.' She folds her arms across her chest, as if to say that ends the subject. Holly waits – a technique Bill Hodges taught her – and Penny finally fills the silence. 'That man could barely blow his own nose without an instruction video. Also *very* immature. I never knew what Bonnie saw in him, and she could never explain it.'

Holly, a fan of the hunks on *Bachelor in Paradise*, has a good idea what Bonnie might have seen in him. She doesn't want to say it and doesn't have to. Penny says it for her.

'He must have been terrific in the sack, a real sixty-minute man.'

'Do you have his address?'

Penny consults her phone. '2395 Eastland Avenue. Although I don't know if he's still there.'

Holly records it. 'Do you have a picture of the note?'

Penny does, says Lakeisha Stone photographed it when Marvin Brown brought the bike. Holly studies it and doesn't like what she sees. Block letters, all caps, carefully made: I'VE HAD ENOUGH.

'Is this your daughter's printing?'

Penny gives a sigh that says she's at her wits' end. 'It might be, but I can't be sure. My daughter doesn't *do* handwriting. None of them do these days except for their signatures, which you can barely read – just scribbles. She doesn't usually print in all big letters, but if she wanted to be . . . I don't know . . .'

'Emphatic?'

'Yes, that. Then she might.'

She could be right, Holly thinks, but if that were the case, might she not have printed in even bigger caps? Not I'VE HAD ENOUGH but I'VE HAD ENOUGH? Maybe even with an exclamation point or two? No, Holly doesn't care for this note at all. She's not ready to believe Bonnie didn't write it, but she's far from ready to believe that Bonnie did.

'Please forward this along with the photos of your daughter. What about you, Penny? Where do you live?'

'Renner Circle. 883 Renner, in Upriver.'

Holly adds it to her notes, where she has also written *P and B argued, P says it got heated.*

'And what do you do?'

'I'm the chief loan officer at the NorBank branch on the turnpike extension at the airport. At least I was, and I assume I will be again. NorBank has temporarily closed three of their stores — we call them stores — and one of them was mine.'

'Not working from home?'

'No. I'm still getting paid, though. One ray of sunshine in all this . . . this *mess*. Which reminds me, I need to give you a check.' She opens her bag and starts rooting through it. 'You must have more questions, too.'

'I will have, but I've got enough to get started on.'

'When will I hear from you?' Penny is writing a check quickly and efficiently, not pausing at any of the fields. And not printing, either, but writing in a small, rolling, tightly controlled script.

'Give me twenty-four hours to get going.'

'If you find out something worth sharing before that, call. Anytime. Day or night.'

'One more thing.' Ordinarily she shies from anything personal, especially if it might seem confrontational, but this morning she doesn't hesitate. She's got hold of this now, like a snarled knot she wants to unpick. 'Tell me about the argument. The one that got heated.'

Penny once more folds her arms over her chest, more tightly this time. Holly knows defensive body language from plenty of personal experience. 'It was nothing. A tempest in a teapot.'

Holly waits.

'We argue from time to time, big deal. What mother and daughter don't?'

Holly waits.

'Well,' Penny says at last, 'this one was a little more serious, maybe. She slammed the door on the way out. She's a goodnatured girl and that was out of character. We had some . . . some warm discussions about Tom, but she never slammed out of the house. And I swore at her. Called her a stubborn bitch. God, I wish I could take that back. Just say, "Okay, Bon, let's forget about it." But you never know, do you?'

'What was it about?'

'There was an excellent position at NorBank. Records and inventory. Collating. Front office, working from home guaranteed, how great does that sound with everything that's going on? I was trying to get her to apply for it, she's excellent with numbers and a real people person, but she wouldn't. I told her about the substantial pay jump she'd get, and the benefits, and the good hours. Nothing got through to her. She could be stubborn.'

Look who's talking, Holly thinks, remembering fights she had with her own mother, especially once she started working with Bill Hodges. There had been some doozies after she and Bill had almost gotten killed while chasing after a doctor who had been possessed – there was really no other way to put it – by Brady Hartsfield.

'I told her if she worked at the bank she could buy some decent clothes for a change and stop dressing like a hippie. She laughed at me. That's when I called her a bitch.'

'Any other arguments? Sore spots?'

'No. None.' Holly knows she's lying, and not just to the private detective she's just hired.

Holly types one more note, then gets up and puts on her mask.

'What will you do first?'

'Call Izzy Jaynes. I think she'll talk to me. She and I go back quite a few years.'

And even before Brown, the pickup truck man, she wants to talk to Lakeisha Stone. Because if Lakeisha and Bonnie were besties – even closies – Lakeisha will have a better fix on how the mother and daughter got along. Door-slamming argument or not, Holly doesn't want to start this by equating her own mother and Bonnie's too closely.

You are not the case, Bill told her once. *Never make the mistake of thinking you are. It never helps and usually makes things worse.*

November 22–25, 2018

1

Em doesn't like this one.

Not that she liked Cary Dressler, and she *loathed* Castro, the spic *maricon*. This girl, though, this Ellen Craslow, is different from either of them. Because she's female? Em doesn't believe it.

She descends the stairs to the basement, carrying the tray in front of her. On it is a pound and a half of liver, uncooked and swimming in its own juices. Price at Kroger: $3.22. Meat is so expensive now, and the last piece was wasted. She came down and found it crawling with maggots and flies. How they got into this sealed room, and so quickly, is beyond her. Even the crack at the foot of the door leading to the kitchen has been sealed.

The girl is standing at the bars of the cell. She's tall, with skin the color of cocoa. Her hair is neat and short and dark. From the foot of the stairs Em could almost believe it's a bathing cap. When she comes closer, she can see that Ellen's lips are cracked and sore-looking in places. But she doesn't cry or beg. She's done neither. So far, at least.

Em takes the plate of liver from the tray and places it on the concrete. She drops to one knee to do this rather than bending. Her sciatica is bad, but bad she can take. When it screams though, when it makes every step agony . . . that is a different matter. She takes the broom and pushes the plate toward the cell. The red liquid sloshes. And as she has done before, Ellen Craslow blocks the pass-through with the side of her foot.

'I've told you, I'm a vegan. You don't seem to listen.'

Em feels an urge to poke her with the broom handle and quells it. Not just because the girl might catch hold of it, either. She must not show emotion. Like Castro and Dressler, this is a caged animal. Livestock. Poking livestock is childish. Being angry with it is childish. What you do with an animal is *train* it.

Ellen refused the protein shake, too. She drank both of the small bottles of water that were in the cage when she woke up, the first all at once. She made the second one last, but both are gone now. From the pocket of her apron, Em takes another. 'When you eat your meat, Ellen, you can have this. Your body doesn't care that you're a vegan. It needs to eat.' She holds the bottle out, displaying it. 'And it needs to drink.'

Ellen says nothing, only stands looking at Em with her hands loosely gripping the bars and her foot blocking the pass-through. That gaze is unnerving. Em doesn't want to feel unnerved, but tells herself that she'd feel the same way if she were at the zoo and locked eyes with a tiger.

'I'll leave the food, shall I? When I come back and the plate is clean – juice, too – you can have the water.'

No reply, and animal or no animal, Professor Emily Harris (emerita) realizes she's angry after all. No, furious. Castro ate; Dressler ate; eventually Ellen will eat, too. She won't be able to help herself. Em turns away and starts for the stairs.

The girl says, 'It's horrible, isn't it?'

Em turns back, startled.

'When people won't do what you want. It's horrible, isn't it? For you, I mean.' And the girl actually smiles!

Bitch, Emily thinks, and then what she would never in a billion years allow herself to say except in her diary: *Stubborn black bitch!*

Em says (gently), 'It's Thanksgiving, Ellen. Give thanks and eat.'

'Bring me a salad,' Ellen says. 'No dressing. That I will eat.'

The nerve! Em thinks. *As if I were a serving girl! As if I were her ladies' maid!*

She does something then she will later regret, because it gives away too much of herself. She takes the bottle of water from her apron pocket, raises it to her lips, and drinks. Then she pours the rest out over the railing.

The girl says nothing.

2

A day later.

Professor Rodney Harris (Life Sciences, emeritus) stands in front of the cell, cogitating. Ellen Craslow looks back at him, calm. Or so she seems. There are a couple of blisters on her lips now, there are pimples on her forehead, and the smooth cocoa loveliness of her skin has turned ashy. But her eyes – a startling green – are brilliant in their deepening sockets.

Roddy is a respected biologist and nutritionist. Before his retirement he was a teacher sometimes revered and more often feared by his students. A bibliography of his published work would fill a dozen pages, and he still keeps up a lively correspondence in various journals with his peers. That he considers himself first among those peers doesn't strike him as conceited. As someone wise once said, *It ain't bragging if it's true.*

He's not angry at this girl the way Em is (she says she isn't, but they have been married for over fifty years and he knows her better than she knows herself), but Ellen certainly perplexes him. She must have been disoriented when she woke up, the way the others were, they use a powerful drug to knock their subjects out, but she didn't *seem* disoriented. If she was hungover – and she must have been that, too – she didn't complain of it. She didn't scream for help, as Cary Dressler did almost at once (*must have made his headache that much worse,* Roddy thinks) and as Jorge Castro had eventually. And of course she has refused to eat, although it's been almost three days now, and over two since she finished off the last of the water she's been allowed.

The liver Em brought down yesterday has darkened and begun to smell. It's still edible but won't be for much longer. Another few hours and she'd probably vomit it back up, which would make the whole thing pointless. Meanwhile, time is flicking past.

'If you don't eat, my dear, you'll starve,' he says in a mild voice his students of yore wouldn't recognize; as a lecturer, Roddy had a tendency to be rapid, excitable, sometimes even shrill. When talking about the wonders of the stomach – serosa, pylorus, duodenum – his voice sometimes rose to a near scream.

Ellen says nothing.

'Your body has already begun to digest itself. It's visible on your face, your arms, the way you stand, slightly slumped . . .'

Nothing. Her eyes on his. She hasn't asked what they want, which is also perplexing and (admit the truth) rather disturbing. She knows who they are, she knows that if they let her go they will be arrested for kidnapping (only the first charge of many), ergo they *can't* let her go, but there has been no bargaining and no begging. Just this hunger strike. She told Em she would gladly eat a salad, but that is out of the question. Salads, whether dressed or undressed, are not sacrament. Meat is sacrament. Liver is sacrament.

'What are we to do with you, dear?' Sadly.

At this point he would expect a prisoner – a *normal* prisoner – to say something ridiculous like *let me go and I won't say a word to anybody.* This girl, hungry and thirsty or not, knows better.

Roddy pushes the plate with the slab of liver on it a little closer. 'Eat that and you'll feel your strength return at once. The feeling will be extraordinary.' He tries a thin joke: 'We'll turn you into a carnivore in no time.'

There's still no response, so he starts for the stairs.

Ellen says, 'I know what that is.'

He turns back. She is pointing to the big yellow box at the far end of the workshop. 'It's a woodchipper. You've got it turned to the wall so I can't see the intake, but I know what it is. My uncle has worked in the woods up north all his life.'

At his age Rodney Harris would have thought himself beyond surprise, but this young woman is full of them. Most extraordinary, almost like discovering a canine prodigy that can count.

'It's how you'll get rid of me, isn't it? I'll go through the hose and into a big bag and the bag will go in the lake.'

He stares, mouth agape.

'How do you . . . why would you think that?'

'Because it's the safest place. There's a TV show, *Dexter*, about a man who kills people and gets rid of them in the Gulf of Mexico. Maybe you've seen it.'

They have seen it, of course.

This is terrible. Like she's reading his mind. *Their* mind, because when it comes to their captives – and the sacrament – he and Em think alike.

'You have a boat. Don't you, Professor Harris?'

This girl was a mistake. She's a sport, an outlier, they might not come across another like her in a hundred years.

He goes upstairs without saying anything else.

3

Em is in her study. It's crammed with so many books on the floor-to-ceiling shelves that there's barely room for her desk. Some of the books have been set aside in a corner to make room for a thick folder with WRITING SAMPLES printed on the cover in neat block letters.

Two framed pictures flank her desktop computer. One is of a very young Roddy and Em, he in a morning suit (rented) and she in the traditional white bridal dress (purchased by her parents). The other shows a much older Roddy and Em, he in a joke admiral's hat and she with a common sailor's Dixie cup cocked rakishly on her beauty shop curls. They are standing in front of their newly purchased (but gently used) Mainship 34. Em has a bottle of cheap champagne in one hand, which she will soon use to christen their boat the *Marie Cather* – *Marie* as in Stopes, *Cather* as in Willa. Their marriage has always been a partnership.

On the screen of her computer, Em's watching Ellen Craslow sitting on the futon in her cage, legs crossed, head in hands, shoulders shaking. Roddy bends over Em's shoulder for a closer look.

'She stood there until you were gone, then just collapsed,' Em says, not without satisfaction.

The girl raises her head and looks up at the camera. Although she's been crying, her eyes look dry. Roddy isn't surprised. It's dehydration at work.

'You heard everything?' he asks his wife.

'Yes. She's intuited a lot, hasn't she?'

'Not intuition, logic. Plus, she recognized the woodchipper. Neither of the others did. What are we going to do, Emmie? Suggestions, please.'

She considers it while they look at the girl in the cage. Neither of them feel pity for Ellen, or even sympathy. She is a problem to be solved. In a way, Roddy thinks the problem is a good thing. They are still relatively new to this. Every solved problem adds to efficiency, as every scientist knows.

At last she says, 'Let's see what happens tomorrow.'

'Yes. I think that's right.'

He straightens up and idly thumbs the thick folder of writing samples. This spring semester's writer-in-residence at Bell's greatly respected (almost legendary) fiction workshop will be a woman named Althea Gibson, author of two novels that reviewed well and sold poorly. As with several previous in-residence authors, Gibson has been more than willing to have Emily Harris do the initial applicant winnowing, and although the pay is a pittance, Em enjoys the work. This was an offer Jorge Castro declined, preferring to go through the stacks of writing samples himself. Thought having Emily do the pre-screening was beneath him. Em has noticed how many fags are uppity, and thinks it's probably compensation. Also . . . all that solitary running.

'Anything good in here?' Roddy Harris asks.

'So far just the usual junk.' Em sighs and rubs at her aching lower back. 'I'm beginning to think that in another twenty years, fiction will be a lost art.'

He bends and kisses her white hair. 'Hang in there, baby.'

4

When Em comes down the stairs at noon on the 24th, the maggots and flies are back on the slab of liver. She looks at them crawling around on a perfectly good cut of meat (well, it *was*) with disgust and dismay. They simply have no business being there so fast. They have no business being there at all!

She pushes the meat toward the pass-through with the broom. And although Ellen looks exhausted, the cracks in her lips bleeding, her complexion the color of clay, she again blocks the hinged panel with her foot.

Em takes a bottle of water from her apron pocket and is delighted by the way the girl's eyes fix on it. And when her tongue comes out in a useless effort to moisten those parched lips . . . that is also delightful.

'Take it, Ellen. Brush off the bugs and eat. Then I'll give you the water.'

For one moment she thinks the stubborn girl means to give in. Then she says what she always says: 'I'm a vegan.'

You're a bitch, is what you are. Emily can barely restrain herself from saying it. The girl is infuriating, and it doesn't help that the goddamned sciatica has kept her up half the night. *An uppity, smartass bitch! BLACK bitch!*

She drops to one knee – back straight, less pain – and picks up the plate. She's unable to suppress a small cry of disgust when a maggot squirms onto her wrist. She carries the plate upstairs without looking back.

Roddy is at the kitchen table, reading a monograph and nibbling trail mix from a cut glass bowl. He looks up, takes off his reading glasses, and massages the sides of his nose. 'No?'

'No.'

'All right. Do you want me to take her the last piece? I can see how much your back hurts.'

'I'm fine. Good to go.' Em tilts the plate. The rotting liver slides into the sink. It makes a squashy sound: *plud.* There's another maggot on her forearm. She swats it off and uses a meat fork to stuff the spoiled meat into the garbage disposal, going at it with short hard jabs.

'Calmly,' Roddy says. '*Calmly*, Em. We are prepared for this.'

'But if she won't eat, it means going out again for a replacement! And it's too soon!'

'We'll be extremely careful, and I can't bear to see you in such misery. Besides, I might have a possibility.'

Em turns to him. 'She exasperates me.'

Nothing so mild as exasperation, my dear one, Roddy thinks. *You are angry, and I think the girl knows it. She may also know your anger is the only vengeance she can ever expect to have.* He says none of that, only looks at her with those eyes she has always loved. Is helpless not to love, even after all these years. He gets up, puts an arm around her shoulders, and kisses her cheek. 'My poor Em. I'm sorry you're in pain and sorry you have to wait.'

She gives him the smile *he* has always loved, is helpless not to love. Even now, with the deepening lines around her eyes and from the corners of her mouth. 'It will work out.'

She turns on the disposal. It makes a hungry grinding sound, not that much different from the sound the chipper in the basement makes when it's running. Then she gets a fresh slab of liver from the fridge.

'Are you sure you don't want me to take it down?' Roddy asks.

'Positive.'

5

In the basement, Em puts the plate of liver on the floor. She sets a bottle of Dasani water down behind it. Ellen Craslow gets up from the futon and blocks the pass-through with the side of her foot before Em can take the broom. Again she says, 'I'm a vegan.'

'I think we have established that,' Em says. 'Think carefully. This is your last chance.'

Ellen looks at Em with haunted, deep-socketed eyes . . . then smiles. Her lips crack open and bleed. She speaks quietly, without heat. 'Don't lie to me, woman. I was all out of chances when I woke up in here.'

6

Roddy is the one who comes down the next day. He's wearing his favorite sportcoat, the one he always wore at conventions and symposia where he had panels to be on or papers to deliver. He knows from the video feed that the liver is still outside the pass-through, but the plate has been moved. He and Em watched as the girl lay on her side, shoulder pressed against the bars, trying to reach the water. She couldn't, of course.

Roddy is holding the requested salad. Ordinarily he would never tease a caged animal, but this girl really has been infuriating. It's not just her unshakable calm. It's the waste of time.

'No dressing. We wouldn't want to violate your dietary principles.'

He sets the salad bowl down, noting the naked greed on her face as she looks at it. He pushes it toward her with the broom. He could let her eat it before putting her out of her misery. He has considered it and decided against. She's made Emily angry.

He pushes it into the cell. She picks it up.

'Thank y—' Her eyes widen as she sees him reach inside the sportcoat. It's a .38. Not much noise and the basement is soundproofed. He shoots her once in the chest. The bowl falls from her hands and shatters. Cherry tomatoes roll here and there. As she goes down he reaches through the bars and puts another bullet into the top of her head, just to make sure.

'What a waste,' he says.

Not to mention the mess to clean up.

July 23, 2021

1

Once Penny is gone, Holly takes a packet of antibacterial wipes from the top drawer of her desk and swabs down both the part of the desk where Penny rested her clasped hands, and the arms of the chair she sat in. Probably overdoing the caution – you can't disinfect everything, it would be crazy to try – but better safe than sorry. Holly only has to think of her mother to know that.

She goes down the hall to the ladies' and washes her hands. When she returns to her office, she reviews her notes and makes a list of the people she wants to talk to. Then she sits tilted back in her chair, hands clasped loosely on her stomach, looking at the ceiling. A vertical crease – what Barbara Robinson calls Holly's think-line – has appeared between her eyes. The missing backpack doesn't concern her; as Penny said, her daughter would have been wearing it. What interests Holly is Bonnie Rae's bike helmet. And the bike itself. Both are *very* interesting to her, for related but slightly different reasons.

After five minutes or so the vertical crease disappears and she calls Isabelle Jaynes. 'Hello, Izzy. It's Holly Gibney. I hope you don't mind me calling your personal phone.'

'Not at all. I was very sorry to hear about your mother, Hol.'

'How did you know?' Izzy wasn't at the Zoom funeral, unless – and this would be just like her – she was lurking.

'Pete told me.'

'Well, thank you. Losing her was tough. And needless.'

'No jabs?'

'No.' Pete probably told Izzy that, too. Holly doesn't know how closely they stay in touch, but she's sure they do. Blue never fades. Bill told her that.

'How is Pete doing?'

'Not bouncing back as fast as I'd hoped.'

'Sorry to hear it. What can I do for you?'

Holly tells her that Penelope Dahl has hired her to look into her daughter's disappearance. She didn't expect Izzy to feel that she was muscling in on a police investigation, and her expectation is fulfilled. Izzy is actually delighted and wishes Holly the best of luck.

'Mrs Dahl doesn't believe Bonnie left town,' Holly says, 'and she rejects the idea of suicide. Vehemently. What's your take?'

'Between us? Not for publication?'

'Of course not!'

'It was a joke, Hols. Sometimes I forget how literal you can be. I think the girl either decided on the spur of the moment to light out for sights unseen and pastures new . . . or she was abducted. If you put a gun to my kitty-cat's head, I'd favor abduction. Possibly followed by rape, murder, and body disposal.'

'Oough.'

'Oough is correct. I notified the right people, and put the State Police in the loop.'

'Did the right people include the FBI?'

'I spoke to the Cincinnati SAC. They won't investigate, they've got bigger fish to fry, but at least it's in their database. If something they *are* investigating touches on the Dahl woman, they'll know. As for here in town, you know what a shitshow it is. Covid is bad enough, but now we've got the Maleek Dutton thing. It's settled a little bit, no one's been breaking store windows or setting cars on fire for the last couple of weeks, but it's still . . . reverberating.'

'That was unfortunate.' It was a lot more than that, but Dutton is a sensitive subject and an old story: young Black man, busted taillight, traffic stop. The officer approaching says keep your hands on the wheel, but Dutton reaches for his phone.

'*Stupid* is what it was. *Unconscionable* is what it was.' Izzy sounds like she's speaking through clenched teeth. 'You didn't hear me say that.'

'No, I didn't.'

'The grand jury cleared the trigger-happy asshole — you didn't hear me say that, either — but at least he's off the force. He's not the only one, either. Between Covid and the trouble in Lowtown, we're down twenty-five per cent. If the governor mandates masks and vaccinations for city and state employees, it will go down more. The thin blue line is thinner than ever.'

Holly makes a sound that might indicate sympathy. She is sympathetic, but only to a point. It was a bad shooting — an indefensible shooting, no matter what the grand jury said — and she will never understand why cops who snap on gloves as a matter of course before injecting ODs with Naloxone are against being vaccinated for Covid. Not all of them refuse the jab, of course, but a sizeable minority do. In any case, she's used to this sort of grousing. Izzy Jaynes is basically a very unhappy person.

'Look, Hols, I know the Dahl woman thinks we let her down. Maybe we did. Probably we did. But they argued all the time, so the neighbors say, and this city's infrastructure is almost underwater. Did you know they're emptying the jails because of Covid? Putting bad guys back on the street? Sometimes I think it's good Bill didn't live to see it.'

I wish he had, Holly thinks. *I wish he'd lived to see anything*. Her mother's death is a fresh grief on top of the one for Bill she still carries.

Izzy sighs. 'Anyway, I'm glad you're taking her on, kiddo. I feel sorry for her, but she's one extra pain in an ass that's already painful. Let me know if I can help.'

'I will.'

Holly ends the call and goes back to looking at the ceiling. She checks her phone to see if Penny has sent her the pics of her daughter. Not yet. She gets down on her knees.

'God, please help me do the best I can for Penny Dahl and for her daughter. If someone took that young woman, I hope she's still alive, and it's your will I should find her. I'm taking my Lexapro, which is good. I'm smoking again, which is bad.' She thinks of Saint Augustine's prayer and smiles into her clasped hands. 'Help me to stop . . . but not today.'

With that taken care of, she opens her Covid drawer. There's a box of fresh masks beside the box of wipes. She takes one and heads out to begin her investigation into the disappearance of Bonnie Rae Dahl.

2

Twenty minutes later Holly is driving slowly up Red Bank Avenue. Just short of Deerfield Park she passes a Dairy Whip where a bunch of kids are skateboarding in the nearly deserted parking lot. She passes John-Boy's Storage Center, Rates By Month And By Year. She passes an abandoned Exxon station that's been sprayed with tags. There's a Quik-Pik, also abandoned, the front windows boarded up.

After a weedy vacant lot, she comes to the auto repair shop where Bonnie's bike was discovered. It's a long building with a sagging roof and rusty corrugated metal sides. The cement parking area out front is sprouting weeds and even a few sunflowers through its cracked surface. To Holly it doesn't look like a building worth saving, let alone buying, but Marvin Brown must have felt differently, because there's a SALE PENDING sign in front. The sign features a photo of a smiling moon-faced man who is identified as George Rafferty, Your City Real Estate Specialist. Holly parks in front of the roll-up doors and notes down the agent's name and number.

She keeps a box of nitrile gloves in the console. Barbara Robinson special-ordered them for her as a birthday present, and they're covered with various emojis: smiley faces, frowny faces, kissy faces and pissy faces. Quite amusing. Holly snaps on a pair, then goes around to the back of her little car and opens the trunk. There's a neatly folded raincoat on top of her toolbox. She won't need that, the day is sunny and hot, but she wants her red rubber galoshes. It isn't Covid she's worried about out here in the open, but there are bushes on both sides of the deserted repair shop, and she's very susceptible to poison ivy. Also, there might be snakes. Holly hates snakes. Their scales are bad, their beady black eyes are worse. *Oough.*

She pauses to consider Deerfield Park across the street. Most of it is a landscaper's dream, but over here on the edge of Red Bank Ave, the trees and bushes have been allowed to grow wild, with greenery actually poking through the wrought-iron fence and invading the space of sidewalk strollers. She sees one interesting thing: a rough downward slash, almost a ravine, topped by a slab of rock. Even from across the street Holly can see it's been heavily tagged, so kids must gather there, possibly to smoke pot. She thinks that rock would have a good view of this side of the avenue, including the auto repair shop. She wonders if any kids were there on the evening Bonnie left her bike, and thinks of the ones she saw goofing off in the parking lot of the Dairy Whip.

She pulls on her galoshes, tucks her pants into them, and walks along the front of the building – past the three roll-up garage doors, then the office. She doesn't expect to find anything, but stranger things have happened. When she reaches the corner she turns and goes back, walking slowly, head bent. There's nothing.

Now for the hard part, she thinks. *The poopy part.*

She starts up the south side of the building, moving slowly, pushing aside the bushes, looking down. There are cigarette butts, an empty Tiparillo box, a rusty White Claw can, an ancient athletic sock. The going is faster along the back, because someone has dumped oil (a big no-no) and there are fewer bushes. She sees something white and pounces on it, but it turns out to be a cracked sparkplug.

Holly turns the far corner and starts wading through more bushes. Some of them have reddish leaves that look suspiciously oily, and she's glad she wore the gloves. There is no bike helmet. She supposes it might have been cast far over the chainlink fence behind the shop, but Holly thinks she'd probably still see it, because it's another vacant lot over there.

At the front corner of the building something glitters deep in a patch of those suspiciously oily leaves. Holly pushes them aside, careful that no leaf should touch her bare skin, and picks up a clip-on earring. A gold triangle. Surely not real gold, just an impulse buy at T.J. Maxx or Icing Fashion, but Holly feels a hot burst of excitement. There are days when she doesn't know why she does this job, and there are days when she knows exactly why. This is one of the latter. She'll have to photograph it and send it to Penny Dahl to be sure, but Holly has no doubt the earring belonged to Bonnie Rae. Perhaps it just fell off – clip-on earrings do that – but maybe it was pulled or jolted off. Possibly in a struggle.

And the bike, Holly thinks. *It wasn't out back or around one of the sides. It was in front. I'll have to confirm that, but I don't think Brown and the real estate man went wading through the bushes like I just did.* To her mind, there's only one scenario where that makes sense.

She tightens her grip on the earring until she feels its sharp corners biting into her palm, and decides to reward herself with a cigarette. She tweezes off her emoji-decorated nitrile gloves and puts them in the footwell of her car. Then she leans against the passenger-side front tire, where hopefully no one passing on the avenue will see her, and fires up. She considers the empty building while she smokes.

When she's finished her cigarette, she butts it on the concrete and tucks it away in a tin cough drop box she keeps in her purse as a portable ashtray. She checks her phone. Penny has sent the pictures of her daughter. There are sixteen of them, including the one of Bonnie on her bike. Holly cares about that one most of all, but she scrolls through the others. There's one of Bonnie and a young man – likely Tom Higgins, the ex-boyfriend – with their foreheads pressed together, laughing. They are in profile to the camera. Holly uses her fingers to enlarge the picture until all she can see is the side of Bonnie's face.

And there on her earlobe, sparkling, is a gold triangle.

3

Holly is much better at talking to strangers – even interrogating them – than she ever thought she would be, but the idea of introducing herself to those laughing, trash-talking boys at the Dairy Whip brings back unpleasant memories. It brings back *trauma*, if you want to call a spade a spade. She was relentlessly teased and made fun of by boys like that in high school. Girls, too, who have their own brands of poisonous cruelty, but Mike Sturdevant was the worst. Mike Sturdevant, who started calling her Jibba-Jibba, because she was (he said) jibba-jibba-*gibbering*. Her mother allowed her to switch high schools – *Oh, Holly, I suppose* – but for the rest of her nightmare years of secondary education, she lived in fear that the nickname would follow her like a bad smell: Jibba-Jibba Gibney.

What if she started jibba-jibba-gibbering when talking to those boys?

I wouldn't, she thinks. *That was another girl.*

But even if that were true (she knows it isn't, not entirely), they might talk more easily to a young man not much older than themselves. Holly has enough self-awareness to know that while this might be so, it's also a rationalization. Nevertheless, she calls Jerome Robinson. At least she won't be interrupting his work; he always pushes back by noon, and it's almost noon now. Isn't 10:50 pretty close to noon?

'Hollyberry!' he exclaims.

'How many times have I told you not to call me that?'

'I never will again, I solemnly promise.'

'Bullshit,' she says, and smiles when he laughs. 'Are you working? You are, aren't you?'

'Stopped dead in the water until I make some calls,' he says. 'Need information. Can I help you? Please say I can. Barbara's clacking away down the hall, making me feel guilty.'

'What is she clacking away on in the middle of summer?'

'I don't know, and she gets grumpy when I ask. And this has actually been going on since last winter. I think she's having meetings with someone about it, whatever it is. I asked her once if it was a guy and she tells me to chill, it's a lady. An old lady. What's up with you?'

Holly explains what's up with her and asks Jerome if he would take the lead in questioning some boys skateboarding at the Dairy Whip. If they're still there, that is.

'Fifteen minutes,' he says.

'Are you sure?'

'Absolutely. And Holly . . . so sorry about your mom. She was a character.'

'That's one way of putting it,' Holly says. She's sitting here with her bottom on hot concrete, leaning against a tire, stupid red galoshes splayed out in front of her, feet sweating, and getting ready to cry. *Again.* It's absurd, really absurd.

'Your eulogy was great.'

'Thanks, Jerome. Are you really s—'

'You asked that already, and I am. Red Bank Ave, across from the Thickets, real estate sign out front. Be there in fifteen.'

She stows her phone in her little shoulder bag and wipes away her latest tears. Why does it hurt so much? Why, when she didn't even like her mother and she's so angry about the stupid way her mother died? Was it the J. Geils Band that said love stinks? Since she has time (and five bars), she looks it up on her phone. Then she decides to explore.

4

The arched entrance to Deerfield Park nearest the big rock is flanked by signs: PLEASE DISPOSE OF PET FECES and RESPECT YOUR PARK! DO NOT LITTER! Holly takes the shady, upward-tending walk slowly, pushing aside a few overhanging branches, always looking to her left. Near the top, she sees a beaten path leading into the undergrowth. She follows it and eventually comes out at the big rock. The area around it is littered with cigarette butts and beer cans. Also nests of broken glass that were probably once wine bottles. *So much for do not litter*, Holly thinks.

She sits down on the sun-warmed rock. As she expected, she has an excellent view of Red Bank Ave: the deserted gas station, the deserted convenience store, the U-Store-It, the Jet Mart further up, and – the star of our show – a repair garage now presumably owned by Marvin Brown. She can see something else as well: the white rectangle of a drive-in movie screen. Holly thinks that anyone sitting up here after dark could watch the show for free, albeit soundlessly.

She's still sitting there when Jerome's used black Mustang pulls in next to her Prius. He gets out and looks around. Holly stands on the rock, cups her hands around her mouth, and calls, *'Jerome! I'm up here!'*

He spots her and waves.

'I'll be right down!'

She hurries. Jerome is waiting for her outside the gate and gives her a strong hug. To her he looks taller and handsomer than ever.

'That's Drive-In Rock where you were standing,' he says. 'It's famous, at least on this side of town. When I was in high school, kids used to go up there on Friday and Saturday nights, drink beer, smoke dope, and watch whatever was playing at Magic City.'

'From the amount of litter up there,' Holly says disapprovingly, 'they still do. What about on weeknights?' Bonnie disappeared on a Thursday.

'I'm not sure there are shows on weeknights. You could check, but the indoor theaters are weekends only since Covid.'

There's another problem, too, Holly realizes. Bonnie exited the Jet Mart with her soda at 8:07, and it would have been mere minutes before she reached the auto repair shop where her bike was found. On July first it wouldn't have been dark enough to start a drive-in movie until at least nine PM, and why would kids gather at Drive-In Rock to watch a blank screen?

'You look bummed,' Jerome says.

'Minor bump in the road. Let's go talk to those kids. If they're still there, that is.'

5

Most of the skateboarders are gone, but four diehards are sitting around one of the picnic tables at the far end of the Dairy Whip parking lot, chowing down on burgers and fries. Holly tries to hang back, but Jerome isn't having that. He takes her elbow and keeps her right beside him.

'I wanted you to take the lead!'

'Happy to help out, but you start. It'll be good for you. Show them your ID card.'

The boys – Holly guesses their average age is somewhere around twelve or fourteen – are looking at them. Not with suspicion, exactly, just sizing them up. One of them, the clown of the group, has a couple of French fries protruding from his nose.

'Hello,' Holly says. 'My name is Holly Gibney. I'm a private detective.'

'Truth or bullshit?' one of them asks, looking at Jerome.

'True, Boo,' Jerome says.

Holly fumbles for her wallet, almost knocking her portable ashtray onto the ground in the process, and shows them her laminated private investigator's card. They all lean forward to look at her awful photograph. The clown takes the French fries from his nose and, to Holly's dismay (*oough*), eats them.

The spokesman of the group is a redhaired, freckled boy with his lime green skateboard propped beside him against the picnic table bench. 'Okay, whatever, but we don't snitch.'

'Snitches are bitches,' says the clown. He's got shoulder-length black hair that needed to be washed two weeks ago.

'Snitches get stitches,' says the one with the glasses and the high-top fade.

'Snitches end up in ditches,' says the fourth. He has a cataclysmic case of acne.

Having completed this roundelay, they look at her, waiting for whatever comes next. Holly is relieved to discover her fear has left. These are just boys not long out of middle school (maybe still in it), and there's no harm in them, no matter what silly rhymes they know from the hip-hop videos.

'Cool deck,' Jerome says to the leader. 'Baker? Tony Hawk?'

Leader Boy grins. 'Do I look like money, honey? Just a Metroller, but it does me.' He switches his attention to Holly. 'Private eye like Veronica Mars?'

'I don't have as many adventures as she does,' Holly says . . . although she's had a few, oh yes indeed. 'And I don't want you to snitch about anything. I'm looking for a missing woman. Her bike was found about a quarter of a mile up the street—' She points. '—at a deserted building that used to be a car repair shop. Do any of you recognize either her or the bike?'

She calls up the picture of Bonnie on her bike. The boys pass her phone around.

'I think I seen her once or twice,' the longhair says, and the boy sitting next to him nods. 'Just buzzing down Red Bank on her bike. Not lately, though.'

'Wearing a helmet?'

'Well duh,' the longhair says. 'It's the law. The cops can give you a ticket.'

'How long since you've seen her?' Jerome asks.

Longhair and his buddy consider. The buddy says, 'Not this summer. Spring, maybe.'

Jerome: 'You're sure?'

'Pretty sure,' the longhair says. 'Good-looking chick. You gotta notice those. It's the law.'

They all laugh, Jerome included.

The leader says, 'You think she took off on her own or somebody grabbed her?'

'We don't know,' Holly says. Her fingers steal to the outside of the pocket of her pants and touch the triangular shape of the earring.

'Come on,' says the boy with the spectacles and the hightop fade. 'Be real. She's good-looking but no teenager. If she just took off, you wouldn't be looking for her.'

'Her mother is very worried,' Holly says.

That they understand.

'Thanks,' Jerome says.

'Yes,' Holly says. 'Thank you.'

They start to turn away, but the redhead with the freckles – Leader Boy – stops them. 'You want to know whose mother is worried? Stinky's. She's half-crazy and the cops don't do anything because she's a juicer.'

Holly turns back. 'Who's Stinky?'

November 27, 2018

It will be a cold winter in this city by the lake, lots of snow, but on this night the temperature is an unseasonable sixty-five degrees. Mist is rising from the seal-slick surface of Red Bank Avenue. The street-lights illuminate a dense cloud cover less than a hundred feet up.

Peter 'Stinky' Steinman rides his Alameda deck down the empty sidewalk at quarter to seven, giving it an occasional lazy push to keep it rolling. He's bound for the Dairy Whip. Ahead is the giant lighted sof' serve cone, haloed in mist. He's looking at that and doesn't notice the van parked on the tarmac of the deserted Exxon station, between the office and the islands where the pumps used to be.

Once upon a time, long long ago (well, three years, which seems like long long ago when you're eleven), young Steinman was known to his peers as Pete rather than Stinky. He was a boy of average intelligence who had nevertheless been gifted with a vivid imagination. On that long-ago day as he walked toward Neil Armstrong Elementary School (where he was currently enrolled in Mrs Stark's third grade class), he was pretending he was Jackie Chan, fighting a host of enemies in an empty warehouse with his excellent kung fu skills. He had already laid a dozen low, but more were coming at him. So absorbed was he ('Hah!' and 'Yugh!' and 'Hiyah!') that he did not notice an extremely large pile of sidewalk excrement left by an extremely large Great Dane. He walked through it and entered Neil Armstrong Elementary in an odiferous state. Mrs Stark insisted he take off his sneakers — one of them shit-stained all the way up to the Converse logo — and leave them in the hall until it was time to go home. His mother made him hose them off and then she threw them in the washing machine. They came out good as new, but by then it was too late. On that day, and forever after, Pete Steinman became Stinky Steinman.

Tonight he's hoping to find his skateboarding pals doing ollies and kick-flips in the parking lot. Two of them are: Richie Glenman (the boy with a habit of sticking French fries up his nose, and sometimes in his ears) and Tommy Edison (redhaired, freckles, the acknowledged leader of their little gang). Two is better than none, but they are out of money, it's getting late, and they're just getting ready to leave.

'Come on, hang out awhile,' Stinky says.

'Can't,' Richie says. 'WWE Smackdown, dude. Can't miss the awesomeness.'

'Homework,' Tommy says glumly. 'Book report.'

The two boys leave, skateboards under their arms. Stinky does a couple of runs, tries a kick-flip and falls off his deck (glad Richie and Tommy aren't there to see). He looks at his skinned elbow and decides to go home. If his mother is upstairs, he can watch the Smackdown himself, keeping the volume down low so he doesn't bother her while she does her accounting shit. She works a lot since she cleaned up her act.

The Whip is open and he'd kill for a cheeseburger, but he only has fifty cents. Plus, Wicked Wanda is on duty. If he asks her for credit – or maybe a buck and a half out of the tip jar – she'll laugh in his face.

He heads back to Red Bank Avenue and once he's outside the misty circle cast by the light at the front of the parking lot – where Wicked Wanda can't see him and laugh, that is – he starts dispatching enemies. Tonight, having reached a more mature age, he's imagining himself as John Wick. It's harder to bring down his enemies when he has his deck under one arm and only one hand with which to cut and chop, but he has great skills, *supernatural* skills, and so—

'Young man?'

He's jerked out of his fantasy and sees an old guy standing just outside the security light at the edge of the parking lot (not to mention the Dairy Whip's lone video surveillance camera). He's hunched over a cane and wearing a cool wide-brimmed hat like in an old black-and-white spy movie.

'Did I startle you? I'm sorry, but I need some help. My wife is in a wheelchair, you see, and the battery died. We have a disability van with a ramp, but I can't push her chair up by myself. If you could help . . .'

Stinky, currently in full hero mode, is perfectly willing to help. He's been told repeatedly not to talk to strangers, but this geezer looks like he'd have trouble knocking over a row of dominoes, let alone pushing a wheelchair up a crip ramp. 'Where is it?'

The old guy points diagonally across the street. Through the rising mist, Stinky can just make out the shape of a van parked on the tarmac of the old Exxon station. And beside it, a wheelchair with someone sitting in it.

Roddy and Emily take turns being the one stranded in the dead wheelchair, and it's really Roddy's turn, but Em's sciatica is now so bad – mostly thanks to the damned stubborn Craslow girl – that she actually *needs* the chair.

'I'll give you ten dollars to help me push her up the ramp and into our van,' the old guy says.

Stinky thinks of the burger he was just wishing for. With a ten-spot he could add fries and a chocolate shake and still have money left over. Plenty. But would Jackie Chan take money for doing a good deed?

'Nah, I'll do it for free.'

'That is very kind.'

They walk into the misty night together, the geezer leaning on his cane. They cross the avenue. When they reach the sidewalk in front of the gas station, the old lady in the wheelchair gives Stinky a weak wave. He returns it and turns to the geezer, who has one hand in the pocket of his overcoat.

'I was just thinking.'

'Yes?'

'Maybe you could give me three bucks for pushing her up the ramp. Then I could go back to the Whip and get a Burger Royale.'

'Hungry, are you?'

'Always.'

The geezer smiles and pats Stinky's shoulder. 'I understand. Hunger must be assuaged.'

July 23, 2021

1

'Are you sure about the night this friend of yours disappeared?' Holly asks. Jerome has purchased the boys milkshakes and they're sprawled on the grass in the picnic area, slurping them up.

'Pretty sure,' the redhead – Tommy Edison – says, 'because his mom called my mom to see if he was staying over and he was absent from school the next day.'

'Nah,' says Richie Glenman. This is the resident clown with the disgusting habit of putting French fries up his nose. Holly has all of their names in her notes. 'It was later. A week or two. I think.'

'I heard he ran away to live with his uncle in Florida,' says the boy with the hightop fade. This is Andy Vickers. 'His mother's a—' He tips an invisible bottle to his mouth and makes a glug-glug sound. 'Got arrested for drunk driving once.'

The boy with the acne shakes his head. He's Ronnie Swidrowski. He looks solemn. 'He didn't run away and he didn't go to Florida. He got grabbed.' He lowers his voice. 'I heard it was Slender Man.'

The others break out laughing. Richie Glenman gives him a shoulder-punch. 'There's no such guy as Slender Man, you douchebag. He's an urban legend, like the Witch of the Park.'

'Ow! You made me spill my shake!'

To Tommy Edison, who seems the brightest, Holly says, 'Do you really think your friend Peter disappeared the night you last saw him?'

'Not positive, that was over two years ago, but I think so. Like I said, he wasn't in school the next day.'

'Skippin,' Ronnie Swidrowski says. 'Stinks did it all the time. Cause his mother's a—'

'Nah, it was later,' Richie Glenman insists. 'I know because I was matching quarters with him in the park after that. Over in the playground.'

They go back and forth about it and Swidrowski starts giving a reasoned and logical argument for the existence of Slender Man, who he hears also got some teacher from the college back in the old days, but Holly has heard enough. The disappearance of Peter 'Stinky' Steinman (if he has in fact disappeared at all) almost certainly has nothing to do with the disappearance of Bonnie Dahl, but she intends to find out a little more, if only because the Dairy Whip and the auto repair shop are just half a mile apart. The Jet Mart, where Bonnie was last seen, is also fairly close.

Jerome gives Holly a look, and she gives him a nod. Time to go.

'You guys have a nice day,' he says.

'You, too,' Tommy Edison says.

The clown points at them with a ketchup-stained finger and says, 'Veronica Mars and John Shaft!'

They all break up laughing.

Halfway across the parking lot, Holly stops and goes back. 'Tommy, the night you and Richie saw him here, he had his skateboard, right?'

'Always,' Tommy says.

Richie says, 'And he still had it a week later when we were matching for quarters. That lame Alameda with the crooked wheel.'

'Why?' Tommy asks.

'Just curious,' Holly says.

It's the truth. She's curious about everything. It's how she rolls.

2

As they walk back up the hill to their cars, Holly takes the earring out of her pocket and shows it to Jerome.

'Whoa! Hers?'

'Almost positive.'

'How come the cops didn't find it?'

'I don't think they looked,' Holly says.

'Well, you win the Sherlock Holmes Award for superior detection.'

'Thank you, Jerome.'

'Which of them did you believe about Stinky Ṣteinman? The redhead or the goofball?'

Holly gives him a disapproving look. 'Why don't we call him Peter? Stinky is an unpleasant nickname.'

Jerome doesn't know Holly's entire history (his sister Barbara knows more), but he knows when he's inadvertently pressed on a sore spot. 'Peter. Got it, got it. Pete now, Pete forever. So was the night they saw him at the Dairy Whip the last time they saw him, or was he matching quarters with Mr French Fries Up the Nose in the park a week later?'

'If I had to guess, I'd say Tommy's right and Richie got his times mixed up. It was two and a half years ago, after all. That's a long time when you're that age.'

They have reached the auto repair shop. Jerome says, 'Let me work Steinman a little. Can I?'

'What about your book?'

'I told you, I'm waiting for information. Editor insists. We're talking Chicago ninety years ago, give or take, and that means mucho research.'

'Are you sure you're not just procrastinating?'

Jerome has a wonderful smile – mucho charming – and flashes it now. 'There might be an element of that, I guess, but chasing after lost kids is more interesting than chasing after lost dogs.' Which is Jerome's usual part-time gig with Finders Keepers. 'You don't really think Dahl and Steinman are related, do you?'

'Different ages and different sexes, over two years apart, so probably not. But what do I always say about probably, Jerome?'

'It's a lazy word.'

'Yes. It—' She gasps and puts a hand to her chest.

'What?'

'We weren't wearing our masks! I never even thought of it! And neither were they!'

'But you're vaxxed, right? Double-vaxxed. And so am I.'

'Do you think *they* were?'

'Probably not,' Jerome says. He realizes what he's said, and laughs. 'Sorry. Old habits die hard.'

Holly smiles. Old habits do indeed die hard, which is exactly why she wants a cigarette.

3

Jerome says he'll talk to the boy's parents. He can at least pin down whether Steinman actually disappeared or went to live with his uncle or what. If Steinman's mother was a juicer, as Andy Vickers suggested, the kid might even have been taken into foster care. The job, as Jerome sees it, is simply to confirm Steinman has nothing to do with Dahl.

Holly promises him a hundred dollars a day, two-day minimum, plus expenses. She's pretty sure he'll get Barbara to do the online stuff, but he'll split with her, even-Steven, so that's okay.

'What are you going to do?' Jerome asks.

'I think I'll take a walk in the park,' she says. 'And think.'

'You do that. It's a skill.'

4

Holly finds the path shooting off to the left and follows it to the big rock overlooking Red Bank Avenue. There she sits down and lights up.

She keeps coming back to Bonnie Dahl's bike helmet. The earring might have dropped off and been lost, but the bike helmet didn't just drop off. If Bonnie decided, pretty much on the spur of the moment, that she was sick enough of arguing with her mother to blow town, why leave her bike and take the helmet? For that matter, why leave a fairly expensive ten-speed where it almost begged to be stolen? It was only luck that it hadn't been . . . assuming Marvin Brown was telling the truth, that is, and Holly thinks she can satisfy herself on that score with reasonable certainty.

The missing bike helmet is the most compelling reason she has to believe that Dahl was abducted. Holly imagines a scenario where Bonnie tried to run from her potential kidnapper and only made it to the far end of the auto repair shop. She struggles. Her earring comes off. She's bundled into her kidnapper's vehicle (in her mind's eye Holly sees a small windowless panel truck) with her helmet still on. Perhaps the man knocks her out, perhaps he ties her up, maybe he even kills her right there, either on purpose or by accident. He leaves a printed note taped to the seat of the bike: *I've had enough.* If someone steals the bike, good. If no one steals it, the assumption will be that she decided to leave town – also good.

Holly doubts if it happened exactly that way (if it happened at all), but it could have; nearing dark, not much traffic on Red Bank Avenue, a brief struggle that might look like nothing but a conversation or a lovers' embrace to someone passing by . . . sure, it could have.

As for the other possibility, leaving town on the spur of the moment, how likely is that, really? A teenager might suddenly decide it was all too much and bug out, Holly entertained such fantasies herself while in high school, but a twenty-four-year-old woman with a job she apparently enjoyed? What about her last paycheck? Is it sitting in her boss's office? And no suitcase, just the stuff in her backpack? Holly doesn't believe it, and she's sure Isabelle Jaynes doesn't, either. But if anyone can give her a state-of-mind check, it will probably be Bonnie's friend and co-worker, Lakeisha Stone.

Holly finishes her cigarette, butts it, and puts it in her little tin box with the other dead soldiers. There are butts scattered all around the big rock, but that doesn't mean she has to add her own filth to the general litter.

She takes her phone out of her purse. She's had it on Do Not Disturb since leaving her office, and she's missed two calls since then, both from someone named David Emerson. The name rings a faint bell, something to do with her mother. He's left a VM but she ignores it for the time being and calls Jerome. She doesn't want to distract him while he's driving, so she keeps it brief.

'If you speak with Peter Steinman's mother, and if the boy is really gone, ask if she has his skateboard.'

'Will do. Anything else?'

'Yes. Watch the road.'

She ends the call and listens to the voicemail.

'Hello, Ms Gibney, this is David Emerson. Call me back as soon as convenient, please. It concerns your mother's estate.' After a pause he adds, 'So sorry for your loss, and thank you for your remarks at her final gathering.'

Now Holly knows why the name was familiar; her mother mentioned Emerson on one of their FaceTime calls after Charlotte was admitted to Mercy Hospital. This was before they put her on a ventilator, when she could still talk. Holly thinks only a lawyer would find a fancy way around saying *funeral*. As for Charlotte's estate . . . Holly hasn't even thought about it.

She doesn't want to speak to Emerson, would like to have one day when she doesn't have to think about anything but chasing the case, so she calls back immediately, pausing only long enough to light another cigarette. Her mother's ironclad dictum, badgered into Holly from the time she was a toddler: *What you don't want to do is what must be done first. Then it's out of the way.* This has stuck with Holly, as many childhood lessons do . . . for better or worse.

It's Emerson himself who answers, so Holly guesses he is one of many now working from home, without the layers of help professional people took for granted pre-Covid.

'Hello, Mr Emerson. This is Holly Gibney, returning your call.' Spread out below her is half a mile of Red Bank Avenue. It interests her quite a bit more than the lawyer.

'Thanks for calling back, and once again, I'm very sorry for your loss.'

Everything over there abandoned except for the U-Store-It, she thinks, *and that doesn't look like it's doing much business. On this side of the street you have the least-used section of the park, where upright citizens fear to tread except in broad daylight. If you planned to grab somebody, what better place?*

'Ms Gibney? Did I lose you?'

'No, I'm here. What can I do for you, Mr Emerson? Something about my mother's estate, wasn't it? There can't be much to discuss there.' *Not after Daniel Hailey*, she thinks.

'I did legal work for your Uncle Henry before he retired, so Charlotte engaged me to write her will, and made me executor. This was after she began to feel unwell and a test showed she was positive for the virus. There's no need for a reading at a family gathering . . .'

What family? Holly thinks. *With cousin Janey dead and Uncle Henry vegetating in Rolling Hills Elder Care, I'm the last pea in the pod.*

'. . . left to you.'

'Pardon me?' Holly says. 'I lost you there for a second.'

'Sorry. I said that with the exception of a few minor bequests, your mother left everything to you.'

'The house, you mean.'

She's not pleased by the idea; she's dismayed. The memories she has of that house (and the one preceding it, in Cincinnati) are dark and sad, for the most part, leading up to that final Christmas dinner where Charlotte insisted that her daughter wear the Santa hat Holly had worn for the holiday as a child. *It's tradition!* her mother had exclaimed as she carved the dry-as-Sahara turkey. So: fifty-five-year-old Holly Gibney in a Santa hat.

'Yes, the house and all the furnishings therein. I'm assuming you'll want to sell?'

Of course she will, and Holly tells him so. Her business is based in the city. Even if it weren't, living at her mother's house in Meadowbrook Estates would be like living in Hill House. Meanwhile, Counselor Emerson has continued – something about keys – and she has to ask him again to rewind.

'I said I have the keys, and I think we should agree on a time when you can come up here and inspect the property. See what you want to keep and what you want to sell.'

Holly's dismay deepens. 'I don't want to keep any of it!'

Emerson chuckles. 'That's not an unusual first reaction in the wake of a loved one's death, but you really must do a walk-through. As Mrs Gibney's executor, I'm afraid I have to insist on that. To see what repairs might need to be made before selling, for one thing, and based on years of experience, I think you *will* find things you want to keep. Could you possibly do it tomorrow? I know that's short notice, and it's a Saturday, but in these situations sooner is usually better than later.'

Holly wants to demur, to say she has a case, but her mother's voice again intrudes: *Is that a reason, Holly, or just an excuse?*

To answer that she has to ask herself if the disappearance of Bonnie Dahl is an *urgent* case, a *race against time* case, like when Brady Hartsfield was planning to blow up the Mingo Auditorium during a rock concert. She doesn't think it is. Bonnie dropped out of sight over three weeks ago. Sometimes missing people who've been abducted are found and saved. More often they are not. Holly would never say so to Penny, but whatever happened to Bonnie Rae has almost certainly already happened.

'I suppose I can do that,' she says, and takes a final monster drag on her cigarette. 'Can you possibly send someone up there today to disinfect the house? I suppose that sounds overly cautious, maybe even paranoid, but—'

'Not at all, not at all. We don't really understand this virus yet, do we? Terrible thing, just terrible. I'll call a company I've done business with before. Insurance issues, you know. I think I can have them in at nine. If so, shall we meet at eleven?'

Holly sighs and stubs out her cigarette. 'That sounds all right. I imagine the disinfecting will be expensive. Especially on a weekend.'

Emerson chuckles again. It's a pleasant one, easy on the ears, and Holly supposes he uses it often. 'I think you'll be able to afford it. Your mother was quite well off, as I'm sure you know.'

Holly isn't exactly shocked to silence, but she's certainly surprised. Shock will come later.

'Holly? Ms Gibney? Still there?'

'I'm afraid I know no such thing,' Holly says. 'She *was* well off. My Uncle Henry was, too. But that was before Daniel Hailey.'

'I don't know that name, I'm afraid.'

'She never mentioned Hailey? The can't-miss Wizard of Wall Street investment counselor that took everything my mother and my uncle had and ran off to one of those non-extradition islands? Along with God knows how many other people's money, including most of mine?'

'Pardon me, Ms Gibney, but I'm not following.'

'Really?' Holly realizes the lawyer's perplexity makes a degree of sense. When it came to unpleasant truths, Charlotte Gibney was a master of omission. 'There *was* money, but it's gone.'

Silence. Then: 'Let's rewind. Your cousin Olivia Trelawney died . . .'

'Yes.' Committed suicide, in fact. Holly had actually driven her much older cousin's Mercedes for awhile, the automotive guided missile Brady Hartsfield used to kill eight people at City Center and wound dozens more. For Holly, fixing up the Benz, changing its color, and driving it was an act of healing. And, she supposes, defiance. 'She left a considerable amount of money to her sister Janey. Janelle.'

'Yes. And when Janelle died so suddenly . . .'

That's one way of putting it, Holly thinks. *Brady Hartsfield blew Janey up, hoping to get Bill Hodges.*

'The bulk of *her* estate went to your Uncle Henry and your mother, with a trust fund set aside for you. It's Henry's share that is paying for his current, um, residence, and will for however long he lives.'

Something is beginning to dawn on Holly. Only that's the wrong metaphor. Something is beginning to *dark* on her.

'Henry's estate will also come to you upon his passing.'

'My mother died rich? That's what you're saying?'

'Quite rich indeed. You didn't know?'

'No. I knew she *was* rich at one time.'

Holly thinks of dominoes falling over in a neat line. Olivia Trelawney's husband made money. Olivia inherited it. Olivia committed suicide. Janey inherited it. Janey got blown up by Brady Hartsfield. Charlotte and Henry inherited it, or most of it. The money getting steadily whittled away by taxes and attorneys' fees, but still an extremely tidy sum. Holly's mother had invested her money and Henry's money with Daniel Hailey of Burdick, Hailey, and Warren. Later, she had also invested most of Holly's funds, with Holly's agreement. And Hailey had stolen it.

So Charlotte had told her daughter, and her daughter had had no reason to disbelieve.

Holly lights another cigarette. How many is that today? Nine? No, eleven. And it's only lunchtime. She's thinking of something in Janey's will that had made her cry. *I am leaving $500,000 in trust for my cousin Holly Gibney, so she can follow her dreams.*

'Ms Gibney? Holly? Still there?'

'Yes. Give me a moment.' But she needs more than a moment. 'I'll call you back,' she says, and ends the call without waiting for a reply.

Did her cousin Janey know that as a frightened, lonely girl, Holly had poetic ambitions? She wouldn't have known from Holly herself, but from Charlotte? From Henry? And what does it matter? Holly wasn't a good poet, no matter how much she desperately wanted to be. She had found something she *was* good at. Thanks to Bill Hodges, she had another dream to follow. A better one. It came late, but better late than never.

One of her mother's pet sayings clangs in her head: *Do you think*

I'm made of money? According to Emerson, Charlotte had been. Not early but later, after Janey died, yes. As for losing it, and losing Henry's, and losing most of Holly's trust fund to the dastardly Daniel Hailey? Holly quickly googles Daniel Hailey, adding Burdick and Warren, the other two partners. She gets nothing.

How had Charlotte been able to pull it off? Was it because Holly had been so grief-stricken at the passing of Bill Hodges and at the same time so entranced by the business of detection, of *chasing the case*? Was it because she trusted her mother? Yes to all three, but even so . . .

'I saw stationery,' she whispers. 'A couple of times I even saw *asset sheets*. Henry helped her trick me. He must have.'

Although Henry, now deep in dementia, would never be able to tell her so, or why.

She calls Emerson back. 'How much are we talking about, Mr Emerson?' This is a question Emerson is duty-bound to answer, because what Charlotte had is now hers.

'Adding in her bank account and the current value of her stock portfolio,' David Emerson says, 'I'd put your inheritance at just over six million dollars. Assuming you outlive Henry Sirois, there will be another three million.'

'And it was never lost? Never stolen by an investment specialist who had my mother's and uncle's power of attorney?'

'No. I'm not sure how you got that idea, but—'

In a growl utterly unlike her usual soft tone of voice, Holly says, '*Because she told me.*'

December 2–14, 2018

1

It's the Christmas season, and along Ridge Road, residents are marking the season in suitably tasteful and subdued fashion. There are no lighted Santas, rooftop reindeer, or lawn tableaux of the Wise Men looking reverently down at the Baby Jesus. There are certainly no houses tricked out in enough flashing lights to make them look like casinos. Such gaucheries may do for other neighborhoods in the city, but not for the genteel houses on Victorian Row between the college and Deerfield Park. Here there are electric candles in the windows, doorposts dressed in spirals of fir and holly, and a few lawns with small Christmas trees studded with tiny white bulbs. These are on timers that click off at nine o'clock, as mandated by the Neighborhood Association.

There are no decorations on the lawn or the front of the brown and white Victorian at 93 Ridge Road; this year neither Roddy nor Em Harris have felt spry enough to put them up, not even the wreath on the door or the big red bow that usually perches atop their mailbox. Roddy is in better shape than Em, but his arthritis is always worse once cold weather arrives, and now that the temperature slides below freezing by most afternoons, he's terrified of slipping on a patch of ice. Old bones are brittle.

Emily Harris isn't well at all. She now actually needs the wheelchair that is usually part of their capture strategy. Her sciatica is unrelenting. Yet there's light at the end of the tunnel. Relief is now close.

Their house has a dining room (all of the Victorians on Ridge Road have dining rooms), but they only use it on the occasions when they have guests, and as they move deeper into their eighties, those occasions are more occasional. When it's just the two of them, they take their meals in the kitchen. She supposes the dining room will be pressed into service if they have their traditional Christmas gathering for Roddy's seminar students and the writing workshop kids, but that will only happen if they feel better.

We will, she thinks. *Surely by next week and perhaps as soon as tomorrow.*

She's had no appetite, the constant pain has taken that, but the aroma coming from the oven causes the smallest pang of hunger in her stomach. It's wonderful to feel that. Hunger is a sign of health. A shame the Craslow girl was too stupid to know that. The Steinman boy certainly had no such problem. Once he got past his initial distaste, he ate like . . . well, like the growing boy he was.

The kitchen nook is humble, but Roddy has dressed the drum table overlooking the backyard with the good linen tablecloth and set two places with the Wedgwood china, the Luxion wine glasses, and their good silver. Everything sparkles. Em only wishes she felt well enough to enjoy it.

She is in her best day dress. She struggled to put it on, but managed. When Roddy comes in with the carafe, he's wearing his best suit. She notes rather sadly that it bags on him a little. They have both lost weight. Which is, she reminds herself, better than gaining it. You don't have to be a doctor to know that fat people rarely get old; you only had to look at the few colleagues of similar ages they still have. Some will be at their Christmas party on the 23rd, supposing they are well enough to have it.

Roddy bends and gives her a kiss on the temple. 'How are you, my love?'

'Well enough,' she says, and presses his hand . . . but lightly, because of his arthritis.

'Dinner in a jiff,' he says. 'In the meantime, let's have some of this.'

He pours into their wine glasses from the carafe, being careful not to spill. Half a glass for him; half a glass for her. They raise them in gnarled hands that were once, back when Richard Nixon was president, young and supple. They touch the rims, producing a charming little chime.

'To health,' he says.

'To health,' she agrees.

Their eyes meet over the glasses – his blue, hers bluer – and then drink. The first sip makes her shudder, as it always does. It's the salty taste underlying the clarity of the Mondavi 2012. Then she drinks down the rest, welcoming the heat in her cheeks and fingers. Even in her toes! The surge of vitality – faint, like her hunger pangs, but undeniable – is even more welcome.

'A spot more?'

'Is there enough?'

'More than enough.'

'Then I will. Just a little.'

He pours again. They drink. This time Em barely notices the salty undertaste.

'Are you hungry, dear one?'

'I actually am,' she says. 'Just a little bit.'

'Then let Chef Rodney finish up and serve out. Save room for dessert.' He drops her a wink and she can't help but laugh. The old rogue!

The broccoli and carrot mix is steaming. The potatoes (mashed, easier on old teeth) are in the warmer. Roddy melts butter in a skillet (he always uses far too much, but neither of them is going to die young), then tilts in the plate of chopped onions and gets them frying. The smell is heavenly, and this time her pang of hunger is stronger. As he stirs the onions, turning them so they are first transparent and then just slightly browned, he sings 'Pretty Little Angel Eyes,' a song from the way-back-when.

She remembers record hops when she was in high school, the boys in sportcoats and the girls in dresses. She remembers doing the Shake to Dee Dee Sharp, the Bristol Stomp to the Dovells, the Watusi to Cannibal & the Headhunters. A name that would be considered *very* politically incorrect today, she thinks.

Roddy takes their plates to the counter and serves out: veg, potatoes, and from the oven, the *pièce de résistance*: a three-pound roast, done to a turn. He shows it to her, simmering in its juices (and a few herbs that are special to Roddy), and she applauds.

He carves the liver into slices, dresses them with fried onions, and brings the plates to the table. Now Em finds herself not just hungry but ravenous. They eat at first without talking much, but as their bellies fill and they slow down, they speak – as they often do – of the old days and those who have either died or moved on. The list grows longer each year.

'More?' he asks. They have eaten a good portion of the roast, but there's still plenty left.

'I couldn't,' she says. 'Oh my goodness, Rodney, you've outdone yourself this time.'

'Have a little more wine,' he says, and pours. 'We'll save dessert for later. That show you like is on at nine.'

'*Haunted Case Files*,' she says.

'That's the one. How bad is your sciatica, dear one?'

'I think a little better, but I'll let you clean up and do the dishes, if you don't mind. I'd like to go through the rest of those writing samples.'

'I don't mind at all. The one who cooks must be the one who cleans, my grandmother used to say. Are you finding anything worthwhile?'

Em wrinkles her nose. 'Two or three prosaists who aren't downright *terrible*, but that's damning with faint praise, wouldn't you say?'

Roddy laughs. '*Very* faint.'

She blows him a kiss and rolls away in the wheelchair.

2

Later – the timers along Ridge Road have turned off all the subdued Christmas lighting – Em is engrossed in *Haunted Case Files*, where tonight's psychic investigator is mapping cold spots in a New England mansion that looks like a decrepit version of their own house. She feels a bit better. It's too early to feel real relief from the liver and the wine . . . or is it? That loosening in her back is definitely there, and the shooting pains down her left leg don't seem quite so vicious.

The blender has been going in the kitchen, but now it stops. Roddy enters a minute later, bearing two chilled sorbet glasses on a tray. He's changed to his pajamas, slippers, and the blue velour robe she gave him for Christmas last year.

'Here we are,' he says, handing her one of the glasses and a long spoon. 'Dessert, as promised!'

He sits down beside her in his easy chair, completing the picture of a couple who has often been pointed out on campus as a good — nay, perfect — example of romantic love's ability to endure.

She raises her glass. 'Thank you, my love.'

'Very welcome. What's going on?'

'Cold spots.'

'*Drafty* spots.'

She gives him a glance. 'Once a scientist, always a scientist.'

'Very true.'

They watch TV and have their dessert, spooning up a mixture of raspberry sorbet and Peter Steinman's brains.

3

Eleven days before Christmas, Emily Harris walks slowly but steadily up from the mailbox at 93 Ridge Road. She climbs the porch steps with a fist planted in the small of her back on the left side, but this is more out of habit than necessity. The sciatica will return, she knows that from sad experience, but for now it's almost totally gone. She turns and looks approvingly at the red bow on the mailbox.

'I'll put the wreath up later,' Roddy says.

She startles and looks around. 'Creep up on a girl, why don't you?'

He smiles and points downward. He's in his socks. 'Silent but deadly, that's me. How's your back, dear one?'

'Quite good. Fine, even. And your arthritis?'

He holds out his hands and flexes his fingers.

'Good on ya, mate,' she says in a passable Aussie drawl. They took a trip to Oz shortly after their double retirement, rented a camper and crossed the continent from Sydney to Perth. *That* was a trip to remember.

'He was a good one,' Roddy says. 'Wasn't he?'

She doesn't need to ask who he's talking about. 'He was.'

Although how long the effects will last, neither of them know. He is the youngest they've ever taken, barely into puberty. There's a great deal about what they've been doing that they don't know, but Roddy says he's learning more each time. Also — and to state the obvious — survival is the prime directive.

Em agrees. There will be no more trips to Australia, probably not even to New York for their once-every-two-years Broadway binge, but life is still worth living, especially when every step isn't an exercise in agony. 'Anything in the paper, dear?'

He slips an arm around her thin shoulders. 'Nothing since the first item, and that was barely more than a squib. Just another runaway or a stranger who came upon a target of opportunity. What do you think about the Christmas party, dear one? Keep or cancel?'

She stretches on her toes to kiss him. No pain.

'Keep,' she says.

July 23, 2021

1

Holly crosses Red Bank Avenue to the defunct auto repair shop, slips into the driver's seat of her Prius, and slams the door. It's been sitting in the sun and is hotter than a sauna, but even though sweat pops on her forehead and the back of her neck almost at once, Holly doesn't start the car to get the AC working. She only stares out through the windshield, trying to get her mind around what she's just found out. *I'd put your inheritance at just over six million dollars*, Emerson said. Plus another three when Uncle Henry dies.

She tries to think of herself as a millionaire, but it doesn't work. Doesn't come close to working. All she can see is Uncle Pennybags, the mustachioed and top-hatted avatar of the Monopoly game. She tries to think of what she might do with her new-found riches. Buy clothes? She has enough. Buy a new car? Her Prius is very reliable, and besides, it's still under warranty. There's no need to help with Jerome's education, he's all set, although she supposes she might help with Barbara's. Travel? She's sometimes daydreamed about going on a cruise, but with Covid running rampant . . .

'Oough,' she mutters. 'No.'

The idea of a new apartment comes to her, but she loves the place she has now. Like Baby Bear's chair and Baby Bear's bed, it's just right. Put more money into the business? Why? Just last year she fielded a $250,000 offer from Midwest Investigative Services to make them an affiliate. With Pete's agreement, she had turned them down. The idea of moving out of the Frederick Building, with its balky elevator and lazy super, has slightly more appeal, but the downtown location is good, and the rent is right.

Not that I have to worry about that anymore, she thinks, and gives a wild little laugh.

Holly finally realizes she's roasting and turns on the engine. She rolls down the windows until the air conditioning gets some traction and looks at her list of the people she wants to interview. That gives her some focus, because the important thing is the case. The money is just pie in the sky, and as for the more troubling implication of David Emerson's bombshell (she remembers her mother calling in tears after Daniel Hailey supposedly robbed the three of them and ran off to St Croix or St Thomas or St Wherever), she won't think about that now. Later she won't be able to help herself, but in the here and now there's a missing woman to find.

Part of her insists she's hiding from an ugly truth. The rest of her refuses that idea. She's not hiding, she's *finding*. At least trying to.

'*Cherchez la femme*,' Holly says, and takes out her phone. She thinks about calling Marvin Brown, who took Bonnie's bike to the Reynolds Library, then has a better idea. Instead of Brown, she reaches out to George Rafferty, the real estate man. Holly explains that Bonnie Dahl's mother has hired her to try and find her daughter, then asks about the day he and Mr Brown found Bonnie's bike.

'Oh my God, I hope she's all right,' Rafferty says. 'Hasn't been in touch with her mom or dad?'

'I hope she is, too,' Holly says, dodging his question. 'Who saw the bike first, you or Mr Brown?'

'Me. I always get to my properties early so I can take a fresh look. That shop, used to be Bill's Automotive and Small Engine Repair, looks like a teardown to me, but the lifts still work and the location—'

'Yes, sir. I'm sure the location is fine.' Holly thinks no such thing; since the turnpike extension was opened in 2010, traffic on Red Bank Avenue has thinned considerably. 'Did you read the note taped to the seat?'

'I sure did. "I've had enough." If I were the girl's parents, something like that would scare me to death. It could mean she was leaving, or it could mean, you know, something worse. Mr Brown and I discussed what to do with the bike, and after we looked at the shop, he put it in his pickup and took it to the library.'

'Because of the sticker on the package carrier.'

'Right. That was a nice bike. I can't remember the brand, but it was nice. All different gears and such. It's a wonder nobody stole it. Kids hang around that part of the park, you know. The part they call the Thickets.'

'Yes, sir, I'm aware.'

'And that ice cream place down the way? Kids there, too. All the time. They play the video games inside and ride their skateboards outside. Have you been a private eye for long?'

It's a term that always makes Holly want to grind her teeth. She's a lot more than an *eye*. 'Quite awhile, yes sir. Just to confirm, you saw the bike first.'

'Right, right.'

'And how long before Mr Brown showed up?'

'Fifteen minutes, maybe a little longer. I make it a point to get to my properties early, so I can check for vandalism, plus any damages that aren't on the sell sheet. Did I tell you that?'

'Yes, sir, you did.'

'So do you think you'll find her? Any leads? Are you hot on the trail?'

Holly tells him it's too early to be sure of anything. Rafferty begins telling her that if she ever has real estate needs herself, this is a prime time to buy and he has a wide selection, both business and residential. Before he can get too far into his spiel, she tells him she has another call coming in and has to take it. Actually she has to make one, to the library at Bell College.

My mother lied. Uncle Henry did, too.

She shuts that down and makes her call.

2

'Reynolds Library, Edith Brookings speaking.'

'Hello. My name is Holly Gibney. I'd like to speak to Lakeisha Stone, please.'

'I'm sorry, but Lakeisha has gone north to spend the weekend with some friends. Swimming and camping in Upsala Village. I should be so lucky.' Edith Brookings laughs. 'Can *I* help you? Or take a message?'

Holly happens to know Upsala Village, a rural community that's home to lots of Amish. It's no more than twenty miles north of her mother's house, where she'll be tomorrow. She might be able to talk to Lakeisha up there. Tomorrow afternoon, if inventorying the house doesn't take too long, Sunday if not. In the meantime, perhaps the Brookings woman *will* be able to help.

'I'm a private investigator, Ms Brookings. Penelope Dahl – Penny – has hired me to look for her daughter.'

'Oh, gee!' She sounds less professional now, and even younger. 'I hope you find her. We're worried to death about Bon!'

'Could I come up to the library and talk to you? It won't take long. Perhaps if you have an afternoon break—'

'Oh, come any time. Come now, if you want. We're not busy at all. Most of the summer sessions have been canceled because of the, you know, the Corona.'

'That's great,' Holly says. 'Thank you.'

As she pulls out onto Red Bank Avenue, she takes another look at that big rock with its view of the street and the drive-in screen a mile or two away. She wonders if Pete Steinman, aka Stinky Steinman, sometimes visited it. It wouldn't surprise her.

3

At the Reynolds Library, Holly gets both Edith Brookings ('Call me Edie') and Margaret Brenner, another of the assistant librarians Penny mentioned. Edie is womaning the main desk, but says they can go in the reading room, where she'll be able to see anyone who has a question or wants to check a book out.

'I wouldn't dare if Matt Conroy was here,' Edie says, 'but he's on vacation.'

'Mad Matt,' Margaret says. She pulls a face and they both giggle into their masks.

'He's not really mad or anything,' Edie says, 'but he's kind of a pill. If you talk to him when he comes back, please don't tell him I said that.'

'Puh-*leeze*,' Margaret says, and they do their giggling thing again. *When the cat's away the mice will play*, Holly thinks. But there's no harm

in these mice; they're just a couple of nice-looking young women who
have had something interesting turn up on an otherwise sleepy day at
work. Unfortunately, they know very little about Bonnie Rae, except
she broke up with her boyfriend, Tom Higgins.

'Anything else, you'd have to ask Keisha,' Margaret says. 'They were
tight.'

Holly plans to do that. She asks for Lakeisha's phone number and
Edie gives it to her.

'Did Bonnie say anything about leaving town?' Holly asks. 'Maybe
just in passing, like wouldn't it be nice?'

The two young women look at each other. Margaret shrugs and
shakes her head.

'Not to me she didn't,' Edie says. 'But you have to understand that
Bonnie keeps pretty much to herself. She's nice, but not what you'd
call a sharing soul.'

'Except for Keisha,' Margaret says.

'Yes, except for her.'

'Let me show you something.' From her pocket Holly takes the
earring and holds it out to them in the palm of her hand. The way
their eyes widen tells her all she needs to know.

'Bonnie's!' Edie says, and touches it with the tip of her finger.
Holly allows this; she knew as soon as she saw it that the earring
wasn't big enough to hope for a fingerprint, including Bonnie Rae's.
'Where was it?'

'In some bushes close to where her bike was found. By itself it
means nothing. It's a clip-on and might have just fallen off.'

'You really should talk to Lakeisha,' Margaret says. 'She'll be back
on Monday.'

'I'll do that,' Holly says, but she doesn't think she'll have to wait
until Monday.

4

The library parking lot is almost dead empty and Holly had no trouble
getting a shady spot, but the interior of her car is still plenty warm.
She gets the AC cranking and calls Bonnie's mom. Penny doesn't even
bother to say hello, just asks if Holly has found out anything. She

sounds both eager and afraid. Holly thinks of that Volvo plastered with Bonnie Rae's smiling pictures and wishes she had better news.

'I'm going to send you a photo of an earring I picked up near where your daughter's bike was found. It's been ID'd as Bonnie's by two women who work with her at the Reynolds, but I want to be sure.'

'Send me the picture! Please!'

'I will, ASAP. While I've got you, do you by any chance have Bonnie's credit card info?'

'Yes. A week or so after she went missing, I went to her apartment and looked at her last two Visa bills. It was that police detective's suggestion. Visa is the only card she has. I thought the bills might tell me something, I don't know what, but there was nothing that stood out. A pair of shoes, two pairs of jeans from Amazon, groceries, some meals she ordered in from DoorDash, pizza from Domino's . . . that kind of thing.'

'What about her phone? Does she pay for that with her Visa?'

'Yes. Her carrier's Verizon, same as mine.'

To Holly, it's the credit card that matters most. 'Text me the number on her card, please. Include the expiration date. Also her cell number.'

Penny says she will. Holly takes a photo of the earring and sends it off. When Penny calls back two minutes later, she's sobbing. Holly calms her as best she can. Eventually Penny gets hold of herself, but Holly knows the woman is starting down a dark road. One that Holly herself has already traveled a bit further. Bonnie Rae might still be alive, but the chances are growing that she's not.

Holly sits with her hands in her lap and cool air from the driver's side vents blowing her fringe around. She needs to think, but the first thing that comes to her is a joke opening: *A new millionaire walks into a bar, and . . .*

And what? It's a joke with no punchline. Which is somehow fitting. She pushes it away and thinks about the case. Why would Bonnie leave her bike on what's probably the most deserted stretch of Red Bank Avenue? Answer: she wouldn't. Why would she leave the note but take her bike helmet? Answer: she wouldn't.

'Leave the gun, take the cannoli,' she murmurs — a line from her favorite gangster movie.

Did someone grab her? Leap out and grab her? If so, then . . .

She calls Marvin Brown, introduces herself, tells him who she is and what she's doing, then asks about the bike – did it look damaged in any way? Brown tells her it looked fine, not a scratch on it. She thanks him, ends the call, and puts her thinking cap back on.

No one leaped out and knocked Bonnie off the bike. The concrete in front of the former Bill's Automotive and Small Engine Repair is so full of cracks and frost heaves it's probably beyond repair. Marvin Brown will have to do a repave job if he really intends to do business there. If the bike had landed on that rough surface, it almost certainly would have been banged up. She'll have to check to be sure, but for the time being she'll take Brown's word. He works with vehicles for a living, after all, and isn't that what a bicycle is, when you get right down to it?

The daughter of a liar walks into a bar. Check that, the daughter of a liar and a thief *walks into a bar. She leaves the gun but takes the cannoli.*

'*Stop* it,' Holly mutters. 'The bike looked good, stay with that. Why does the bike look good?'

It seems to her that the answer is as plain as the blue eyes she sees in her rearview mirror. Because Bonnie stopped there. Stopped and got off. Why stop if she didn't mean to head downtown to one of those fly-by-night, we-take-cash bus lines? Because she saw someone she knew? Because someone needed help? Or was pretending to need help?

Bill Hodges still sometimes speaks to her, and he does so now. *If you go any farther out on that limb, Holly, it's going to break off.*

His voice is right, so she backs up . . . but not all the way. The bike's pristine condition suggests Bonnie Rae stopped of her own accord. Whether that was because she actually meant to leave it there or for some other reason is still an open question.

But again: why leave the bike and take the helmet?

Her phone bings with a text. It's Bonnie's Visa info and her phone account. Holly can't sit still anymore. She gets out of her car, calls Pete Huntley, and begins pacing around the library parking lot, sticking to the shady areas as much as she can. That sun is still like a hammer – *oough.*

The first thing Pete says is, 'You took the case after all. Jesus, Holly, after your mother . . .' He starts coughing.

'Pete, are you all right?'

He gets it under control. 'I'm fine. Well, not fine but no worse than I was when I got up this morning. Holly, your mother just died!'

Yes, and left me quite the fortune, Holly thinks. *A new millionaire walks into a bar and . . . something funny happens.*

'Working is good for me. And I'm going up to Meadowbrook Estates tomorrow. It seems I inherited a house I don't want.'

'Your mother's, right? Well, good for you. It's a seller's market. Assuming you want to get rid of it.'

'I do. Are you in the market?'

'Dream on, Gibney.'

'How did you know I took the case?'

'Tall, dark, and handsome has already been on the phone to me.' Pete means Jerome. 'He wanted me to look up an address he was too lazy to look up himself.'

Holly finds this a trifle irritating. 'We have an address-finder app, and since we pay for it, we should use it once in awhile. Besides, *you* need something to do as well, Pete. Besides coughing and wheezing.' Holly's latest turn around the parking lot has brought her back to her Prius. She thinks of her cigarettes in the center console, thinks of coughing and wheezing, and walks on. 'What address did he want?'

'A Vera Steinman. She lives in one of those tract houses near Cedar Rest Cemetery. What do *you* want?'

'I have Bonnie Dahl's Visa and Verizon information. I need to know if there's been any activity on either account.'

'I can get that, I have a source, but it's not strictly legal. In fact—' There's a honk as Pete blows his nose. '—it's not legal at all. Which means it will cost, and itemizing it on the Dahl woman's expense account could be risky.'

'I don't think you need to use your source,' Holly says. 'I bet Izzy will check for you.'

There's a pause, except for the rasp of Pete's breathing. To Holly it doesn't sound good. 'Really?'

'She practically gave me the case, and I wasn't all that surprised. You know how it is in the PD now?'

'FUBAR. Which means—'

'I know what it means.'

'Tell you something, Gibney, when I see what's going on with the cops now I'm so friggin glad I pulled the pin.'

'Tell Izzy that if we find out something substantive, we'll loop her in.'

'Yeah? Will we?'

'I haven't decided,' Holly says primly.

'What's this Vera Steinman got to do with the Dahl girl?'

'Probably nothing.' Holly could tell Pete that at twenty-four, Bonnie Rae is hardly a girl, but it would do no good. Pete is old-school. She once heard him complaining to Jerome about the Miss America Pageant dropping the swimsuit competition, and his go-to word for breasts is either *bazams* or *jahoobies*. 'Pete, I have to go.'

'If you catch the Corona running around, Holly, we'll be shut down a lot longer.'

'I hear you, Pete. Will you call Izzy?'

'Yeah. Good luck, Hols. Really sorry about your mom.'

She walks slowly to her Prius, thinking. Suppose someone was waiting who knew Bonnie's routine. Did the old boyfriend know it? Maybe. Probably. And the bike. She keeps coming back to the bike, out front and just begging to be stolen. If it had been, would the missing helmet bother her so much?

'No,' she says. 'It would not.'

She gets in the car, re-starts the engine, then smiles. She's thought of a punchline for her joke.

December 4–19, 2020

1

On December 4th, Bell College President Hubert Crumley announces that he is sending all students home early because of rampant Covid infections on campus. On the 7th – Pearl Harbor Day – he decrees that the spring semester will consist of remote classes only.

Roddy Harris is horrified.

'That's all right for you literary types,' he says to Emily. 'Most writing has been done in a lockdown environment since time immemorial, but aren't we supposed to follow the science, according to the great Dr Fauci? What about lab time, for God's sake? Bio labs? Chemistry and physics labs? What about *them*? Labs are *science*!'

'This too shall pass, my dear,' Em says.

'Yes, but when? And in the meantime, what to do? I need to talk to Hamish about this.'

Hamish Anders is the head of the Life Sciences Department, and Em doubts if Roddy's fulminations – which is what they are – will move him much. She and Roddy still take active roles in the doings of their respective colleges, but their status is largely honorary. She understands that, and is happy with her little job of reading applications to the Writer's Workshop, especially without Jorge Castro to get in her way. It keeps her busy, it keeps her sharp, and there is the occasional gem in those piles of slush. But something else is troubling her.

'No Christmas party this year,' she says. 'We haven't missed since 1992 – almost thirty years! It's a shame.'

Roddy hasn't even considered that. 'Well . . . . it's not an official lockdown, dear. So people *might* come . . .' He sees her eye-roll. 'At least a few?'

'I don't think so. Even if they did, how would they eat canapes and drink champagne indoors with their masks on?' Something else occurs to her then. 'And *The BellRinger*! Those anti-establishment dodos who think they're reporters would have a ball with that!'

The BellRinger is the campus newspaper.

Em frames a headline with her hands. 'Old Profs Party While America Burns with Fever! How does that sound to you?'

He has to laugh, and Emily joins in. Winter is hard on old joints and bones, and they are having the usual aches and pains, but overall they're doing very well. The real pain will return, they know this from experience, but in the meantime, Peter Steinman has been good to them.

Of course planning ahead is important, and they have already started making a list of possibles. Roddy likes to say that God wouldn't have given us brains unless he wanted us to use them. Not that either of them believes in God, or a happily-ever-afterlife, which is an excellent reason to extend this one as long as possible.

'No Christmas party, on top of everything else!' Roddy exclaims. 'Damn this *plague*!'

She gives him a hug.

2

A week later Emily comes out to the garage, where Roddy is affixing the 2021 state ID stickers on the license plates of their Subaru wagon. Next to it is the van with the blue and white license plates from the next state over. Roddy starts it up every once in awhile to freshen the battery, but the van is only used on special occasions. The Wisconsin disability plates weren't stolen, because stolen plates have a tendency to be reported. He created them in his basement workshop and would defy anyone to tell the difference between them and the real thing.

'What are you doing out here without a coat?' Roddy asks.

'I've had an idea,' she says, 'and couldn't wait to tell you. I think it's a good one, but you be the judge.'

He listens and declares it not just a good idea but an excellent idea. Genius, in fact. He gives her a hug that's maybe a bit too strong.

'Easy, big boy,' Em says. 'The sciatica is sleeping. Don't wake it up.'

3

The Harrises' annual Christmas party happens after all. It's held on the Saturday before Christmas. The attendance is the best in years, and no one has to wear a mask. Some of the partygoers arrive from other states (one actually orbits in from Bangladesh), but most are from nearby. President Crumley comes and so does this year's writer-in-residence, Henry Stratton (Emily would never say it, but thinks it's nice to have a straight white male holding down the job again).

It's a Zoom party, of course, but with a special touch that caused Roddy to raise his estimation of Em's idea from excellent to genius. They can't serve food and drink to the party attendees in Maine or Colorado or Bangladesh, but here in this city they absolutely can – especially to those living along Victorian Row between the school and the park.

They use the websites of the English and Life Sciences Departments to advertise for one-night-only help, explaining what the job would entail. The stipend offered is small (the Harrises are financially comfortable but not rich), but they still have plenty of takers. It's the novelty of the thing, Emily says. Plenty of campus employees – even a few instructors! – sign up for duty as Santa's elves. They spread out on the night of the party dressed in Santa hats and Santa beards. Some even add black boots and tip-of-the-nose Santa glasses. Santa's elves are reverse trick-or-treaters, each bearing a small tray of canapes to local partygoers. And sixpacks of Iron City beer in lieu of champagne.

The party is a roaring success.

A Santa's elf also comes to 93 Ridge Road, home of the Harrises – Emily insisted. Roddy lets her in. It's a darned pretty elf with lots of blond hair and lively brown eyes above her white beard. Her red Santa pants accentuate long legs which Roddy admires surreptitiously (but not too surreptitiously for Em). Emily shows the elf into the living room, where both Harrises have set up their laptops – the better to Zoom with, my dear. Em takes the plate of canapes. Roddy takes the sixpack of IC.

On their laptops, Henry Stratton and his girlfriend are tipsily harmonizing on 'Santa Claus Is Coming to Town' from their own Victorian (once the residence of Jorge Castro and his 'friend').

'Aren't you just the cutest elf ever?' Roddy says.

'Watch him, he's a shark,' Emily says. The elf laughs and says she will. Emily shows her back to the door. 'Do you have more stops to make?'

'A couple,' says the elf, and points to her bike at the end of the walk. A cooler, presumably holding two more cellophane-wrapped plates of canapes and two more sixpacks, has been bungee-corded to the package carrier. 'I'm glad it's warm enough to bicycle. Professor, this was such a fantastic idea!'

'Thank you, dear. Very kind of you to say.'

The elf gives Emily a shy side-glance. 'I took your Early American Writers the year before you retired. That was an awesome class.'

'I'm glad you enjoyed it.'

'And this year I finally decided to apply for the workshop. You know, the Writer's Workshop? You'll probably come across my submission, if you're reading them for Mr Stratton—'

'I am, but if you're applying for the fall semester next year, I think we'll have somebody new.' She lowers her voice. 'We've asked Jim Shepard, although I doubt if he'll agree to come.'

'That would be amazing, but I probably won't make the cut, anyway. I'm not very good.'

Em pretends to cover her ears. 'I pay no attention to what writers say about their work. It's what the work says about the writer that matters.'

'Oh. I suppose that's very true. Well, I better get going. Enjoy your party!'

'We will,' Em says. 'What's your name, dear?'

'Bonnie,' the elf says. 'Bonnie Dahl.'

'Do you ride your bike everywhere?'

'Except in bad weather. I have a car, but I love my bike.'

'Very aerobic. Do you live close by?'

'I have a little condo apartment by the lake. I work at the Reynolds and pick up other work – odd jobs, like – when I can.'

'Should you be looking for another odd job in the near future, I might have something you could help me with.' She wonders if Bonnie's response will be *awesome* or *amazing*.

'Really? That would be awesome!'

'Are you computer-friendly? Working in the library, you must be. I can hardly turn mine on without Roddy to help me.' Emily speaks this lie with a disarming smile.

'I can't fix them, but work with them, sure!'

'May I have your number, just in case? No promises, mind.'

Bonnie complies happily. Em could put it in her iPhone contacts as quick as winking, but in her current persona as a computer illiterate, she scratches it on a napkin featuring a dancing and obviously inebriated St Nick and the words *HAPPY HOLIDAZE!*

'Merry Christmas, Bonnie. Perhaps I'll see you again.'

'Cool! Merry Christmas!'

She goes down the walk. Emily closes the door and looks at Roddy.

'Nice legs,' he says.

'Dream on, Lothario,' she replies, and they both laugh.

'Not only an elf, an aspiring writer,' Roddy says.

Em snorts. 'Awesome. Cool. *Amayyyzing*. I doubt if she could write an original sentence if someone put a gun to her head. But it's not her brains we'd be interested in. Would we?'

'Oh, don't say *that*,' Roddy says, and they both laugh some more.

They have a little list of possibles for next fall, and this Santa's elf would make a good addition.

'As long as she's not vegan,' Roddy says. 'We don't need another one of *those*.'

Emily kisses his cheek. She loves Roddy's dry sense of humor.

July 23, 2021

Vera Steinman lives on Sycamore Street, which is devoid of sycamores. Devoid of any trees, in fact. There are plenty in the manicured and well-watered acres beyond Sycamore Street's dead end, but they are sequestered behind the gates and meandering rock walls of Cedar Rest Cemetery. In this neighborhood of treeless streets named for trees, there are only tract houses standing almost shoulder to shoulder and broiling in the sun of late afternoon.

Jerome parks at the curb. There's a Chevrolet occupying the cracked driveway. It's at least ten years old, maybe fifteen. The rocker panels are rusty and the tires are bald. A faded bumper sticker reads WHAT WOULD SCOOBY DO? Jerome has called ahead and started to explain that he came across Peter Steinman's name while pursuing another case, but she stopped him right there.

'If you want to talk about Peter, by all means drop by.' Her voice was pleasant, almost musical. The sort of voice, Jerome thought, that you'd expect from a well-paid receptionist in an upscale law or investment firm downtown. What he thinks now is that this little house standing on a dead lawn is no upscale anything.

He pulls up his mask and rings the bell. Footsteps approach. The door opens. The woman who appears looks like a perfect match for the upscale voice: light green blouse, dark green skirt, hose in spite of the heat, auburn hair pulled back from her face. The only thing that doesn't fit is the whiff of gin on her breath. More than a whiff, actually, and there's a half-full glass in her hand.

'You're Mr Robinson,' she says, as if he might not be sure himself. In the direct sunlight he sees her smooth middle-aged good looks may be due in large part to the magic of makeup. 'Come in. And you can take off the mask. Assuming you've been vaccinated, that is. I've had it and recovered. Chock-full of antibodies.'

'Thank you.' Jerome steps inside, takes off his mask, and shoves it into his back pocket. He hates the fucking thing. They're in a living room that's neat but dark and spare. The furniture looks strictly serviceable. The only picture on the wall is a humdrum garden scene. Somewhere an air conditioner is thumping.

'I keep the shades down because the AC is on its last legs and I can't afford to replace it,' she says. 'Would you like a drink, Mr Robinson? I'm having a gin and tonic.'

'Maybe just some tonic. Or a glass of water.'

She goes into the kitchen. Jerome sits in a slingback chair – gingerly, hoping it won't give way under his two hundred pounds. It creaks but bears up. He hears a rattle of ice cubes. Vera Steinman comes back with a glass of tonic and her own glass, which has been refreshed. He will tell Holly when he calls her that night that in spite of what one of the Dairy Whip skateboys said, he had no idea he was dealing with a deep-dish daily drunk until the end of their conversation. Which came suddenly.

She sits in the boxy living room's other chair, puts her drink on the coffee table, where there are coasters and a spread of magazines, and smooths her skirt over her knees. 'How can I help you, Mr Robinson? You seem very young to be chasing after missing children.'

'It's actually a missing woman,' he says, and gives her the rundown on Bonnie Dahl – where her bike was found, how he and Holly ('my boss') went down to the Dairy Whip to talk to the boys skateboarding there, and how Peter's name had come up.

'I don't think Peter's disappearance has anything to do with Bonnie Dahl's, but I'd like to make sure. And I'm curious.' He rethinks that word. 'Concerned. Have you heard from your son, Mrs Steinman?'

'Not a word,' she says, and takes a long swallow of her drink. 'Maybe I should buy a Ouija board.'

'So you think he's . . .' Jerome finds himself unable to finish.

'Dead? Yes, that's what I think. In the daytime I still hold out hope, but at night, when I can't sleep . . .' She holds up her glass and takes a deep swallow. 'When not even a bellyful of this stuff will *let* me sleep . . . I know.'

A single tear trickles down her cheek, cutting through the makeup and showing paler skin beneath. She wipes it away with the back of her hand and takes another swallow. 'Excuse me.'

She goes into the kitchen, still walking perfectly straight. Jerome hears the clink of a bottleneck. She returns and sits down, careful to sweep the back of her skirt so it won't wrinkle. Jerome thinks, *She dressed for me. Got out of her PJs and housecoat and dressed for me.* He can't know this, but he does.

Vera Steinman talks for the next twenty minutes or so, sipping away at her drink and taking a second pause to refill her glass. She doesn't slur. She doesn't wander off-topic. She doesn't stagger or weave on her trip to and from the kitchen.

Because Peter disappeared before Covid and the current turmoil in the city's police department, his case was quite thoroughly investigated. The conclusion, however, was the same. The investigating detective, David Porter, believed (or said he believed) that Peter had run away.

Part of Detective Porter's reasoning was based on his interview with Katya Graves, one of two guidance and health counselors at Breck Elementary School. A year or so before Peter's disappearance his grades had slipped, he was often tardy and sometimes absent, and there had been several incidents of acting out, one resulting in a suspension.

In Graves's meeting with the boy after the suspension had run its two-day course, the counselor persisted past the usual no-eye-contact mumbles, and finally the dam burst. His mother was drinking too much. He didn't mind his friends calling him Stinky, but he hated it when they made fun of his mom. Her husband had left her when Peter was seven. She lost her job when he was ten. He hated the jokes, and sometimes he hated her. He told Ms Graves he thought often about hitching to Florida to live with his uncle, who had a home in Orlando, near Disney World.

Vera says, 'He never showed up there, but Detective Porter still thought he was a runaway. I bet you know why.'

Of course Jerome knows. 'They never found his body.'

'No,' she agrees. 'Not to this day, and there's no more exquisite torture than hope. Excuse me.'

She goes into the kitchen. The bottle clinks. She returns, walking straight, skirt swishing, hose whispering. She sits. Good posture. Clear speech. She tells Jerome that Peter's photo can be found among thousands of others on the Center for Missing and Exploited Children's website. He can be found on the FBI's Kidnappings & Missing Persons website. On the Global Missing Children's Network. On Missing Kids. org. On the Polly Klaas Foundation website, Polly Klaas being a twelve-year-old kidnapped from a slumber party and subsequently murdered. And for months after Vera reported Peter missing, his picture was shown on the assembly room screen of the city PD at every rollcall.

'Of course I was questioned as well,' Vera says. The smell of gin is now very strong. Jerome thinks it isn't just coming from her mouth, but actually seeping from her pores. 'Parents murder children all the time, don't they? Mostly stepfathers or natural fathers, but sometimes mothers get into the act, as well. Diane Downs, for instance. Ever seen the movie about her? Farrah Fawcett was in it. I was given a polygraph, and I suppose I passed.' She shrugs. 'All I could tell them was the truth. I didn't kill him, he just went out one night on his skateboard and never came back.'

She tells Jerome about the meeting she had with Katya Graves after Graves's talk with Peter. 'She said anytime that was convenient for me, which was funny because anytime was convenient, me being between jobs. I lost the last one because of a DUI. While I was out of work Peter and I lived on savings and the monthly checks I get from my ex-husband – child support and alimony. Sam can't stand me, but he was very good about those payments. Still is. He knows Peter is missing, but he still sends the support checks. I think it's superstition. He loves Peter. It was me he couldn't stand. He asked me once why I drank so much, was it him? I told him not to flatter himself. It wasn't him, it wasn't childhood trauma, it wasn't anything, really. It's a stupid question. I drink, therefore I am. Excuse me.'

When she comes back – perfectly straight, sweeping the back of her skirt before sitting down, knees together – she tells Jerome that she learned from Ms Graves how Peter's friends were making fun of him because his mommy was a drunk who lost her job and had to spend a night in the clink.

'That was hard to hear,' she says. 'It was my bottom. At least then. I didn't know how deep a bottom could be. Now I do. The Graves woman gave me a list of AA meetings and I started going to them. Got a new job at Fenimore Real Estate. It's one of the biggest firms in the city. The boss is an ex-drunk, and he hires lots of people who are getting sober, or trying to. Life was better that last year, Mr Robinson. Peter's grades improved. We stopped arguing.' She pauses. 'Well, no, not *entirely*. You can't *not* argue with your kid.'

'You don't have to tell me,' Jerome says, 'I was one.'

She laughs loudly and humorlessly at that, making Jerome realize that she's not somehow magically metabolizing all that gin, that yes-sir-ree-sir, she's really drunk. As a skunk. Yet she doesn't seem it, and how can that be? Practice, he supposes.

'That's why it's stupid to think Peter ran off because of my drinking. Just three weeks before he disappeared, I picked up a one-year sobriety chip. I don't suppose I'll ever get another. I didn't start boozing again until six weeks or so after he disappeared. During that six weeks I practically wore out the carpet on my knees, praying to my higher power to bring Peter back.' She gives another loud and humorless bark of laughter. 'I might as well have spent that time praying the sun would come up in the west. When it really sank in that he was gone for good, I reacquainted myself with the local liquor store.'

Jerome doesn't know what to say.

'He's listed as missing because that makes it simple for the police, but I think Detective Porter knows he's dead as well as I do. Luckily for me, there really *is* a higher power.' She raises her glass.

'What night did he go missing, Ms Steinman?'

She doesn't have to think about her answer. Jerome supposes it's engraved on her memory. 'November 27th, 2018. Not a thousand days ago, but getting there.'

'One of the boys at the Dairy Whip said you called his mother.'

She nods. 'Mary Edison, Tommy's mom. That was at nine o'clock, half an hour after he was supposed to be in. I had numbers for several of his friends' parents. I was a good mother to him during that last year, Mr Robinson. Conscientious. Trying to make amends for the years when I wasn't so good. I thought maybe Peter was planning to stay over with Tommy and forgot to tell me. It made sense . . . sort of . . . because school started late the next day. Some kind of teacher meeting about what to do if there was a violent incident, Peter told me. That I *do* remember. When Mrs Edison said Peter wasn't there, I waited another hour, hoping. I got on my knees and prayed to that higher power guy that he'd come in with some nutty story about why he was late . . . even with beer on his breath . . . just to see him, you know?'

Another tear, which she wipes away with the back of her hand. Jerome isn't sorry he came, but this is hard. He can almost smell her pain, and it smells like gin.

'At ten o'clock, I called the police.'

'Did he have a phone, Mrs Steinman?'

'Oh sure. I tried that even before I called Mary Edison. It rang in his room. He never took it when he was skateboarding. He was afraid he'd fall and break it. I told him if he broke his phone I wouldn't be able to afford a replacement.'

Jerome recalls what Holly asked him to find out. 'What about his board? Any idea about that?'

'The skateboard? It's in his room.' She stands up, sways briefly, then catches her balance. 'Would you like to see his room? I keep it the same as it was. You know, like a crazy mom in a horror movie.'

'I don't think you're crazy,' Jerome says.

Vera leads him down a short hall. There's a laundry room on one side, clothes heaped in careless piles in front of the washer, and Jerome thinks he's just had a glimpse of the real Vera, the one who's confused and lost and often half in the bag. Maybe all in the bag.

Vera sees him looking and closes the laundry room door.

Pete's room has PETE STEINMAN H.Q. Dymo-taped to the door. Below it is a *Jurassic Park* velociraptor with a word balloon coming out of its toothy mouth: **Keep Out Or Risk Being Eaten Alive**.

Vera opens the door and holds out a hand like a model on a game show.

Jerome goes in. The single bed is neatly made – you could bounce a dime off the top blanket. Over it is a poster of Rihanna in a come-hither pose, but at the age the boy was when he blinked out of the known world, his interest in sex hadn't yet overshadowed the child's hunger for make-believe . . . especially, Jerome thinks, when the child in question was known as Stinky to his peers. Flanking the window (which looks out on the almost identical house next door) are posters of John Wick and Captain America. On the dresser is Peter's cell phone in its dock and a Lego model of the *Millennium Falcon.*

'I helped him build that,' Vera says. 'It was fun.' At last Jerome detects the faintest slur: not *was fun* but *wash fun.* He's almost relieved. Her capacity is . . . well, he doesn't exactly want to think about it. Propped in the corner to the left of the dresser is a blue Alameda skateboard, its surface scuffed by many rides. A helmet rests on the floor next to it.

Jerome points to it. 'Could I . . .?'

'Be my guest.' *Gesh.*

Jerome picks up the board, runs his hand over the slightly dipped fiberglass surface, then turns it over. One wheel looks slightly bent. Written in fading Magic Marker, but still perfectly legible, is the owner's name and address and telephone number.

'Where was it?' Jerome asks, suddenly sure he knows the answer: on the cracked pavement of the abandoned auto repair shop where Bonnie Rae's bike was found. Only that turns out not to be the case.

'In the park. Deerfield. They searched it for his, you know, body, and one of them found it in some bushes near Red Bank Avenue. I think that's where someone took him to kill him and do whatever else to him first. Or else, it was a foggy night, maybe someone hit him with a car and took the body away. To bury. Some drunk like me. I just hope, you know . . . please God, he didn't suffer. Excuse me.'

She heads back to the kitchen, posture still perfect, but now there's an appreciable hip-sway in her walk. Jerome looks at the skateboard a little longer, then puts it back in the corner. He's no longer sure there's no connection between Steinman and Dahl. The similarities of location and artifacts left behind may be coincidental, but they certainly exist.

He goes back to the living room. Vera Steinman comes out of the kitchen with a fresh drink.

'Thanks very much for—'

Jerome gets that far before Vera's knees buckle. The glass falls from her hand and rolls across the rug, spilling what smells like straight gin.

Jerome ran track and played football in high school, and his reflexes are still good. He catches her under the arms before she can go all the way down in what might have been a nose- and tooth-breaking face-plant. She feels completely boneless in his grip. Her hair has come loose and hangs around her face. She makes a growling noise that might or might not be her son's name. Then the seizures begin, taking her and shaking her like a rat in a dog's mouth.

January 6, 2021

1

'That's enough,' Em says to Roddy. 'Turn it off.'

'My dear,' Roddy says, 'this is *history*. Don't you agree, Bonnie?'

Bonnie Rae is standing in the doorway of Em's downstairs study nook with stacks of last year's Christmas cards forgotten in her hands. She is staring at the television, transfixed, as a mob storms the Capitol, breaking windows and scaling walls. Some wave the Stars and Bars, some the Gadsden rattlesnake flag, the one that says DON'T TREAD ON ME, many more with Trump banners the size of bedsheets.

'I don't care, it's awful, turn it off.'

It *is* awful, she means that, but it's also awfully exciting. Emily thinks Donald Trump is a boor, but he's also a sorcerer; with some abracadabra magic she doesn't understand (but in her deepest heart envies) he has turned America's podgy, apathetic middle class into revolutionaries. Intellectually they disgust her. But there is another side to her, usually expressed only in her diary, and the experiences of the last nine years have changed her at an age when personality change is supposed to be next to impossible. She would never say so, but this political sacrilege fascinates her. A part of her hopes they break into offices, haul out elected representatives of both parties, and string them up. Let them feed the birds. What else are they good for?

'Turn it *off*, Rodney. Watch it upstairs, if you must.'

'As you like, dear.'

Roddy reaches for the controller on the table next to him, but it slips from his hand and thumps to the carpet as a reporter says, 'Do you call this a riot or an actual insurrection? At this point it's impossible to tell.'

He picks the controller up awkwardly, not grasping it but holding it between the edges of his palms. Then, with a grimace, he thumbs the off button, killing the reporter's voiceover in mid-speculation. He puts the controller back on the table and turns to Bonnie. 'What do you think, my dear? Riot or insurrection? Is this the twenty-first century's version of Fort Sumter?'

She shakes her head. 'I don't know what it is. But I bet if Black people were doing that, the police would be shooting them.'

'Pooh,' Emily says. 'I don't believe that for a minute.'

Roddy gets up. 'Emily, would you work some of your magic on my hands? They don't care for this cold weather.'

'In a few minutes. I want to get Bonnie started.'

'That's fine.' He leaves the room and soon they hear him ascending the stairs, which he does without pause. There's no arthritis in his knees or hips. At least not yet.

'I've put a file on your laptop titled CHRISTMAS AND NEW YEAR'S,' Bonnie says. 'The names and addresses of everyone who sent you and Professor Harris a card is in it. There's a lot of them.'

'Fine,' Emily says. 'Now we need some sort of letter . . . I don't know what you'd call it . . .' She knows very well, and she already has a complete contact list on her phone. She could transfer it to her computer in a jiff, but Bonnie doesn't need to know that. Bonnie needs to see her as the stereotypical elderly academic: head in the clouds, losing a few miles an hour off her mental fastball, and largely helpless outside her own field of expertise. And harmless, of course. Would never dream of insurrectionists hanging elected representatives of the United States government from lampposts. Especially the blacks (a word which in her mind she will *never* capitalize) and the fanny-fuckers. Of which there are more every day.

'Well, if you were a business,' Bonnie lectures earnestly, 'I suppose you'd call it a form letter. I prefer to think of it as a *core* letter. I can show you how to personalize each response to include not just thank yous – if there was a gift – and Happy New Year wishes, but personal details about families, promotions, awards, whatever.'

'Marvelous!' Em exclaims. 'You're a genius!' Thinking, *As if any teenager couldn't do the same thing, between* Call of Duty *sessions and posting pictures of his penis to his girlfriend on WhatsApp.*

'Not really,' Bonnie says. 'It's pretty basic.' But she flushes with pleasure. 'If you dictate the core letter, I'll keyboard it.'

'Excellent idea. Just let me think how I want to word it while I see what I can do about poor Roddy's hands.'

'His arthritis is pretty bad, isn't it?'

'Oh, it comes and goes,' Em says. And smiles.

2

Roddy is lying on their bed with his gnarled hands clasped on his chest. She doesn't like seeing him that way; it's how he'd look in his coffin. But dead men don't smile the way he's smiling at her. He is still *such* a charmer. She closes the bedroom door and goes to her vanity. From it she takes an unlabeled jar.

'I'm thinking we should scratch her from the list,' Roddy says as she returns to the bed and sits beside him.

'Someone has nevertheless been fascinated by firm breasts and a slim waist,' Em says, unscrewing the lid of the jar. 'Not to mention those long legs.' Inside the jar is a yellow jelly-like substance. There wasn't a great deal of fat on the late Peter Steinman, but they harvested what there was.

'Of course she's good-looking,' Roddy says impatiently, 'but it's not that. We've never taken someone we've had a close association with. It's dangerous.'

'I worked in the same department as Jorge Castro,' she points out. 'In fact, I was *questioned*.' She widens her eyes. 'Also, you bowled in that league, the Golden Oldies . . .'

'Not these days.' He lifts his hands. 'As for you being questioned about Castro, everyone in your department was. It was routine. This might not be the same. She works in our *house*.'

This, of course, is true. Emily called the girl on Boxing Day and offered her part-time employment, updating her computer to make her correspondence easier, also to create a spreadsheet containing the names of the current Writer's Workshop applicants.

Em swipes a finger into the yellow substance that lined Peter Steinman's abdomen not all that long ago. 'Hold 'em out, sweetie.'

Roddy holds out his hands, the fingers slightly twisted, the knuckles more than slightly swollen. 'Easy, easy.'

'Just a little pain, then sweet relief,' she says, and begins coating his fingers with the lotion, paying particular attention to the knuckles. Several times he grimaces and sucks in breath, making a snakelike hissing.

'Now flex,' she says.

He closes his hands slowly. 'Better.'

'Of course.'

'A bit more, please.'

'There isn't much left, hon.'

'Just a little.'

She swipes her finger again, creating a clear glass comma at the bottom of the jar. She transfers the lotion to Roddy's left palm and he begins rubbing it into his fingers, now flexing them almost naturally.

'Her employment is short-term,' Emily says, 'and she understands that. She'll be back at the library full-time as soon as the extended Christmas break ends and the spring semester begins. And of course she'll be working on her writing, with my encouragement.'

'Is she any good?'

'I haven't seen any yet, but guessing by the subject matter, I would say not.'

'The subject matter being?'

She leans close and whispers, 'Vampires in love.'

Rodney actually giggles.

'But in the course of our conversations, I've also learned a great deal about her, and it's all good. She's quits with her boyfriend, and even though she instigated the breakup, it's still painful to her. She wonders if there's something wrong with her, a character flaw, that makes her unable to participate in a stable relationship.'

Roddy scoffs. 'Based on what she's told me – yes, she does talk to me – the boyfriend, this Tom, was the very definition of a loser. She's well rid of him, I'd say.'

'I'm sure you're right, but this is about how she feels and what it means to us. She also has a relationship with her mother that I'd describe as fraught. Not at all uncommon, young women and their mothers often butt heads, but also good for us. Do you know what she said to me? "My mother is a controlling bitch, but I love her."

Also . . . keep rubbing those hands, dear, work that stuff deep into the joints . . . also, the head librarian at the Reynolds, name of Conroy, has fixed upon our Bonnie. According to her, he has a bad case of Roman hands and Russian fingers.'

Roddy gives a brief cackle. 'Haven't heard that one in awhile.'

'If we wait until October or November, as we usually do, she will have left our employment – our *part-time, seasonal* employment – nine or even ten months before. If we're questioned, and I suppose we might be, we can tell the absolute truth.' Em ticks off the points on her fingers, which are almost as slim as they were when she was a girl wearing shin-length skirts and bobby sox. 'Unhappy breakup with boyfriend. A need to escape mother's influence. Best of all, sexual harassment in the workplace. You see how good all this is? How she might just decide to up stakes and leave?'

'I suppose she might,' he says. 'When you put it like that.'

'*And* we know her routine. She always takes the same route from the library.' She pauses, then continues in a lower voice. 'I know you like looking at her breasts. I don't mind.'

'My father used to say a man on a diet can still read a menu. So yes, I've looked. She has what my students – the male ones – would call a fine rack.'

'Aesthetic issues aside, those breasts amount to almost four per cent of her body fat.' She holds up the almost empty jar. 'That's a lot of arthritis relief, honeybun. Not to mention my sciatica.' She screws on the lid. 'So. Have I convinced you?'

He flexes his fingers rapidly, and without apparent pain. 'Let's say you've given me food for thought.'

'Good. Now give me a kiss. I have to go downstairs and resume pretending to be a computer illiterate. And you have a riot to watch.'

July 23, 2021

1

Jerome calls Holly at quarter past six from outside the Steinman house and tells her of his adventures. He says he had to take Vera to the hospital himself, because all of the Kiner ambulances, plus those from the city's Emergency Services Department, were on Covid calls. He carried her to his car, wedged her into the passenger bucket seat, buckled her up, and drove to the hospital as fast as he dared.

'I rolled down the window, thinking the fresh air might revive her a little. I don't know if it worked, she was still pretty soupy when we got there, but it saved me the expense of getting the Mustang steam cleaned. She vomited twice on the way, but down the side. Which will wash off. That stink is a lot harder to get off the carpeting.'

He tells Holly that Vera also vomited twice while she was seizing. 'I got her on her side before she spewed the second time. Which was good because it cleared her airway, but at first she wasn't breathing. That scared the crap out of me. I gave her mouth-to-mouth. She might have started again on her own, but I was afraid she might not.'

'You probably saved her life.'

Jerome laughs. To Holly it sounds shaky. 'I don't know about that, but I've rinsed my mouth out half a dozen times since and I can still taste gin-flavored puke. When I got to her house she said I could take off my mask, she'd had Covid and was chock-full of antibodies. I hope she was right. I don't know if even a double dose of Pfizer would stand up to that kind of soul kiss.'

'Why are you still there? Didn't they keep her overnight?'

'Are you kidding? There's not a single available bed in that place. There was a car-crash guy lying in the hall, moaning and covered with blood.'

My mother died in a hospital just like that, Holly thinks. *She was rich.*

'Did they do *anything* for her?'

'Pumped her stomach, and when she could say her name they sent her home with me. No paperwork or anything, just your basic wham-bam-thank-you-ma'am. Crazy. It's like all the systems are breaking down, you know?'

Holly says she does.

'I got her inside – she could walk – and to her bedroom. She said she could undress herself and I took her word for it but when I looked in, she was lying there fully dressed and snoring. Puke all down the side of my car, but she never got a speck on her clothes, which were nice. I think she dressed for me.'

'You're probably right. You wanted to talk to her about her son, after all.'

'The nurse said there were also a few half-digested pills in the stuff they pumped out of her. I'm not sure she was trying to kill herself, but she might have been.'

'You saved her life,' Holly says. No *probably* this time.

'This time, maybe. What about next time?'

Holly has no good answer for that.

'If you could have seen her, Holly . . . I mean before she went down . . . perfectly put together, totally coherent. But knocking back gin like they were going to outlaw it next week. I could have left thinking that she was perfectly okay, except for a hangover tomorrow. How is that possible?'

'She's built up a tolerance. Hers must be higher than most. You say Peter's skateboard was in his room?'

'Yeah. There was a search party combing the park, looking for him . . . or his body . . . and one of them found it in the bushes. I didn't get a chance to ask her, but I'd bet you anything they found it in the Thickets. Which is not far from where the Dahl woman's bike was found. I think Dahl and Steinman might be related, Holly. I really do.'

Holly was about to make herself a Stouffer's chipped beef on toast for supper – her go-to comfort food – when Jerome called. Now she drops the frozen packet into a pot of boiling water. According to the box you can microwave it, which is quicker, but Holly never does it that way. Her mother always said that microwaves were first-class food ruiners, and like so many of her mother's teachings, it has stuck with her only child. *Oranges are gold in the morning and lead at night. Sleeping on your left side wears out your heart. Only sluts wear half-slips.*

'Holly? Did you hear me? I said I think Dahl and the Steinman boy might—'

'I heard you. I need to think about it. Did he have a helmet for skateboarding? I should have asked those boys, but I never thought of it.'

'You didn't think of it because *they* weren't wearing them,' Jerome says. 'Neither was Peter Steinman, if he was going out to meet his friends that night. They would have called him a pussy.'

'Really?'

'Absolute. He didn't take his phone and he didn't wear his helmet. It was in his room next to his board. I don't think he *ever* wore it. Looked like it just came out of the box. Not a scratch on it.'

Holly stares at the bag of chipped beef, turning over and over in the boiling water. 'What about the uncle in Florida?' She answers her own question. 'Mrs Steinman would have called him, of course.'

'She did and the detective in charge – Porter – also did. She tried, Holly. With herself and with her boy. Quit drinking for a year. Got another job. It's a fucking tragedy. Do you think I should stay over with her? Steinman? The living room smells pretty bad and the couch doesn't look what you'd call comfy, but I will if you think I should.'

'No. Go home. But before you do I think you should go back in, check her breathing, and check the medicine cabinet. If she's got tranquilizers or pain pills or stuff for depression, like Zoloft or Prozac, dump them down the toilet. The booze too, if you want. But that's only a stopgap. She can always get new prescriptions and they sell booze everywhere. You know that, right?'

Jerome sighs. 'Yeah. I do. Hols, if you could have *seen* her before she went down . . . I thought she was okay. Sad for sure, and drinking too much, but I really thought . . .' He trails off.

'You did what you could. She's lost her only child, and unless there's a miracle, she's lost him for good. She'll either cope – go back to her meetings, sober up, get on with her life – or she won't. That Chinese proverb about how you're responsible for someone if you save their life is so much poop. I know that's hard, but it's the truth.' She stares at the boiling water. 'At least, as I understand it.'

'One thing might help her,' Jerome says.

'What's that?'

'Closure.'

Closure is a myth, she thinks . . . but doesn't say. Jerome is young. Let him have his illusions.

2

Holly eats her chipped beef on toast at her tiny kitchen table. She thinks it's the perfect meal because there's hardly anything to clean up. She feels bad for Jerome, and terrible for Peter Steinman's mother. Jerome was right when he called it a tragedy, but Holly is wary of lumping the missing woman and the missing boy together. She knows perfectly well what Jerome is thinking about: a serial, like Ted Bundy or John Wayne Gacy or the Zodiac. But most serials are fundamentally uncreative, not capable of getting past some unresolved psychological trauma. They go on picking versions of the same victim until they're caught. The so-called Son of Sam killed a number of women with dark wavy hair, possibly because he couldn't kill Betty Broder, the woman who birthed him and then abandoned him.

Or maybe Berkowitz just liked seeing their heads explode, the Bill Hodges in her head remarks.

'Oough,' Holly says.

But Bonnie Rae and Peter Steinman are too different to be the work of one person. She's sure of it. Or almost sure; she's willing to admit the similar locations and the abandoned modes of transportation, bike and skateboard.

That reminds her to check with Penny about Bonnie's clothes. Are any of them missing? Did she possibly have a suitcase of duds stashed somewhere, maybe with her friend Lakeisha? Holly takes out her notebook and scratches a reminder to ask that. She'll call tonight, try to set up an appointment with Lakeisha for the following afternoon, but she'll save her important questions for when they are face to face.

She rinses her plate and puts it in her dishwasher, the smallest Magic Chef the company makes, perfect for the single lady with no man in her life. She returns to the table and lights a cigarette. Nothing, in Holly's opinion, finishes a meal as perfectly as a smoke. They also aid the deductive process.

Not that I have anything to deduce, she thinks. *Maybe after I dig a little deeper, but all I can do now is speculate.*

'Which is dangerous,' she tells her empty kitchen.

Silver bells tinkle, which means it's her personal (the office ring is the standard Apple xylophone). She expects it to be Jerome, with something he forgot to tell her, but it's Pete Huntley.

'You were right about Izzy. She was delighted to give me what she found out about the Dahl girl's credit and phone. On the Visa, no activity. On the Verizon account, ditto. Iz went back in to see if there were any charges in the last ten days. There haven't been. Her last credit card purchase was jeans from Amazon on June 27th. Isabelle says when you call Dahl's phone, you can no longer leave a voicemail, just get the robot telling you the mailbox is full. And there's no way to track it.'

'So Bonnie or someone else took out the SIM card.'

'It sure wasn't a case of nonpayment. The phone bill was paid on July 6th, five days after the girl disappeared. *All* her bills were paid on the 6th. Ordinarily the bank pays on the first Monday of the month, but that Monday was the official holiday, so . . .'

'Was it NorBank?'

'Yeah. How did you know?'

'It's where her mother works. Or did until some of the branches shut down. She says when they re-open, she expects to be rehired. How much is in Bonnie Dahl's account?'

'I don't know because Isabelle doesn't. It would take a court order to get that info, and Iz doesn't see the point in trying for one. Neither do I. It's not what's important. You know what is, right?'

Holly knows, all right. Financially speaking, Bonnie Rae Dahl is dead in the water. Which is probably a terrible metaphor under the circumstances. 'Pete, you sound better. Not coughing so much.'

'I *feel* better, but this Covid is a real ass-kicker. I think if I hadn't gotten those shots, I'd be in the hospital. Or . . .' He quits there, no doubt thinking of his partner's mother, who didn't get the shots.

'Go to bed early. Drink fluids.'

'Thank you, nurse.'

Holly ends the call and lights another cigarette. She goes to the window and looks out. It's still hours until dark, but the sunlight has taken on the evening slant that always feels rueful to her, and a little sad. *Another day older, another day closer to the grave*, her mother used to say. Her mother who is now *in* her grave.

'She stole from me,' Holly murmurs. 'She stole the trust fund I got from Janey. Not all of it, but most of it. My own mother.'

She tells herself that's the past. Bonnie Rae Dahl may still be alive. But.

No action on her Visa. No calls made from her phone. Holly supposes a trained secret agent – one of John le Carré's 'joes' – could slip away like that, shedding the ties to modern life the way a snake sheds its skin, but a twenty-four-year-old college librarian? No. Not unlikely, just no.

Bonnie Rae Dahl is dead. Holly knows it.

3

Holly has an ill-formed (and totally unscientific) idea that exercise can offset some of the damage she's doing to her body by renewing her smoking habit, so after speaking with Pete she takes a two-mile walk in the latening light, ending up at the south end of Deerfield Park. The playground is full of kids swinging and teeter-tottering, sliding and hanging upside-down from the jungle gym. She watches them in an unguarded way no man could get away with in this century of sexual hyper-awareness, not consciously thinking about her new case, subconsciously thinking of nothing else. She has a nagging sensation that she's forgetting something, but refuses to chase it. Whatever it is will make itself known eventually.

She calls Lakeisha Stone when she gets home. The woman who answers sounds exuberant and high on life (other substances possible). In the background Holly can hear music – it might be Otis Redding – and people laughing. There are occasional whoops. *Other substances probable*, Holly thinks.

'Hi, whoever you are,' Lakeisha says. 'If this is some car warranty offer or how I can improve my credit rating—'

'It's not.' Holly introduces herself, explains why she's calling, and asks if she could meet with Lakeisha tomorrow afternoon, lateish. She says she has to be close to Upsala Village on family business. Would that be convenient?

It's a much less exuberant Lakeisha who says that she'd be happy to talk to Holly. She's with friends at the campground on Route 27, the one with the Indian name – does Holly know it? Holly says she doesn't, and doesn't say that these days *Indian* is considered a pejorative at best, racist at worst. She says she's sure the GPS on her phone will take her right there.

'Nothing about Bonnie? No word?'

'No word at all,' Holly says.

'Then I don't know how I can help you, Ms Gibney.'

'You can help me with one thing right now. Do you think she ran away?'

'God, no.' Her voice wavers. When she speaks again, all traces of exuberance are gone. 'I think she's dead. I think some sick bastard raped her and killed her.'

4

That night Holly prays on her knees, being sure to name-check her friends and saying that she's sorry she resumed her smoking habit and hopes that God will help her quit again soon (but not just yet). She tells God she doesn't want to think about her mother tonight – what Charlotte did and why she did it. She ends by asking for any help God can give her in the case of the missing woman and concludes by saying she hopes that Bonnie Rae is still alive.

She gets into bed and looks up into the darkness, wondering what was nagging her at the park. As sleep approaches, ready to take her in, it comes to her: have there been other disappearances in the vicinity of Deerfield Park?

She thinks it might be interesting to find out.

February 8, 2021

January has been bitterly cold, but February brings unseasonably warm temperatures, as if to make up for three weeks of lake-effect snow and teeth-clattering near-zero weather. On this Monday afternoon, with the mercury in the mid-fifties, Roddy Harris decides to rid the Subaru wagon of the built-up encrustations of salt, which will eventually rot out the rocker panels and undercarriage if allowed to stay. Em suggests he take it to the Drive & Shine on the Airport Extension, but Roddy says he'd rather get out in the fresh air while the fresh air is bearable. She asks about his arthritis. He insists it isn't bothering him, says he feels fine.

'Not bothering you *now*,' Em says, 'but you'll be moaning about it tonight, I bet, and you'll be stuck with Bengay because the good stuff is down to dribs and drabs. We should save what's left for an emergency.' *If my back or your neck locks up again* is what she means.

'I'll wear my gloves,' he tells her, and Em sighs. Roddy is a dear man, the light of her life, but when he decides to do something, there's no swaying him.

He enters the garage by the back door, gets the hose, and attaches it to the faucet bib on the side of the house. Then he returns to back the car out. There are three buttons on the garage wall. One opens the left bay, where the van they seldom use is parked. One opens the right bay, home to the Harrises' Subaru runabout. The third button opens both bays, and Roddy has an irritating habit of pushing that one. *Because it's in the middle instead of at the bottom or top* is what he tells himself when both doors go rattling up instead of the one he wants. *It's not forgetfulness, just bad design, pure and simple.*

He gets in the wagon and backs to where the hose is waiting with the spray attachment already screwed on. Roddy is looking forward to this little chore. He loves the way the high-pressure blast cleans away the caked-on clots of road salt. He lifts the nozzle, then stops. There's someone standing at the head of the driveway, looking at him. She's a pretty girl wearing a red coat and a matching knitted scarf and hat. Her facemask is also red and so are her galoshes – a Christmas present, as it happens, because the girl has admired her good friend Holly's pair on several occasions. In one hand she's holding a slim file folder against her chest.

'Are you Professor Harris?' she asks.

'I am indeed,' he says. 'One second, young lady.' He opens the driver's door of the Subaru. The remote for the garage is clipped to the visor. This one has two buttons instead of three. He pushes one and the lefthand door trundles down, enclosing the van. He doubts she even noticed it, it's him she's looking at, but always safe, never sorry.

He approaches her with a smile and holds out a hand. Mostly these days she greets people with a Covid-aware elbow bump, but he's wearing gloves and she's wearing mittens (not really necessary on a day this warm, nor is the scarf, but the ensemble makes a fashion statement), so it's okay.

'What can I do for you this fine mild day?'

Barbara Robinson smiles. 'It's actually your wife I was hoping to see. I wanted to ask her about something.'

Based on the folder she's holding so protectively to her bosom, he guesses it's the Writer's Workshop she's interested in. He could tell her that she's probably too young for the program – most of the wannabe writers who attend are in their twenties and thirties. He could also tell her it seems more and more likely that there won't *be* a workshop program this fall. Jim Shepard has passed, and few other pro writers have expressed an interest. The department's current scribbler in residence, Henry Stratton, has also turned down a return engagement. He told English Department head Rosalyn Burkhart that the idea of remote learning in an intensive writing program was absurd. According to Emily, who got it from Rosalyn, Stratton said it would be like making love while wearing boxing gloves.

But let Em give pretty Little Red Riding Hood the bad news; he is just a humble (and retired) biology prof.

'I'm sure she'll be happy to speak with you, Miss—'

'I'm Barbara. Barbara Robinson.'

'Very nice to meet you, Barbara. Just ring the bell. My wife is elderly, but her hearing is acute.'

Barbara smiles at this. 'Thank you.' She starts up the walk to the house, then turns back. 'You should do your van, too. My dad had one when I was little, and the muffler fell off on the Interstate. He said the salt ate right through it.'

So she did *see it*, Roddy thinks. *I really have to be more careful.*

'I appreciate the tip.'

Would she remember? Did she see anything she shouldn't have seen? Roddy thinks not. Roddy thinks Little Red Riding Hood, aka Barbara Robinson, is only interested in whatever uncut gems of writing she's carrying in her folder. Dreaming of being the next Toni Morrison or Alice Walker. But he will have to be even more careful in the future. *All the fault of that button in the wrong place*, he thinks. *Idiotic engineering. My memory is fine.*

He turns on the hose and directs it at the side of the Subaru. The salt begins to wash away, revealing the gleaming green paint beneath. He was looking forward to this, but now not so much. The girl, pretty as she is in her red gear, has darkened his mood.

Barbara gives him a final wave, goes up the front walk, and rings the bell. The door opens and Em stands there, looking no more than seventy in a green silk dress, her hair fresh from the beauty parlor that morning. Hair Today is supposed to be closed because of the pandemic, but Helen makes exceptions for longtime customers who tip well through the year and remember her at Christmas.

'Yes? May I help you?'

'I wonder if I could talk to you. It's about . . .' Barbara gulps. 'It's about writing.'

Em looks at the folder, then gives Barbara an apologetic smile. 'If it concerns the Writer's Workshop, they are not taking any new applications. The fall–winter program is rather up in the air, I'm afraid. This sickness, you know.'

'No, it's not that.'

Emily gazes at her visitor for a moment: pretty, sturdy, obviously healthy, and – of course – young. She looks over the girl's shoulder and sees Roddy looking at them as the hose sprays the driveway. *That will freeze if the temperature drops tonight,* she thinks. *You should know better.* Then she returns her eyes to the girl in red. 'What's your name, my dear?'

'Barbara Robinson.'

'Well, Barbara, why don't you come inside and tell me what it *is* about.'

She stands aside. Barbara walks into the house. Em closes the door. Roddy continues washing the trim green wagon.

July 24, 2021

1

Holly arrives at Meadowbrook Estates forty-five minutes before the time she and Counselor Emerson agreed on. *Holly is early for everything,* Uncle Henry liked to say. *She'll be early to her own funeral.* For that one she'll probably be right on time – no choice – but she signed on to her mother's Zoom funeral fifteen minutes early, which more or less proves Uncle Henry's point.

She doesn't go directly to the house but stops on the corner of Hancock Street, keeping an eye on the step van parked in her late mother's driveway. The van is bright red except for the company name on the side: A.D. CLEANING, in yellow. As the owner and chief sleuth (*gumshoe, hawkshaw, dick,* and *keyhole-peeper* are less dignified terms) of a private investigation company, Holly has seen such vans a time or two before. A.D. stands for After Death.

In this case they will only be vacuuming and wiping down every surface with disinfectant (must not neglect the light switches, flush handles, even the door hinges). After violent deaths, and after the police forensic units have done their work, the A.D. crew comes in to clean up blood and vomit, cart away broken furniture, and of course fumigate. The last is particularly important when it comes to meth labs. Holly might actually know one or two members of this crew, but she doesn't want to see or talk to them. She rolls down her window, lights a cigarette, and waits.

At ten forty, two A.D. employees come out with their bulky cases slung over their shoulders. They are wearing gloves, coveralls, and masks. Regular N95s, not the gas masks sometimes necessary after violent deaths. The lady in this house died of so-called natural causes, and in the hospital, so it's strictly a Covid wipedown, easy-peasy, quick in and quick out. They exchange a nod. One of them tapes an envelope – red, like the step van – to the front door. They hop in their van and drive away. Holly reflexively lowers her head as they go by.

She puts her cigarette butt in her traveling ashtray (freshly cleaned that morning but already containing three dead soldiers) and drives down to 42 Lily Court, the house her mother bought six years ago. She pulls the envelope off the door and opens it. The enclosed sheets of paper (only two; following a suicide or murder there would have been many more) detail the services performed. The last line reads ITEMS REMOVED: 0. Holly believes that, and David Emerson must also have believed it. A.D. has been around for years, they're bonded, their reputation in this less than pleasant but utterly necessary field is impeccable . . . and besides, what did her mother have to steal? Her dozens of china figurines, including the Pillsbury Doughboy and the leering Pinocchio that used to give Holly the horrors as a little girl?

For a millionaire she lived cheap, Holly thinks. This awakens feelings that aren't a part of her usual emotional spectrum. Resentment? Yes, but mostly it's anger and disappointment.

She thinks, *The daughter of a liar walks into a bar and orders a mai-tai.*

Of course a mai-tai. On the rare occasions when she orders a drink, that's the one Holly orders because it makes her think of palm trees, turquoise water, and white sand beaches. Sometimes in bed at night (not often, but sometimes) she imagines a bronze lifeguard in tight bathing trunks sitting up on his tower. He looks at her and smiles and what follows, follows.

Holly has her key, but she has no urge to go in and see that china Pinocchio with his Alpine hat and his leering little smile that says *I know all about your fantasy lifeguard, Holly. I know how you dig your fingernails into his back when you—*

'When I come, so what, who cares,' she mutters as she sits on the step to wait for the lawyer.

In her mind, her mother replies, sad as always when her untalented and unglamorous daughter fails to come up to the mark: *Oh, Holly.*

Time to open the door, not to the house but in her mind. To think about what happened and *why* it happened. She supposes she already knows. She's a detective, after all.

2

Elizabeth Wharton, mother of Olivia Trelawney and Janelle 'Janey' Patterson, died. Holly met Bill Hodges at the old lady's funeral. He came with Janey, and he was kind. He treated Holly – gasp! – as a regular person. She had *not* been a regular person, isn't a regular person now, but she's closer to regular than she was. Thanks to Bill.

Janey died after that funeral. Brady Hartsfield blew her up. And Holly – a forty-something lonely woman with no friends, living at home with her mother – actually helped to catch Brady . . . although as it turned out, Brady wasn't done with any of them. Not with Bill, not with Holly, not with Jerome and Barbara Robinson.

It was Bill who convinced her she could be her own person. He never said it out loud. He never had to. It was all in the way he treated her. He gave her responsibilities and simply assumed she would fulfill them. Charlotte didn't like that. Didn't like *him*. Holly barely noticed. Her mother's cautions and disapprovals became background noise. When she was working with Bill, she felt alive and smart and useful. Color came back into the world. After Brady there was another case to chase, another bad guy to go after, Morris Bellamy by name. Morris was looking for buried treasure and willing to do anything to get it.

Then . . .

'Bill got sick,' Holly murmurs, lighting a fresh cigarette. 'Pancreatic.' It still hurts to think of that, even five years later.

There was another will, and Holly discovered Bill had left her the company. Finders Keepers. It hadn't been much, not then. Nascent. Struggling to get on its feet.

And me struggling to stay on mine, Holly thinks. *Because Bill would have been disappointed if I fell down. Disappointed in me.*

It was around then – she can't remember exactly, but it had to be not long after Bill passed – that Charlotte called her in tears and told her the dastardly Daniel Hailey had scarpered off to the Caribbean with the millions Janey had left to her and to Henry. Also with most of Holly's trust fund, which she had thrown into the pot at her mother's urging.

There was a family meeting where Charlotte kept saying things like *I can't forgive myself, I'll never be able to forgive myself*. And Henry kept telling her it was all right, that they both still had enough to live on. Holly did as well, he said, although she might consider giving up her apartment and living on Lily Court with her mother for awhile. Taking up residence in the guest room, in other words, where her mother had more or less replicated Holly's childhood room. *Like a museum exhibit*, Holly thinks.

Had Uncle Henry really said *easy come, easy go* at that meeting? Sitting on the step, smoking her cigarette, Holly can't remember for sure, but she thinks he did. Which he *could* say, because the money actually hadn't gone anywhere. Not his, not Charlotte's, not Holly's.

And of course you'll have to close the business, Charlotte had said. That Holly *can* remember. Oh yes. Because that was the purpose of it all, wasn't it? To put a stop to her fragile daughter's crazy plan to run a private detective agency, an idea put into her head by the man who had almost gotten her killed.

'To get me back under her thumb,' Holly whispers, and mashes her cigarette out so hard that sparks fly up and bite the back of her hand.

3

She's thinking about lighting another one when Elaine from next door and Danielle from across the street come over to tell her how sorry they are for her loss. They both attended the funeral. Neither are wearing masks, and they exchange an amused look (an *oh, Holly* look for sure) when Holly quickly pulls hers up. Elaine asks if she's going to list the house for sale. Holly says probably. Danielle asks if she is perhaps thinking of having a yard sale. Holly says probably not. She's feeling the onset of a headache.

That's when Emerson pulls up in his no-nonsense Chevrolet. A Honda Civic parks behind him, two women inside. Emerson is also early, only by five minutes or so, but thank God. Danielle and Elaine head off to Danielle's house, chatting away, exchanging gossip plus whatever invisible creepy-crawlies might or might not be colonizing their respiratory systems.

The women who exit the Honda are roughly Holly's age, Emerson quite a bit older, sporting showy white wings on the sides of his swept-back hair. He's tall and cadaverous, with dark circles under his eyes that suggest to Holly either insomnia or an iron deficiency. He's toting a very lawyerly briefcase. She's glad to see all three are wearing no-frills N95 masks, and instead of his hand, he offers an elbow. She gives it a light bump. Each of the women raises a hand in greeting.

'Pleased to meet you face to face, Holly – may I call you Holly?'

'Yes, of course.'

'And I'm David. This is Rhoda Landry, and the pretty lady next to her is Andrea Stark. They work for me. Rhoda's my notary. Have you been inside yet?'

'No. I was waiting for you.' *Did not want to face Pinocchio and the Pillsbury Doughboy alone*, she thinks. It's a joke, but like many jokes it's also true.

'Very kind,' he says, although why it would be Holly doesn't know. 'Would you like to do the honors?'

She uses her key, the one her mother gave to her with great ceremony, telling her *for goodness sake take care of it, don't lose it like the library book you left on the bus*. The library book in question, *A Day No Pigs Would Die*, was recovered from the bus company's lost and found the next day, but Charlotte was still bringing it up three years later. And later still. At sixteen, eighteen, twenty-one, in her *fifties*, God save the Queen, it was still *remember the time you lost that library book on the bus?* Always with the rueful laugh that said *Oh, Holly*.

The smell of potpourri hits her as soon as the door is open. For a moment she hesitates – nothing brings back memories, both good and bad, so strongly as certain aromas – but then she squares her shoulders and steps inside.

'What a nice little place,' Rhoda Landry says. 'I love a Cape Cod.'

'Cozy,' Andrea Stark adds. Why she's here Holly doesn't know.

'I've got some things for you to look over and a few papers for you to sign,' Emerson says. 'The most important is an acknowledgement that you have been informed of the bequest. One copy of that goes to the IRS and one to County Probate. Would the kitchen work for you? That's where Charlotte and I did most of our business.'

Into the kitchen they go, Emerson already fumbling with the catches of his briefcase, the two women looking around and taking inventory, as women are apt to do in a house that isn't their own. Holly is also looking around, and hearing her mother everywhere her eyes stop. Her mother's voice, always starting with *how many times have I told you.*

The sink: *How many times have I told you to never put a juice glass in the dishwasher until you rinse it?*

The refrigerator: *How many times have I told you to make sure the door is closed tight?*

The cupboards: *How many times have I told you to never put away more than three plates at a time if you don't want them to chip?*

The stove: *How many times have I told you to double-check that everything is off before you leave the kitchen?*

They sit at the table. Emerson gives her the papers he needs her to sign, one by one. There's the acknowledgement that she has been informed of the bequest. There's an acknowledgement that she has been provided a copy of Charlotte Anne Gibney's last will and testament (which Emerson gives her now). There's the acknowledgement that she has been informed of her mother's various investment assets, which include a very valuable stock portfolio, Tesla and Apple shares being the pick of the litter. Holly signs an employment agreement authorizing David Emerson to represent her in probate court. Rhoda Landry notarizes each document with her big old stamping gadget, and Andrea Stark witnesses them (so that's what she's here for).

When the signing ritual is done, the women offer Holly murmured condolences and make their exit. Emerson tells Holly he'd be happy to take her to lunch, except for his pending appointment. Holly tells him that's perfectly fine. She doesn't want to eat with Emerson; what she wants is to see the back of him. Her headache is getting worse, and she wants a cigarette. *Craves* one, actually.

'Now that you've had some time to think about it, are you still leaning toward selling the house?'

'Yes.' Not just leaning, either.

'With furnishings or without? Have you thought about that?'

'With.'

'Still . . .' From his briefcase he takes a small stack of red tags. Printed on them is SAVE. 'If you find there are things you want after going through the place, you can put these tags on them. Just peel off the back, you see?'

'Yes.'

'For instance, your mother's china figurines in the front hall, you might want those as keepsakes . . .' He sees her face. 'Or perhaps not, but there might be other things. Probably will be. Based on my previous experience in such cases, legatees often let things go they later wish they had held onto.'

You believe that, Holly thinks. *You believe it to your very soul, because you're a holder-onner, and holder-onners are never able to understand let-goers. They are tribes that just can't understand each other. Sort of like vaxxers and anti-vaxxers, Trumpers and Never Trumpers.*

'I understand.'

He smiles, perhaps believing he's convinced her. 'The last thing is this.'

He takes a slim folder from his briefcase. It contains photographs. He spreads them out before her like a cop laying out a perp gallery for a witness. She views them with amazement. It's not perps she's looking at but jewelry lying on swatches of dark cloth. Earrings, finger rings, necklaces, bracelets, brooches, a double string of pearls.

'Your mother insisted I take these for safekeeping before she went to the hospital,' Emerson says. 'A bit irregular, but it was her wish. They're yours now, or will be once Charlotte's will is probated.' He hands her a sheet of paper. 'Here's the inventory.'

She glances at it briefly. Charlotte has signed, Emerson has co-signed, and Andrea Stark – whose job description, apparently, is Professional Witness – has also signed. Holly looks back at the photos and taps two of them. 'This is my mother's wedding ring, and this is her engagement ring, which she hardly ever wore, but I don't recognize *any* of this other stuff.'

'She seems to have been quite the collector,' Emerson says. He sounds a bit uncomfortable, but really not very. Death reveals secrets. Surely he knows this. He has been, as they say, around the block a few times.

'But . . .' Holly stares at him. She thought – hoped – she was prepared for this meeting, even for touring her dead mother's house and the museum exhibit guest room, but *this*? No. 'Is it valuable or costume?'

'You'll have to have it appraised to determine the value,' Emerson says. He hesitates, then adds something less lawyerly. 'But according to Andrea, it's not costume.'

Holly doesn't reply. What she's thinking is that this goes beyond deceit. Maybe beyond forgiveness.

'I'll continue to hold these pieces in the firm's safe until the will is probated, but you should keep this. I have a copy.' He means the inventory. There have to be at least three dozen items on it, and if those are real gems, the total value must be . . . Jesus, a lot. A hundred thousand dollars? Two hundred thousand? *Five?*

Under the patient tutelage of Bill Hodges, she has trained her mind to follow certain facts and not flinch when they lead to certain conclusions. Here is one fact: Charlotte apparently had jewelry worth a great deal of money. Here is another: Holly has never seen her mother wearing any of said sparklers; did not even know they existed. Conclusion: At some point following her mother's inheritance, and probably after the money had supposedly been lost, Charlotte became a secret hoarder, like a cave-bound goblin in a fantasy story.

Holly sees him to the door. He looks at the china figurines and smiles. 'My wife loves stuff like this,' he says. 'I think she's got every gnome and pixie-sitting-on-a-mushroom ever made.'

'Take a few for her,' Holly says. *Take them all.*

Emerson looks alarmed. 'Oh, I couldn't. No. Thank you, but no.'

'At least take this one.' She picks up the hateful Pinocchio and slaps it into his palm with a smile. 'I'm sure the estate is paying you—'

'Of course—'

'But take this from me. For your kindness.'

'If you insist—'

'I do,' Holly says. Seeing that poopy little long-nosed fucker going away will be the best thing that's happened to her since arriving at 42 Lily Court.

Closing the door and watching through the window as Emerson goes to his car, Holly thinks, *Lies. So many lies.*

Holly goes back to the kitchen and gathers up her copies of the legal papers. Feeling like a woman in a dream – a new millionaire walks into a bar, so on and so on – she goes to the second drawer to the left of the sink, where there are still Baggies, aluminum foil, Saran wrap, bread ties (her mother never threw them away), and other assorted rickrack. She roots around until she finds a big plastic chip clip and attaches it to the papers. Then she takes a teacup – HOME IS WHERE

THE HEART IS printed on the side – back to the table. Her mother never allowed smoking in the house; Holly used to do it in her bathroom with the window open. Now she lights up, feeling both residual guilt and a certain naughty pleasure.

Once she sat at a table very like this one, in her parents' house on Bond Street in Cincinnati, filling out college applications: one to UCLA, one to NYU, one to Duke. Those were her dream choices, worth every penny of the application fees. Places far away from Walnut Hills High, where she had never been known as Jibba-Jibba. Away from her mother, father, and Uncle Henry, too.

She was accepted at none of them, of course. Her grades were strictly mediocre and her SATs were abysmal, possibly because the day she took them she had a migraine headache up top and menstrual cramps down below, both probably brought on by stress. The only acceptance she got was from State U, which was not surprising. Getting accepted at State was like striking out the pitcher in a baseball game. And even from State there was no offer of scholarship help.

Your father and I certainly can't afford to send you and you'd be paying a loan back until you're forty, Charlotte said. Back then it was probably true. *And if you flunked out you'd still owe the money.* The subtext being that of *course* Holly would flunk out; college would be just too much pressure for such a fragile child. Hadn't Charlotte once found Holly curled up in the tub, refusing to go to school? And look what happened after she took the SATs! Came home, had a crying jag, spent half the night throwing up!

Holly ended up working for Mitchell Fine Homes and Estates and taking community college classes at night. Most of them were computer science courses, although she snuck in an English class or two. All was going pretty well – she was often unhappy, but had come to accept that, like a birthmark or a turned-in foot – until Frank Mitchell, Jr, the boss's son, began to bother her.

'Bother my fanny!' Holly tells the empty kitchen. 'He hounded me! For sex!'

When she told her mother some of what was going on at the office, Charlotte advised her to laugh it off. Men were men, she said, went through life following their peckers, and they never changed. Coping with them wasn't pleasant, but it was part of life, you had to take the bitter with the sweet, what could not be cured must be endured, so on and so on.

Dad's not that way, Holly had said, to which her mother waved one hand in an airy gesture of dismissal that said *of course he's not* and *he wouldn't dare* and *I'd like to see him try it*. A lot to convey in a simple hand gesture, but Charlotte had managed.

What Holly didn't tell her was that she had almost given in, had almost given the bulgy-eyed trout-faced son of a so-and-so what he wanted. *Nobody likes you here*, Junior Mitchell said. *You're standoffish and you do substandard work. Without me you'd be out on your ass. So how about a little payback, huh? I think once you try it, you'll like it.*

They went into his office, and Junior started to unbutton her blouse. The first button . . . the second . . . the third . . . and then she slapped him, a real roundhouse, putting everything she had into it, knocking his glasses off and making his lip bleed. He called her a useless bitch and said he could get her arrested for assault. Gathering courage she hadn't known she possessed, speaking in a coldly certain voice that sounded nothing like her usual one (which was so quiet that people often had to ask her to repeat herself), she told him that if he tried that, when the police came she'd tell them he tried to rape her. And something in his face – a kind of instinctive grimace – made her think that the police might believe her side of the story, because Frank Jr had been in trouble before. Trouble of this sort. In any case, that was the end of it. For him, at least. Not for Holly, who came in early one day a week later, trashed his office, then curled up in her shitty little cubicle with her head on her desk. She would have crawled under the desk, but there wasn't room.

A month in a 'treatment center' followed (her parents had found money enough for *that*), then three years of counseling. The counseling ended when her father died, but she continued to take various medications which left her functional but seeing the world as if through a cellophane wrapper.

What cannot be cured must be endured: the gospel according to Charlotte Gibney.

4

Holly puts out her cigarette under the tap, rinses the teacup, sets it in the drainer, and goes upstairs. The first door on the right is the guest room. Except not really. The wallpaper's wrong, for one thing, but it's still creepily like the room she lived in as a teenager in Cincinnati. Charlotte perhaps believed her mentally and emotionally unstable daughter would come to realize she wasn't meant to live among people who didn't understand her problems. As Holly steps inside she thinks again, *Museum exhibit. There should be a sign saying HABITAT OF A SAD GIRL, TRISTIS PUELLA.*

That her mother loved her Holly still has no doubt. But love isn't always support. Sometimes love is taking the supports away.

Over the bed is a poster of Madonna. Prince is on one wall, Ralph Macchio as the Karate Kid on another. If she looked on the shelves below her tidy little sound system (*Ludio Ludius*, the little sign would say), she'd find Bruce Springsteen, Van Halen, Wham!, Tina Turner, and of course the Purple One. All on cassettes. The tartan coverlet, which she always hated, is on the bed. Once there was a girl who lived among these things, and looked out the window at Bond Street, and played her music, and wrote her poems on a blue portable Olivetti typewriter. What followed the typewriter was a Commodore PC with a tiny screen.

Holly looks down and sees she is holding those red tags with SAVE printed on them. She can't even remember picking them up.

'I'm glad I came here,' she says. 'It's wonderful to be home.'

She goes to the *Star Wars* wastebasket (*Bella Siderea*, the little sign would say – how the old Latin comes back) and drops the tags into it. Then she sits down on the bed with her hands clasped between her thighs. So many memories here. The question is simple: face or forget?

Face, of course, and not because she's a different person now, a better person, a courageous person who has faced horrors most people wouldn't believe. Face because there is no other choice.

5

After her breakdown, after the so-called 'treatment center,' Holly answered an ad from a small publisher who wanted to hire a indexer for a series of three doorstop-sized books about local history written by a Xavier University prof. She was nervous when the interview began – scared stiff, more like it – but the editor, Jim Haggerty, was so obviously at sea when it came to indexing that Holly was able to tell him how she'd proceed without stuttering and getting all tangled up in her own words, as she had so often in her high school classes. She said she would first create a concordance, then make a computer file, then categorize and alphabetize. After that the work would go back to the author, who would vet, edit, and return it to her for any final changes.

'I'm afraid we don't have a computer just yet,' Haggerty said, 'only a few IBM Selectrics. Although I suppose we'll have to get one – wave of the future, and all that.'

'I have one,' Holly said. She sat forward, so excited by the possibilities that she forgot this was a job interview, forgot Frank Jr, forgot about going through four years of high school known as Jibba-Jibba.

'And you'd use it for indexing?' Haggerty looked bemused.

'Yes. Take the word *Erie*, for instance. That's a category, but it can refer to the lake, the county, or to the Erie Native American tribe. Which would have to be cross-referenced with Cat Nation, of course, and Iroquois. Even more! I'd have to go over the material again to get a handle on that, but you see the way it works, right? Or wait, take Plymouth, that's a really interesting one—'

Haggerty stopped her there and told her she could have the job on spec. *He knew an index-nerd when he saw one*, Holly thinks as she sits on the bed.

That first job, an earn-while-you-learn situation if ever there was one, led to more indexing jobs. She moved out of the house on Bond Street. She bought her first car. She upgraded her computer and took more classes. She also took her pills. When she was working, she felt bright and aware. When she wasn't, that sense of living in a cellophane bag returned. She went on a few dates, but they were clumsy, awkward affairs. The obligatory kiss goodnight too often made her think of Frank Jr.

When the indexing work ran thin (the publisher of the doorstop history books went broke), Holly worked for the local hospitals, which were loosely affiliated, as a medical transcriptionist. To this she added claims filing for Cincinnati District Court. There were the obligatory visits home, more of them after the death of her father. She listened to her mother complain about everything from her finances to the neighbors to the Democrats who were ruining everything. Sometimes on these visits Holly thought of a line from one of the *Godfather* movies: *Just when I thought I was out they pull me back in.* At Christmas, she and her mother and Uncle Henry sat on the couch and watched *It's a Wonderful Life.* Holly wore her Santa hat.

6

Time to go.

Holly gets up, starts to leave the room, hears her mother's imperative voice (*Leave it like you found it – how many times have I told you?*), and goes back to smooth out the tartan coverlet. For who? A woman who is dead? It's one of those laugh-or-cry situations, so Holly laughs.

I'm still hearing her. Will I be hearing her forever?

The answer is yes. To this day she won't lick frosting from the beaters (*you can get lockjaw that way*), she'll wash her hands after handling paper money (*nothing so germy as a dollar bill*), she won't eat an orange at night, and she'll never sit on a public toilet seat unless absolutely necessary, and then always with a frisson of horror.

Never talk to strange men, that was another one. Advice Holly followed until meeting Bill Hodges and Jerome Robinson, when everything changed.

She starts for the stairs, then thinks of the advice she gave Jerome about Vera Steinman, and goes down the hall to her mother's room. There's nothing she wants here – not the framed pictures on the wall, not the clutter of perfumes on the dresser, not any of the clothes or shoes in the closet – but there *are* things she should get rid of. They'll be in the top drawer of the night table next to Charlotte's bed.

On the way, she diverts to the wall where the framed pictures form a kind of gallery. There are none of Charlotte's late (and not much lamented) husband, and only one of Uncle Henry. The rest are mother-and-daughter photos. Two in particular have caught Holly's eye. In one she's about four, wearing a jumper. In the other she's nine or ten, wearing the kind of skirt that was all the rage back then: a wraparound with a showy gold safety pin to hold it closed. In her bedroom she hadn't been able to remember why she hated the coverlet, but now, looking at these pictures, she understands. Both the jumper and the skirt are tartans, she had blouses that were tartan, and (maybe) a sweater. Charlotte just loved tartans, would dress Holly and exclaim, 'My Scottish lassie!'

In both pictures – in almost all of them – Charlotte has an arm slung around Holly's shoulders. Such a gesture, a kind of sideways hug, can be seen as protective or loving, but looking at it repeated over and over in photographs where Charlotte's daughter progresses from two to sixteen, Holly thinks it can convey something else as well: ownership.

She goes to the night table and opens the top drawer. Mostly it's the tranquilizers she wants to get rid of, and any prescription pain meds, but she'll take everything else as well, even the Every Woman's multi-vites. Flushing them down the commode is a no-no, but there's a Walgreens on the way back to the Interstate, and she's sure they'll be happy to dispose of them for her.

She's wearing cargo pants with voluminous pockets, which is fortunate; she won't have to go back downstairs to get a gallon-sized Baggie from the rickrack drawer. She begins stuffing the bottles into her pockets without looking at the labels, then freezes. Beneath her mother's pharmacy is a stack of notebooks she remembers well. The top notebook has a unicorn on the cover. Holly takes them out and thumbs through one at random. They are her poems. Terrible limping things, but each one from the heart.

> I lie in my leafy bower to watch the clouds go by,
> I think of my love so far away, I won't see him for many a day,
> I close my eyes and sigh.

Even though she's by herself, Holly can feel her cheeks heating up. This stuff was written years ago, it's the juvenilia of an untalented juvenile, but her mother not only kept it, but kept it close by, possibly reading her daughter's bad poetry before turning out the light. And why would she do that?

'Because she loved me,' Holly says, and the tears start, right on cue. 'Because she missed me.'

If only that were all. If not for the crying and wailing about the dastardly Daniel Hailey. She had sat at the kitchen table of this house on Lily Court while Charlotte and Henry explained how they had been gulled. There had been much breast-beating. There had been *stationery* and *spreadsheets*. Charlotte must have told Henry what they would need to convince Holly of their lie and Henry had supplied it. He had gone along, as he always did with Charlotte.

Holly thinks that if Bill had been at that family meeting, he would have seen through the deception almost at once. (*Not a deception, a con*, she thinks. *Call it what it was.*) But Bill hadn't been there. Holly should have seen through it herself, but she was new at the game then, and in spite of the dizzying amount they were talking about – a *seven-figure* amount – she hadn't really cared. She had been absorbed in her new love of investigation. Besotted, in fact. Not to mention blinded by grief.

If I had investigated my own family instead of hunting for lost dogs and chasing bail-jumpers, things might have been different.

So on and so on.

Meanwhile, what will she do with the notebooks, those embarrassing relics of her youth? Maybe keep them, maybe burn them. She'll make that decision after the case of Bonnie Rae Dahl is either wrapped up or just peters away to nothing, as some cases do. But for now . . .

Holly puts them back where they came from and slams the drawer shut. On her way out of the room, she looks at the pictures on the wall again. She and her mother in each one, no sign of the mostly absent father, most with her mother's arm around her shoulders. Is that love, protectiveness, or an arresting officer's come-along? Maybe all three.

7

Halfway down the stairs, the pockets of her cargo pants bulging with pill bottles, Holly has an idea. She hurries back to her room and yanks the tartan coverlet off the bed. She balls it up and carries it downstairs.

In the living room is an ornamental hearth containing a log that never burns because it's really not a log at all. It's supposed to be gas-fired but hasn't worked in years. Holly spreads the coverlet on the hearth, then goes into the kitchen for a trashcan-sized plastic bag from under the sink. She shakes it out as she walks to the front hall. She sweeps all the ceramic figurines into the bag and takes them into the living room.

The money is still all there. Holly has to give her mother that much. Even her trust fund – the part Holly threw into the so-called invest-ment opportunity – is still there. She feels sure her mother bought the jewelry out of her own share of the inheritance, but that doesn't change the fact that her mother's only reason for making up the whole thing was so Finders Keepers would fail. Would die a crib death. Then Charlotte could say *Oh, Holly. Come and live with me. Stay for awhile. Stay forever.*

And had she left a letter? An explanation? Justifications for what she'd done? No. If she'd left such a letter with Emerson, he would have given it to her. It all hurts, but maybe that hurts the most: her mother didn't feel any need to explain or justify. Because she had no doubt that what she had done was right. As she felt that refusing to be vaccinated against Covid was right.

Holly begins throwing the figurines into the fireplace, really heaving them. Some don't shatter, but most do. All the ones that hit the not-log do.

Holly doesn't take as much pleasure from this as she expected. It was more satisfying to smoke in a kitchen where smoking had always been verboten. In the end she dumps the rest of the figurines from the trash bag onto the coverlet, picks up a few shards that have escaped the fireplace, and bundles the coverlet up. She hears the pieces clinking inside and that *does* give her a certain grim pleasure. She takes the coverlet around to the garbage hutch on the side of the house and stuffs it into one of the cans.

'There,' she says, dusting her hands. '*There.*'

She goes back into the house, but with no intention of circling through all the rooms. She's seen what she needs to see and done what needs to be done. She and her mother aren't quits, will never be quits, but getting rid of the figurines and the coverlet was at least a step toward prying that come-along hold from around her shoulders. All

she wants from 42 Lily Court are the papers on the kitchen table. She
picks them up, then sniffs the air. Cigarette smoke, thin but there.

Good.

Enough of memory lane; there's a case to chase, a missing girl to
be found. 'A new millionaire jumps in her car and drives to Upsala
Village,' Holly says.

And laughs.

February 8, 2021

1

Emily checks out Barbara's red coat, hat, and scarf and says, 'Aren't you pretty! All done up like a Christmas package!'

Barbara thinks, *How funny. It's still okay for a woman to say things like that, but not a man.* Professor Harris's husband, for instance. He did give her a good looking over, but you can't MeToo a man for that. You'd have to MeToo almost all of them. Besides, he's old. Harmless.

'Thank you for seeing me, Professor. I'll only take a minute of your time. I was hoping for a favor.'

'Well, let's see if I can do you one. If it's not about the writing program, that is. Come in the kitchen, Ms Robinson. I was just making tea. Would you like a cup? It's my special blend.'

Barbara is a coffee drinker, gallons of the stuff when she's working on what her brother Jerome calls her Top Secret Project, but she wants to stay on this elderly (but sharp-eyed, very) woman's good side, so she says yes.

They pass through a well-appointed living room into an equally well-appointed kitchen. The stove is a Wolf – Barbara wishes they had one at home, where she'll be just a little longer, before going off to college. She has been accepted at Princeton. A teapot is huffing away on the front burner.

While Barbara unwinds her scarf and unbuttons her coat (really too warm for them today, but it *does* give her a good look – young woman perfectly put together), Emily spoons some tea from a ceramic cannister into a couple of tea balls. Barbara, who has never drunk anything but bag tea, watches with fascination.

Emily pours and says, 'We'll just let that steep a bit. Only for a minute or so. It's strong.' She leans her narrow bottom against the counter and crosses her arms below a nearly bosomless bosom. 'Now how may I help you?'

'Well . . . it's about Olivia Kingsbury. I know she sometimes mentors young poets . . . at least she used to . . .'

'She still might,' Emily says, 'but I rather doubt it. She's very old now. You might think *I'm* old – don't look uncomfortable, at my age I have no need to varnish the truth – but compared to Livvie, I'm a youngster. She's in her late nineties now, I believe. So thin it wouldn't take a strong wind to blow her away, just a puff of breeze.'

Em removes the tea balls and sets a mug in front of Barbara. 'Try that. But take off your coat first, for heaven's sake. And sit down.'

Barbara puts her folder on the table, slips off her coat, and drapes it over the back of the chair. She sips her tea. It's foul-tasting, with a reddish tinge that makes her think of blood.

'How do you find it?' Em asks, bright-eyed. She takes the chair across from Barbara.

'It's very good.'

'Yes. It is.' Emily doesn't sip but gulps, although their mugs are still steaming. Barbara thinks the woman's throat must be leather-lined. *Maybe that's what happens to you when you get old*, she thinks. *Your throat gets numb. And you must lose your sense of taste, too.*

'You are, I take it, an acolyte of Calliope and Erato.'

'Well, not so much Erato,' Barbara says, and ventures another sip. 'I don't write love poetry, as a rule.'

Emily gives a delighted laugh. 'A girl with a classical education! How unusual and delectably rare!'

'Not really,' Barbara says, hoping she won't have to drink this whole mug, which looks bottomless. 'I just like to read. The thing is, I love Olivia Kingsbury's work. It's what made me want to write poetry. *Dead Certain . . . End for End . . . Cardiac Street . . .* I've read them all to bits.' This isn't just a metaphor; her copy of *Cardiac Street* did indeed fall to pieces, parted company with its cheap Bell College Press binding and went all over the floor. She had to buy a new copy.

'She's very fine. Won a batch of prizes in her younger years and was shortlisted for the National Book Award not long ago. I believe in 2017.' Em knows it was 2017, and she was actually quite pleased when Frank Bidart won instead. She has never cared for Olivia's poetry. 'She lives just down the street from us, you know, and . . . aha! The picture clarifies.'

Her husband, the other Professor Harris, comes in. 'I'm going to gas up our freshly washed chariot. Do you want anything, my love?'

'Just the Sheepherder's Special,' she says. 'A cup of ewe.'

He laughs, blows her a kiss, and leaves. Barbara may not like the tea she's been given (hates it, actually), but it's nice to see old people who still love each other enough for silly jokes. She turns back to Emily.

'I don't have the courage to just walk up to her house and knock on her door. I barely had the guts to come here — I almost turned around.'

'I'm glad you didn't. You dress up the place. Drink your tea, Ms Robinson. Or may I call you Barbara?'

'Yes, of course.' Barbara takes another sip. She sees that Emily has already finished half her cup. 'The thing is, Professor—'

'Emily. You Barbara, me Emily.'

Barbara doubts if she can manage calling this sharp-eyed old lady by her given name. Professor Harris's mouth is smiling, and there's a twinkle — so to speak — in her eye, but Barbara isn't sure it's an amused twinkle. More of an *assessing* one.

'I went to the English Department at Bell and spoke with Professor Burkhart — you know, the department head—'

'Yes, I know Roz pretty well,' Emily says drily. 'For the last twenty years or so.'

Barbara flushes. 'Sure, yes, of course. I went to her about maybe getting an introduction to Olivia Kingsbury, and she said I should talk to you, because you and Ms Kingsbury were friends.'

Livvie may think we're friends, Emily thinks, *but that would be stretching the truth. Stretching it until it snapped, actually.* But she nods.

'We had side-by-side offices for many years and were quite collegial. I have signed copies of all her books, and she has signed copies of mine.' Emily gulps tea, then laughs. '*Both* of mine, to say fair and true. She has been considerably more prolific, although I don't believe she's published anything lately. Looking for an introduction, are you? I suspect rather more. You want her to mentor you, which is understandable, you being a *fan* and all, but I fear you will be disappointed. Livvie's mind is still sharp, at least so far as I can tell, but she's very lame. Can hardly walk.'

Which doesn't explain why Olivia did not attend last year's Christmas party, which she could have done from her computer – she does have one. But Livvie (or the woman who works for her) did not refuse the elf-delivered beer and canapes; they were happy enough to take the food and drink. Emily has a resentment about that. As Roddy would say, *I have marked her in my book. Black ink rather than blue.*

'I don't want mentoring,' Barbara says. She manages another sip of tea without grimacing, then touches her folder, as if to be sure it's still there. 'What I want, *all* I want, is for her to read a few of my poems. Maybe just two, even one. I want to know . . .' Barbara is horrified to realize her eyes have filled up with tears. 'I *need* to know if I'm any good, or if I'm just wasting my time.'

Emily sits perfectly still, just looking at Barbara. Who, now that she's said what she came to say, cannot meet the old woman's eyes. She looks into the brackish brew in her cup instead. So much is left!

At last Emily says, 'Give me one.'

'One . . .?' Barbara honestly doesn't understand.

'One of your poems.' Emily sounds impatient now, as she did in her teaching days when faced with a dullard. Of which there were many, and she had no patience with them. She stretches out a blue-veined hand. 'One you like, but one that's short. A page or less.'

Barbara fumbles open her folder. She has brought an even dozen poems, and they are all short. Thinking that if Ms Kingsbury *did* agree to look (a long shot, Barbara knows), she wouldn't want to look at any like 'Ragtime, Rag Time,' which runs to almost eighteen pages.

Barbara starts to say something conventional, like *are you sure*, but one look at Professor Harris's face, especially her bright eyes, convinces her not to be so foolish. It wasn't a request but a demand. Barbara opens her folder, fumbles through the few poems with a hand that's not quite steady, and selects 'Faces Change.' It has to do with a certain terrible experience the year before, one she still has nightmares about.

'You'll have to excuse me for a bit,' the professor says. 'I don't read in company. It's rude and it hampers concentration. Five minutes.' She starts to leave the room with Barbara's poem in her hand, then points to the cannister beside the tea. 'Cookies. Help yourself.'

Once Barbara hears a door close on the far side of the living room, she carries her mug to the sink and pours all but a single swallow down the drain. Then she lifts the lid of the cookie jar, sees macaroons, and helps herself to one. She's far too nervous to be hungry, but it's the polite thing to do. She hopes so, at least. This whole encounter has a strange off-kilter feel to her. It started even before she came in, with the way the male Professor Harris hurried to close the lefthand garage door, almost as if he didn't want her looking at the van.

As for the female Professor Harris . . . Barbara never expected to get past the front door. She'd explain her business, ask Professor Harris if she would speak to Olivia Kingsbury, and be on her way. Now she is sitting alone in the Harris kitchen, eating a macaroon she doesn't want and saving the last sip of awful tea, for which she'll offer her thanks, just as her mother taught her.

It's more like ten minutes before Emily comes back. She doesn't leave Barbara hanging when she does; even before sitting down she says, 'This is very good. Almost extraordinary.'

Barbara doesn't know what to say.

'You've packed quite the load of fear and loathing into nineteen lines. Does it have to do with your experience as a black woman?'

'I . . . well . . .' The poem actually has nothing to do with her skin color. It has to do with a creature that called itself Chet Ondowsky. It looked human, but it wasn't. It would have killed her if not for Holly and Jerome.

'I withdraw the question,' Emily says. 'It's the poem that should speak, not the poet, and yours speaks clearly. I was just surprised. I was expecting something quite a bit more jejune, given your age.'

'Oh my,' Barbara says, channeling her mother. 'Thank you.'

Emily comes around to Barbara's side of the table and lays the poem on top of Barbara's folder. Close up she has a cinnamony smell that Barbara doesn't quite like. If it's perfume, she maybe should try another brand. Only Barbara doesn't think it's perfume, she thinks it's *her*.

'Don't thank me yet. This line doesn't work.' She taps the fourth line of the poem. 'It's not only clumsy, it's banal. *Lazy*. You can't cut it, the poem is already as brief as it needs to be, so you must replace it with something better. These other lines tell me you are capable of that.'

'All right,' Barbara says. 'I'll think of something.'

'You should. You will. As for this last line, what would you think about changing *This is the way birds stitch the sky closed at sunset* with *This is how*? Save a word.' She picks up a spoon by the bowl and begins to jab it up and down. 'Long poems can provoke deep feelings, but a short one must *stab* and *stab* and be done! Pound, Williams, Walcott! You agree?'

'Yes,' Barbara says. She would probably have agreed to anything at this moment – it's just so *weird* – but this she actually does agree with. She doesn't know Walcott but will look for him or her later.

'All right.' Emily puts the spoon down and resumes her seat. 'I will speak to Livvie and tell her you have talent. She may say yes, because talent – especially young talent – always engages her. If she says no, it will be because she is now too infirm to take on a mentee. Will you give me your telephone number and email address? I'll pass them on to her, and I'll send her a copy of this poem, if you don't mind. Make that little change – just scratch it in, please, and don't bother with the bad line for now. I'll take a picture of it with my phone. Does that sound like a plan?'

'Sure, yes.' Barbara scratches out *the way* and adds *how*.

'If you don't hear back from her in a week or two, I may be in touch. If, that is, you might consider me as . . . an interested party.'

She doesn't use the word *mentor*, but Barbara is sure from the pause that's what she means, and on the basis of a single poem!

'That's wonderful! Thank you so much!'

'Would you like a cookie for the ride home?'

'Oh, I walked,' Barbara says. 'I walk a lot. It's good exercise, especially on nice days like this, and it gives me time to think. Sometimes I drive to school, I got my driver's license last year, but not so much. If I'm late, I ride my bike.'

'If you're walking, I insist you take two.'

Emily gets Barbara the cookies. Barbara lifts her mug and takes the final sip as Emily turns around. 'Thank you, Professor . . . Emily. The tea was very good.'

'Glad you enjoyed it,' Emily says, with that same thin smile. Barbara thinks there's something knowing about it. 'Thank you for sharing your work.'

Barbara leaves with her red coat unbuttoned, her red scarf hanging loose instead of wrapped, her knitted red beret cocked rakishly on her head, facemask forgotten in her pocket.

Pretty, Emily thinks. *Pretty little pickaninny.*

Although that word (and others) comes naturally to mind, if spoken aloud it would surely sully her reputation for the rest of her life in these Puritanical times. Yet she understands and forgives herself, as she forgave herself for certain unkind thoughts about the late Ellen Craslow. Emily Dingman Harris's formative years occurred in an era when the only black people you saw in the movies or on TV were the servants, where certain candies and jump-rope rhymes contained the n-word, where her own mother was the proud owner of an Agatha Christie first edition with a title so racist that the book was later retitled *Ten Little Indians* and still later as *And Then There Were None*.

It's my upbringing, that's all. I am not to blame.

And that little girl is talented. Indecently talented for one so young. Not to mention a blackie.

2

When Roddy comes back from his errand, Emily says, 'Do you want to see something amusing?'

'I live for amusement, dear one,' he says.

'It's science and nutrition you live for, but I think this *will* amuse you. Come with me.'

They go into Emily's study nook. It was here that she read Barbara's poem, but that wasn't all she did. Em goes to **CAMS**, keyboards the password, and selects the one hidden behind a panel above the refrigerator. It gives a view of the whole kitchen at a slight downward angle. Emily fast-forwards to the point where Emily leaves the room with Barbara's poem in her hand. Then she pushes play.

'She waits until she hears me close the study door. Watch.'

Barbara gets up, takes a quick look around to make sure she's alone, then pours her tea down the drain. Before going back to the table and resuming her seat, she takes a macaroon from the cookie jar.

Roddy laughs. 'That *is* amusing.'

'But not surprising. I filled my tea ball from the top of the cannister, where it's fresh. The English Breakfast at the bottom has been there for I don't know how long. Seven years? Ten? That's the stuff I used for her, and it must have been stronger than hell. You should have seen her face when she took the first sip! Ha–ha–ha, wonderful! Now wait. You'll like this, too.'

She fast-forwards again. She and the girl discuss the poem at double speed, then Em goes to the cookie jar. The girl raises her cup . . . holds it in front of her mouth . . .

'There!' Em says. 'You see what she did?'

'Waited for you to turn so you could see her finishing what you'd think was the whole cup. Clever girl.'

'*Sneaky* girl,' Em says admiringly.

'But why give her the old tea?'

She gives him her *I don't suffer dullards* look, but this one is softened by love. 'Curiosity, my dear, simple curiosity. You are curious about your various experiments in biology as applies to nutrition and aging; I'm curious about human nature. This is a resourceful girl, bright and pretty. And . . .' She taps his deeply lined brow. 'She has a good brain. A *talented* brain.'

'You're not suggesting putting her on the list, are you?'

'I'd have to find out a good deal of background before considering such a thing. Which is what this was made for.' She pats the computer. 'But probably not. Still . . . in a pinch . . .'

She lets it dangle.

July 24, 2021

1

Both parking lots of the Kanonsionni Campground, the one for cars and the one for campers and RVs, are full, pandemic be damned. The campground itself looks jammed. Holly drives a quarter of a mile further up Old Route 17 and parks on the shoulder. She calls Lakeisha Stone, who says she'll be waiting on the shady side of the campground store. Holly says she's up the road a little way, give her five or ten minutes.

'I'm sorry about the parking,' Lakeisha says. 'I think half the cars in the lot are ours. We've got a gang this year. Most of us work at the college, or went there.'

'I don't mind,' Holly says. 'I can use the walk.' This is true. She can't seem to get the smell of her mother's potpourri out of her nose . . . or maybe it's her mind she can't get it out of. She hopes the fresh air will flush it away. And maybe it will flush away nasty emotions she doesn't want to admit to.

She keeps thinking about the first months after Bill died. What remained of her trust fund went into Finders Keepers over her mother's howls of protest. She remembers praying for clients. She remembers shuffling bills like a blackjack player on speed, paying what had to be paid, putting off what could be put off even when the bills came with FINAL NOTICE stamped on them in red. Meanwhile, her mother bought jewelry.

Holly realizes she's walking so fast that she's almost jogging and makes herself stop. Just ahead looms the campground's sign, a grinning

Native American chief in a gaudy red, white, and blue headdress holding out what's probably supposed to be a peace pipe. Holly wonders if the people who put it up realize how absurdly racist that is. Surely not. They probably think old Chief Smoke-Um Peace Pipe is a way to honor the Native Americans who once lived on Lake Upsala and who now live on a reservation miles from where they once hunted and fi—

'Quit it,' she whispers. She takes a moment to close her eyes and mutter a prayer. It's the one most commonly associated with recovering alcoholics, but it's good for lots of other things and lots of people. Including her.

'Grant me the serenity to accept the things I cannot change.'

Her mother is dead. The terrible days of looming insolvency are past. Finders Keepers is a paying concern. The present is for finding out what happened to Bonnie Rae Dahl.

Holly opens her eyes and starts walking again. She's almost there.

2

Thanks to her work indexing those doorstop histories, Holly knows that Kanonsionni means 'longhouse' in the old Iroquois tongue, and there is indeed a longhouse in the center of the campground. Half of it is a store and half of it seems to be for group gatherings. Right now the latter part is full of boys and girls singing 'The Night They Drove Old Dixie Down' while the choir director (if that's what he is) chords along on an electric guitar. It's not Joan Baez, but their voices rising on the afternoon air are plenty sweet. A softball game is going on. A gang of men is throwing horseshoes; a clang shivers the hot summer air and one of them shouts, '*A leaner, by God!*' The lake is full of swimmers and splashers. People stream in and out of the store, munching munchies and drinking sodas. Many are wearing campground souvenir tee-shirts with Big Chief Smoke-Um Peace Pipe on the front. There are few masks in evidence. Although Holly is wearing hers, she feels a burst of happiness at the sight of all this exuberant, barefaced activity. America is coming back, Covid-ready or not. That worries her, but it also gives her Holly hope.

She walks around to the shady side of the longhouse and there's

Lakeisha Stone, sitting on the bench of a picnic table whose surface is covered with incised initials. She's wearing a light green coverup over a dark green bikini. Holly thinks she's Bonnie's age, give or take a year, and she looks absolutely smashing – young and vital and sexy. Holly supposes Bonnie looked the same. It would be nice to believe she still does.

'Hello,' she says. 'You're Lakeisha, aren't you? I'm Holly Gibney.'

'Keisha, please,' the young woman says. 'I bought you a Snapple. It's the kind with sugar. I hope that's okay.'

'Wonderful,' Holly says. 'That was very thoughtful.' She takes it, screws off the cap, and sits down beside Keisha. 'May I be snoopy and ask if you're vaccinated?'

'Double. Pfizer.'

'Moderna,' Holly says. It's the new meet-and-greet. She takes off her mask and holds it in her hand for a moment. 'I feel silly wearing it out here, but I had a death in the family recently. It was Covid.'

'Oh, I'm so sorry to hear. Someone close?'

'My mother,' Holly says, and thinks, *Who bought jewelry she didn't wear.*

'That's awful. Was she vaxxed?'

'She didn't believe in it.'

'Girl, that's harsh. How are you doing with it?'

'As they always say on the TV shows, it's complicated.' Holly stuffs her mask in her pocket. 'Mostly I'm concentrating on the job, which is finding Bonnie Dahl, or finding out what happened to her. I won't keep you from your friends for long.'

'Don't worry about it. They're all playing softball or swimming. I'm a lousy baller and I've spent most of the day in the lake. Take all the time you want.' There's an outbreak of cheering at the softball game. Keisha looks over. Someone waves at her. She waves back, then turns to Holly. 'A bunch of us have gotten together here for the last three years and I was really looking forward to it. Since Bonnie disappeared . . .' She shrugs. 'Not so much.'

'Do you really think she's dead?'

Keisha sighs and looks at the water. When she looks back, her brown eyes – beautiful eyes – are filled with tears. 'What else could it be? It's like she dropped off the face of the earth. I've called everyone I can think of, all our friends, and of course her mother called me. Nothing. She's my best friend, and not a *word*?'

'The police have her down as a missing person.' Of course that's not what Izzy Jaynes thinks. Or Pete Huntley.

'Of course they do,' Keisha says, and takes a drink from her own bottle of Snapple. 'You know about Maleek Dutton, right?'

Holly nods.

'That's a perfect example of how Five-O operates in this town. Kid got killed for a busted taillight. You'd expect them to take a little more interest in a white girl, but no.'

That's a minefield Holly doesn't want to walk into. 'May I record our talk?' *Never call it an interview*, Bill Hodges said. *Cops do interviews. We just talk.*

'Sure, but there's not much I can tell you. She's gone and it's wrong. That's the extent of what I know.'

Holly thinks Keisha knows more, and although she doesn't expect any great breakthrough here, she has that Holly hope. And curiosity. She sets her phone on the scarred table and pushes record.

'I'm working for Bonnie's mother, and I'm curious as to how they got along.'

Keisha starts to reply, then stops herself.

'Nothing you say will go back to Penny. You have my word on that. I'm just crossing *t*'s and dotting *i*'s.'

'Okay.' Keisha gazes down toward the lake, frowning, then sighs and looks back at Holly. 'They didn't get along, mostly because Penny was always looking over Bonnie's shoulder, if you know what I mean.'

Holly knows, all right.

'Nothing Bonnie did was quite right with her mom. Bon said she hated to drive her mother anywhere because Penny would always tell her she knew a shorter way, or one with less traffic. She'd always be telling Bonnie to get over, get over, you want the lefthand lane. You feel me?'

'Yes.'

'Also, Bonnie said, Penny'd always be pumping the invisible brake on the passenger side or stiffening up if she felt like Bon was getting too close to the car in front of her. Irritating as hell. One time Bonnie got a red streak in her hair, very cute . . . at least *I* thought so . . .

but her mother said it made her look slutty. And if she'd ever gotten a tattoo, like she talked about . . .'

Keisha rolls her eyes. Holly laughs. She can't help it.

'They fought about her job at the library all the time. Penny wanted her to work at the bank where *she* worked. She said the pay and the benefits would be much better, and except for in-person meetings she wouldn't have to wear a mask seven hours a day. But Bonnie liked working at the libe, and like I said, we have a good gang. Everybody friends. Except for Matt Conroy, that is. He's the head librarian, and kind of a pill.'

'Grabby?' Holly's thinking of something she's heard from one of the other librarians, neither of whom are here today. 'Touchie-feelie?'

'Yeah, but he's actually been a little better this year, maybe because of that assistant prof in the Sociology Department. You probably didn't hear about that, the administration kept it pretty quiet, but we hear everything in the library. It's gossip central. This guy grabbed some grad student's ass, there was a witness, and the prof got fired. That's around the time Matt started to behave.' She pauses. 'Although he never misses an opportunity to peek up a girl's skirt. Not unusual, except he's pretty fucking blatant about it.'

'Could you see him having anything to do with Bonnie's disappearance?'

Keisha gives a delighted laugh. 'Lord, no. He's what my mama calls a stuffed string. Bonnie outweighs him by at least thirty pounds. If Matt grabbed *her* ass, she'd flip him over her shoulder or hip him into the wall.'

'She knows judo, or some other martial art?'

'No, nothing so serious, but she took a self-defense class. I took it with her. That was something else her mother bitched about. Called it a needless expense. Bon just couldn't do anything right in her mother's eyes. And when it came to Mrs D. wanting her to work at her bank, they had a couple of real screamers.'

'No love lost.'

Keisha considers this. 'You could say that, sure, but there was plenty of love left. Do you get that?'

Holly thinks of the dog-eared poetry notebooks in the drawer of her mother's night table and says she does.

'Keisha, would Bonnie have left town to get away from her mother? All that constant carping and complaining, those arguments?'

'There was a woman police who asked me that same question,' Keisha said. 'Didn't come see me, just called on the phone. Two or three questions and then it was thanks, Ms Stone, you've been a great help. Typical. The answer to your question is not a chance. If I gave you the idea that Bon and Mrs D. were at each other's throats, I didn't mean to. There was arguing and sometimes yelling but no physical stuff, and they always made up. So far as I know, at least. What went on between them was more like a stone you can't get out of your shoe.'

Holly is struck by this, wondering if that was what Charlotte was to her: a stone in her shoe. She thinks of Daniel Hailey, a thief who never was, and decides it was quite a bit more.

'Ms Gibney? Holly? Are you still there, or are you gathering wool?' Keisha is smiling.

'I guess I was. Did she have a cash reserve that you know of? I ask because there's been no action on her credit card.'

'Bonnie? No. What she didn't spend went into the bank, and I think maybe she had a few investments. She liked the stock market, but she was no plunger.'

'She didn't have any clothes at your place? Ones that are now gone?'

Keisha's eyes narrow. 'What exactly are you asking?'

Holly is a shy person as a rule, but that changes when she's chasing a case. 'I'll be blunt. I'm asking if you're covering for her. You're her best friend, I can tell you're loyal to her, and I think you'd do it if she asked.'

'Kind of resent that,' Keisha says.

Holly, who has gotten hesitant of touching since Covid, puts a hand on the young woman's arm without even thinking about it. 'Sometimes my job means asking unpleasant questions. Penny and Bonnie may not have had an ideal relationship, but the woman is paying me to find her because she's half out of her mind.'

'All right, I hear you. No, Bon didn't keep any clothes at my place. No, she didn't have a secret cash stash. No, Matt Conroy didn't grab her. He also asked around – college employment office, campus security, a few library regulars. Did his due diligence, I'll give him that.

The note she supposedly left? It's bullshit. And leave her bike? She loved that bike. Saved for it. I'm telling you someone stalked her, grabbed her, raped her, killed her. My sweet Bonnie.'

This time the tears fall and she lowers her head.

'What about the boyfriend? Tom Higgins. Know anything about him?'

Keisha utters a harsh laugh and looks up. '*Ex*-boyfriend. Wimp. Loser. Stoner. Bonnie's mother was right about him, at least. Definitely not the kidnapping type. No idea what Bon saw in him to begin with.' Then she echoes Penny: 'The sex must have been great.'

Holly is back on *someone stalked her*. That seems more and more likely, which would mean it wasn't an impulse crime. Ergo, Holly needs to look at the Jet Mart footage again, very carefully. But it ought to wait until tomorrow, when her eyes and mind are fresh. This has been a long day.

'Have you been a private detective for long?'

'A few years,' Holly says.

'Is it interesting?'

'I think so, yes. Of course there are dull stretches.'

'Is it ever dangerous?'

Holly thinks of a certain cave in Texas. And of a thing that pretended to be a man falling down an elevator shaft with a diminishing scream. 'Not often.'

'It's interesting to me, you being a woman and all. How did you get into it? Were you on the cops? You don't seem like the cop type, is all.'

Another clang from the horseshoe pit followed by yells of delight. The kids in the meeting hall are now singing 'Tonight,' from *West Side Story*. Their young voices soar.

'I was never a cop,' Holly says. 'As to how I got into the business . . . that's complicated, too.'

'Well, I hope you succeed on this. I love Bonnie like a sister, and I hope you find out what happened to her. But I can't help feeling bitter. Bonnie's got a well-off mama with a cushy bank job. She can afford to pay you. It's wrong to feel that way, I know it is, but I can't help it.'

Holly could tell Keisha that Penny Dahl probably isn't well-off, she's been furloughed from her job thanks to Covid, and while she may still be getting a check from NorBank, no way can it be her full salary. She could say those things but doesn't. Instead she does what she does best: keeps her eyes on Keisha's face. Those eyes say *tell me more*. Keisha does, and in her distress, or anger, or both, she loses some of her careful I'm-talking-to-a-white-lady diction. Not much, just a little.

'What do you think Maleek Dutton's mama has? She works in the Adams Laundry downtown. Husband left her. She got twin girls about to go into middle school and they'll need clothes. School supplies, too. Her oldest has a job at Midas Muffler and helps what he can. Then she loses Maleek. Shot in the head, brains all over his bag lunch. And you know that saying about how a grand jury would indict a ham sandwich, if the prosecutor asked them nice? They didn't indict the cop that shot Maleek, did they? I guess he was just peanut butter and jelly.'

No, but he *did* lose his job. Holly doesn't say that, either, because it wouldn't be enough for Lakeisha Stone. Nor enough for Holly herself. And to Isabelle Jaynes's credit, it wasn't enough for her. As for the cop? Probably working a security gig, or maybe he caught on at the state prison, guarding the cells instead of inhabiting one.

Keisha makes a fist and bangs it softly on the scarred surface of the picnic table. 'No civil suit, either. No money for one. *Black News* got up a fund, but it won't be enough to hire a good lawyer. Old story.'

'Too old,' Holly murmurs.

Keisha shakes her head, as if to clear it. 'As for finding Bonnie, go with God's love and my good wishes. I mean that with all my heart. Find whoever did it, and . . . do you carry a gun, Holly?'

'Sometimes. When I have to.' It's Bill's gun. 'Not today.'

'Well if you find him, put a bullet in him. Put it right in his mother-fucking ballsack, pardon my French. As for Maleek? Nobody's looking for *his* justice. And nobody's looking for Ellen Craslow, either. Why would they? Just Black folks, you know.'

Holly is thrown back to the Dairy Whip parking lot, talking to those boys. The leader, Tommy Edison, was redhaired and as white as vanilla ice cream, but what he said then and what Keisha said just now are voices in two-part harmony.

You want to know whose mother is worried? Stinky's. She's half-crazy and the cops don't do anything because she's a juicer.

She thinks of Bill Hodges, sitting with her one day on the steps of his little house. Bill saying *Sometimes the universe throws you a rope. If it does, climb it. See what's at the top.*

'Who's Ellen Craslow, Keisha?'

3

Holly lights a cigarette as soon as she gets back to her car. She takes a drag (the first one is always the best one), blows smoke out the open window, and pulls her phone out of her pocket. She fast-forwards to the last part of her conversation with Keisha, the Ellen Craslow part, and listens to it twice. Maybe Jerome was right about it being a serial. No jumping to conclusions, but there *is* a pattern of sorts. It just isn't sex or age or color. It's location. Deerfield Park, Bell College, maybe both.

Ellen Craslow was a janitor, swapping her time between the Life Sciences building and the Bell College restaurant and rathskeller. The Belfry is in the Memorial Union, a central spot where students tend to get together when they're not in class. Keisha's library gang gathers there for their coffee breaks, lunch hours, and often for beers when the day's work is done. It makes sense, because the Reynolds Library is nearby, making it a quick walk on those winter days when the snow and wind come howling off the lake.

According to Keisha, Ellen was bright, personable, probably a lesbian, although not one with a partner, at least currently. Keisha said she once asked if Ellen had thought about taking classes, and Ellen said she had no interest.

'She said life was her classroom,' Keisha says from Holly's phone. 'I remember that. She said it like she was joking, but also not. Do you know what I mean?'

Holly said she did.

'She was happy with her little trailer in a trailer park on the edge of Lowtown, said it was just fine for her, and she was happy with her job. She said she had everything a girl from Bibb County, Georgia, could want.'

Keisha got used to seeing Ellen sweeping in the Belfry or buffing floors in the lobby of Davison Auditorium, or up on a ladder, changing bulbs, or in the women's bathroom, filling the paper towel dispensers or scrubbing graffiti off the stalls. If she was alone, Keisha said, she always stopped to talk to Ellen, and if all of them – the library crew – were together, they always made room for her in their conversation if she wasn't working in Life Sciences or too busy. Not that Ellen would sit with them, but she was happy to join them for a little talk, or maybe a quick cup of coffee, which she would drink on her feet, standing hipshot. Keisha remembered once they were arguing about *No Exit*, which the theater club was putting on in the Davison, and Ellen said in an exaggerated Georgia accent, 'Ah *dig* that existential shit. It be life as we know it, my homies.'

'How old was she?' Holly asks from her phone.

'Maybe . . . thirty? Twenty-eight? Older than most of us, but not a lot older. She fit right in.'

Then one day she wasn't there. After a week, Keisha thought Ellen must be on vacation. 'I never thought about her that much, though.' Her recorded voice sounds embarrassed. 'She was on my radar, but out toward the edge of the screen, if you know what I mean.'

'Not a friend, just an acquaintance.'

'That's right.' Sounding relieved.

After a month or so Keisha asked Freddy Warren, the Union's head janitor, if Ellen had been switched to Life Sciences full-time. Warren said no, one day she just didn't show up. Or the next. Or at all. One lunch hour, Keisha and Edie Brookings dropped into the college's employment office to find out if they knew where Ellen had gone. They didn't. The woman they spoke to said that if Ellen got in touch with Keisha to get an address. Because Ellen had never picked up her last check.

'Did you follow up? Maybe check her residence?'

A long, long pause. Then Keisha said, low: 'No. I guess I assumed she just wasn't up for another winter by the lake. Or went home to Georgia.'

'When did this happen?'

'Three years ago. No, less. It was in the fall, and had to've been right around Thanksgiving, because the last time I saw her – or one of the last, I can't be sure – the tables in the Belfry all had paper turkeys on them.' A long pause. 'When I say no one looked for her, I guess that includes me. Doesn't it?'

There's a little more – Holly showed Keisha the photo of the earring and Keisha also confirmed it was Bonnie's – but nothing of substance, so Holly shuts off her phone. She's smoked her cigarette down to the filter. She mashes it out in her portable ashtray and immediately thinks about lighting another one.

Keisha hadn't connected Ellen Craslow with Bonnie Dahl, probably because they disappeared years apart. The connection she made was Ellen and Maleek Dutton, because both were Black. And she was embarrassed, as if telling the story about a woman suddenly being not there made her realize that she wasn't so different from the people – probably most of them in the city – who didn't care much about one more young Black man shot at a traffic stop.

But there was a huge difference between a young man shot dead in his car and an acquaintance who just dropped out of the mix. Holly could have told Keisha that, but she had been too full of her own thoughts – troubled thoughts – to do more than thank Keisha for her time and tell her that she, Holly, would get in touch if she had more questions or if the case resolved.

There's probably a perfectly reasonable explanation for Ellen Craslow's disappearance. Janitorial work is a skill, but Holly thinks it's probably a high turnover job. Ellen could have moved on to someplace warmer, just as Keisha said – Phoenix or LA or San Diego. She could have gotten an urge to see her mama again and eat some of her mama's home cooking. Except she never picked up her last check and Peter Steinman disappeared around the same time. Ellen lived in Lowtown (*on the edge*), but she worked at the college, which is only a couple of miles from the Dairy Whip. Less, if you cut through the park.

As for Bonnie Rae Dahl, her bike was found in front of an abandoned repair shop approximately between the college and the Whip.

Holly starts her car, makes a careful U-turn, and drives past the campground, where summer vacationers are enjoying themselves beneath the benevolent gaze of Chief Smoke-Um Peace Pipe.

4

It would be a long drive back to her apartment in the city, too long after the day Holly has put in. 42 Lily Court is closer, but she has no desire to spend the night in her dead mother's house and smelling her dead mother's potpourri. She registers at a Days Inn near the turnpike and gets a take-out chicken dinner from Kountry Kitchen. She didn't bring a change of clothes, so after eating in her room, she walks to a nearby Dollar General and buys fresh underwear. To this she adds an extra-large sleep shirt with a big smiley face on it.

Back in her room – not fancy, but comfortable enough, and the air conditioner doesn't rattle too badly – she calls Barbara Robinson, feeling she has troubled Barbara's big brother enough for one weekend. Barbara is almost as good at sussing out information on her computer as Holly is herself (she's willing to admit that Jerome is better than either of them). Besides, she wants to know how Barbara's doing. Holly hasn't seen much of her this summer, although Barbara *was* at Charlotte's Zoom funeral.

'Hey, Hol,' Barbara says. 'What's going on? How are you doing with your mother and all?' It's the right question under the circumstances, but Holly thinks Barbara sounds distracted. It's how she sounds if you try to talk to her when she's reading one of her endlessly long fantasy novels.

'I'm doing well. How are you?'

'Fine, fine.'

'Jerome had quite a time, wouldn't you say?'

'He did? What's up with Jerome?' No noticeable excitement in Barbara's voice.

'Had to take a woman to the hospital. He was asking her some questions for me and she OD'd on booze and pills. He didn't tell you?'

'Haven't seen him.' Distracted for sure.

'As for what's going on, I'm looking for a missing woman, and came across another one in the process. The name of the second one is Ellen Craslow. I was wondering if you could do a little digging and see if you could find out anything about her. I'd do it myself, but the WiFi at the motel where I'm staying is super poopy. It's kicked me off twice already.'

A long pause. Then: 'I'm kinda busy, Hols. Could Pete do it?'

Holly is surprised. This is a girl who used to love playing Nancy Drew, but seemingly not tonight. Or maybe, considering what she went through last year, not at all.

'Are you thinking about Ondowsky? Because it's nothing like that.'

Barbara laughs, which is a relief. 'No, I've pretty much put that to bed, Hol. I'm just really really busy. Kind of under the gun, if you want to know the truth.'

'Is it your special project? Jerome said you had one.'

'It is,' Barbara says, 'and I'll tell you all about it soon. Maybe even next week. You, Jerome, my folks, my friends. I promise. But not now. I don't want to jinx it.'

'Say no more. I'll talk to Pete. It'll give him something to do besides taking his own temperature every fifteen minutes.'

Barbara giggles. 'Does he do that?'

'It wouldn't surprise me.'

'Are you really doing okay with your, you know, your . . .'

'Yes,' Holly says firmly. 'Really okay. And I'll let you get on with whatever it is you're doing. Not to sound like your mother, but I hope some college prep is involved, because it won't be long.'

'College prep may eventually play a part.' Barbara sounds amused. 'And listen, if this woman is really important, I can—'

'No, no, it's probably nothing.'

'And we're good, right?'

'Always, Barb. Always.'

She ends the call, wondering just what Barbara's special project could be. Writing is Holly's best guess, something carried in the genes. Jim Robinson, their father, spent ten years as a newspaper reporter on the Cleveland *Plain Dealer*; Jerome is writing a book about his notorious great-grandfather; so why not?

'As long as you're happy,' Holly murmurs. 'Not having nightmares about Chet Ondowsky.'

She flops down on the bed – comfy! – and calls Pete. 'If you feel well enough to give me a hand, I could use one.'

Pete replies in a voice that's a little less clogged and raspy. 'For you, Hols, anything.'

It's hyperbole and she knows it, but it still makes her feel warm inside.

5

Before signing off, Pete reminds her it's the weekend, and he may not
be able to get the stuff she wants until Monday, probably Monday
afternoon. Holly, who works all the time when she's working, sees
weekends mostly as an annoyance. She has three missed calls from
Penny and three voicemails. The VMs are basically the same — *where
are you, what's happening*. She'll call and update her, but first she wants
a cigarette.

She dumps her clogged portable ashtray in a trashcan by the motel
office, then smokes beside the ice machine. When she started this nasty
habit as a teenager, you could smoke everywhere, even on airplanes.
Holly believes the new rules are a big improvement. It makes you think
about what you're doing and how you're killing yourself by inches.

She calls Penny and gives her a progress report that's accurate but
far from complete. She relates a version of her conversation with Keisha
Stone that omits the part about Ellen Craslow, and although she tells
Penny about talking to the Dairy Whip Gang, she doesn't mention
Peter 'Stinky' Steinman. She will if Craslow and Steinman turn out to
be connected, but not until then. Penny's frame of mind is dire enough
without planting the idea of a serial killer in her head.

Holly undresses, puts on the smiley-face shirt (it comes almost to
her knees), flumps down onto the bed, and turns on the TV. She stops
channel surfing long enough to watch some of an old musical on
TCM, then turns it off. In the bathroom she washes her hands thoroughly and brushes her teeth with her finger, scolding herself for not
getting a toothbrush along with undies and the nightshirt.

'What cannot be cured must be endured,' she murmurs. Will she
sleep tonight after such an eventful day, or will her thoughts turn to
her mother as she lies there listening to the drone of semis on the
turnpike, a sound that always makes her feel lonely? Oddly enough,
she thinks she will sleep. Holly knows herself well enough to understand she'll never have complete closure with her mother, and that
Charlotte's lies — *a new millionaire walks into a bar wondering how her
mother could do what she did* — may rub at her for a long time to come
(especially the hidden stash of jewelry), but does anyone ever get
complete closure? Especially from a parent? Holly doesn't think so, she

thinks closure is a myth, but at least she got a little of her own today, smoking in the kitchen and breaking those fracking figurines.

She gets down on her knees, closes her eyes, and starts her prayer as she always does, telling God it's Holly . . . as if God doesn't know. She thanks God for safe travel, and for her friends. She asks God to take care of Penny Dahl. Also Bonnie and Pete and Ellen, if they are still ali—

Something bombs her then and her eyes fly open.

Maybe it's not location, or not *just* location.

She sits on the edge of the bed, turns on the light, and calls Lakeisha Stone. It's Saturday night and she expects her call will go to voicemail. There may be a dance in the longhouse, or – perhaps more likely – Keisha and her friends will be drinking in a local bar. Holly is delighted when Keisha answers.

'Hi, it's Holly. I have one more quick question.'

'Ask as many as you want,' Keisha says. 'I'm in the campground laundry, watching a drier full of towels go around and around and around.'

Why's a fine-looking young woman like you doing laundry on a Saturday night is a question Holly doesn't ask. What she asks is, 'Do you know if Ellen Craslow had a car?'

Holly is expecting Keisha to say she doesn't know or can't remember, but Keisha surprises her.

'She didn't. I remember her saying she had a Georgia driver's license, but it was expired and that was a hell of a good way to get in trouble if you were stopped. Driving while Black, you know. Like Maleek Dutton. She wanted to get one from here but kept putting it off. Because the DMV was always so crowded, she said. She rode the bus to and from work. Does that help?'

'It might,' Holly says. 'Thank you. I'll let you get back to watching your towels—'

'Oh, something else,' Keisha says.

'What?'

'Sometimes, if the weather was good, she'd skip the bus and go to the NorBank close to her place.'

Holly frowns. 'I don't—'

'They rent bikes,' Keisha says. 'There's a line of them out front. You just pick the one you want and pay with your credit card.'

6

Holly finishes her prayer, but now it's really just a rote recitation. Her mind is on the case. If anything keeps her awake tonight it will be that, not thinking about Charlotte's Millions. In her mind she sees Deerfield Park, with Ridge Road on one side and Red Bank Avenue on the other. She thinks of the Belfry, the deserted repair shop, and the Dairy Whip. She thinks, *location, location, location*. And she thinks that none of them had a car.

Well, Bonnie did, but she didn't use it for going back and forth to work. She rode her bike. Ellen also rode a bike when she didn't take the bus. And Pete Steinman had his skateboard.

Lying in the dark, hands clasped on her stomach, Holly asks herself the question these two similarities raise. It's crossed her mind before, but only as a hypothetical. Now it's starting to feel a lot more practical. Is it just the ones she knows about, or are there more?

February 12, 2021

1

Barbara stands outside 70 Ridge Road, one of the smaller Victorians on the smoothly sloping street. The temperature has dropped thirty degrees since the day she saw Professor Harris washing what he had (rather grandiloquently) called his chariot, and today her red winter gear — coat, scarf, hat — are a necessity instead of a fashion statement. She is once more holding her folder of poems, and she's scared to death.

The woman inside that house is her idol, in Barbara's opinion the greatest American poet of the last sixty years. She actually *knew* T.S. Eliot. She corresponded with Ezra Pound when he was in St Elizabeths Hospital for the criminally insane. Barbara Robinson is just a kid who's never published anything except for a few boring (and no doubt banal) editorials in the high school newspaper.

What is she doing here? How dare she?

Emily Harris thought the poem she'd looked at was good — *quite the load of fear and loathing packed into nineteen lines,* she'd said. She'd even suggested a couple of corrections that seemed like good ones, but Emily Harris hadn't written *End for End* or *Cardiac Street.* What Emily Harris had written were two books of literary criticism published by the college press. Barbara checked online.

This morning, after she'd started to believe she would hear nothing, she had gotten an email from Olivia Kingsbury.

I have read your poem. If your schedule permits, please come and visit with me at 2 PM this afternoon. If your schedule does not permit, please reply to my email address. I am sorry about the short notice. It had been signed *Olivia.*

Barbara reminds herself that she has been invited, and that has to mean *something*, but what if she makes an ass of herself? What if she can't even open her mouth, only stare like a complete dummocks? Thank God she didn't tell her parents or Jerome where she was going this afternoon. Thank God she hadn't told *anyb*—

The door of 70 Ridge Road opens, and a fabulously old woman emerges, swaddled in a fur coat that comes down to her ankles and walking on two canes. 'Are you just going to stand there, young woman? Come in, come in. I have no tolerance for the cold.'

Feeling outside herself – *observing* herself – Barbara walks to the porch and mounts the steps. Olivia Kingsbury holds out a frail hand. 'Gently, young woman, gently. No squeezing.'

Barbara barely touches the old poet's fingers, thinking something that's both absurdly grandiose and very clear: *I am touching greatness.*

They go inside and down a short wood-paneled hall. As they do, Olivia pats her enormous fur coat. 'Faux, faux.'

'Fo?' Barbara says, feeling stupid.

'Faux *fur*,' Olivia says. 'A gift from my grandson. Help me off with it, will you?'

Barbara slips the coat off the old poet's shoulders and folds it over her arm. She holds it tightly, not wanting it to slip away and fall on the floor.

The living room is small, furnished with straight-backed chairs and a sofa that sits in front of a television with the largest screen Barbara has ever seen. She somehow didn't expect a TV in a poet's house.

'Put it on the chair, please,' Olivia says. 'Your things as well. Marie will put them away. She's my girl Friday. Which is fitting, since this is Friday. Sit on the couch, please. The chairs are easier for me to get out of. You are Barbara. The one Emily emailed me about. I am pleased to meet you. Have you been vaccinated?'

'Um, yes. Johnson and Johnson.'

'Good. Moderna for me. Sit, sit.'

Still feeling outside herself, Barbara takes off her outerwear and puts it on the chair, which has already been mostly swallowed by the improbable fur coat. She can't believe such a tiny woman could wear it without collapsing under its weight.

'Thank you so much for giving me some of your time, Ms Kingsbury. I love your work, it—'

Olivia holds up one of her hands. 'No fangirl remarks necessary, Barbara. In this room we are equals.'

As if, Barbara thinks, and smiles at the absurdity of the idea.

'Yes,' Olivia says. '*Yes.* We may or may not have fruitful discussions in this room, but if we do, they must be as equals. You'll call me Olivia. That might be hard for you at first, but you'll get used to it. And you may take off your mask. If I were to catch the dread disease in spite of our vaccinated state, and die, I would make very old bones.'

Barbara does as she has been told. There's a button on the table beside Olivia's chair. She pushes it, and a buzzer sounds deeper in the house. 'We'll have tea and get to know each other.'

At the idea of drinking more tea, Barbara's heart sinks.

A trim young woman dressed in fawn-colored slacks and a plain white blouse comes in. She's holding a silver tray with tea things on it and a plate of cookies. Oreos, in fact.

'Marie Duchamp, this is Barbara Robinson.'

'Very nice to meet you, Barbara,' Marie says. Then, to the old poet, 'You have ninety minutes, Livvie. Then it's naptime.'

Olivia sticks out her tongue. Marie returns the favor. Barbara is startled into laughter, and when the two women laugh with her, that sense of otherness mostly slips away. Barbara thinks this could be all right. She will even drink the tea. At least the cups are small, not like the bottomless mug she was faced with in the Harris house.

When Marie leaves, Olivia says, 'She's a boss, but a good boss. Without her, I'd be in assisted living. There is no one else.'

This Barbara knows, from her online research. Olivia Kingsbury had two children by two different lovers, a grandson by one of those children, and she has outlived all of them. The grandson who gave her the enormous fur coat died two years ago. If Olivia lives until the following summer, she will be a hundred years old.

'Peppermint tea,' Olivia says. 'I'm allowed caffeine in the morning, but not the rest of the day. Occasional arrhythmia. Will you pour out, Barbara? A plink of cream – it's the real stuff, not that wretched half and half – plus the veriest pinch of sugar.'

'To make the medicine go down,' Barbara ventures.

'Yes, and in the most delightful way.'

Barbara pours for both of them and at Olivia's urging takes a couple of Oreos. The tea is good. There's none of the strong, murky flavor that caused her to sneak most of Professor Harris's brew down the sink. It's actually sort of delightful. The word *sprightly* comes to mind.

They drink their tea and eat their cookies. Olivia munches two, spilling some crumbs down her front which she ignores. She asks Barbara about her family, her school, any sports in which she has participated (Barbara runs track and plays tennis), whether or not she has a boyfriend (not currently). She doesn't discuss writing at all, and Barbara begins to think she won't, that she has only been invited here today to break the monotony of another afternoon with no one to talk to but the woman who works for her. This is a disappointment, but not as big a one as Barbara might have expected. Olivia is sharp, gently witty, and *current*. There's that big-screen TV, for instance. And Barbara was struck by Olivia's casual use of the word *fangirl*, which isn't one you expected to hear coming from an old lady.

It will only be later, walking home in a daze, that Barbara will realize that Olivia was circling the thing that has brought Barbara here, as if to outline its size and shape. Taking her measure. Listening to her talk. In a gentle and tactful manner, Barbara has been interrogated, as if at a job interview.

Marie comes for the tea things. Olivia and Barbara thank her. As soon as she's gone, Olivia leans forward and says, 'Tell me why you write poetry. Why do you even want to?'

Barbara looks down at her hands, then back up at the old poet sitting across from her. The old poet whose face is little more than a skin-covered skull, who has forgotten or ignored the Oreo crumbs littering the bodice of her dress, who is wearing blocky old-lady shoes and pink support hose, but whose eyes are bright and completely *here*. Barbara thinks they are fierce eyes. Raging, almost.

'Because I don't understand the world. I hardly even *see* the world. It makes me crazy sometimes, and I'm not kidding.'

'All right, and does writing poems make the world more under-standable and less crazy?'

Barbara thinks of how Ondowsky's face changed in the elevator and how everything she thought she understood about reality fell to ruin when that happened. She thinks of stars at the edge of the universe, unseen but burning. Burning. And she laughs.

'No! *Less* understandable! *More* crazy! But there's something about doing it . . . I can't explain . . .'

'I think you can,' the old poet says.

Well, maybe. A little.

'Sometimes I write a line . . . or more than one . . . once in awhile a whole poem . . . and I think, "There. I got that right." And it satisfies. It's like when you have an itch in the middle of your back, and you don't think you'll be able to reach it, but you can, just barely, and oh man, that . . . that sense of *relief* . . .'

The old poet says, 'Destroying the itch brings relief. Doesn't it?'

'Yes!' Barbara almost shouts it. '*Yes!* Or even like with an infection, a swelling, and you . . . you have to . . .'

'You have to express the pus,' Olivia says. She jerks a thumb like a hitchhiker. 'They don't teach that at the college, do they? No. The idea that the creative impulse is a way to get rid of poison . . . or a kind of creative defecation . . . no. They don't teach that. They don't dare. It's too earthy. Too *common*. Tell me a line you wrote that you still like. That gave you that feeling of finally relieving the itch.'

Barbara thinks it over. She has stopped being nervous. She's engaged. 'Well, there's a line in the poem Professor Harris sent you that I still like – *This is the way birds stitch the sky closed at sunset*. It's not perfect, but—'

Olivia holds up a hand like a traffic cop. 'In the poem I read you wrote in *how*. *This is* how *birds stitch the sky closed at sunset.*'

Barbara is amazed. Olivia has quoted the line exactly, although the poem isn't in front of her. 'Yes. It was Professor Harris who suggested the change from *this is the way* to *this is how*. So I put it in.'

'Because you thought her version of the line was better?'

Barbara starts to say yes, then pauses. This feels like a trap question. No, that's not right, this woman doesn't ask questions to trap (although Barbara thinks Emily Harris might). But it could be a test question.

'I did then, but . . .'

'But now you're not so sure. Do you know why?'

Barbara thinks it over and shakes her head. If it's a test question, she guesses she just failed.

'Could it be because your original version contains words that continue the *rhythm* of the poem? Could it be *this is the way* swings and *this is how* clunks, like a dead key on a piano?'

'It's just one word . . . well, two . . .'

'But in a poem every word counts, doesn't it? And even in free verse, *especially* in free verse, the rhythm must always be there. The heartbeat. Your version is poetry. Emily's is prosy. Did she offer to help you with your work, Barbara?'

'I guess, in a way. She said, I think this was it, that if I didn't hear back from you, I might consider her as an interested party.'

'Yes. That's Emily as I've come to know her. Emily all over. She's managerial. She would begin by making suggestions, and eventually your poems would become her poems. At best collaborations. She's all right at what she does now that she's semi-retired, going through writing samples for the fiction workshop, but as a teacher, or a mentor, she's like a driving instructor who always ends up taking the wheel from the student. She can't help it.'

Barbara bites her lip, considering, and decides to risk taking it a little further. 'You don't like her?'

It's the old poet's turn to consider. Finally she says, 'We're collegial.'

That's not an answer, Barbara thinks. *Or maybe it is.*

'When I was teaching poetry at Bell many years ago, we were next door neighbors in the English Department, and when she left her door open, I sometimes overheard her student conferences. She never raised her voice, but often there was a . . . a kind of browbeating going on. Most adults can stand up to that sort of thing, but students, especially those who are eager to please, are a different matter. Did *you* like her?'

'She seemed all right. Willing to talk to a kid who basically just barged in.' But Barbara is thinking of the tea, and how nasty it was.

'Ah. And did you meet her husband, the other half of their storied love match?'

'Briefly. He was washing his car. We didn't really talk.'

'The man is crazy,' Olivia says. She doesn't sound angry, and she doesn't sound like she's making a joke. It's just a flat declaration, like *the sky is cloudy today.* 'Don't take my word for it; before he retired, he was known in Life Sciences as Rowdy Roddy the Mad Nutritionist. For a few years before he finally stepped down – although he may still have lab privileges,

I don't know about that – he had an eight-week seminar called Meat Is Life. Which always made me think of Renfield in *Dracula*. Have you read it? No? Renfield is the best character. He's locked in a madhouse, eating flies and repeating "the blood is the life" over and over.

'Fuck me, I'm rambling.'

Barbara's mouth drops open.

'Don't be shocked, Barbara. You can't write well without a grasp of profanity and the ability to look at filth. To sometimes exalt filth. All I'm saying – not out of jealousy, not out of possessiveness – is you would do well to steer clear of the Professors Harris. Her, especially.' She eyes Barbara. 'Now if you have me down for a jealous old woman slandering a former colleague, please say so.'

Barbara says, 'All I know is her tea is *horrible*.'

Olivia smiles. 'We'll close the subject with that, shall we? Are those your poems in that folder?'

'Some of them. The shorter ones.'

'Read to me.'

'Are you sure?' Barbara is scared. Barbara is delighted.

'Of course I am.'

Barbara's hands are shaking as she opens her folder, but Olivia doesn't see; she has settled back in her chair and closed those fierce eyes. Barbara reads a poem called 'Double Image.' She reads one called 'The Eye of December.' She reads one called 'Grass, Late Afternoon':

> 'The storm is finished. The sun returns.
> The wind says, When I blow
> tell your million shadows
> to say "Eternity, eternity."
> So that is what they do.'

After that one the old poet opens her eyes and yells for Marie. Her voice is surprisingly strong. Barbara thinks with dismay that she has been found wanting and is going to be escorted out by the woman in the fawn-colored slacks.

'You have another twenty minutes, Livvie,' Marie says.

Olivia ignores that. She's looking at Barbara. 'Are you attending classes in person, or are you Zooming?'

'Zooming for now,' Barbara says. She hopes she won't cry until she gets out of here. She thought it was going so well, that's the thing.

'When can you come? Mornings are best for me. I'm fresh then . . . or as fresh as is possible these days. Are they possible for you? Marie, get the book.'

Marie leaves, giving Barbara just enough time to find her voice. 'I have no classes until eleven.'

'Assuming you're an early riser, that's perfect.'

As a rule Barbara is far from an early riser, but she thinks that's about to change.

'Can you come from eight until nine? Or nine thirty?'

Marie has returned with an appointment book. She says, 'Nine. Nine thirty is too long, Livvie.'

Olivia doesn't stick out her tongue, but she makes an amusing face, like a child who's told she must eat her broccoli.

'Eight to nine, then. Monday, Tuesday, and Friday. Wednesdays are for the goddam doctors and Thursdays are for the motherfucking physical therapy chick. The *harpy*.'

'I can do that,' Barbara says. 'Of course I can do that.'

'Leave the poems you brought. Bring more. If you have books of mine you want signed, bring them next time and we'll get that nonsense out of the way. I'll see you out.' She gropes for her canes and begins the slow process of getting up. It's like watching an Erector Set building constructed in slow motion. Marie moves to help her. The old poet waves her away, almost falling back into her chair in the process.

'You don't have to—' Barbara begins.

'Yes,' Olivia says. She sounds out of breath. 'I do. Walk with me. Throw my coat over my shoulders.'

'Faux, faux,' Barbara says, without meaning to. The way she writes some lines – often the best lines – without meaning to.

Olivia doesn't just laugh at that, she cackles. They move slowly down the short hall, the old poet almost invisible beneath the fur coat. Marie stands watching them. *Probably ready to pick up the pieces if she falls and shatters like an old porcelain vase*, Barbara thinks.

At the door, one of those frail hands grasps Barbara's wrist. In a low voice carried on a waft of faintly bad breath, she says, 'Did Emily ask you if your poems were about what she likes to call "the Black experience"?'

'Well . . . she did say something . . .'

'The poem I saw and the ones you read me weren't about being Black, were they?'

'No.'

The hand on her wrist tightens. 'I'm going to ask you a question, young lady, and don't you lie to me. Don't you *dare*. Give me your promise.'

'I promise.'

The old poet leans close, looking up into Barbara's young face. She whispers: 'Do you understand that you are good at this?'

Barbara thinks, *On the basis of three or four poems, you know this how?* But she whispers back, 'Yes.'

2

She walks home in a daze, thinking of the last thing Olivia said to her. 'Gifts are fragile. You must never entrust yours to people who might break it.'

She doesn't say who she might be thinking of, and Barbara doesn't need her to. She has what she needs and doesn't expect to return to the Harris house again.

July 25, 2021

1

Holly walks into her office and all the furniture is gone. Not just the desk and the chairs, but her desktop computer, the TV, and the carpet. Her mother is standing at the window and looking out, just as Holly does when she has — Charlotte's phrase — *her thinking cap on*. Charlotte turns around. Her eyes are sunken deep in their sockets and her face is a grayish yellow. She looks as she did the last time Holly spoke to her in the hospital, just before she slipped into a coma.

'Now you can come home,' Charlotte says.

2

When Holly opens her eyes she's at first not sure where she is, only relieved that it's not in her empty office. She looks around and the world — the real one — clicks into place. It's a room on the second floor of a Days Inn, halfway back to the city. Her mother is dead. *I'm safe* is her first waking thought.

She goes into the bathroom to urinate, then just sits on the toilet for a little while with her face in her hands. She's a terrible person for equating safety with her mother's death. Charlotte's lies don't change that.

Holly showers and puts on her clean underwear while her mother tells her that new-bought garments should always be washed before they're worn; *Oh, Holly — you don't know who may have handled it, how many times have I told you that?*

Two slips of paper have been pushed under her door. One is the

bill for her night's stay. The other is headed BREAKFAST BUFFET
NOTICE. It says that if the room's occupants are vaccinated, they are
free to enjoy the breakfast buffet 'in our pleasant dining area.' If not,
will they please take a tray back up to their room.

Holly has never exactly enjoyed a motel breakfast buffet, but she's
hungry, and since she's been vaxxed, she eats it in the little dining
area, where the only other occupant is an overweight man staring at
his phone with sullen concentration. Holly skips the scrambled eggs
(motel breakfast buffet eggs are always wet or cooked to death) in
favor of a single rubbery pancake, a cardboard bowl of Alpha-Bits,
and a cup of bad coffee. She takes a breakfast pastry in a cellophane
wrapper and eats it next to the ice machine after her first cigarette
of the day. According to the time-and-temperature sign in front of
the bank across the service road, it's already seventy-five degrees at
only seven in the morning. Her mother is dead and it's going to be
a scorcher.

Holly goes back to her room, figures out the little coffee maker –
one cup won't be enough, not after that awful dream – and opens her
iPad. She finds the Jet Mart security video and looks at it. She wishes
the fracking lens of the camera wasn't so fracking dirty. Did no one
ever think to clean it? She goes into the bathroom, shuts the door,
turns off the lights, sits on the lid of the toilet, and looks at the footage
again, holding the iPad three inches from her face.

She leaves the bathroom, pours herself some coffee – not as bad as
the buffet coffee but almost – and drinks it standing up. Then she goes
back, closes the bathroom door, turns out the light, and looks at the
video for a third time.

8:04 PM on the night of July first, a little more than three weeks
ago. Here comes Bonnie, riding down Red Bank Avenue from the
direction of the college at the top of the ridge. Off with the helmet.
Shake out the hair. Helmet placed on the seat of a bike which will
later be found abandoned further down the avenue, just begging to be
stolen. She walks into the store—

Holly backs the footage up. Off with the helmet, shake out the hair,
and *freeze it*. Before Bonnie's hair falls back against the sides of her
face, Holly sees a flash of gold. She uses her fingers to enlarge the

image and there can be no doubt: one of the triangular earrings Holly found in the undergrowth.

'That girl is dead,' Holly whispers. 'Oh God, she's dead.'

She re-starts the video. Bonnie gets her soda from the cooler, inspects the snacks, almost buys a package of Ho Hos, changes her mind, goes to the counter. The clerk says something that makes them both laugh and Holly thinks, *This is a regular stop for her.* Holly needs to talk to that clerk. Today, if possible.

Bonnie stows her drink in her backpack. Says something else to the clerk. He gives her a thumbs-up. She leaves. Puts on her helmet. Mounts up. Pedals away with a final quick wave to the clerk. He raises his in return. And that's it. The time-stamp at the bottom of the screen says 8:09.

Holly gets up, reaches for the bathroom light switch, then settles back onto the closed lid of the john. She starts the video again, this time ignoring Bonnie and the clerk. She wishes the security camera had been mounted a little lower, but of course the purpose was to catch shoplifters, not monitor the traffic on Red Bank Avenue. At least she doesn't have to watch the traffic going uphill, just the vehicles going in the direction of the abandoned auto shop where the bike was found. She can only see their lower halves; the top of the store's front window cuts off the rest.

Bonnie's abductor – Holly no longer doubts there *was* an abductor – could have already been in place at the auto shop, but he might also have followed her, then gone ahead to get in place while she made her regular halfway-point stop.

Doing it that way would minimize the time he was parked and waiting for her, she thinks. *Less chance of being noticed and possibly attracting suspicion.*

Eight o'clock on a weeknight, and the turnpike extension has sucked most of the downtown traffic away. *Which is,* she thinks, *why so many of the businesses on that stretch of Red Bank are closed, including the gas station, the Quik-Pik, and the auto repair shop.*

She counts only fifteen cars going downhill past the store, plus two pickup trucks and a van. Holly rewinds the footage and goes again, this time stopping as the van passes. Bonnie is frozen at the snack rack. The clerk is putting cigarettes into one of the slots in the display behind the counter.

Holly once more brings the screen close to her face and uses her fingers to enlarge the image. Damn dirty camera lens! Plus the top half of the van is cut off by the top of the store window. She can make out the driver's left hand on the wheel and it's a white hand, if that were any help, but it's really not. She shrinks the image back to its original size. The van is either dirty white or light blue. There's a stripe down the side, along the bottom of the driver's side door and the body of the van. The stripe is definitely a dark blue. She wonders if either Pete or Jerome could tell her what kind of van it is. She doesn't really think so, but if you were going to kidnap a young woman, a van might be just the thing. God, if only she could see the license plate!

Holly sends the vid to Pete and Jerome, asking if either of them can identify the make of the van, or at least narrow it down. The WiFi is better this morning, and before checking out she goes to the city PD's Reported Missing website, specifying 2018. There are almost four hundred thousand residents of the city by the lake, so she's not surprised to find over a hundred names on the list. Peter Steinman's is among them. Ellen Craslow's is not, probably because she had no one to report her gone; Keisha just assumed she'd quit her job, probably to go back to Georgia. Next to the names of five souls who were reported missing is the date they were found, along with one word: DECEASED.

3

On her drive back to the city, Holly is nagged by the thought of her Dollar General underwear, bought new but unwashed, and it comes to her that her mother really isn't dead after all and won't be until Holly herself dies. She gets off at the Ridgeland exit, checks her iPad notes at a red light, and drives to Eastland Avenue, which is not far from Bell College. It doesn't escape her that Bonnie's case keeps leading her back to the area of the college.

On the south side of the ridge are those stately Victorian homes curving down to the park; on this side there's student housing, mostly three-decker apartment buildings. Some have been kept up pretty well, but many more are running to seed with peeling paint and scruffy yards. There are discarded beer cans in some of those yards, and in one there's a twenty-foot-high balloon man, bowing and scraping and waving its long red arms. Holly guesses it might have been pilfered from a car dealership.

She passes through a two-block commerce area aimed at college students: three bookstores, a couple of head shops (one called Grateful Dead), lots of pizza-burger-taco joints, and at least seven bars. On this hot Sunday, still shy of noon, most of the joints are closed and there's little foot traffic. Beyond the shops, restaurants, and dive bars, the apartment houses recommence. The lawn of 2395 Eastland has no balloon man out front; instead there are at least two dozen flamingos stuck in the parched grass. One wears a beret that's been tied on with a piece of ribbon; the head of another is buried in a cowboy hat; a third is standing in a fake wishing well.

College student humor, Holly thinks, and pulls in at the curb.

There are only two stories to this house, but it rambles all over the place, as if the original builder could never bring himself to stop. There are five cars crammed into the driveway, bumper to bumper and side by side. A sixth is on grass which strikes Holly as too tired and near death to complain.

A young guy sits on the concrete front step, head hung low, smoking either a cigarette or a doob. He looks up when Holly gets out of her car – blue eyes, black beard, long hair – then lowers his head again. She weaves her way through the flamingos, which probably struck some young man or men as the height of Juvenalian wit.

'Hello there. My name is Holly Gibney, and I wondered—'

'If you're a Mormon or one of those Adventists, go away.'

'I'm not. Are you by any chance Tom Higgins?'

He looks up at that. The bright blue eyes are threaded with snaps of red. 'No. I am not. Go away. I have the world's worst fucking hangover.' He waves a hand behind him. 'Everyone else is still sleeping it off.'

'Saturday Night Fever followed by Sunday Morning Coming Down,' Holly ventures.

The bearded young man laughs at that, then winces. 'You say true, grasshopper.'

'Would you like a coffee? There's a Starbucks down the street.'

'Sounds good, but I don't think I can walk that far.'

'I'll drive.'

'And will you pay, Dolly?'

'It's Holly. And yes, I will pay.'

4

Having a strange man – big, bearded, and hungover – in her car might have put Holly's nerves on edge under other circumstances, but this young man, Randy Holsten by name, strikes her as about as dangerous as Pee-wee Herman, at least in his current state. He rolls down the passenger window of Holly's Prius and holds his face out into the hot breeze, like a shaggy dog eager for every passing scent. This pleases her. If he throws up, it will be outside rather than in. Which makes her think of Jerome's drive to the hospital with Vera Steinman.

The Starbucks is thinly populated. Several of the customers also look hungover, although perhaps not as severely as young Mr Holsten. She gets him a double cap and an Americano for herself. They take chairs outside in the scant shade of the overhang. Holly lowers her mask. The coffee is strong, it's good, and it takes the curse off the motel brew she drank earlier. When Holsten begins showing signs of slightly improved vitality, she asks him if Tom Higgins is also sleeping it off in the House of Flamingos.

'Nope. He's in Lost Wages. At least as far as I know. Billy and Hinata went on to LA, but Tom stayed. Which doesn't surprise me.'

Holly frowns. 'Lost wages?'

'Slang, my sister. For Las Vegas. A town made for such as Monsewer Higgins.'

'When did he go there?'

'June. Middle of. And left owing his share of the rent. Which I can tell you was Tom all over.'

Holly thinks of Keisha's short and brutal summing up of Tom Higgins's character: *Wimp. Loser. Stoner.*

'You're sure it was the middle of June? And these other two went with him?'

'Yeah. It was just after the Juneteenth block party. And yeah, the three of them went in Billy's 'Stang. Tom Terrific is the kind of dude who'll suck on his fellow dudes until there's nothing more to suck. I guess they wised up. Speaking of sucking on people, can I have another one of these?'

'I'll pay, you get. One for me, too.'

'Another Americano?'

'Yes, please.'

When he comes back with their coffees, Holly says, 'It sounds like you didn't like Tom much.'

'I did at first. He's got a certain amount of charm – I mean, the girl he was going with was *way* out of his league – but it wears off in a hurry. Like the finish on a cheap ring.'

'Nicely put. You're feeling better, aren't you?'

'A little.' Holsten shakes his head . . . but gently. 'Never again.'

Until next Saturday night, Holly thinks.

'What's this about, anyway? What's your interest in Tom?'

Holly tells him, leaving Ellen Craslow and Peter Steinman out of it. Randy Holsten listens with fascination. Holly is interested to see how quickly the red is leaving his eyes. The older she gets, the more the resilience of the young amazes her.

'Bonnie, yeah. That was her name. She's missing, huh?'

'She is. Did you know her?'

'Met her is all. At a party. Maybe once or twice before. The party must have been New Year's. She was steppin dynamite. Legs all the way up.' Holsten shakes one hand, as if he's touched something hot. 'Tom brought her, but our place wasn't exactly her *milieu*, if you know what I mean.'

'Didn't like the flamingos?'

'They're a new addition. I haven't seen her since that party. She broke up with him, you know. I talked to her a little. You know, just your standard party blah-blah – and I think the breakup was like, happening then. Or about to happen. I was in the kitchen. That's where we talked. Maybe she came out to get away from the babble, maybe to get away from Tom. He was in the living room, probably trying to score dope.'

'What did she say?'

'Can't remember. I was pretty drunk. But if you're thinking he might have done something to her, forget it. Tom isn't the confrontational type. He's more the can-you-loan-me-fifty-until-next-Friday type.'

'And you're sure he hasn't been back since June?' She tells him what she told Keisha. 'I'm just crossing *t*'s and dotting *i*'s here.'

'If he did I haven't seen him. Don't think so. Like I said, Vegas is his kind of town.'

'Do you have his number?'

He finds it on his phone and Holly adds it to her notes, but she's already close to taking Tom Higgins off her list of possible suspects, and he was never high on it anyway. Not that she has a list.

'If you call him, you'll get one of those robots that just repeats the number and tells you to leave a message.'

'He monitors his calls.'

'Guys like Tom, that's what they do. He owes money, I think. Not just the back rent.'

'How much of that does he owe?'

'His share for two months. June and July. Five hundred dollars.'

Holly gives him a card from her purse. 'If you think of anything, maybe something she said when you were talking at the party, give me a call.'

'Man, I don't know. I was pretty fried. All I can be sure of is that she was fine-looking. Out of Tom's league, like I said.'

'I get it, but just in case.'

'Okay.' He puts the card in the back pocket of his jeans, where Holly guesses it will probably stay until it goes through the wash and comes out lint. Randy Holsten smiles. It's charming. 'I think Tommy was starting to bore her. Ergo, breakup.'

Holly gives him a lift back to the rambling apartment building. He's improved enough to keep his head inside. He thanks her for the coffee and she asks him again to call her if he thinks of anything, but it's just a rote exercise. She's pretty sure she's gotten everything from Holsten that he has to give, which amounts to nothing but a phone number that will probably lead nowhere.

Still, when she gets back to the commerce area of Eastland Avenue, she pulls into an empty parking space – there are plenty – and calls Tom Higgins's number. It's two hours earlier in Las Vegas, but not *that* early. There's one ring, followed by the robo-voice Holsten warned her of. Holly identifies herself, says Bonnie Dahl has disappeared, and asks if Tom will call her back (she calls him Mr Higgins). Then she drives home, showers again, and throws her Dollar General underwear in the washing machine.

5

While the washer is doing its thing, Holly gets on Twitter and plugs in the name Craslow. She's not expecting a long list – it's not a name she's ever heard before – and only gets a dozen hits. Two Twitter Craslows feature thumbnail pictures of Black people, a man and a woman. Two are whites, both women. The other eight feature either blank silhouettes or cartoon avatars.

Holly uses Facebook, Instagram, and Twitter routinely in her work. Bill didn't teach her; he was old-school. She can send messages on Twitter to the dozen Craslows from one of her several social media aliases, something simple: *I'm looking for information about Ellen Craslow, from Bibb County, Georgia. If you know her, please reply.* Even if the Craslow from whom she's hoping to get information isn't on Twitter, chances are good one of the twelve is related and will pass the message on. Easy-peasy, nothing to it, she's done it before when looking for missing people (mostly bail-jumpers) and lost pets. There's no reason not to now, but she pauses, frowning at the list of names on her desktop computer.

Why the hesitation?

No concrete reason she can think of, but her gut says don't do it. She decides to table this logical next step and think it over. She can do that while she makes a trip to Jet Mart and talks to the clerk who waited on Bonnie.

Her phone rings as she's leaving. She thinks it will be either Penny, asking for another update, or possibly Tom Higgins calling from Las Vegas, assuming that's where he is. But it's Jerome, and he sounds excited.

'You think someone grabbed her in that van, Holly. Don't you?'

'I think it's possible. Can you tell me anything about it?'

'I've looked at a lot of car sites, and it might be a Toyota Sienna. *Might* be. The lens of that surveillance camera was mighty dirty—'

'I know.'

'—and you can only see the bottom half. But it's not a Chevy

Express. Take that to the bank. Could be a Ford, but if it was Final Jeopardy, I'd say it was a Sienna.'

'Okay, thanks.' Not that it's much help.

'There was something funny about it.'

'Really? What?'

'I don't know. I've looked at it a dozen times and I still don't know.'

'The stripe? The blue one down low?'

'No, not that, lots of vans have stripes. Something else.'

'Well, if you figure it out, let me know.'

'Wish we had a license plate.'

'Yes,' Holly says. 'Wouldn't that be nice?'

'Holly?'

'I'm still here.' Now heading for the elevator.

'I think it's a serial. I really do.'

6

She's pulling out of the parking garage when her phone rings again. The screen says UNKNOWN NUMBER. She puts her car in park and takes the call. She's pretty sure Mr Unknown Number is Tom Terrific.

'Hello, this is Holly Gibney, how can I help?'

'Tom Higgins.' In the background she can hear electronic boops, electronic beeps, and jangling bells. Casino sounds. Any doubt that Tom Higgins isn't in Las Vegas departs. 'You can help by telling me what you mean about Bonnie being missing.'

'Wait one. Let me park.' Holly pulls into a vacant space. She never talks on her phone while she's driving unless she has absolutely no choice and thinks people who behave otherwise are idiots. It's not just against the law, it's dangerous.

'Where did she go?'

Holly thinks of asking him what part of *missing* he doesn't understand. Instead, she tells him that Bonnie's mother hired her, and what she's found out so far. Which isn't much. When she finishes there's a long moment of silence. She doesn't bother to ask if he's still there; the boops and beeps continue.

At last he says, 'Huh.'

Is that all you've got? Holly thinks.

'Do you have any idea where she might have gone, Mr Higgins?'

'Nope. I dumped her last winter. She was asking – without asking, you know how some women are – for a long-term commitment, and I was already planning this trip.'

I heard the dumping was the other way around, Holly doesn't say.

'Does it seem likely to you that she'd leave without telling anyone?'

'According to you, she told everyone,' Tom says. 'She left a note, didn't she?'

'Yes, but on the spur of the moment? Leaving her bike for anyone to steal? Was she that impulsive?'

'Sometimes . . .' This careful answer suggests to Holly that he's saying what he thinks she wants to hear.

'Without taking any clothes? And without using a credit card or her phone for the last three weeks?'

'So what? She probably got sick of her mother. Bonnie hated her like poison.'

Not according to Keisha. According to Keisha, there was love lost between them but plenty of love left. Penny is driving around with her daughter's picture plastered on her car, after all.

'She probably hasn't called anybody because then her mother would send out the Royal Canadian Mounties. Or someone like you. Can't wait to get her back there and start running her life again.'

Holly decides to change the subject. 'Are you enjoying Las Vegas, Mr Higgins?'

'Yeah, it's great.' Animation replaces caution. 'It's a happening town.'

'It sounds like you're in a casino.'

'Yeah, Binion's. I'm just waiting tables right now, but I'm working my way up. And the tips are fantastic. Speaking of work, my break's almost over. Good talking to you, Miz Gibley. I'd say I hope you find Bonnie, but since you're working for the Queen Bitch, I can't really do that. My bad, I guess.'

'One more thing before you go, please?'

'Make it quick. My asshole boss is waving.'

'I spoke with Randy Holsten. You owe five hundred dollars of back rent.'

Tom laughs. 'He can whistle for it.'

'I'm the one who's whistling,' Holly says. 'I know where you work.

I can have my lawyer call the management and ask that your wages be attached in that amount.' She doesn't know if she can actually do that, but it certainly sounds good. She's always been more inventive on the phone. More assertive, too.

Neither caution nor animation this time. Injury. 'Why would you do that? You're not working for Randy!'

'Because,' Holly says in the same prim voice she used with Jerome, 'you don't strike me as a good person. For all sorts of reasons.'

A moment's silence, except for the boops and beeps. Then: 'Right back atcha, bitch.'

'Goodbye, Mr Higgins. Have a nice day.'

7

Holly drives across town to the Red Bank Avenue Jet Mart, feeling strangely happy, strangely light. She thinks, *A bitch walks into a bar and orders a mai-tai.*

Not even discovering that the clerk she wants isn't on duty can put a dent in her good mood. She should have expected it, anyway; if the guy has enough seniority to know Bonnie as a regular, it's not surprising that he'd have Sundays off. She describes the man she's looking for to the current clerk, a young man with an unfortunate wall eye.

'That's Emilio,' the young man says. 'Emilio Herrera. He'll be on tomorrow, three to eleven. Eleven's when this dump closes up.'

'Thank you.'

Holly considers driving up to the college and asking some questions about Ellen Craslow at the Belfry and the Life Sciences building, but what would be the point? It's not just a Sunday in midsummer but a Sunday in *Covid* midsummer. Bell College of Arts and Sciences will be as dead as Abe Lincoln. Better to go home, put her feet up, and think. About why she felt hesitant about getting in touch with the Craslows she found on Twitter. About whether the van on the security footage means anything. Sometimes a cigar is just a smoke and a van is just a van. About whether or not she actually has stumbled across the track of a serial killer.

Her phone rings. It's Pete Huntley. Once she's back in her apartment building garage, she lights a cigarette and calls him back.

'I don't know what kind of van that is,' he says, 'but there's something funny about it.'

'Only you don't know exactly what.'

'Yeah. How did you know that?'

'Because Jerome said the same thing. Why don't you talk to him? Maybe between the two of you, you can figure it out.'

8

Holly can't sleep that night. She lies on her back, hands folded between her breasts, looking up into the dark. She thinks about Bonnie's bike, just begging to be stolen. She thinks about Peter Steinman, known as Stinky to his friends. Skateboard abandoned but returned to his mother. Does Bonnie's mother have Bonnie's bike? Of course she does. She thinks about Keisha, saying love was lost but plenty was left. And she thinks about Ellen Craslow. *That's* what's keeping her awake.

She gets up, goes to her desktop, and opens Twitter. Using her favorite alias – LaurenBacallFan – she messages each of the dozen Craslows, asking if any of them have information about Ellen Craslow from Bibb County, Georgia. She attaches each query to each Craslow's last tweet. This doesn't allow for privacy, but so what? None of them have more than a dozen followers. With that done she goes back to bed. For awhile she still can't sleep, nagged by the idea that it was somehow a wrong move, but how can it be? Not doing it would have been the wrong one. Right?

Right.

At last she drops off. And dreams of her mother.

February 15, 2021–March 27, 2021

1

Barbara and Olivia Kingsbury begin their meetings. There is always tea brought by Marie Duchamp, who seems to have an endless supply of white shirts and fawn-colored slacks. There are always cookies. Sometimes ginger snaps, sometimes shortbread fingers, sometimes Chips Ahoy, most commonly Oreos. Olivia Kingsbury is partial to Oreos. Every morning at nine Marie appears in the doorway of the living room and tells them that it's time to stop. Barbara shoulders her backpack and heads for school. She can Zoom her classes from home but has permission to use the library, where there are fewer distractions.

By mid-March, she is giving Olivia a kiss on the cheek before leaving.

Barbara's parents know that she has a special project of some kind and assume it's at school. Jerome guesses it's somewhere else but doesn't pry for details. Several times Barbara comes close to telling them about her meetings with Olivia. What mostly holds her back is *Jerome's* special project, the book he's writing about their great-grandfather, a book that's going to be published. She doesn't want her big brother to think she's copying him, or trying somehow to draft off his success. Also, it's *poetry*. That seems pretty frou-frou to Barbara compared to her brother's sturdy, well-researched history of Black gangsters in Depression-era Chicago. *Further* also, it's her own thing. Secret, like the diary she kept in her early teen years, read over when she was seventeen (as much of it as she could bear, at least) and then burned one day when everyone was gone.

To each meeting – each *seminar* – she brings a new poem. Olivia insists on it. When Barbara says some of the new ones aren't good, aren't *finished*, the old poet waves her objections away. Says it doesn't matter. Says the important thing is to keep the channel open and the words flowing. 'If you don't,' she says, 'your channel may silt up. And then dry up.'

They read aloud . . . or rather Barbara does; Olivia picks the poems but says she has to save what remains of her voice. They read Dickey, Roethke, Plath, Moore, Bishop, Karr, Eliot, even Ogden Nash. One day she asks Barbara to read 'The Congo,' by Vachel Lindsay. Barbara does, and when she's finished, Olivia asks Barbara if she finds the poem racist.

'Oh sure,' Barbara says, and laughs. 'It's racist as hell. "Fat black bucks in a wine-barrel room"? Are you kidding me?'

'So you don't like it.'

'No. I *loved* it.' And peals laughter again, partly in amazement.

'Why do you?'

'The rhythm! It's like tromping feet! Boomlay, boomlay, boomlay, *boom*. It's like a song you can't get out of your head, a total earworm.'

'Does poetry transcend race?'

'Yes!'

'Does it transcend racism?'

Barbara has to think. In this room of tea and cookies, she always has to think. But it excites her, almost exalts her. She never feels more alive than she does in the presence of this wrinkled old woman with the raging eyes.

'No.'

'Ah.'

'But if I could write a poem like this about Maleek Dutton, I totally would. Only the boomlay-boom would be a gunshot. He's the kid who—'

'I know who he was,' Olivia says, and gestures to the television. 'Why don't you try doing that?'

'Because I'm not ready,' Barbara says.

2

Olivia reads Barbara's poems and has Marie make copies of every one, and when Barbara comes again – not every time, only sometimes – she will tell her to make a change or find another word. She always says the same two things, either 'You were not present when you wrote this' or 'You were the audience instead of the writer.' Once she tells Barbara that she is only allowed to admire what she writes a single time: during the act of composition. 'After that, Barbara, you must be ruthless.'

When they're not talking about poems and poets, Olivia encourages Barbara to talk about her life. Barbara tells her about growing up UMC – it's what her father calls the upper middle class – and how she's sometimes embarrassed to be treated well and sometimes both ashamed and angry when people look right through her. She doesn't just assume it's the color of her skin; she knows it. Just as she knows that when she's in a shop, the people who work there are watching to see if she's going to steal something. She likes rap and hip-hop, but the phrase *my nigga* makes her uncomfortable. She thinks she shouldn't feel that way, she even likes the YG joint, but she can't help it. She says those words should make whites uncomfortable, not her. Yet there it is.

'Tell that. Show it.'

'I don't know how.'

'Find a way. Find the images. No ideas but in things, but they must be the true things. When your eye and heart and mind are in harmony.'

Barbara Robinson is young, barely old enough to vote, but terrible things have happened to her. She went through a brief suicidal period. What happened with Chet Ondowsky last Christmas in the elevator was even worse; it amputated her concept of reality. She would tell Olivia about these things even though they are too fantastic to be believed, but each time she approaches the subject – almost throwing herself in front of an oncoming truck in Lowtown, for instance – the old poet raises a hand like a cop stopping traffic and shakes her head. She is allowed to talk about Holly, but when Barbara tries to tell about how Holly saved her from being blown up at a rock show in Mingo Auditorium, the hand goes up again. *Stop.*

'This is not psychiatry,' Olivia says. 'It is not therapy. It is *poetry*, my dear. The talent was there before awful things happened to you, it came with the original equipment just as your brother's did, but talent is a dead engine. It runs on every unresolved experience – every unresolved *trauma*, if you like – in your life. Every conflict. Every mystery. Every deep part of your character you find not just unlikeable but loathsome.'

One hand goes up and makes a fist. Barbara can tell it hurts Olivia to do that, but she does it anyway, closing her fingers tight, nails digging into the thin skin of her palm.

'Keep it,' she says. 'Keep it as long as you can. It's your treasure. You will use it up and then you will have to rely on the memory of the ecstasy you once felt, but while you have it, keep it. Use it.'

She doesn't say the new poems Barbara brings her are good or bad. Not then.

3

Mostly it's Barbara who talks, but on a few occasions Olivia changes it up and reminisces, with a mixture of amusement and sadness, about literary society in the fifties and sixties, which she calls 'the gone world.' Poets she's met, poets she's known, poets she's loved, poets (and at least one Pulitzer-winning novelist) she's gone to bed with. She talks about the pain of losing her grandson, and how that's one thing she cannot write about. 'It's like a stone in my throat,' she says. She also talks about her long teaching career, most of it 'up the hill,' meaning Bell College.

One day in March when Olivia is talking about Sharon Olds's six-week residency and how wonderful it was, Barbara asks about the poetry workshop. 'Didn't there used to be both fiction *and* poetry? Like in Iowa?'

'Exactly like Iowa,' Olivia agrees. Her mouth tucks into a bed of wrinkles, as if she's tasted something disagreeable.

'Weren't there enough applicants to keep it going?'

'There were plenty of applicants. Not as many as for the fiction work-shop, of course, and it always ran at a loss, but since the fiction workshop makes a profit, the two balanced out.' The creases in her mouth deepen. 'It was Emily Harris who moved that it be shut down. She pointed out that if it was, we could afford not only to lure more high-profile fiction writers to come but add considerably to the overall English Department budget. There were protests, but Emily's point of view carried the day, although I believe she was emerita even then.'

'That's a shame.'

'It is. I argued that the prestige of the Bell Poetry Workshop made a difference, and Jorge — I *liked* that man — said it was part of our responsibility. "We must carry the torch," he said. That made Emily smile. She has a special one for such occasions. It's small, no teeth showing, but in its way it's as sharp as a razor blade. She said, "Our responsibility is wider than a few would-be poets, dear Jorge." Not that he was her dear anything. She never liked him and I imagine she was delighted when he decamped. Probably resented him even coming to that meeting.' She pauses. 'I invited him, actually.'

'Who was Jorge? Was he on the faculty?'

'Jorge Castro was our fiction writer-in-residence in the 2010–2011 academic year, and part of 2012. Until, as I say, he decamped.'

'Did he write *The Forgotten City*? That's on our summer reading list.' Not that Barbara plans to read it; she will be done with high school in June.

'Yes. It's a fine novel. All three of his novels are good, but that's probably the best. He was passionate about the virtues of poetry, but couldn't vote when the time for that came around. Not a faculty member, you see.'

'What do you mean, he decamped?'

'That's a strange story, sad and more than a little mysterious. It's off the subject you are here to discuss — if Jorge ever wrote poetry, I never saw it — but I'll tell you if you want to hear it.'

'Please.'

Marie comes in just then and tells Olivia and Barbara that it's time. The old poet raises her hand in that *stop* gesture. 'Five more minutes, please,' she says.

And tells Barbara the story of Jorge Castro's strange disappearance in October of 2012.

4

On the last Saturday of March, Barbara's phone rings while she's curled up in the living room, reading *The Forgotten City*, by Jorge Castro. It's Olivia Kingsbury. She says, 'I think I owe you an apology, Barbara. I may have made a bad mistake. You will decide. Can you come and see me?'

July 26, 2021

1

Holly is up with the sun. She has a bowl of oatmeal and fruit, then goes to her computer and opens Twitter. She has gotten one reply to her Craslow query. Elmer Craslow (Eagles fan, MAGA fan, Nyack Strong!) says he's never heard of Ellen Craslow, of Bibb County, Georgia. Holly isn't terribly disappointed. She has eleven more chances. In baseball it's three strikes and you're out.

As she's putting on her sneakers in preparation for her morning walk – it's when she does her best thinking – her phone trills. It's Jerome, and he sounds excited. In a voice slightly muffled by the mask he's wearing, he tells her he's in an Uber, headed for the airport. He's going to New York.

Holly is alarmed. 'In a *plane?*'

'That's the usual way one travels a thousand miles,' he says, and laughs. 'Relax, Hollyberry, I've got my vax card and I'll be wearing my mask the whole time I'm in the air. In fact I'm wearing one now, as you can probably tell.'

'Why New York?' But of course she knows. 'Your book!'

'The editor called me last night. He said he could send the contract, or I could come and sign it today and he'd hand me a check for a hundred thousand dollars! He says that's not the way it's usually done, but he got the green light to make an exception. Is that crazy, or what?'

'It's crazy and wonderful, as long as you don't get sick.'

'According to the statistics, New York's actually safer than our town, Hols. I can't get there for lunch – too bad, publisher's lunch is sort of a tradition – but he says we can get together this afternoon for burgers and a beer. My agent will be there – I've never even met her except for Zoom, also crazy. He said in the old days he would have taken us to Four Seasons, but the best he can manage now is the Blarney Stone. Which is good enough for me.'

He's babbling, but Holly doesn't mind. What she minds is the idea of him traveling on a plane where the air is recirculated and anyone might have Covid, but she can't help being delighted by his over-the-moon happiness. *Spur-of-the-moment trip to New York City in the summer of Covid*, she thinks. *It's good to be young and today it's good to be Jerome.*

'Enjoy yourself, and whatever you do, don't lose that check.'

'My agent will handle that,' he says. 'Whoo, this is so far out! We're almost at the terminal, Hollyberry.'

'Fly well and when you go to the restaurant, make sure to sit outsi—'

'Yes, Mom. One more thing while I've got you. I printed out a MapQuest of Deerfield Park and the surrounding area. Marked it in red where Bonnie and Pete Steinman were last seen. We don't know about Ellen Craslow, but we know she worked on campus, so I marked the Union. Barbara can give it to you if you want. I left it on my desk.'

'I know the locations,' Holly says with some asperity. She thinks of Uncle Henry saying *I didn't fall off a skidder yesterday*.

'Yeah, but seeing them like that is creepy. You should find out if there are more. We're here. I gotta go.'

'When do you come back?'

'I might stay a couple of days or I might come back tomorrow.'

'If you're thinking about Broadway, the shows are clo—'

'Gotta bounce, Hollyberry.' And boom, he's gone.

'I hate it when you call me that.' But she's smiling. Because she really doesn't, and Jerome knows it.

2

She's on her walk when her phone rings again. 'Who's your daddy?' Pete Huntley inquires.

'Not you, Pete. But you sound happy. Plus, not sick.'

'I have risen from the ashes of Covid a new man,' he says, then spoils it with a coughing fit. 'Almost. I found your chick, Holly.'

She stops. 'You found Ellen Craslow?'

'Well, not *her*, but I got her LKA.' Last known address. 'Also her picture, which I will send to you ASAP. Called the personnel office at Bell as soon as they opened, so ain't you proud of me?'

'Very proud. What's the address?'

'11114 MLK Boulevard. That's about as far out of Lowtown as you can get and still be in it.'

'Peter, thank you.'

'No, it's the job.' Sounding serious now. 'You think they're related, don't you? Dahl, Craslow, the kid Jerome was tracking?'

'I think they *might* be.'

'Not going to talk to Isabelle about it, are you?'

'Not yet.'

'Good. You run with it, Hol. I'll do what I can from here. Kinda quarantined, you know?'

'Yes.'

'I can be Mycroft Holmes to your Sherlock. How are you doing with your mom?'

'Getting there,' Holly says. She ends the call.

Five seconds later her phone bings with an incoming text from Pete. She waits until she gets back to her apartment to look at the picture because she wants her iPad with its bigger screen. What he's sent is Ellen Craslow's Bell College ID card, which is still valid – it doesn't expire until October. The photo shows a Black woman with a cap of dark hair. She's neither smiling nor scowling, only looking at the camera with a calmly neutral expression. She's pretty. Holly thinks she looks like she might be in her late twenties or early thirties, which is in line with what Keisha told her. Below her name is BELL COLLEGE ARTS & SCIENCES CUSTODIAL STAFF.

'Where are you, Ellen?' Holly murmurs, but what she's thinking now is *Who took you?*

3

Half an hour later she's cruising slowly down Martin Luther King Boulevard. She's left the stores, churches, bars, convenience stores, and restaurants behind. Pete said the address was almost as far out of Lowtown as it was possible to get and still be in it. It's also about as far out of the city as it's possible to get and still be in it; soon MLK will become Route 27. Ahead of her she can see fields where cows are grazing, also a couple of silos. She's starting to think Pete must have given her the wrong address even though her GPS claims she's going right, but then she comes to Elm Grove Trailer Park. A stake fence surrounds it. The trailers are neat and well-kept. They are in various pastel colors, a plot of grass in front of each one. There are many flowerbeds. An asphalt lane winds among the trailers. Her GPS announces that she has arrived at her destination.

At the head of this lane is a cluster of mailboxes with numbers running from 11104 to 11126. Holly drives slowly into the trailer park, stopping when a couple of kids in bathing suits, one white and one Black, chase a bouncing beachball across the lane without so much as a look. She takes her foot off the brake, then tromps it again as a small yellow dog chases after the kids. In front of a sky-blue trailer with a picture of Barack Obama taped inside the storm door, a woman wearing a sunhat against the day's increasing heat is watering her flowers from a can.

In the middle of the trailer park is a green building with a sign over the door reading OFFICE. Next to it is another green building with a sign reading LAUNDRY. A woman wearing a headwrap is going in with a plastic basket of clothes. Holly parks, dons her mask, and goes into the office. There's a counter with a plaque on it reading STELLA LACEY MANAGER. Behind the counter, a stout lady is playing solitaire on her computer. She glances around at Holly and says, 'If you're looking for a vacancy, I'm sorry. We're at full occupancy.'

'Thank you, but I'm not. My name is Holly Gibney. I'm a private investigator, and I'm trying to locate a woman.'

At the words *private investigator*, Stella Lacey loses interest in her game and becomes interested in Holly.

'Really? Who? What did she do?'

'Nothing that I know of. Do you recognize her?'

Holly offers her phone. Lacey takes it and holds it close to her face. 'Sure. That's Ellen Caslow!'

'Craslow,' Holly says. 'I wonder if you remember exactly when she left.'

'Why do you care?'

'I'd like to know where she went. She worked at the college. Bell?'

'I know Bell,' Lacey says, sounding a bit resentful – the subtext being *I'm not stupid*. 'I think Ellen was a janitor there.'

'A custodian, yes. Ms Lacey, I just want to make sure she's okay.'

Lacey's resentment – if that's what it was, not just Holly's imagination – disappears. 'Okay, I hear that. Do you know which trailer was hers?'

'11114 is the address I have.'

'Right, right, one of the ones behind the laundry, by the kiddie pool. Just let me check.' The solitaire game goes away. A spreadsheet replaces it. Lacey scrolls, peers, puts on a pair of glasses, and scrolls again. 'Here we are. Ellen Craslow. She was renting by the half-year. Paid for July through December of 2018. Then gone.'

She turns to Holly and whips off her glasses.

'I remember now. Phil – my husband – held that trailer vacant through January of '19 because she was a good tenant. No yelling, no arguments, no loud music, no cops showing up at two in the morning. That's the kind of tenant we prefer, and the *only* kind we lease to long-term.'

'I'm sure.'

'We have people who've been here for a long time, Ms Gibley. Why, Mr and Mrs Cullen have been here for I'm going to say twenty years. We like the older folks, Phil and me. Ellen was only in her twenties, but she said she was the quiet type, so we took a chance. And she was as good as her word.' She shakes her head. 'We lost a month on that unit. Just standing empty. I think Phil was smit with her, not that he would have gotten anywhere even if he'd been thirty instead of sixty. I believe she batted for the other side, if you know what I mean.'

'I do.' That also agrees with Keisha's impression.

'She's really missing? Not just from here, I mean?'

Holly nods. 'Since around Thanksgiving in 2018.'

'And someone's just getting around to looking for her now? Why am I surprised? That's how it goes with Black folks.'

'The thing is, nobody reported her missing,' Holly says. 'Maybe she's not. She was from Georgia and might have gone home. I'm trying to track down her relatives, but really, I just got started.'

'Well then, you go on with your bad self. And by the way, you don't need that mask. Corona, that's all just a big old hoax.'

'What happened to Ellen's things, do you know?'

'You know what, I don't. Of course the trailers are furnished, but she must have had her own stuff, right?'

'You'd think,' Holly agrees.

'Phil's in Akron this week. At the trailer show. But if she left a bunch of stuff, he would have told me. He always does. We have a good clientele here, Ms Gibby, but every now and then someone does kind of . . .' She raises her hand and makes the first two fingers trot. 'Sometimes then we find leftover things, which go to the First Baptist or the Goodwill. If they're worth saving, that is.'

'How long was she here?'

Lacey puts on her glasses and calls up a different spreadsheet. 'She came in March of 2016. Two and a half years? Yeah, she must have had stuff. Want me to call Phil? Although I'm sure he would have told me.'

'That would be great,' Holly says. 'Are there any neighbors around 11114 who would remember her?'

Lacey considers. 'What about Mrs McGuire, in 11110? That's not right next door, but only across the kiddie pool. I think Ellen and Imani McGuire used to be friends. Did their laundry together, you know? Women talk plenty then. And she'll be home. Her husband still works part-time at the city impound, but Imani's retired from some other city job. These days she just knits and watches TV. That old girl knits up a storm. Sells it, too, at craft fairs and such. She might know where Ellen went.'

Not if Ellen got snatched in the vicinity of Deerfield Park, Holly thinks. *That's miles from here*. But she'll talk to Imani McGuire. Holly is a fan of Michael Connelly's detective hero, Harry Bosch, and especially of Bosch's number one maxim: get off your ass and go knock on doors.

'I'll talk to Phil and see if he knows what happened to her stuff. I'm pretty sure her trailer was empty – you know, except for the mod cons – when we rented it in February of '19. You could talk to the Joneses, they live there now, but they're both working folks. And why would they know anything? Ellen was long gone when they moved in.' She shakes her head. 'Missing over two years! What a shame! You come back, Ms Gibsy, I'll call Phil right now.'

'Thank you.'

'And ditch the mask, that's my advice. Corona's just make-believe to sell magic pillows on the TV news.'

4

Imani McGuire is tall and thin, with an afro so white it makes the top of her head look like a dandelion puff. Her trailer is a doublewide, painted canary yellow. There's a beautiful rag rug on the floor of the living area, concentric circles of green and cinnamon. The walls – some composition stuff that's supposed to look like wood and really doesn't – are dressed in photographs showing the McGuires at various stages of their lives. The one holding pride of place is a wedding photo. The groom is in Navy dress whites. The bride, with an afro that's black instead of white, bears a striking resemblance to Angela Davis. Imani is perfectly willing to talk, but she has a question.

'Are you vaxxed?'

'I am.'

'Double?'

'Yes. Moderna.'

'Take off your mask, then. I got my second shot in April.'

Holly takes it off and puts it in her pocket. There are his-and-hers La-Z-Boy recliners on the rag rug, facing a TV whose screen isn't much bigger than the screen of Holly's iPad Pro. Draped over the padded arm of one is a half-finished sweater the same bright yellow as the trailer's exterior. Below it is a basket filled with skeins of the same yellow.

Imani picks her needlework up and drapes it over her lap. On the TV, Drew Carey is extolling prizes on *The Price Is Right*. Imani raises the remote and snaps the TV off.

'I'm sorry to interrupt your day.'

'Oh no, I love some company,' Imani says, 'and besides, they already spun the wheel. That's the best part. After that comes the Showcase Round, and you tell me why some fat old man on Social Security wants a couple of motorcycles and camping gear. I bet they sell those prizes if they win. I know I would.' Her needles are already flying, the sweater growing appreciably before Holly's eyes.

'That's going to be beautiful.'

'Hell of a thing to be knitting on a day when the temperature's s'posed to be in the nineties, but cold weather always comes . . . or did, they got the climate so screwed up it's hard to tell what's gonna happen from one year to the next. But if the snow flies and the lake freezes, someone'll buy this at the church sale. I have more put away, plus scarves and mittens. I get good money for these things, more than Yardley makes, but working at the impound keeps him out of my hair . . . and me out of his, I suppose. Works both ways. Fifty-two years is a hell of a long walk from the altar, let me tell you. And some of it's stony. Now how can I help you?'

Holly tells how Keisha got to know Ellen Craslow, and how Ellen just dropped out of sight: there one day, gone the next. 'I put her name out to the other Craslows who are on Twitter, but so far I've only heard from one, and he was no help.'

'Nor will any of the others, based on what I know about her. She's gone anyplace but Traverse, Georgia. She is a sweetie, Miz Gibney—'

'Holly. Please.'

Imani nods. 'A sweetie, smart as a whip, and *strong*. She'll find her way.'

'You say she won't go back to her hometown, where I assume she has people. Why is that?'

'There's family, all right, but she is dead to them and they to her. You won't get anything on Facebook.'

'What happened?'

For what seems like a long time there's only the click of Imani's needles. She's frowning down at the yellow sweater. Then she looks up. 'Is your kind of investigator bound by confidentiality? Like a lawyer or a priest or a doctor?'

Holly thinks this isn't a real question but a test. She has an idea Imani knows. And in any case, it doesn't matter. Honesty really is the best policy. 'I have some degree of privilege, but not as much as lawyers or priests. Under certain circumstances I'd have to talk to the police or the district attorney's office about a case, but they aren't involved in this.'

Holly leans forward. 'What you say to me stays with me, Ms McGuire.'

'Call me Immi.'

'All right.' Holly smiles. She's got a good one. Jerome tells her she doesn't use it enough.

'I'm gonna take you at your word, Holly. Because I cared for that girl. Certainly felt sorry for her troubles. I just want you to know that I'm no tattletale and no backfence gossip.'

'Noted,' Holly says. 'May I turn on my phone and record this?'

'No you may not.' *Click-click* go the needles. 'I don't think I'd tell you at all if you were a man. I've never told Yard. But women, we know more than they do. Don't we?'

'Yes. Yes we do.'

'All right, then. Ellen – she was always an Ellen, never an Ellie – she was in her family's bad books ever since twelve or thirteen, when she gave up eating meat, or any meat products. Total vegetarian. No, that's not right. Total *vegan*. Her family was part of one of those hard-shell bunches, the First Unreformed Church of I Know Better, and when she quit eating flesh they quoted the Bible at her left and right. The pastor counseled her.'

Imani puts a satiric emphasis on *counseled*.

'I'm a fallen-away hardshell myself, and I know you can always find scripture to support what you believe, and they found plenty. In Romans it says the weak person eats only vegetables. Deuteronomy, the Lord has promised you shall eat meat. Corinthians, eat whatever is sold in the meat market. Huh! They must have loved that one in Wuhan, where this damn plague came from. Then when she was fourteen, they caught her with another girl.'

'Oh-oh,' Holly says.

'Oh-oh is right. She tried to run away, but they brought her back. Her family. Don't suppose you know why?'

'Because she was their cross to bear,' Holly says, thinking of times when her own mother said something similar, always prefacing it with a sigh and an *Oh, Holly*.

'So. You know.'

'Yes I do,' Holly says, and something in her voice opens the door to the rest of the story, which Imani might not have told her otherwise.

'When she was eighteen, she got raped. They wore masks, those stocking things people wear when they go skiing, but she recognized one of them by his stutter. He was from her church. Sang in the choir. Ellen said he had a good voice, and didn't stutter when he sang. Excuse me.'

She raises the back of one hand and wipes at her left eye. Then the needles resume their synchronized flight. Watching the sun flash on them is hypnotic.

'You know what they kept talking about? Meat! How they were giving her the meat, and didn't she like it, wasn't it good? Wasn't it something she couldn't get from some *girl*? She said one of them tried to put his doodad in her mouth, told her to go on and eat the meat, and she told him he'd lose it if he did. So that boy fetched her a wallop upside her head and for the rest of the business she was only about a quarter conscious. And guess what came of that?'

Holly knows this, too. 'She got pregnant.'

'Indeed she did. Went on down to Planned Parenthood and got it taken care of. When her folks found out – I don't know how, she didn't tell them – they told her she wasn't part of the family anymore. She was ex-com-*mu*-nicated. Her daddy said she was a murderer no different from Cain in Genesis, and told her to go where Cain went, to the east of Eden. But Traverse, Georgia, was no Eden to Ellen, furthest thing from it, and she didn't go east. She went north. Worked ten years' worth of blue-collar jobs and wound up here, up to the college.'

Holly sits silent, looking at the needles. It occurs to her that next to Ellen Craslow, she hasn't had it so bad. Mike Sturdevant hung Jibba-Jibba on her but he never raped her.

'She didn't tell me that all at once. It came out in pieces. Except the last part, about the rape and the abortion. That came out all at once. She was looking down at the floor the whole time. Her voice cracked once or twice, but she never cried. We were in that laundry room by the office, all by ourselves. When she was done I put two fingers under her chin and said, "Look at me, girl," and she did. I said, "God sometimes asks us to pay up front in this life, and you paid a high cost. From now on you are going to have a good life. A blessed life." *That* was when she cried. Here, have a Kleenex.'

Until she takes it and wipes her eyes, Holly hasn't realized she's crying herself.

'I hope I was right about that,' Imani says. 'I hope that wherever she is, she's fine. But I don't know. For her to leave so sudden like she did . . .' She shakes her head. 'I just don't know. The woman who came for her things – clothes, her laptop computer, her little TV, her knick-knack ceramic birds and suchlike – she said Ellen was going back to Georgia, and that didn't sound right to me. Not that going back *south* means going back *home*, there's a lot more Georgia than one little shit-splat of a town, pardon my French. That woman might have said something about Atlanta.'

'What woman?' Holly asks. All of her interior lights have flashed on.

'I can't remember her name – Dickens, Dixon, something like that – but she seemed all right.' Something in Holly's expression troubles her. 'Why wouldn't she be? I walked across to check up on her when I saw her going in and out, and she was friendly enough. Said she knew Ellen from the college, and she had her keys. I recognized the lucky rabbit's foot Ellen kept on her keyring.'

'Was this woman driving a van? One with a blue stripe down low on the side?'

Holly is sure the answer will be yes, but she's disappointed. 'No, a little station wagon. I don't know what kind, but Yard would, working in the impound and all. And he was here. He stood on the stoop when I went over, just to make sure everything was all right. Did I do wrong?'

'No,' Holly says, and means it. There was no way Imani could have known. Especially when Holly herself isn't entirely sure that something unlucky happened to the already unlucky Ellen Craslow. 'When did this woman come?'

'Well, gee. It's been awhile, but I think it was after Thanksgiving but before Christmas. We'd just had the first real snowfall, I know that, but that probably isn't any help to you.'

'What did she look like?'

'Old,' Imani says. 'Older than me by maybe ten years, and I just passed seventy. And white.'

'Would you recognize her if you saw her again?'

'I might,' Imani says. She sounds dubious.

Holly gives her one of her Finders Keepers cards and asks her to have her husband call if he can remember what kind of car it was.

'I actually helped her carry out the laptop computer and some of the clothes,' Imani says. 'Poor old lady looked like she was in pain. She said she wasn't, but I know sciatica when I see it.'

March 27, 2021

When Barbara arrives at the old poet's Victorian home on Ridge Road, red-cheeked and glowing from her two-mile bike ride, Marie Duchamp is sitting on the couch with Olivia. Marie looks worried. Olivia looks distressed. Barbara probably looks mystified because that's how she feels. She can't imagine what Olivia feels she needs to apologize for.

Marie is first to speak. 'I encouraged her, and I took the envelope to Federal Express. So if you want to blame someone, blame me.'

'That's nonsense,' Olivia says. 'What I did was wrong. I just had no idea . . . and for all I know you will be pleased . . . but either way I had no right to do what I did without your permission. It was unconscionable.'

'I don't get it,' Barbara says, unbuttoning her coat. 'What did you do?'

The two women – one in the healthy prime of life, the other a shrunken doll-woman soon to be a centenarian – look at each other, then back at Barbara.

'The Penley Prize.' Olivia's mouth is doing that trembly, inward-drawing thing that always makes Barbara think of an old-fashioned string purse.

'I don't know what that is,' Barbara says, more mystified than ever.

'The full name is the Penley Prize for Younger Poets. It's jointly sponsored by New York publishers known as the Big Five. I'm not surprised you don't know of it because you are essentially self-taught and don't read the writers' magazines. Why would you, when there's no paying market for poetry? But most English majors in the writing courses know about it, just as they know about the New Voices Award or the Young Lions Fiction Award. The Penley Prize is open for submissions each year on March first. They get thousands, and the response is rapid. Because most of the submissions are awful moon-and-June stuff, I suppose.'

Now Barbara understands. 'You . . . what? Sent them some of my poems?'

Marie and Olivia share a glance. Barbara is young, but she knows guilt when she sees it.

'How many?'

'Seven,' Olivia says. 'Short ones. The rules specify no more than two thousand words. I was just so impressed by your work . . . its anger . . . its terror . . . that . . .' She doesn't seem to know how to continue.

Marie takes Olivia's hand. 'I encouraged her,' she says again.

They expect her to be angry, Barbara realizes. She's not. A little shocked is all. She has kept her poetry secret not because she's ashamed of it, or worried people will laugh (well . . . maybe a little), but because she's afraid showing it to anyone other than Olivia would lessen the pressure she feels to write more. And there's something else, or rather someone: Jerome. Although she's actually been writing poems – mostly in her journal – since she was twelve, long before he started.

Then, in the last two or three years, something changed. There has been a mysterious jump not just in ability but in ambition. It makes her think of a documentary she saw about Bob Dylan. A folk singer from Greenwich Village in the sixties said, 'He was just another guitar player trying to sound like Woody Guthrie. Then all at once he was Bob Dylan.'

It was like that. Maybe her brush with Brady Hartsfield had something to do with it, but she doesn't believe that's all. She thinks something – a previously dormant circuit in her brain – just fired up.

Meanwhile they're looking at her, absurdly like a pair of middle school girls who have been caught smoking in the school bathroom, and she can't have it.

'Olivia. Marie. Two girls in my class took naked selfies – for their boyfriends, I guess – and the pictures turned up on the Internet. *That's* embarrassing. This? Not so much. Did you get a rejection letter? Is that what this is about? Can I see it?'

They exchange another of those looks. Olivia says, 'The Penley judges compile a longlist of finalists. The number varies, but it's always a *very* long list. Sometimes sixty, sometimes eighty, this year it's ninety-five. Ridiculous to have so many, but . . . you are on it. Marie has the letter.'

There's a single sheet of paper on the endtable next to where Marie sits. She hands it to Barbara. It's fancy paper, heavy in her hand. At the top is an embossed seal featuring a quill pen and an inkpot. The addressee is Barbara Robinson, C/O Marie Duchamp, 70 Ridge Road.

'I'm surprised you're not angry,' Olivia says. 'And grateful that you're not, of course. It was such a high-handed thing to do. Sometimes I think my brains have fallen out of my ass.'

Marie jumps in. 'But I—'

'Encouraged her, I know,' Barbara murmurs. 'It *was* high-handed, I guess, but I was the one who just turned up one day with my poems. That was high-handed, too.' Not exactly how it went down, and she barely hears herself, anyway. She's scanning the letter.

It says the Penley Prize Committee is pleased to inform Ms Barbara Robinson of 70 Ridge Road that she has been placed on the Penley Prize longlist, and if she wishes to be considered going forward, would she please submit a larger body of poems, no more than five thousand words *in toto*, by April 15th. No poems of 'epic length,' please. There's also a puff paragraph about previous winners of the Penley Prize. Barbara knows three of the names from her reading. No, four. It ends with congratulations 'on your superior work.'

She puts the letter aside. 'What's the prize?'

'Twenty-five thousand dollars,' Olivia says. 'More than many fine poets make from their poetry in their entire lifetime. But that isn't the important part. A collection of the winner's work is published, not by a small press but by one of the houses that participate. This year it's Random House. The book always attracts notice. Last year's winner appeared on TV with Oprah Winfrey.'

'Is there any chance I could . . .' Barbara stops. Even to say it feels like crazy-talk.

'Very unlikely,' Olivia says. 'But should you be shortlisted, attention would be paid. The chances that your collection would be published by a small press would be fairly high. The only question is whether or not you want to proceed. You certainly have enough poems for the longlist submission, and if you continue to write I'm sure you'd have enough for a book.'

There's no question about what she wants, now that a few of the poems have been seen by strangers and been met with approval; the question is how to go about it. She says, 'I really would have let you submit, you know. If you had asked me. Like the song says, a girl can dream.'

Olivia's cheeks go rose-pink. Barbara might not have believed the old poet had enough circulation to blush, given her powered-down state, but apparently she does. 'It was very wrong,' she repeats. 'I had Marie use her name on the envelope because mine would have been recognized and I didn't want to put my thumb on the scales, so to speak. I thought you might get a few words of encouragement. That was all I hoped for.'

Words of encouragement you would have shown me, Barbara thinks, *and then you would have been in the same uncomfortable position of having shared my poems without my permission . . . only with less to show for it than this amazing letter.*

She smiles. 'You two didn't think this out very well, did you?'

'No,' Marie says. 'We just . . . your poems . . .'

'You've also read them, I take it?'

Marie's blush is much stronger than Olivia's. 'All of them. They are wonderful.'

'Although you still have far to go,' Olivia quickly adds.

Barbara reads the letter over more closely. Her surprise is giving way to a new emotion. It takes her a second to recognize what it is. She's thrilled.

'We should send the poems,' she says. 'Might as well grab for the brass ring. You'll help me pick them out, Olivia, won't you?'

The old poet smiles, mostly with relief. Barbara had no idea they thought she might be such a diva. That they did is sort of cool. 'That would be my pleasure. The key, I believe, is your poem "Faces Change," with its sense of horror and dislocation. There are a number of poems that share that leitmotif, that questioning of identity and reality. Those are the strongest.'

'It has to be a secret for now. Just between the three of us. Because of my brother. He's supposed to be the writer in the family, and I'm pretty sure his book about our great-grandfather is going to be published. I told you about it, right?'

'Yes,' Olivia says.

'If he does get it published, and if he gets good money for it – his agent says he might – I can talk about this. If I should make the shortlist, that is. If I don't, he never has to know. Okay?'

'Would he really be jealous?' Marie asks. 'Of *poetry*?'

'No.' Barbara doesn't even have to think about it. 'J doesn't have a jealous bone in his body. He'd be happy for me. But he's been working so hard on this book, I don't think the words come as easy for him as they sometimes do for me, and I won't steal any of his spotlight. I love him too much to do that, even a little bit.' She hands the letter back to Marie. 'This letter stays here. But I'm glad you did what you did.'

'You are generous,' Olivia says. 'Other than in their work, poets rarely are. Marie, what would you think about the three of us splitting a can of Foster's Lager, if only to celebrate the fact that we're still friends?'

'I think that's a wonderful idea,' Marie says, getting up. 'But that's another secret we three have to keep.' She tilts her head to Olivia. 'From her doctor.'

She leaves for the kitchen. Barbara says, 'You're the generous one, Olivia. I'm glad to have you for a friend as well as a teacher.'

'Thank you. I must have done something right, because some providence saved the best student for last.'

It's Barbara's turn to blush, not with shame but with happiness.

'Tell me what you're reading,' Olivia says. School is in session.

'You suggested the beats, so that's who I'm reading. I got an anthology at the college bookstore. Ginsberg, Snyder, Corso, Ed Dorn . . . I love him . . . Lawrence Ferlinghetti . . . is he still alive?'

'Died a month ago. He was older than I am. I want you to read some prose, if you're game. It may help you. James Dickey to start with. You know his poems, and there's a famous novel, *Deliverance*—'

'I saw the movie. Men going down a river in canoes.'

'Yes, but don't read that one. Read *To the White Sea*. Lesser known, but I think better. For your purposes. I want you to read at least one

Cormac McCarthy novel, *All the Pretty Horses* or *Suttree*. Will you do that?'

'All right.' Although she's reluctant to leave the beats behind, with their mixture of innocence and cynicism. 'I'm actually reading prose now. That book you told me about, *The Forgotten City*, by Jorge Castro. I like it.'

Marie comes back with three glasses and an enormous can of Foster's on a tray.

'I suppose Jorge finally went to South America,' Olivia says. 'He used to talk about going back to his roots, which was bullshit. He spoke Spanish like a native but he was born in Peoria and raised there. I think he was ashamed of that. Did I tell you I saw him shortly before he disappeared? Running. He always ran at night, to the park and back again. Even in the rain, and it was raining that night. I suppose he must have been planning to leave even then. I certainly never saw him again, but I remember because I was writing a poem and it turned out to be a good one.' She sighs. 'Freddy Martin – his partner – was devastated. Freddy left shortly after, I think to look for Jorge. The love of his life. Came back broken-hearted and with a monkey on his back. Stayed six months and then left again. The Wicked Witch of the West said it best. What a world, what a world!'

'Enough of sadness,' Marie says, pouring. 'Let's drink to good times and great expectations.'

'Good times only,' Olivia says. 'Leave the future out of it. The only person unhappier than a writer whose expectations aren't fulfilled is one whose dreams come true.'

Barbara laughs. 'I'll take your word for it.'

They clink glasses and drink.

July 26, 2021

1

When Holly pulls into the handkerchief-sized Jet Mart parking lot at quarter past three, she sees the man she wants to interview is on duty. Excellent. She pauses long enough to hunt something on her iPad, then gets out of her car. On the lefthand side of the door there's a bulletin board under the overhang. WELCOME TO A JET MART NEIGHBORHOOD! it proclaims. It's covered with notices of apartments to rent, cars and washing machines and game consoles for sale, a lost dog (*WE LOVE OUR REXY!*), and two lost cats. There's also one lost girl: Bonnie Rae Dahl. Holly knows who put that one up, and hears Keisha Stone saying *love lost but plenty of love left.*

She goes in. The store is currently empty except for her and the clerk, Emilio Herrera by name. He looks to be Pete's age, maybe a little younger. He's perfectly willing to talk. He's got a round face and a charmingly cherubic smile. Yes, Bonnie was a regular customer. He liked her and is very sorry that she has gone missing. Hopefully she will get in touch with her mama and her friends soon.

'She'd come in most nights around eight,' Herrera says. 'Sometimes a little earlier, sometimes a little later. She always had a smile and a good word, even if it was just *how are you doing* or *what do you think about the Cavs* or *how's your wife.* You know how few people take the time to do that?'

'Probably not many,' Holly says. She herself isn't apt to be chatty with people she doesn't know; mostly contents herself with *please* and *thank you* and *have a nice day. Holly keeps herself to herself,* Charlotte used to say, with a little grimacing smile meant to convey *she can't help it, you know.*

'Not many is right,' Herrera says. 'But not her. Always friendly, always a good word. She'd get a diet soda, sometimes one of those sweets in the rack there. She was partial to Ho Hos and Ring Dings, but mostly she'd pass them by. Young women are figure-conscious, as you probably know.'

'Was there anything unusual about that night, Mr Herrera? Anything at all? Someone outside who might have been watching her? Maybe standing where the video wouldn't pick him up?'

'Not that I saw,' Herrera says, after doing Holly the courtesy of giving it some thought. 'And I believe I would have. Convenience stores like this, especially on quiet streets like Red Bank Ave, are prime targets for robbers. Although this place has never been hit, grace of God.' He crosses himself. 'But I keep an eye out. Who's coming, who's going, who's loitering. Didn't see anyone like that on the last night that girl you're looking for was in here. Not that I can remember, at least. She got her soda, put it in her backpack, put on her helmet, and off she went.'

Holly opens her iPad and shows him what she downloaded before she came in. It's a picture of a 2020 Toyota Sienna. 'Do you remember a van like this? That night or any other night? It would have had a blue stripe running down low, along the side.'

Herrera studies the picture carefully, then hands it back. 'Seen plenty of vans like that, but it doesn't ring a bell. You know, about that night. Which you know is now almost a month ago, right?'

'Yes, understood. Let me show you something else. It might refresh your memory.'

She plays the security video from the night of July first, and freezes it when the van is in the background. He studies it and says, 'Wow. I better clean the lens of that camera.'

Kind of locking the barn door after the horse has been stolen, Holly doesn't say. 'You're sure you don't remember a van like that, maybe on other nights?'

'I'm sorry, ma'am. I don't. Vans are pretty common.'

It's what Holly expected. Another *t* crossed, another *i* dotted. 'Thank you, Mr Herrera.'

'I wish I could have been more help.'

'What about this boy? Do you recognize him?' She shows him a picture of Peter Steinman. It's a group shot of his middle school band club, which she found online (everything's online these days). Holly has enlarged it so that Peter, standing in the back row with a pair of cymbals, is relatively clear. Better than the Jet Mart security footage, anyway. 'He was a skateboarder.'

Herrera peers, then looks up when a middle-aged woman comes in. He greets her by name and she returns the greeting. Then he gives the iPad back to Holly. 'He looks familiar, but that's all I can say. Those skateboard kids come in all the time. They buy candy or chips, then ride their boards down the hill to the Whip. Do you know the Dairy Whip?'

'Yes,' Holly says. 'He's missing, too. Since November of 2018.'

'Hey, you don't think we've got some kind of predator in the neighborhood, do you? John Wayne Gacy type?'

'Probably not. This young man and Bonnie Dahl are probably not even related.' Although she's finding this ever tougher to believe. 'I don't suppose you can think of any other regulars who just suddenly stopped showing up, can you?'

The woman customer – Cora by name – is now waiting to pay for an Iron City sixer and a loaf of Wonder Bread.

'Nope,' Herrera says, but he's not looking at Holly anymore, who isn't a customer. Cora is.

Holly can take a hint, but before moving away from the counter, she gives Emilio Herrera one of her cards. 'My number's on there. If you think of anything that might help me locate Bonnie, would you give me a call?'

'Sure,' Herrera says, and pockets the card. 'Hey, Cora. Sorry to keep you waiting. What about this Covid, huh?'

Holly buys a can of Fanta before leaving. She doesn't really want it, but it seems only polite.

2

Holly checks Twitter as soon as she's back in her apartment. There is one new response, from Franklin Craslow (Christian, Proud NRA

Member, South Is Gonna Rise Again). It's brief. *Ellen killed her baby and will burn in hell. Leave us alone.*

Us, Holly assumes, meaning the Craslow clan from Bibb County.

She calls Penny Dahl. It's not a call she wants to make, but it's time to tell Penny what she now believes, that Bonnie may have been abducted. Possibly by someone in a van who was waiting for her at the former Bill's Automotive and Small Engine Repair. Possibly by someone she knew. Holly emphasizes the *may* in *may have been*.

She expects sobs, but there are none, at least for the time being. This is, after all, exactly what Penny Dahl has been afraid of. She asks Holly if there's a chance Bonnie might still be alive.

'There's always a chance,' Holly says.

'Some fucker took her.' The vulgarity surprises Holly, but only for a moment. Anger instead of tears. Penny makes Holly think of a bear who's lost a cub. 'Find him. Whoever took my daughter, you find that fucker. No matter what it costs. I'll get the money. Do you hear me?'

Holly suspects that tears will come later, when what Holly has told Penny has had a chance to sink in. It's one thing to have the worst fear a mother can feel locked inside; it's quite another to hear it spoken aloud.

'I'll do my best.' It's what she always says.

'Find him,' Penny repeats, and ends the call without saying goodbye.

Holly goes to the window and lights a cigarette. She tries to think of what her next step should be and comes to the conclusion (reluctantly) that right now she doesn't have one. She knows of three missing people and feels their disappearances are related, but in spite of certain similarities, she has no proof of that. She's at a dead end. She needs the universe to throw her a rope.

3

That evening Jerome calls from New York. He's excited and happy, and why not? The lunch went well, the check duly handed over. His agent will deposit it to his account (minus her fifteen per cent), but he actually held it in his hand, he tells her, and ran his fingers over the embossed numbers.

'I'm rich, Hollyberry. I'm freaking *rich*!'

You're not the only one, Holly thinks.

'Are you also drunk?'

'No!' He sounds offended. 'I had two beers!'

'Well, that's good. But on this one occasion, I suppose you'd have a right to get drunk.' She pauses. 'As long as you didn't get all sloppy and vomit on 5th Avenue, that is.'

'The Blarney Stone is on 8th, Hols. Near Madison Square Garden.'

Holly, who's never been to New York and doesn't want to go, says that's interesting.

Then, channeling his younger sister without knowing it, Jerome tells her it's not really the money that's blowing his mind. 'They're going to publish it! It started as a college paper, it turned into a book, and now it's going to be published!'

'That's wonderful, Jerome. I'm so glad for you.' She wishes her friend – who once saved her life and Bill's life in a snowstorm – could always be this happy, and knows that's not the way life works. Maybe just as well. If it did, happiness wouldn't mean anything.

'What's going on with the case? Have you made any progress?'

Holly fills him in on everything. Most of it is about Ellen Craslow, but she doesn't neglect Tom Higgins being out of the picture. When she finishes, Jerome says, 'I'd give a hundred bucks to know who the old lady was. The one who cleaned out Ellen Craslow's trailer. Wouldn't you?'

'Yes.' Holly's thinking (and with a smile) that Jerome could actually afford to give a thousand, considering his recent windfall. For that matter, so could she. She is *dives puella* – a rich girl, just like in the Hall and Oates song she used to love. 'To me the most interesting thing is all the Black people living in that trailer park. Not surprising, because it's at the western edge of Lowtown, but the old lady was white.'

'What's next for you?'

'I don't know,' Holly says. 'How about you, Jerome?'

'I'm going to stay in New York awhile longer. Until Thursday at least. My editor – I love saying that – wants to talk about some stuff, a few changes in the manuscript, plus he wants to brainstorm a book jacket concept. He says the head of publicity wants to talk about a possible tour. A *tour*! Do you believe that?'

'I do,' Holly says. 'I'm so glad for you.'

'Can I tell you something? About Barb?'

'Of course.'

'I'm pretty sure she's writing, too. And I think she's getting some-where with it. Wouldn't it be crazy if we both turned out to be writers?'

'No crazier than the Brontës,' Holly says. 'There were three of them. Charlotte, Emily, and Anne. All writers. I loved *Jane Eyre*.' This is true, but the one Holly especially loved as an unhappy teenager was *Wuthering Heights*. 'No idea what Barbara might be writing?'

'I'd say poetry. Just about has to be. It's about all she's been reading since she was a sophomore. Listen, Holly, I want to go for a walk. I think I could fall in love with this city. For one thing, they get it — there are actually pop-up vaccine sites.'

'Well, don't get mugged. Keep your wallet in your front pocket, not the back. And call your mother and father.'

'Already did.'

'What about Barbara? Have you talked to her?'

'I will. If she's not too busy with her secret project to take my call, that is. I love you, Holly.'

This isn't the first time he's said it, but it always makes her feel like crying. 'I love you, too, Jerome. Enjoy the rest of your big day.'

She ends the call. She lights a cigarette and goes to the window.

She *puts her thinking cap on*.

Much good does it do her.

4

Roddy Harris comes back from his usual Monday evening visit to Strike Em Out Lanes around quarter to nine. He and Emily take good care of themselves (often in ways of which dimwitted society would not approve), but his once strong hips have grown rather fragile as he advances deeper into his eighties, and it's been almost four years since he last rolled a ball down a hardwood lane. He still goes on most Mondays, though, because he likes to root for his team. The Golden Oldies play in the Over 65 League. Most of the men with whom he bowled when he joined the Oldies are gone, but a few are left, including Hugh Clippard, once of the Sociology Department.

Hugh has to be pushing eighty himself these days, he's made a pile in the stock market, and he's still got a wicked hook. Too bad it's to the Brooklyn side.

Emily comes out of her little office as soon as she hears the front door close. He kisses her on the cheek and asks how her evening was.

'Not wonderful. We may have a slight problem, dear. You know I monitor certain people's tweets and posts.'

'Vera Steinman,' he says. 'And the Dahl woman, of course.'

'I also check in every now and then with the Craslows. There's not much and they never talk about Ellen. Nobody asks about Ellen, either. Until yesterday.'

'Ellen Craslow,' Roddy says, shaking his head. 'That bitch. That . . .' For a moment the word he wants escapes him. Then it comes. 'That *intransigent* bitch.'

'She certainly was. And someone calling herself LaurenBacallFan has been asking for information about her on Twitter.'

'After almost three *years*? Why now?'

'Because I'm positive that LaurenBacallFan runs a private investigation firm. Her real name is Holly Gibney, the firm is called Finders Keepers, and Penelope Dahl has engaged her services.'

He is paying close attention now, looming over her upturned face. He's seven inches taller than Emily, but she's his equal in intellect, maybe in some ways his superior. She's . . . again the word dances away from him, but he catches it as he always does. *Almost* always.

Emily is *sly*.

'How did you find out?'

'Mrs Dahl is very chatty on social media.'

'Chatty Penny,' he says. 'That girl, that Bonnie, was a mistake. Worse than the goddam Mexican, and we can excuse ourselves for that, because—'

'Because he was the first. I know. Come in the kitchen. There's half a bottle of red left from dinner.'

'Wine before bed gives me acid. You know that.' But he follows her.

'Just a splash.'

She gets it from the fridge and pours – a splash for him, a bit more for her. They sit facing each other.

'Bonnie probably *was* a mistake,' she admits. 'But the heat brought back my sciatica . . . and the headaches . . .'

'I know,' Roddy says. He takes her hand across the table and gives it a gentle squeeze. 'My poor dear with her migraines.'

'And you. I saw you struggling so for words sometimes. And your poor hands, the way they were shaking . . . we had to.'

'I'm fine now. The shakes are gone. And any . . . any *mental muddiness* I might have been dealing with . . . that's gone, too.'

This is only half-true. The shakes are gone, true enough (well, sometimes the minutest tremble when he's very tired), but there are those words that sometimes dance just out of reach.

Everyone sometimes has those blank spots, he tells himself when it happens. *You've researched it yourself. It's a temporarily fouled circuit, transient aphasia, no different from a muscle cramp that hurts like Satan and then lets go. The idea that it might be incipient Alzheimer's is ridiculous.*

'In any case it's done. If there's fallout, we'll deal with it. The good news is that I don't believe we'll have to. This Gibney woman has had some notable successes – yes, I looked her up – but when those occurred she had a partner, ex-police, and he died years ago. Since then she mostly looks for lost dogs, chases bail-jumpers, and works on a contingency basis with certain insurance companies. *Small* ones, none of the majors.'

Roddy sips his wine. 'Apparently she was smart enough to find Ellen Craslow.'

Emily sighs. 'That's true. But two disappearances almost three years apart don't make a pattern. Still, you know what you always say – the wise man prepares for rain while the sun shines.'

Does he always say that? He thinks he does, or used to. Along with *one monkey don't make no sideshow*, a thing his father used to say, his father had that fabulous sky-blue Packard—

'Roddy!' The sharpness of her tone brings him back. 'You're wandering!'

'Was I?'

'Give me that.' She takes the jelly glass with its splash of wine from in front of him and pours it down the sink. From the freezer she takes a parfait glass containing a cloudy gray concoction. She sprays whipped cream from a can on top and puts it in front of him with a long-handled dessert spoon. 'Eat.'

'Do you not want to share?' he asks . . . but his mouth is already watering.

'No. You have it all. You need it.'

She sits across from him as he begins to spoon the mixture of brains and vanilla ice cream greedily into his mouth. Emily watches. It will bring him back. It *has* to bring him back. She loves him. And she needs him.

'Listen to me carefully, love. This woman will hunt around for Bonnie, find nothing, take her fee, and go her way. If she *should* present a problem – one chance in a hundred if not in a thousand – she is unmarried and seems to have no significant other, based on what I've read. Her mother died earlier this month. Her only other living relative, an uncle, is in an elder care center with Alzheimer's. She has a business partner, but he's apparently *hors de combat* with Covid.'

Roddy eats a little faster, wiping a dribble that runs down a seam at the side of his mouth. He believes he can already sense a greater clarity in what he's seeing and in what she's saying.

'You found all that on that Twitter platform?'

Emily smiles. 'There and a few other places. I have my little tricks. It's like that TV show we watch. *Manifest*. Where the characters keep saying "everything is connected." It's a silly show, but *that's* not silly. My point is simple, dear one. This is a woman who has no one. This is a woman who must feel quite normally depressed and grief-stricken after losing her mother. If a woman like that were to commit suicide by jumping in the lake, leaving a suicide note behind on her computer, who would question it?'

'Her business partner might.'

'Or he might understand completely. I'm not saying it will come to that, only—'

'That we should prepare for rain while the sun is shining.'

'Exactly.' The parfait is almost gone, and surely he's had enough. 'Give me that.'

She takes it and finishes it herself.

5

Barbara Robinson is in her bedroom, reading in her jammies by the light of her bedside lamp, when the phone rings. The book is *Catalepsy*, by Jorge Castro. It isn't as good as *The Forgotten City*, and the title seems deliberately off-putting – a writer's declaration that he is 'literary' – but it's pretty good. Besides, the working title of her book – *Faces Change* – isn't exactly *Favorite Fireside Poems for Young & Old*.

It's Jerome, calling from New York. It's quarter past eleven where she is, so it must already be tomorrow in the eastern time zone.

'Hey, bro. You're up late, and you're not partyin, unless it's with a bunch of mutes.'

'No, I'm in my hotel room. Too excited to sleep. Did I wake you?'

'No,' Barbara says, sitting up in bed and propping an extra pillow behind her. 'Just reading myself to sleep.'

'Sylvia Plath or Anne Sexton?' Teasing.

'A novel. The guy who wrote it actually taught up the ridge for awhile.' *Up the ridge* meaning Bell College. 'What's going on with you?'

So he tells her everything he already told his parents and Holly, spilling it out in an exuberant rush. She is delighted for him, and says so. She marvels over the hundred thousand dollars, and squeals when he tells her about the possible tour.

'Bring me along! I'll be your gofer!'

'I might take you up on that. What's going on with you, Barbarella?'

She almost tells him everything, then holds back. Let this be Jerome's day.

'Barb? You still there?'

'It's been pretty much the same old same old.'

'Don't believe it. You're up to something. What's the big secret? Spill.'

'Soon,' she promises. 'Really. Tell me what's up with Holly. I kind of blew her off the other day. I feel bad about that.' But not too bad. She has an essay to write, it's important, and she hasn't made much progress. Much? She hasn't even started.

He recaps everything, ending with Ellen Craslow. Barbara says *yes* and *wow* and *uh-huh* in all the right places, but she's just half-listening. Her mind has drifted back to that damned essay again, which has to be in the mail by the end of the month. And she's sleepy. She doesn't connect the disappearances J is telling her about with the one Olivia Kingsbury told her about, even though Jorge Castro's novel is facedown on her comforter.

He hears her yawn and says, 'I'll let you go. But it's good to talk to you when you're actually paying attention.'

'I always pay attention to you, my dear brother.'

'Liar,' he says, laughing, and ends the call.

Barbara puts Jorge Castro aside, unaware that he is part of a small and extremely unlucky club, and turns out her light.

6

That night Holly dreams of her old bedroom.

She can tell by the wallpaper it's the one on Bond Street in Cincinnati, but it's also the museum exhibit she imagined. Those little plaques are everywhere, identifying objects that have become artifacts. LUDIO LUDIUS next to the sound system, BELLA SIDEREA beside the wastebasket, CUBILE TRISTIS PUELLA on the bed.

Because the human mind specializes in connectivity, she wakes thinking of her father. She doesn't often. Why would she? He died a long, long time ago, and was never much more than a shadow even when he was home. Which was seldom. Howard Gibney was a salesman for Ray Garton Farm Machinery, Inc., and spent his days traveling the Midwest, selling combines and harvesters and Ray Garton TruMade tractors, all in bright red, as if to make sure nobody mistook Garton farm gear for John Deere equipment. When he was home, Charlotte made sure he never forgot who, in her words, *kept the home fires burning.* In flyover country he might have been a sales dynamo, but at home he was the original Mr Milquetoast.

Holly gets up and goes to her bureau. The records of her working life – the life she has made for herself – are either at Finders Keepers on Frederick Street or in her little home office, but she keeps certain other records (certain *artifacts*) in the bottom drawer of this bureau. There aren't many, and most bring back memories that are a mixture of nostalgia and regret.

There's the plaque she received as second prize in a speaking contest in which several city elementary schools participated. (This was when she was young enough and still confident enough to stand up in front of large groups of people.) She recited a Robert Frost poem, 'Mending Wall,' and after complimenting her, Charlotte told her she could have won first prize if she hadn't stumbled over several words halfway through.

There's a photograph of her trick-or-treating with her father when she was six, he in a suit, she wearing a ghost costume that her father made. Holly vaguely recalls that her mother, who usually took her (often dragging her from house to house), had the flu that year. In the picture, Howard Gibney is smiling. She thinks she was smiling, too, although with that sheet over her head it's impossible to tell.

'I was, though,' Holly murmurs. 'Because he didn't drag me so he could get back home and watch TV.' Also, he didn't remind her to say thank you at every house but simply assumed she would do so. As she always did.

But it isn't the plaque she wants, or the Halloween photograph, or the pressed flowers, or her father's obituary, carefully clipped and saved. It's the postcard. Once there were more – at least a dozen – and she assumed the others were lost. After discovering her mother's lie about the inheritance, a less palatable idea has come to her: that her mother stole these souvenirs of a man Holly can remember only vaguely. A man who was under his wife's thumb when he was there (which was seldom) but who could be kind and amusing on the rare occasions when it was just him and his little girl.

He took four years of Latin in high school and won his own award – first prize, not second – for a two-page essay he wrote in that language. The title of his essay was 'Quid Est Veritas – What Is Truth?' Over Charlotte's strong, almost strident, objections, Holly took two years of Latin in high school herself, all that was offered. She did not shine, as her father had done in his pre-salesman days, but she carried a solid B average, and remembered enough to know that *tristis puella* was sad girl and *bella siderea* was star wars.

What she thinks now – what is clear to her now – is that she took Latin as a way of reaching out to her father. And he had reached back, hadn't he? Sent her those postcards from places like Omaha and Tulsa and Rapid City.

Kneeling in front of the bottom drawer in her pajamas, she searches through these few remnants of her *tristis puella* past, thinking even that last card is also gone, not filched by her mother (who had completely erased Howard Gibney from her own life) but lost by her own stupid self, probably when she moved to this apartment.

At last she finds it, stuck in the crack at the back of the drawer. The picture on the front of the card shows the Gateway Arch in St Louis. The message, no doubt written with a Ray Garton Farm Machinery ballpoint, is in Latin. All of his postcards to her were written in Latin. It was her job – and her pleasure – to translate them. She turns this one over and reads the message.

Cara Holly! Deliciam meam amo. Lude cum matre tua. Mox domi ero. Pater tuus.

It was his one accomplishment, something that made him even prouder than selling a new tractor for a hundred and seventy grand. He had told her once that he was the only farm machinery salesman in America who was also a Latin scholar. He said that in Charlotte's hearing, and she had responded with a laugh. 'Only you would be proud of speaking a dead language,' she said.

Howard had smiled and said nothing.

Holly takes the card back to bed and reads it again by the light of the table lamp. She can remember figuring out the message with the help of her Latin dictionary, and she murmurs the translation now. 'Dear Holly! I love my little girl. Have fun with your mother. I will be home soon. Your father.'

With no idea she's going to do it until it's done, Holly kisses the card. The postmark is too blurry to read the date, but she believes it was sent not too long before her father died of a heart attack in a motel room on the outskirts of Davenport, Iowa. She remembers her mother complaining – *bitching* – about the cost of having the body sent home by rail.

Holly puts the card on the bedside table, thinking she will restore it to the bureau drawer in the morning. *Artifacts*, she thinks. *Museum artifacts*.

She's saddened by how few memories she has of her father, and dully angry at the realization that her mother's shadow has all but blotted him out. *Did* Charlotte steal the other cards, as she had stolen Holly's inheritance? Only missed this one, perhaps because a younger and much more timid version of Holly had been using it for a bookmark or put it in the satchel (tartan, of course) that she carried everywhere back then? She will never know. Did he spend so much time on the road because he didn't want to come home to his wife? She'll never know that, either. What she does know is that he was always glad to come home to *cara Holly*.

What she also knows is they gave a little life to a dead language. It was their thing.

Holly turns out the light. Goes to sleep.

Dreams of Charlotte in Holly's old bedroom.

'Remember who you belong to,' Charlotte says.

She goes out and locks the door behind her.

May 19, 2021

1

Barbara enters the hospital lobby in a hurry, not quite running only because Marie has told her this is no emergency, just routine. At the main desk of Kiner Memorial, she asks which floor oncology is on. The woman at the desk directs her to the west bank of elevators. Barbara emerges in a pleasant lounge with pleasant pictures on the walls (sunsets, meadows, tropic isles) and pleasant music wafting down from overhead speakers. Plenty of people are sitting here, hoping for good news and fearing the opposite. All are wearing masks. Marie is reading a paperback John Sandford novel. She's saved a chair for Barbara.

'Why didn't you *tell* me?' is the first thing Barbara says.

'Because it would have worried you needlessly when you didn't have to worry at all,' Marie says. She's perfectly calm. Fawn-colored slacks and white shirt as usual, minimal makeup perfectly applied, not a hair out of place. 'What Olivia wanted you to worry about is your poetry.'

'I'm worried about *her!*' Barbara tries to keep her voice down, but several people look around.

'Olivia has cancer,' Marie says. 'What she calls, no surprise, ass-cancer. She's had it for a very long time. Dr Brown — her oncologist — says it's a cancer you die with, not the kind you die of. At her advanced age it just crawls along. Over the last two years it's crawled a little faster.'

'Malignant?' She whispers the word.

'Oh yes,' Marie says, still calm. 'But it hasn't metastasized and may not. She used to get its growth checked twice a year. This year it will be three times. Assuming she lives another year, that is. Olivia herself likes to say her equipment package is long past the warranty. I called you here because she has something to tell you. Are you missing school?'

Barbara waves this aside. She's a senior, she's carrying an A average, she can take a day off any old time she wants to.

'What's up?'

'She'll tell you that herself.'

'Is it about the Penley?'

Marie only picks up her novel and begins reading again. Barbara didn't bring a book. She takes out her phone, goes to Instagram, looks at a few boring posts, checks her email, and puts it away again. Ten minutes later Olivia comes out of swinging doors behind which is machinery Barbara doesn't want to know about. Olivia is walking with both of her canes. Her satchel purse swings from one thin shoulder. An orderly is holding her arm.

She reaches Barbara and Marie, thanks the orderly, and plops down with a sigh and a wince. 'I have once more survived the indignity of being entombed in a noisy machine while my poop-chute is examined,' she tells them. 'Old age is a time of casting away, which is bad enough, but it's also a time of escalating indignities.' Then, just to Barbara: 'I'm assuming Marie informed you of the cancer, and why we kept it from you.'

'I still wish you'd told me,' Barbara says.

Olivia looks tired (tired unto death, Barbara thinks), but she also looks interested. 'Why?'

Barbara has no answer. This woman will be a hundred in the fall, and somewhere behind those doors there may be bald children who won't live to see their tenth birthday. So why indeed?

'Can you scream, Barbara?' The eyes above her mask, which is imprinted with red, white, and blue peace signs, are as bright as ever.

'What? Why?'

'Have you ever screamed? A full-out, full-throated scream, the kind that leaves you hoarse afterward?'

Barbara thinks of her history with Brady Hartsfield, Morris Bellamy, and Chet Ondowsky. Especially Ondowsky. 'Yes.'

'You won't scream here, this is no place for screaming, but perhaps later. Here you must be quiet. I could have waited until we got home to have Marie call you, but the older I get the poorer my impulse control becomes. Besides, I didn't know how long the MRI would take. So I asked Marie to ask you to come here.'

She slides her big purse from her shoulder and fumbles it open. From inside she takes an envelope with a quill-and-inkpot logo Barbara recognizes at once. Her heart, which has been beating rapidly ever since she got Marie's call, goes into overdrive.

'I took the liberty of opening this in order to give you bad news gently, if the news was bad. It isn't. There are fifteen poets under the age of thirty on the Penley shortlist. You are one of them.'

Barbara sees her hand take the envelope. She sees her hand open it and pull out the heavy sheet of folded paper inside. She sees the same logo on top of the letter, which begins *The Penley Committee is pleased to inform you*. Then her eyes blur with tears.

2

They go back to Ridge Road in Marie's car. Barbara sits in back. The radio, tuned to Sirius XM, plays a constant stream of forties tunes. Olivia sings along with some of them. Barbara guesses when they were first popular, Olivia wore penny loafers and did her hair in a pageboy. On the drive, Barbara reads the letter over and over again, making herself understand it's real.

When they get to the house, Barbara and Marie help Olivia out of the car and up the steps, a slow process accompanied by several loud farts. 'Just backfiring,' Olivia says matter-of-factly. 'Clearing the exhaust system.'

In the foyer, with the door shut, Olivia faces Barbara with a cane gripped in each hand. 'If you want to scream, now would be a good time. I'd do it myself, but I no longer have the lungpower.'

Barbara is still in the running to win the Penley, and to be published by Random House. She thinks it would be nice, she could certainly use the money for college, but that isn't the important part. Olivia has all but assured her that her poems will be published even if she doesn't win. They will be read. Not by multitudes, but certainly by people who love what she loves.

She draws in breath and screams. Not with horror, but for joy.

'Good.' Olivia is smiling. 'How about another? Can you manage that?'

She can. Marie puts an arm around her shoulders and they scream together.

'Excellent,' Olivia says. 'Just so you know, I've mentored two young men who were longlisted for the Penley, but you, Barbara Robinson, are the first to be shortlisted, and by far the youngest. There are more hurdles to jump, however, and they're high ones. Remember that you're in the company of fourteen men and women of immense talent and dedication.'

'You need to rest, Olivia,' Marie says.

'I will. But first we have things to discuss.'

July 27, 2021

1

At quarter to eleven in the morning, the universe throws Holly a rope.

She's in her office (all furniture reassuringly in place), filling out an insurance company payment invoice. Every time she sees a jolly insurance ad on TV – the Aflac duck, Flo the Progressive lady, Doug and his emu – Holly mutes the sound. Insurance ads are a laugh a minute. The companies themselves, not so much. You can save them a quarter of a million dollars on a bogus claim and still have to bill them two, three, sometimes four times before you get paid. When filling out invoices of this sort, she often thinks of a line from some old folk song: a handful of gimme and a mouthful of much obliged.

The phone rings just as she's finishing the last few lines of the poopy three-page form. 'Finders Keepers, Holly Gibney speaking, how can I help?'

'Hi, Ms Gibney, this is Emilio Herrera. From Jet Mart? We talked yesterday.'

'Yes we did.' Holly sits up straight, the invoice forgotten.

'You asked me if any other of my regulars ever just stopped showing up.'

'And have you thought of someone, Mr Herrera?'

'Well, maybe. Last night before I went to bed I was switching around the channels for something to watch while I waited for my melatonin to work, and *The Big Lebowski* was on AMC. I don't suppose you've ever seen it.'

'I have,' Holly says. Three times, in fact.

'Anyway, that made me think of the bowling guy. He used to come in all the time. He'd buy snacks and soda and sometimes Rizla papers. Nice kid – seemed like a kid to me, I'm pushing sixty – but his picture could have been in the dictionary next to *stoner*.'

'What was his name?'

'I don't really remember. Cory, maybe? Cameron? This was five years ago at least, maybe more.'

'What did he look like?'

'Skinny. Long blond hair. He kept it tied back, probably because he drove a moped. Not a motorcycle and not really a scooter, just a kind of bike with a motor. The new ones are electric, but this one ran on gasoline.'

'I know what they are.'

'And it was *noisy*. I don't know if something was wrong with the motor or if that was just the way mopeds like that are supposed to sound, but it was really noisy, *blak-blak-blak,* like that. And covered with stickers, silly stuff like NUKE THE GAY WHALES and I DO WHATEVER THE LITTLE VOICES TELL ME TO. Also Grateful Dead stickers. He was a Deadhead kind of guy. Used to come in just about every weeknight in warm weather – you know, April to October. Sometimes even November. We used to talk about movies. He always got the same thing. Two or three candybars and a P-Co'. Sometimes rolling papers.'

'What's a P-Co'?'

'PeruCola. Kind of like Jolt. Do you remember Jolt?'

Holly certainly does. For awhile in the eighties, she was a Jolt fiend. 'Their motto was "all the sugar and twice the caffeine."'

'That's the one. P-Co' was all the sugar and about nine times the caffeine. I think he'd go up to Drive-In Rock and watch the movies at Magic City – you can see the screen really well from up there, he said—'

'I've been there, and you can.' Holly is excited now. She turns over the pain-in-the-butt insurance payment invoice and scribbles *Cory or Cameron, moped w/funny stickers.*

'He said he only went up on weeknights, because there were too many kids on the weekends, goofing off and grab-assing around. A nice enough young fellow, but a stoner. Did I already say that?'

'You did, but that's okay. Go on.' She scribbles *Drive-In Rock* and then *RED BANK AVENUE!!!*

'So I said what's the point when there's no sound and he said – I got a kick out of this – he said "It doesn't matter, I know all the dialogue." Which was probably true of the movies they show there. Oldies, you know. And actually there are movies where *I* know all the dialogue.'

'Really?' Of course really. Holly knows long stretches from at least sixty movies herself. Maybe a hundred.

'Yes. You know, you're gonna need a bigger boat, get busy living or get busy dying, stuff like that.'

'You can't handle the truth.' Holly can't resist saying.

'Right, that's a famous one. Tell you something, Ms Gibney, in my business the customer is always right. Unless it's kids wanting cigarettes or beer, that is. But it doesn't stop me from thinking, does it?'

'Of course not.'

'And what I thought about this kid is that he was speedballing. I think he'd go up there, smoke some dope to get high, then chug a can of P-Co' to put chrome on it. They quit making that soda two or three years ago, and I'm not surprised. I tried a can of it once and just *jittered*. Anyway, that guy was a regular. Like clockwork. He'd get off his shift, drive his blatty little moped here, buy his candy and soda, sometimes rolling papers, talk a little, then off he went.'

'And when did he stop coming in?'

'I don't know exactly. I've been working at that Jet Mart a long time. Seen em come and seen em go. But Trump was running for president, I remember that because we joked about it. Seems like the joke was on us.' He pauses, perhaps thinking over what he just said. 'But if you voted for him, I'm only kidding.'

Like fun you were, Holly thinks. 'I voted for Clinton. You called him the bowling guy?'

'Sure, because he worked at the Strike Em Out. It was right on his shirt.'

2

They talk a little more, but Herrera can't remember anything else of value. It shouldn't be hard to find out the bowling guy's name, though. Holly cautions herself that it may not mean anything. And yet . . .

same store, same street, no car, about the same time of evening when Bonnie Rae went missing. And Drive-In Rock, where Holly herself was sitting after finding Bonnie's earring.

She checks her iPad and sees that Strike Em Out Lanes opens at eleven AM. They'll know the bowling guy's name. She heads for the door, then gets another idea. Imani McGuire didn't allow her to record their interview, but Holly recapped the high points on her phone afterward. She opens that recording now, but even as she's about to push play, the name of Imani's husband comes to her. Yard, impound yard.

She finds the number for the city impound and asks if Mr Yardley McGuire is there.

'Speaking.'

'Mr McGuire, my name is Holly Gibney. I spoke with your wife yesterday—'

'About Ellen,' he says. 'Immi says you had a good talk. Don't suppose you tracked Ellen down, did you?'

'No, but I may have stumbled across someone else who went missing a few years earlier. Might not be connected, but it could be. He drove a moped that was covered with stickers. One of them said NUKE THE GAY WHALES. Another one might have been a Grateful Dea—'

'Oh sure, I remember that moped,' Yard McGuire says. 'It was here for a year at least, maybe longer. Jerry Holt finally took it home and gave it to his middle kid, who'd been yelling for one. But he tuned it up first, because—'

'Because it was noisy. Went *blak-blak-blak*.'

Yard laughs. 'Yuh, pretty much just like that.'

'Where was it found? Or abandoned?'

'Gee, no idea. Jerry might know. And listen, Miz Gibney, it wasn't like Jer stoled it, all right? The license plate was gone, and if there was a registration number, nobody bothered to run it through DMV.org. Not for a little kettle-burner like that.'

Holly gets Jerry Holt's number, thanks Yardley, and tells him to give her best to Imani. Then she calls Holt. After three rings she gets voicemail, leaves a message, and asks him to call back. Then she walks around her office, running her hands through her hair until it looks like a haystack after a windstorm. Even without knowing the bowling guy's name she's ninety per cent sure that he's another victim of the person she's coming to think of as the Red Bank Predator. It's unlikely that the predator is an old white lady with sciatica, but possibly the old lady is covering up for someone? Cleaning up after someone? Maybe even her son? God knows such things have happened before. Holly recently read a story about an honor killing where an old lady held her daughter-in-law's legs so her outraged son could behead her. The family that slays together stays together – that type of thing.

She thinks of calling Pete. She even thinks of calling Isabelle Jaynes at the cop shop. But she doesn't think seriously of calling either one. She wants to roll this herself.

3

The lot of Strike Em Out Lanes is big but sparsely populated. Holly parks and as she's opening her door, her phone rings. It's Jerry Holt.

'Sure, I remember that bike. When nobody came for it after a year – no, more like sixteen months – I gave it to my kid. Does someone want it back?'

'No, nothing like that. I just—'

'Good, because Greg wrecked it doing jumps in a gravel pit near here. Damn idiot broke his arm. My wife gave me sixteen kinds of hell.'

'I just want to know where it was found. Do you happen to know that?'

'Oh yeah,' Holt says. 'It was on the worksheet. Deerfield Park. In that overgrown part they call the Thickets.'

'Near Red Bank Avenue,' Holly says. More to herself than to Jerry Holt.

'That's right. One of the groundskeepers found it.'

4

There are two signs on the bowling alley doors. One says OPEN. The other says NO MASK? NO PROBLEM! Holly pulls hers up and goes in. The foyer is decorated with dozens of framed group shots of children. Above them is a sign reading KIDS BOWL FOR HEALTH!

Holly can think of healthier activities – swimming, running, volleyball – but she supposes every little bit helps.

There are twenty lanes, all but three dark. The sound of the few balls is loud. The crash of the pins when the balls hit is even louder, like the part of a Hollywood action movie when a disposable character cuts the red wire instead of the blue one.

A lanky longhair in an orange-striped Strike Em Out shirt is at the counter, pulling an early afternoon beer for one of the bowlers. For a wild moment Holly thinks she's found Cory-or-Cameron – alive, well, and undisappeared – but when he turns to her, she sees the nametag pinned to his shirt says DARREN.

'Want shoes? What size?'

'No thank you. My name is Holly Gibney. I'm a private investigator—'

His eyes widen. 'Shut *up*!'

Holly takes this as an expression of surprised respect rather than an actual command and pushes on. 'I'm looking for information about someone who used to work here a few years ago. A young man. His name might have been—'

'Can't help you. I've only been here since June. Summer job. You want to talk to Althea Haverty. Owns the place. She's in the office.' He points.

Holly walks to the office as more pins explode and a woman gives an exultant whoop. She knocks. Someone inside says 'Yow,' which Holly takes as an invitation and opens the door. She would have opened it even if the person inside had said *go away*. She's chasing the case, and when she's doing that her natural timidity disappears.

Althea Haverty is an extremely large woman who sits behind a cluttered desk like a meditating lady Buddha. She's got a handful of papers in one hand. A laptop is open in front of her. Holly's pretty sure from the sour way she's looking at the papers that they're bills.

'What's the problem? Pinsetter on Eleven shit the bed again? I told Darren to shut that lane down until Brock comes to fix it. I swear that kid has popcorn for brains.'

'I didn't come to bowl.'

Holly introduces herself and explains what she wants. Althea listens and puts her papers aside. 'You're talking about Cary Dressler. He was

the best worker I ever had in here since my son moved to California.
Got along with the customers and had a way of cutting off the day-drinkers
when they'd had enough without getting them all pissed off. And sched-
uling? A champ! He was a doper, but these days aren't they all? And it
never got in the way. Never late, never called in sick. Then one day he's
just gone. Boom. Like that. You're looking for him, huh?'

'Yes.' Penny Dahl is the client, but Holly is now looking for all of
them. The missing. What they call *desaparecidos* in South America.

'Well, it ain't his folks paying your bills, I don't have to be a detective to know that.' Althea puts her hands behind her head and stretches,
jutting out a truly mammoth bosom that shades half her desk.

'Why do you say that?'

'He came here from some little shitpot town in Minnesota. Stepfather
tuned up on him a lot, he said. Mother turned a blind eye. He finally
got sick of it and put on his traveling shoes. No sob story, Cary was
matter-of-fact about it. Good attitude. All that young man cared about
was movies and working here. Plus dope, probably, but I'm the original don't-ask-don't-tell mama. Besides, it was just the bud. Do you
think something happened to him? Something bad?'

'I think it's possible. Can you help me pinpoint when he left? I
talked to a Jet Mart clerk where Cary used to stop on his way home
. . . to some apartment, I'm guessing . . . but the only thing the clerk
seemed sure of is that it happened around the time when Trump was
running for president the first time.'

'Fucking Democrats fucking stole his second term, pardon my
Spanglish. Wait a minute, wait a minute.' She opens the top drawer of
her desk and begins pawing through it. 'I hate to think something
happened to Cary, the league situation just isn't the same without him.'

Rummage, rummage, rummage.

'I mean, fucking Covid has killed a lot of the leagues – it would
be ridiculous if it wasn't also killing my business – but without Cary
here the matches and seedings were getting jumbled up even before
Covid hit. Cary was just so fucking good at . . . ah. I think this is it.'

She plugs a flash drive into her laptop, puts on a pair of glasses,
hunts and pecks, shakes her head, hunts and pecks some more. Holly
has to restrain herself from going around the desk and finding whatever
the woman's looking for herself.

Althea peers at the screen. Reflected in her spectacles Holly sees what looks like a spreadsheet. She says, 'Okay. Cary started here in 2012. Too young to serve alcohol until his birthday, but I hired him anyway. Glad I did. He got his last paycheck on September 4th, 2015. Six years ago, almost! Time sure does zip by, doesn't it? Then he was gone.' She whips off her glasses and looks at Holly. 'My husband had to take over for him. That was before Alfie had his heart attack.'

'Do you have a picture of Cary?'

'Come out to the Bowlaroo with me.'

The Bowlaroo turns out to be a restaurant where a tired-looking woman (masked, Holly's glad to see) is serving burgers and beer to a couple of bowlers. The tile walls are decorated with more framed photos. A couple feature smiling men holding up score sheets showing Xs all the way across. Above these is a sign reading 300 CLUB! Most of the others are groups of bowlers wearing league shirts.

'Look at this place,' Althea laments, gesturing at the empty booths, tables, and counter stools. 'This used to be a good business, Holly. If it goes on like this, I'll be *out* of business. All because of some fake flu. If the fucking Democrats hadn't stolen the election . . . okay, here he is. That's Cary, right up front.'

She has stopped near a photo of seven older men – white hair on four, chrome-domes on three – and one young man with his long blond hair tied back. The young man and one of the older guys are holding up a trophy. Underneath it says GOLDEN OLDIES WINTER LEAGUE CHAMPS 2014–2015.

'Can I take a picture?' Holly asks, already raising her phone.

'Be my guest.'

Holly snaps it.

'He's in a couple others, too. Check this one out.'

In the one she's pointing at, Cary is standing with six smiling women, two of whom look like they could eat young Mr Dressler with a spoon. According to their shirts, they are the Hot Witches, champs of the Ladies Division in 2014.

'They wanted to call themselves the Hot Bitches, but Alfie put his foot down on that. And here he is with one of the Beer League teams. They bowl for a case of Bud.'

Holly takes more pictures.

'Cary'd roll with any league team that showed up a man or woman short. If it was during his shift, that was. He worked from eleven in the morning, when we open, to seven at night. He was very popular, and a good bowler – 200 average – but he'd pull back when he was subbing. He fit in with any team, but these guys were his favorites and they were the ones he rolled in with most often.' She has led Holly back to the Golden Oldies. 'Because they played in the afternoons, when this place was pretty dead even before fucking Covid. The Oldies could do afternoons because they were retired, but I think Cary had something to do with it, too. Maybe a lot.'

'Why do you say that?'

'Because after he stopped working here, the Oldies switched to Monday nights. We had a slot and they took it.'

'Is it possible that Cary might have talked to any of those guys about his plans for quitting and maybe leaving town?'

'I guess he might've. Anything's possible.'

'Do they still play? I mean, the men in this picture?'

'Some do, but at least a couple are gone.' She taps a smiling white-haired man who's holding a red marbled ball that looks custom. 'Roddy Harris still comes most weeks, but these days he just watches. Bad hips, he says, and arthritis in his hands. This one is dead . . . this one I think had a stroke . . . but this guy still plays.' She taps the man holding up the trophy with Cary. 'In fact, he's the team captain. Was then, is now. Hugh Clippard's his name. If you want to talk to him, I can give you his address. We've got the addresses of all the team members, in case they win something. Or if there's a complaint.'

'Do you get a lot of those?'

'Girlfriend, you'd be surprised. Competition gets pretty hot, especially in the winter leagues. I remember a match between the Witches and the Alley Sallies that ended in a fight. Punching, scratching, hair-pulling, beer spilled everywhere, what a mess. All about a little bitty line foul. It was Cary who got them broken up. He was good at that, too. Gee, I miss him.'

'I *would* like Mr Clippard's address. And his phone number, if you have it.'

'I do.'

She follows Althea Haverty back to her office. Holly doesn't for a minute believe Cary Dressler told any of the Oldies about his plans to leave, because she doesn't think he had such plans. His plans were changed, perhaps permanently. But if an old woman cleaned out Ellen's trailer, it's possible that one of these old men knew her. Might even be related to her, either by blood or marriage. Because the Red Bank Avenue Predator isn't picking his victims at random, or not entirely at random. He knew Ellen was on her own. He knew Cary was on his own. He might have known Pete Steinman's mother had a booze problem. He knew Bonnie had recently broken up with her boyfriend, her father was out of the picture, and Bonnie's relationship with her mother was strained. In other words, the Predator had information. Was picking his targets.

Holly is better than she used to be – more grounded, more emotionally stable, less prone to self-blame – but she still suffers from low self-esteem and insecurity. These are character flaws, but the irony is this: they make her a better detective. She's perfectly aware that her suppositions about the case could be entirely wrong, but her gut tells her they're right. She doesn't want to know if Cary confided in one of the Golden Oldies about his plans to leave the city; she wants to know if any of them know or may even be married to a woman who suffers from sciatica. Unlikely, but as Muskie used to say to Deputy Dawg on the old cartoon show, 'It's possible, it's possible.'

'Here you go,' Althea says, and hands Holly a sheet of notepaper. Holly folds it into one of the flap pockets of her cargo pants.

'Anything else you can tell me about Cary, Ms Haverty?'

Althea has picked up the sheaf of bills again. Now she puts them down and sighs. 'Just that I miss him. I bet the Oldies – those like Clippard, who were here when Cary was here – miss him, too. The Witches miss him, even the kids who came on buses for their once-a-month PE outings miss him, I bet. Especially the girls. He was a stoner, and I bet that wherever he is he believes in the fake flu just like you do, Holly – no, I'm not going to argue with you about it, this is America, you can believe whatever you want to believe – I'm just saying he was a good worker, and there are less and less of them around. That Darren, for instance. He's just putting in time. Do you think he could make out a tourney sheet? Not if you put a gun to his head.'

'Thank you for *your* time,' Holly says, and offers an elbow.

Althea looks amused. 'No offense, but I don't do that.'

Holly thinks, *my mother died of that fake flu, you gullible bitch.*

What she says, and with a smile, is 'None taken.'

5

Holly slow-walks across the lobby, listening to the roll of balls and the crash of tenpins. She is about to push open the foyer door, bracing herself for the wave of heat and humidity that will strike her, then stops, eyes wide and amazed.

My God, she thinks. *Really?*

May 19, 2021

Marie and Barbara have coffee. Olivia, with her episodes of heartbeat arrhythmia over the last few years, has caffeine-free Red Zinger iced tea. When they're all seated in the living room, Olivia tells Barbara what lies ahead as regards the Penley Prize. She speaks more hesitantly than usual. Barbara finds this troubling, but there's no slurring and what Olivia says is as sharp and on-point as ever.

'They drag it out as if it were one of those television competitions like *Dancing with the Stars* instead of a poetry award that hardly anyone cares about. Around the middle of June, the shortlist will be winnowed to ten. In mid-July they will announce the five finalists. The winner will be declared – with relief and an appropriate flourish of trumpets, one assumes – a month or so later.'

'Not until *August*?'

'As I said, they drag it out. At least you won't be required to submit any more poems, which is good in your case. Correct me if I'm wrong, but I believe your cupboard may be almost bare. The last two you showed me seemed – forgive me for saying it – a little forced.'

'They might have been.' Barbara knows they were. She could feel herself pushing the lines instead of being pulled through them.

'You are *allowed* to send a few more – a vague term the people in charge should know better than to use – but I suggest you not do so. You've sent your best. You agree?'

'Yes.'

'You need to go to bed, Olivia,' Marie says. 'You're tired. I can see it in your face and hear it in your voice.'

To Barbara, Olivia always looks tired — except for those raging eyes — but she supposes Marie sees better and knows more. She should; she has a practical nursing license and has been with Olivia for almost eight years.

Olivia holds up a hand without looking at her caregiver. The palm is almost devoid of lines. *Like a baby's*, Barbara thinks.

'If you are one of the final five, you'll be required to write a statement of poetic purpose. An essay. You saw that on the website, did you not?'

Barbara did but only skimmed that part, never having expected to get as far as she has. But the mention of the Penley Prize website raises an idea that she should have thought of before.

'Are the fifteen finalists listed on their website?'

'I don't know, but I should think so. Marie?'

Marie already has her phone out and must have the Penley Prize website in her favorites, because it only takes her a few seconds to find the answer to Barbara's question. 'Yes. They're here.'

'Damn,' Barbara says.

'You still intend to keep this a secret?' Marie asks. 'Because having made it this far is one hell of an accomplishment, Barb.'

'Well, I *was* going to. At least until Jerome signs his contract. I guess the cat's out of the bag, huh?'

Olivia snorts a laugh. 'Be serious. The Penley Prize is hardly *New York Times* material or breaking news on CNN. I imagine the only people who check that website are the finalists themselves. Plus friends and family. Perhaps a favorite teacher or two. The wider world takes no notice. If you think of literature as a town, then those who read and write poetry are the poor relations who live in shanties across the tracks. I think your secret is safe. May I return to the essay I mentioned?' She reaches to put her glass of iced tea on the endtable. She doesn't get it all the way on and it almost falls, but Marie has been watching and catches it.

'Sure, go ahead,' Barbara says. 'Then you better lie down.'

Marie gives her an emphatic nod.

'A statement of poetic purpose, not to exceed five hundred words.

You may no longer be in competition when the finalists are announced, hence no need to write about why you do what you're doing, but it won't hurt to be thinking about it. Will you do that?'

'Yes.'

Although Barbara has no idea what she'll say, if it comes to that. The two of them have talked about poetry so much and Barbara has soaked it up, so glad to be told that yes, what she's doing is important, that yes, it is a serious matter. To be told *yes*. But what would be the most important things to put in a two- or three-page essay when it all seems important? Vital, even?

'You'll help me with it, won't you?'

'Not at all,' Olivia says, sounding surprised. 'Anything you say about your work needs to come from your own heart and mind. Understood?'

'Well . . .'

'Well nothing. Heart. Mind. Subject closed. Now tell me – are you still reading prose? *To the White Sea*, perhaps?'

'Olivia, enough,' Marie says. 'Please.'

Again the hand goes up.

'I read it. Now I'm on *Blood Meridian*, by Cormac McCarthy.'

'Oh my, that's a dark one. A spill of terror. But full of vision.'

'And I'm reading *Catalepsy*. That's by Professor Castro, the one who taught here.'

Olivia chuckles. 'He was no professor, but he was a good teacher. Gay, did I tell you that?'

'I think so.'

Olivia gropes for her glass of iced tea. Marie puts it in her hand with a longsuffering look. She's apparently given up on getting Olivia to the chairlift and upstairs to bed. The lady is engaged, her speech quick and clear again.

'Gay as gay could be. Attitudes about that were a little less tolerant ten years ago, but most members of the faculty – including at least two who have now come out – accepted him for what he was, with his white shoes, flamboyant yellow shirts, and beret. We enjoyed his sharp Oscar Wilde wit, which was the armor he wore to protect his basic kindness. Jorge was a very kind man. But there was at least one member of the faculty who didn't like him at all. May even have loathed him. I believe if she had been department chairman instead of Rosalyn Burkhart, she would have found some way to toss him out on his ear.'

'Emily Harris?'

Olivia gives Barbara a sour, inturned smile that's very unlike her usual one. 'None other. I don't think she has much use for people who aren't white, which is one reason I made sure to steal you away from her even though I'm older than God, and I *definitely* know she doesn't like those who are, in Emily's words, "a bit loose in the loafers." Help me up, Marie. I believe I'm going to fart again when you do. Thank God at my age farts are relatively odorless.'

Marie helps her up. Olivia has her canes, but after sitting so long, Barbara isn't sure she could walk without Marie's help. 'Think about that essay, Barbara. I hope you'll be one of the fortunate five asked to write one.'

'I'll put my thinking cap on.' It's something her friend Holly sometimes says.

Halfway to the stairs, Olivia stops and turns back. Her eyes are no longer fierce. She's gone back in time, a thing that happens more often this spring. 'I remember the department meeting when the future of the Poetry Workshop was discussed and Jorge spoke up – very eloquently – in favor of keeping it. I remember it like it was yesterday. How Emily smiled and nodded while he spoke, as if saying "good point, good point," but her *eyes* didn't smile. She meant to have her way. She's very determined. Marie, do you remember her Christmas party last year?'

Marie rolls her eyes. 'Who could forget?'

'What about it?' Barbara asks.

'Olivia—' Marie begins.

'Oh hush, woman, this will only take a minute and it's such a great story. The Harrises have a party a few days before Christmas every year, Barbara. It's tra-*di*-tional, y'know. They've had it since God was a baby. Last year, with Covid running wild, the college shut down and it seemed that the grand tradition would be broken. But was Emily Harris going to let that happen?'

'I'm guessing not,' Barbara says.

'You're guessing right. They had a *Zoom* party. Which Marie and I chose not to attend. But Zooming wasn't good enough for our Emily. She hired a bunch of young people to dress up in fucking *Santa* outfits and deliver goody-baskets to the partygoers who were in town. We got a basket ourselves even though we chose not to Zoom in. Didn't we, Marie? Beer and cookies, something like that?'

'Indeed we did, a pretty blond delivered. Now for God's sake—'

'Yes, boss, yes.'

With Marie helping her, the old poet makes her slow way to the stairs, where she settles – with another fart – into the chairlift. 'At that meeting about the Poetry Workshop, when it looked . . . only for a minute or two . . . like Jorge might sway the voting members, Em never lost that smile of hers, but her eyes . . .' Olivia laughs at the memory as the chair starts to rise. 'Her eyes looked like she wanted to kill him.'

July 27, 2021

1

KIDS BOWL FOR HEALTH, reads the sign over the group shots of the school children who came here to bowl in the days before Covid made an end to such outings. Holly looks around to make sure she's not observed. Darren – the young man now doing Cary Dressler's job – is leaning beside the beer taps, studying his phone. Althea Haverty is back in her office. Holly is afraid the picture she wants may be glued to the wall, but it's on a hook. She worries that nothing will be written on the back, but there is, and neatly printed: *5th Street Middle School Girls, May 2015.*

Holly puts the picture back on its hook, and then – because she's Holly – carefully straightens it. A dozen girls in dark purple shorts, which Holly recognizes as the 5th Street Middle PE uniform. Three rows, four girls in each. They are sitting cross-legged in front of one of the lanes. In the middle row, smiling, is Barbara Robinson, topped by the medium-length afro she wore back then. She would have been twelve, a sixth grader if Holly's not mistaken. Cary Dressler isn't in the photo, he's not in any of the KIDS BOWL FOR HEALTH photos, but if he started working at eleven, when the Strike Em Out opened, he would have been on duty when the kids came in.

Holly goes out to her car, barely noticing the heat and for once not wanting a cigarette. She gets the air conditioning cranking and finds the photo she took of the Golden Oldies, the one that features team captain Hugh Clippard and Cary holding up the trophy. She sends it to Barbara with a brief message: *Do you remember this guy?*

With that done, the little nicotine bell begins to ring. She lights up, places her portable ashtray on the console, and gets rolling. It's time to start knocking on doors. Starting with Hugh Clippard's.

2

The Victorians on the graceful downhill curve of Ridge Road are nice, but the ones on Laurel Close deeper into Sugar Heights are nicer. If, that is, one's definition of nice includes not just expensive but *really* expensive. Holly couldn't care less. As far as she's concerned, if the appliances in her apartment work and the windows don't leak, all is fine; a groundskeeper (or a crew of them) would just be an annoyance. There is such a fellow outside of the Clippard residence, which is a Tudor with a big, velvety lawn. The groundskeeper is mowing the grass as she pulls in at the curb.

Holly thinks, *A new millionaire parks and watches a man on a riding mower clip the Clippards' grass.*

She calls Hugh Clippard's number. She's prepared to leave a message, but he answers and listens while Holly gives a brief version of her interest in Cary Dressler.

'What a great young man!' Clippard exclaims when she finishes. He is, Holly will discover, an exclamatory sort of fellow. 'Happy to talk to you about him. Come on around back. My wife and I are out by the pool.'

Holly pulls into the driveway and gives the groundskeeper a wave. He gives her a return flick and keeps on trucking. Or mowing. For the life of her Holly can't see what there is to mow. To her the grass already looks like the surface of a freshly vacuumed billiard table. She takes her iPad — it has a bigger screen for the picture she wants to show Clippard — and walks around the house, pausing to peek into a dining room with a table that looks long enough to seat a football team (or a bowling league).

Hugh Clippard and his wife are on matching loungers in the shade of a vast blue umbrella. The pool, the same shade of blue, isn't Olympic size, but it's no kiddie pool, either. Clippard is wearing sandals and tight-fitting red trunks. He sees her and bounces up. His belly is flat and rippled with a modified sixpack. His hair is long and white, slicked back sleek and wet against his skull. Holly's first impression is that he's seventy. When he gets close enough to shake hands, she sees that he's quite a bit older, but in awesome shape for a Golden Oldie.

He grins at her hesitation to take his hand, showing perfect white teeth that probably didn't come cheap. 'We're both vaccinated, Ms Gibney, and we plan to get the boosters as soon as the CDC approves them. May I assume you have also had the jab?'

'Yes.' Holly shakes his hand and lowers her mask.

'This is my wife, Midge.'

The woman under the big umbrella is at least twenty years younger than Clippard, but not in such sculpted shape. There's a little round bulge under her one-piece bathing suit. She takes off her sunglasses, gives Holly a desultory wave with them, then returns to her paperback, which is titled, not very subtly, *The Subtle Art of Not Giving a F*ck*.

'Come on in the kitchen,' Clippard says. 'It's *sweltering* out here. You okay, Midge?'

The only answer is another desultory wave. This time without looking up. She clearly doesn't give a f*ck.

The kitchen — reached through glass sliders — is about what Holly expected. The fridge is a Sub-Zero. The clock over the granite counter is a Perigold. Clippard pours them each a glass of iced tea and invites her to tell him in more detail about why she's here. She does, touching on Bonnie — the Jet Mart connection — but focusing on Cary.

'Did he say anything to you about his plans? Confide in any way? I'm asking because Ms Haverty said you guys were his favorite league to bowl with.'

Holly doesn't expect any help from his answer. There might be something, never say never and all that, but one look at Midge Clippard has told her that she's not the old woman Imani McGuire saw cleaning out Ellen Craslow's trailer.

'Cary!' Clippard exclaims, shaking his head. 'He was a hell of a good guy, I can tell you that much, and he could roll a ball, too!' He raises a finger. 'But he never took advantage. He always matched his skills to those of the teams we bowled against.'

'How often did he substitute in?'

'Pretty often!' Clippard adds a chuckle that is in its own way exclamatory. 'They don't call us the Golden Oldies for nothing! Someone was usually out with a strained back, pulled hammy, stiff neck, some darn old thing. Then we'd yell for Cary and give him a round of applause if he could roll in with us. He wasn't always able to, but he usually managed. We liked him and he liked us. Want to hear a secret?'

'I love secrets.' This is true.

Hugh Clippard lowers his voice to a near-whisper that is exclamatory in its own way. 'Some of us used to buy weed from him! He didn't always have great stuff, but it was usually good stuff. Small Ball wouldn't touch it, but most of us weren't averse to a joint or a bowl. Back then it wasn't legal, you know.'

'Who's Small Ball?'

'Roddy Harris. We called him that because he rolled with a ten-pounder. Most of us used twelves or fourteens.'

'Was Mr Harris allergic to marijuana?'

'No, just *crazy*!' Clippard shouts, and bursts out laughing. 'A good guy and a decent bowler, but nutty as a fruitcake! We also called him Mr Meat! Roddy makes that Atkins guy look like a vegetarian! Claims meat restores brain cells and certain vegetable products, cannabis included, destroys them.'

Clippard stretches and the sixpack ripples, but she sees wrinkles encroaching on the insides of his arms. *Time*, she thinks, *really is the avenger.*

'Gosh, this takes me back! Most of these guys are gone! When I started with the Oldies, I was teaching at Bell College, living downtown and day-trading on the side. Now I'm in the investment business full-time, and as you can see, business has been good!' He sweeps his arm around, presumably indicating the kitchen with its high-priced appliances, the backyard pool, perhaps even the younger wife. Who's not quite young enough to be called a trophy wife, Holly gives him credit for that.

'Trump is an idiot and I'm glad he's gone, *dee*-lighted, the guy couldn't find his ass with both hands and a flashlight, but he was good for the markets. More iced tea?'

'No, thank you. This is fine. Very refreshing.'

'As to your question, Ms Gibney, I can't remember Cary ever talking to me about plans to leave town or change jobs. I may have forgotten something he said about those things, this goes back six, seven, even nine years I guess, but that young man seemed perfectly happy to me.

Crazy about the movies and always riding that noisy little moped of his. You say someone found it in Deerfield Park?'

'Yes.'

'Crazy! Hard to believe he'd leave it behind! That was his trademark!'

'May I show you a picture? You'll have seen it before – it's hanging in the Bowlaroo.' She calls it up on her iPad. Clippard bends over it.

'Winter Championship, right,' he says. 'Those were the days! Haven't won it since, but last year we came close.'

'Can you identify the men in the picture? And do you by any chance have their addresses? And phone numbers?'

'Memory challenge!' Clippard cries. 'Let's see if I'm up to it!'

'May I record on my phone?'

'Knock yourself out! This is me, of course, and this is Roddy Harris, also known as Small Ball and Mr Meat. He and his wife live on Victorian Row. Ridge Road, you know. Roddy was Life Sciences, and his wife, don't recall her name, was in the English Department.' He moves his finger to the next man. 'Ben Richardson is dead, heart attack two years ago.'

'Was he married? Wife still in town?'

He gives her an odd look. 'Ben was divorced when he started rolling with us. *Long* divorced. Ms Gibney, do you think one of our guys had anything to do with Cary's disappearance?'

'No, no, nothing like that,' Holly assures him. 'I'm just hoping one of them might be able to tell me where Cary went.'

'Got it, got it! Moving right along! This baldy with the big shoulders is Avram Welch. He's in one of those Lakeside condos. Wife died some years back, if you're wondering. Still bowls.' He moves to another baldy. 'Jim Hicks. We called him Hot Licks! Ha! He and his wife moved to Racine. How'm I doing?'

'Terrific!' Holly exclaims. It seems to be catching.

Midge wanders in. 'Having fun, kids?'

'You betchum bobcats!' Clippard cries, either not catching the faint note of sarcasm in his wife's voice or choosing to ignore it. She pours herself a glass of iced tea, then stands on tiptoe to get a bottle of brown liquor from a cabinet where other bottles stand shoulder to shoulder. She pours a dollop into her glass, then holds the bottle out to them, one eyebrow raised.

'Why not?' Clippard nearly shouts. 'God hates a coward!'

She pours a shot into his glass. It goes swirling down.

'What about you, Ms Gibley? A little Wild Turkey will get that iced tea right up on its feet.'

'No thank you,' Holly says. 'I'm driving.'

'Very law-abiding of you,' Midge says. 'Ta-ta, kids.'

Out she goes. Clippard gives her a look that might or might not be mild distaste, then returns his attention to Holly. 'Do you bowl yourself, Ms Gibney?' He gives her name a slight emphasis, as if to correct his wife in absentia.

'I don't,' Holly admits.

'Well, league teams are usually just four players, and that's how we play it in the tourney finals, but during the regular season we sometimes bowled with five or even six guys, assuming the other team rolled with the same number. Because in the Over Sixty-Fives, someone is almost always on the DL. Sometimes two or three. By DL I mean—'

'The Disabled List,' Holly says, and doesn't bother telling him it's now called the Injured List. She's all at once wanting to get out of here. There's something almost frantic about Hugh Clippard. She doesn't think he's coked up, but it's like that. The sixpack . . . the tight little buns in the red swimsuit . . . the tan . . . and the encroaching wrinkles . . .

'Who's this one?'

'Ernie Coggins. Lives in Upriver with his wife. He still bowls with us on Monday nights, if her caregiver can come in. Advanced degenerative disc disease, poor woman. Wheelchair-bound. But Ernie's in great shape. Takes care of himself.'

Now Holly understands what's bothering her, because it's bothering him. Most of the men in the photo are falling apart, and if eighty is their median age, why would they not be? The equipment wears out, which seems to be something Hugh Clippard doesn't want to admit. He is, as they say, sitting in the denial aisle.

'Desmond Clark isn't in the picture – guess he wasn't there when it was taken. Des and his wife are dead, too. They were in a light plane crash down in Florida. Boca Raton. Des was piloting. Damn fool tried to land in heavy fog. Missed the runway.' Nothing exclamatory about this; Clippard speaks in what's almost a monotone.

He takes a big slug of his spiked iced tea and says, 'I'm thinking of quitting.'

For a moment she believes he's talking about booze, then decides that's not it. 'Quitting the Golden Oldies?'

'Yes. I used to like that name, but these days it kind of grates on me. The only ones in this picture I still roll with are Avram and Ernie Cog. Small Ball comes, but just to watch. It's not like it used to be.'

'Nothing is,' Holly says gently.

'No? No. But it should be. And could be, if people would only take care of themselves.' He's staring at the picture. Holly is looking at him and realizes that even the sixpack is starting to show wrinkles.

'Who is this last one?'

'That's Vic Anderson. Slick Vic, we used to call him. He had a stroke. He's in some care home upstate.'

'Not Rolling Hills, by any chance?'

'Yes, that's the name.'

The fact that one of the old bowlers is in the same care home as Uncle Henry feels like a coincidence. Holly finds that a relief, because seeing a picture of Barbara Robinson in the Strike Em Out foyer felt more like . . . well . . . fate.

'His wife moved up there so she could visit him more often. Sure you don't want a little pick-me-up, Ms Gibney? I won't tell if you won't.'

'I'm fine. Really.' Holly stops recording. 'Thank you so much, Mr Clippard.'

He's still looking at her iPad. He seems almost hypnotized. 'I really didn't realize how few of us are left.'

She swipes away the picture and he looks up, as if not entirely sure where he is.

'Thank you for your time.'

'Very welcome. If you locate Cary, ask him to drop by sometime, will you? At least give him my email address. I'll write it down for you.'

'And the numbers of the ones that are still around?'

'You bet.'

He tears a sheet from a pad that's headed JUST A NOTE FROM MIDGE'S KITCHEN, grabs a pen from a cup full of them, and jots, consulting the contacts on his phone as he does. Holly notes that the numbers and the e-address show the slightest tremble of the hand writing them. She folds the sheet and puts it in her pocket. She thinks again, *time the avenger*. Holly doesn't mind old people; it's something about the way Clippard is handling his old age that makes her uneasy.

She basically can't wait to get the frack out.

3

There's only one (and oh-so-tony) shopping center in Sugar Heights. Holly parks there, lights a cigarette, and smokes with the door open, elbows on her thighs and feet on the pavement. Her car is starting to stink of cigarettes, and not even the can of air freshener she keeps in the center console completely kills the odor. What a nasty habit it is, and yet how necessary.

Just for now, she thinks, and then thinks again of Saint Augustine praying that God should make him chaste . . . but not yet.

Holly checks her phone to see if Barbara has answered her message with the attached photo of Cary Dressler and the Golden Oldies. She hasn't. Holly looks at her watch and sees it's only quarter past two. There's plenty of day left in the day, and she has no intention of wasting it, so what next?

Get off her ass and knock on doors, of course.

There were eight bowling Oldies in 2015, including Desmond Clark, the one not in the picture. Three of them don't need to be checked out. Four, if she counts Hugh Clippard. He looks capable of overpowering Bonnie and the skateboard kid – about Ellen, Holly's less sure – but for the time being she puts him aside with the two who are dead and Jim Hicks (living in Wisconsin . . . although that should be checked out). That leaves Roddy Harris, Avram Welch, and Ernie Coggins. There's also Victor Anderson, but Holly doubts if a stroke victim is sneaking out of Rolling Hills to abduct people.

She knows it's very unlikely that *any* of the Golden Oldies is the Red Bank Predator, but she's more and more convinced that the presumed abductions of Dressler, Craslow, Steinman, and Bonnie Rae Dahl were planned rather than random. The Predator knew their routines, all of which seem to have Deerfield Park as their epicenter.

The bowlers knew Cary. She doesn't need to mention the other *desaparecidos*, unless she gets a feeling — what Bill Hodges would have called *a vibe* — that questions about Cary are making someone nervous. Or defensive. Maybe even guilty. She knows the tells to look for; Bill taught her well. Better to keep Ellen, Pete, and Bonnie as hole cards. At least for the time being.

It never once crosses her mind that Penny Dahl has outed her on Facebook, Instagram, and Twitter.

4

While Holly is smoking in the parking lot of the Sugar Heights Boutique Shopping Mart, Barbara Robinson is staring uselessly into space. She's shut off all notifications on her computer and phone, allowing only calls from her parents and Jerome to ring through. Those little red check-me-out circles by the text and mail icons are too tempting. The Penley Prize Essay — a requirement for the five finalists — has to be in the mail by the end of the month, and that's only four days away. Make it three, actually; she wants to take her essay to the post office on Friday and make absolutely sure of that postmark. Being eliminated because of a technicality after all this would be crazy-making. So she bends to the work.

Poetry is important to me because

Horrible. Like the first line of a middle school book report. Delete.

Poetry matters because

Worse. Delete.

My reason for

Delete, delete, *delete*!

Barbara shuts off her computer, spends some more time staring into space, then gets up from her desk and shucks off her jeans. She pulls on a pair of shorts, adds a sleeveless tee, ties back her hair in a sloppy ponytail, and goes running.

It's too hot to run, the temperature's got to be topping ninety, but it's all she can think of to do. She circles the block . . . and it's a long one. By the time she gets back to the house where she will live with her parents only until she starts college and begins another life, she's sweating and gasping for breath. Nevertheless, she goes around the block again. Mrs Caltrop, who is watering her flowers under an enormous sunhat, looks at her like she's crazy. Probably she is.

In front of her computer, looking at the blank screen and the flashing cursor that seemed to mock her, she felt frustrated and – face it – scared. Because Olivia refuses to help. Because her mind was as blank as the screen. But now, running full out with sweat darkening her shirt and trickling down the sides of her face like extravagant tears, she realizes what was beneath the fright and frustration. She's angry. She feels fucking toyed with. Made to jump through hoops like a circus dog.

Back in the house – for the time being all hers, with her mother and father at their respective jobs – she takes the stairs two at a time, leaves a path of her clothes in the hallway on her way to the bathroom, then gets in the shower with the handle turned all the way to C. She lets out a scream and clutches herself. She sticks her throbbing face in the cold spray and screams again. It feels good to scream, as she learned on that day two months ago when she did it with Marie Duchamp, so she does it a third time.

She gets out of the shower shivering and covered with goosebumps but feeling better. *Clearer.* She towels up and down until her skin is glowing, then goes back to her room, picking up her clothes on the way. She tosses them on the bed, goes naked to her computer, reaches for the button that turns it on, then thinks *No. Wrong.*

She grabs one of her school notebooks from the shelf beside her desk, flips past scribbled notes on Henry VII and the Wars of the Roses, and comes to a blank page. She tears it out almost carelessly, not ignoring the frayed edge but glad of it. She's thinking of something Olivia said in one of their morning meetings. She told Barbara it came from a Spanish writer named Juan Ramón Jiménez, but she, Olivia, first heard it from Jorge Castro. She said Jorge claimed it was the cornerstone of everything he ever wrote or hoped to write: *If they give you ruled paper, write the other way.*

Barbara does that now, writing her essay quickly across the blue ruled lines. According to the Penley requirements, it is *not to exceed 500 words*. Barbara's is much shorter than that. And it turns out Olivia is here to help her after all, with something else she said on one of those morning meetings that have changed her life. Maybe more than college ever will.

I write poetry because without it I am a dead engine. She pauses only for a moment, then adds: *That I should be asked to write an essay about my poetry after sending so much of it to you is idiotic. My poetry is my essay.*

She folds the ragged-edged sheet twice and stuffs it in an envelope that's already stamped and addressed. She throws on some clothes, runs back down the stairs, and goes out the door, leaving it open. She sprints down the block, probably ruining her cold shower with fresh sweat. She doesn't care. She needs to do this before she can change her mind. Doing that would be wrong, because what she's written is right.

There's a mailbox on the corner. She drops the envelope inside, then bends over, grasping her knees and breathing hard.

I don't care if I win or lose. I don't care, I don't care.

She may regret what she wrote later, but not now. Standing at the mailbox, bent over with her wet hair hanging in her face, she knows it's the truth.

The work matters.

Nothing else. Not prizes. Not being published. Not being rich, famous, or both.

Only the work.

July 1, 2021

8:03.

Bonnie Rae Dahl bikes down Red Bank Avenue and turns in at the Jet Mart.

8:04.

She dismounts, takes off her helmet, and shakes out her hair. She puts the helmet on the seat and goes in.

'Hey, Emilio,' she says, and gives him a smile.

'Hey,' he responds, and gives it right back.

She goes past the Beer Cave to the back cooler, where the soft drinks are waiting. She grabs a Diet Pepsi. She starts back down the aisle, then pauses at the rack of snack cakes – Twinkies, Ho Hos, Yodels, Little Debbies. She picks up a package of Ho Hos, considering. Emilio is putting cigarettes into the rack behind the counter. Outside, a van passes the store, heading downhill.

8:05.

Roddy Harris is driving the van. He's got the hypo of Valium in the pocket of the sportcoat he's wearing. Emily is already in the wheelchair, ready to go . . . and tonight she needs it. Her sciatica has returned with a vengeance. Roddy pulls onto the cracked tarmac of what used to be Bill's Automotive and Small Engine Repair with the van's sliding door facing the abandoned shop.

'One Christmas elf, coming right up,' he says.

'Just hurry,' Emily snaps. 'I don't want to miss her. This is *agony*.'

She turns the wheelchair to face the door. Roddy presses a button and the door rolls back. The ramp slides out. Emily rides it down to the pavement. Roddy puts on the four-way flashers and gets out. They have debated the flashers at great length and have finally decided they have to take the risk. They can't afford to miss her. Em is bad and Roddy isn't in great shape himself. His hips hurt and his hands are stiff, but the real problem is his mind. It keeps drifting. It's not Alzheimer's, he refuses to believe that, but he's definitely gotten muzzy. A fresh infusion of brains will put him right. And the rest will put Em right. Especially the Christmas elf's liver, that's the holy grail, the sacrament, but no part of the animal must be wasted. It isn't just his motto; it's his mantra.

8:06.

Bonnie has put the package of Ho Hos back, not without regret. She comes to the counter, billfold in hand. She carries it in her hip pocket, like a man.

'Why don't you think again about those Ho Hos?' Emilio says as he rings her up. 'You're in good shape, they won't hurt you.'

'Get thee behind me, Satan. My body is a temple.'

'If you say so,' Emilio replies. 'At Jet Mart – this one, anyway – the customer is always right.'

They both laugh. Bonnie pockets her change, slides her backpack off one shoulder, and puts her bottle of soda inside. She plans to sip it while watching *Ozark* on Netflix. She zips the pack closed and shoulders it.

'Have a good night, Emilio.'

He gives her a thumbs-up.

8:07.

Bonnie puts on her helmet, mounts her bike, and pauses just long enough to adjust one of her pack's straps. Not far down the hill, across from the part of the park known as the Thickets, Emily is piloting her wheelchair around the rear of the van. The pavement is cracked and uneven. Each time the wheelchair dips and sways there's an explosion of pain in her lower back. She presses her lips together to keep from crying out, but she can't help moaning.

'Flag her down!' It's part whisper, part growl. 'Don't fail, Roddy, please don't fail!'

Roddy has no intention of failing. If Bonnie won't stop for him, he'll kick her off her bike as she tries to pass by. Assuming, of course, that his hips are up to the task. What he would give to be fifty again! Even sixty!

He turns to Em and sees something he doesn't like. The wheelchair's guide-light is still on, shining down on the pavement. Hard to believe a wheelchair has a dead battery if the light is still working! And the girl is coming, speeding down the hill.

'Turn off the light!' he whispers. 'Emily, turn off the goddam guide-light!'

She does, just in time. Because here's the girl, their Christmas elf.

Roddy steps off the sidewalk, waving his arms. 'Can you help us, please? We need help!'

Bonnie speeds past, and she's too far into the street for him to even think about karate-kicking her off the bike. He has an instant to see all their planning going to waste, diminishing as the bike's flashing red taillight diminishes downhill. But then the girl brakes, swerves, and comes back. He doesn't know if it was him waving his arms, the four-way flashers, the desire to be a good Samaritan, or all three. He's just relieved.

She pedals slowly, a little wary at first, but there's more than enough light left in the day for her to see who was waving her down. 'Professor Harris? What's up? What's wrong?'

'It's Em. Her sciatica is very bad, and the battery in her wheelchair died. Is it possible you could help me get her inside? The ramp is on the other side. I want to take her home.'

'Bonnie?' Emily asks weakly. 'Bonnie Dahl, is that you?'

'It is. Oh my God, Emily, I'm so sorry!'

Bonnie dismounts her bike and pushes down the kickstand. She hurries to Emily and bends over her. 'What happened? Why did you stop *here*?'

A car passes. It slows; Roddy's heart stops. Then it speeds up again.

Emily has no good answer for Bonnie's question, so she just moans.

'We need to get her around to the other side,' Roddy repeats. 'Can you help me push?'

He bends as if to take one of the wheelchair's rear handles, but Bonnie hips him aside and grabs both. She turns the wheelchair and pushes it around the back of the van. Emily whimpers at each bounce and jounce. Roddy skirts the ramp, leans in the open driver's side door, and kills the four-way flashers. *That's one less thing to worry about*, he thinks.

'Should I call someone?' Bonnie asks. 'My phone—'

'Just get me up the ramp,' Emily gasps. 'I'll be fine once I get home and take a muscle relaxant.'

Bonnie positions the wheelchair facing the ramp and takes a deep breath. She'd like to pull it back first and get a running start, but the pavement is too uneven. *One hard push*, she thinks. *I'm strong enough, I can do this.*

'Should I help?' Roddy asks, but he's already moving behind Bonnie rather than toward the wheelchair's handles. His hand dips into his pocket. He flips the small protective cap off the tip of the hypo with no trouble; he's done this before, both in numerous practice runs and four times when it's the real thing. The van blocks what's happening here from the street and he has no reason to think everything won't go well. They are almost home free.

'No, I can do it. Stay back.'

Bonnie bends like a runner in the starting blocks, gets a good grasp on the rubber handgrips, and pushes. Halfway up the ramp, just as she thinks she won't be able to finish the job, the wheelchair's motor hums to life. The guide-light comes on. At the same moment she feels a wasp sting the back of her neck.

Emily rolls into the van. Roddy expects Bonnie to collapse, just as the others did. He has every reason to expect that; he's just injected 15 milligrams of Valium less than two inches from elf-girl's cerebellum. Instead, she straightens up and turns around. Her hand goes to the back of her neck. For a moment Roddy thinks he's given her a diluted dose, maybe even no dose at all, only water. It's her eyes that convince him that isn't true. A younger and much brawnier Roddy Harris, then an undergraduate, worked two summers in a Texas slaughterhouse — it was where he began to formulate his theories about the near-magical properties of flesh. Sometimes the bolt gun they used to put the cows down wouldn't be fully charged, or would be aimed slightly off-target. When that happened, the cows looked like Bonnie Dahl does now, eyes floating in their sockets, faces slack with bewilderment.

'What . . . did you do? What . . .'

'Why won't she go down?' Emily asks shrilly from the open van door. 'Be quiet,' he says. 'She will.'

But instead of going down, Bonnie blunders toward the back of the van, arms held out for balance. And toward the street beyond, presumably. Roddy tries to grab her. She pushes him away with surprising strength. He stumbles backward, trips over a protruding lip of pavement, and lands on his ass. His hips howl. His teeth click together, catching a scrap of his tongue between them. Blood trickles into his mouth. In this fraught moment he enjoys the taste even though he knows his own blood is useless to him. *Any* blood without flesh is useless to him.

'She's getting away!' Emily cries.

Roddy loves his wife, but in that moment he hates her, too. If there were people on the other side of Red Bank Avenue instead of tangled undergrowth, they would be coming out to see what all the ruckus was about.

He scrambles to his feet. Bonnie has veered away from the van and Red Bank Avenue. Now she's blundering across the front of the abandoned repair shop, one hand sliding along the rusty roll-up door to keep from going down, taking a drunk's big loose swaying strides. She makes it all the way to the end of the building before he can throw a forearm around her neck and yank her back. She still tries to fight him, twisting her head from side to side. Her bike helmet thuds against his shoulder. One of her earrings flies off. Roddy is too busy to notice; his hands are, as they say, full. Her vitality is nothing short of remarkable. Even now Roddy thinks he can't wait to taste her.

He drags her back toward the van, gasping for breath, heart beating not just in his chest but thrumming in his neck and pulsing in his head.

'Come on,' he says, and gets her turned around. 'Come on, elf, come on, come on, c—'

One flailing elbow connects with his cheekbone. Sparks flash in front of his eyes. He loses his hold on her but then – thank God, thank God – her knees buckle and she finally drops. He turns to Emily. 'Can you help me?'

She gets partway up, winces, and plops back down. 'No. If my back locks up all the way, I'll only make matters worse. You'll have to do it yourself. I'm sorry.'

Not as sorry as I am, Roddy thinks, but the alternative is jail, head-lines, a trial, cable news 24/7, and finally prison. He seizes Bonnie under the arms and drags her toward the ramp, his back groaning, his hips threatening to simply lock up. Part of the problem is her pack. He gets it off. It has to weigh at least twenty pounds. He hands it up to Emily, who manages to take it and hold it in her lap.

'Open it,' he says. 'Get her phone if it's in there. You have to . . .' He doesn't finish, needing to save his breath for the job at hand. Besides, Em knows the drill. Right now they have to get out of here, and with any luck, they will. *If anyone deserves some luck after what we've been through, it's us*, he thinks. The idea that Bonnie has had even worse luck this evening never crosses his mind.

Em is already taking the SIM card out of Bonnie's phone, effectively killing it.

He drags Bonnie up the ramp. Emily reverses the wheelchair to give him room. She's already unzipped the backpack and started rummaging inside. He'd like to pause and catch his breath, but they've been here too long already. Far too long. He kicks Bonnie's legs away from the door. It would have hurt her if she was conscious, but she's not.

'The note. The note.'

It's waiting in the back pocket of the passenger seat, in a clear plastic envelope. Emily has printed it, working from various notes Bonnie has made during her brief term of employment. It's not an exact replica, but printing doesn't need to be. And it's short: *I've had enough*. The note probably won't matter if the bike is stolen, but even then it might if the thief is caught. Roddy puts it on the seat of her bike and wipes the sleeve of his sportcoat across it, in case paper takes fingerprints (on that the Internet seems divided).

He gets into the driver's seat, whooping for breath. He pushes the button that retracts the ramp and closes the door. His heart is beating at an insane rate. If he has a heart attack, will Emily be able to drive the van back to 93 Ridge Road and get it in its garage bay? Even if she can, what about the unconscious girl?

Em will have to kill her, he thinks, and even in his current state — body aching all over, heart speeding, head pounding — the thought of all that meat going to waste gives him a pang of regret.

8:18 PM.

July 27, 2021

1

'Just look at this,' Avram Welch says. He's wearing cargo shorts (Holly has several pairs just like them) and pointing at his knees. There are healed S-shaped scars on both. 'Double knee replacement. August 31st, 2015. Hard to forget that day. Cary was at the Strike Em Out the last time I came, in the middle of August – me there just to watch, my knees were too bad by then to even think about throwing a ball – and gone the next time I went. Does that help any?'

'It absolutely does,' Holly says, although she doesn't know if it does or not. 'When was the next time you went back to the bowling alley after your op?'

'I know that, too. November 17th. It was the first round of the Over Sixty-Fives tournament. I still couldn't play, but I came to cheer the Oldies on.'

'You have a good memory.'

They are sitting in the living room of Welch's third-floor Sunrise Bay condominium apartment. There are boats in bottles everywhere, Welch has told her that building them is his pastime, but the place of honor is held by the framed photograph of a smiling woman in her mid-forties. She's dressed in a pretty silk dress and wearing a lace mantilla over her chestnut hair, as if she's just come from church.

Welch points at the picture now. 'I ought to remember. It was the next day that Mary was diagnosed with lung cancer. Died a year later. And do you know what? She never smoked.'

Hearing of a non-smoker who's died of lung cancer always makes

Holly feel a little better about her own habit. She supposes that makes her a poopy person.

'I'm very sorry for your loss.'

Welch is a small man with a big potbelly and skinny legs. He sighs and says, 'Not as sorry as I am, Ms Gibney, and you can take that to the bank. She was the love of my life. We had our disagreements, as married people do, but there's a saying: "Don't let the sun go down on your anger." And we never did.'

'Althea says you all liked Cary. The Golden Oldies, I mean.'

'*Everybody* liked Cary. He was a Tribble. I don't suppose you know what I mean by that, but—'

'I do. I'm a *Star Trek* fan.'

'Right, okay, right. Cary, you couldn't *not* like him. Kind of a space cadet, but friendly and always cheerful. I suppose the dope helped with that. *He* was a smoker, but not cigarettes. He puffed the bud, as the Jamaicans say.'

'I think some of the other members of your team might also have puffed the bud,' Holly ventures.

Welch laughs. 'Did we ever. I remember nights when we'd go out back and pass a couple of joints around, getting stoned and laughing. Like we were back in high school. Except for Roddy, that is. Old Small Ball didn't mind us doing it, he was no crusader, sometimes he even came along, but he didn't do pot. Didn't believe in it. We'd smoke up, then go back inside, and do you know what?'

'No, what?'

'It made us *better*. Hughie the Clip especially. When he was stoned, he lost that Brooklyn hook of his, and he'd put it bang in the pocket more often than not. *Bwoosh!*' He flings his hands apart, simulating a strike. 'Not Roddy, though. Without the magic smoke, the prof was the same one-forty bowler as he ever was. Isn't that a riot?'

'Absolutely.'

Holly leaves the Sunrise Bay having learned just one thing: Avram Welch is also a Tribble. If he were to turn out to be the Red Bank Predator, everything she's ever believed, both intellectually and intuitively, would fall to ruin.

Her next stop is Rodney Harris, retired professor, one-forty bowler, also known as Small Ball and Mr Meat.

2

Barbara is reading a Randall Jarrell poem called 'The Death of the Ball Turret Gunner' and marveling at its five lines of pure terror when her phone rings. Only three callers can currently get through, and since her mom and dad are downstairs, she doesn't even look at the screen. She just says 'Hi, J, what do you say?'

'I say I'm staying in New York for the weekend. But not the city. My agent has invited me to spend the weekend in Montauk. Isn't that cool?'

'Well, I don't know. I have an idea that sex and business don't mix.'

He laughs. She has never heard Jerome laugh so easily and frequently as he has during their last few conversations, and she's glad for his happiness. 'You can be cool on that score, kiddo. Mara's in her late fifties. Married. With children and grandchildren. Most of whom will be there. I've told you all that already, but you've been lost in the clouds. Do you even remember Mara's last name?'

Barbara admits she does not, although she's sure Jerome has told her.

'Roberts. What is *up* with you?'

For a moment she's silent, just looking at the ceiling, where fluorescent stars glow at night. Jerome helped her put them up when she was nine.

'If I tell you, will you promise not to be mad? I haven't told Mom and Dad yet, but I guess once I tell you, I better tell them.'

'Just as long as you ain't pregnant, sis.' His voice says he's joking and not joking at the same time.

It's Barbara's turn to laugh. 'Not pregnant, but you could say that I'm expecting.'

She tells him everything, going all the way back to her initial meeting with Emily Harris, because she was too afraid to approach Olivia Kingsbury on her own. She tells him about her meetings with the old poet, and how Olivia submitted her poems to the Penley Prize Committee without telling her, and how she's still in the running for the prize.

She finishes and waits for jealousy. Or lukewarm congratulations. She gets neither, and is ashamed she ever felt she had to hold back. But maybe it was better that she did, because Jerome's reaction – a

babbling and excited mixture of questions and congratulations –
delights her.

'So *that's* it! That's where you've been at! Oh my God, Ba! I wish
I was there so I could hug the shit out of you!'

'That would be mondo nasty,' she says, and wipes her eyes. The
relief is so great she feels she could float up to her stick-on stars, and
she thinks how good her brother is, how generous. Did she forget
that, or was her head so full of her own concerns that she blocked it
out?

'What about the essay? Did you kill?'

'I did,' Barbara says. Thinking, *You bet I did. They'll read it and toss
it in what Dad calls the circular file.*

'Great, great!'

'Tell me again about the woman whose son disappeared. I can listen
now. You know, with both ears. I wasn't before.'

He tells her not just about Vera Steinman, but recaps the whole
case. He finishes by saying Holly may have, purely by accident, un-
covered a serial killer who operates on the Red Bank Avenue side of
Deerfield Park. Or at the college. Or both.

'And I figured something out,' he says. 'It was bugging the hell out
of me, but it finally clicked into place. You know, like one of those
inkblot pictures that you stare at and stare at, and all at once you see
it's the face of Jesus or Dave Chappelle.'

'What?'

He tells her. They talk a little more, and then Barbara says she wants
to tell her mother and father about the Penley Prize.

'Before you do that, I need you to do something for me,' he says.
'Go down to Dad's old study, where I've been working on the book,
and find the orange flash drive. It's sitting next to the keyboard. Can
you do that?'

'Sure.'

'Plug it in and send me the folder marked PIX, P-I-X. Mara is
thinking the publishers will want photos in the middle of the book,
and they may want to use them for promotion, too.'

'For your tour.'

'Yeah, except if Covid doesn't go away, it's apt to be a virtual tour
on Zoom and Skype.'

'Happy to do it, J.'

'One of em's a photo of the Biograph Theater, with *Manhattan Melodrama* on the marquee. The Biograph is where John Dillinger was shot. Mara thinks it would make a great cover. And Barbara . . .'

'What?'

'I'm so happy for you, sis. I love you.'

Barbara says she feels the same and ends the call. Then she cries. She can't remember ever being quite this happy. Olivia has told her happy poets are usually bad poets, but right now Barbara doesn't care.

July 2, 2021

Bonnie wakes up thirsty and with a mild headache, but nothing like the hangover symptoms Jorge Castro and Cary Dressler felt on waking. Roddy used an injectable ketamine solution on them, but switched to Valium for Ellen and Pete. It's not because of the vicious mornings-after they suffered, he couldn't care less about those, but postmortem samples showed incipient damage to Castro's and Dressler's cellular structure in the thorax and lymph nodes. It hadn't reached their livers, thank God, the liver being the center of regeneration, but those damaged lymph nodes were still worrying. Cellular damage there can conceivably pollute the fat, which he uses for his arthritic hands and Emily uses on her left buttock and leg to soothe the sciatic nerve.

There are many uses for the brains of their livestock, and such organs as the heart and kidneys, but the liver is what matters most, because it is the consumption of the human liver that preserves vitality and lengthens life. Once the liver has been fully awakened, that is, and calf's liver triggers that awakening. Human liver would undoubtedly be even more efficacious, but that would mean taking two people each time, one to donate a liver and the other to feed on it before being slaughtered, and the Harrises have decided that would be much too dangerous. Calf's liver serves very well, being close to the human liver at a cellular level. Pigs' liver is even closer, the DNA nearly indistinguishable, but with pigs there's the danger of prions. The risk is negligible, but neither Rodney or Emily wants to die with prions eating holes in their valuable brains.

Bonnie knows none of this. What she knows is that she's thirsty and her head hurts. Another thing she knows: she's a prisoner. The cell she's in appears to be at one end of someone's basement. It's hard for her to believe it's below the tidy Victorian home of the Professors Harris, but harder not to believe it. The basement is big, lit by fluorescents that have been turned down to a soothing yellow glow. The space in front of the cage is bare, clean cement. Beyond is a flight of stairs, and beyond that is a workshop containing machines she doesn't know the names of, although it seems fairly obvious that they're power tools for cutting and sanding, things like that. The biggest item, on the far side of the room, is a metal box equipped with a hose that goes into the wall next to a small door. She assumes it's an HVAC unit for heating and air conditioning.

Bonnie sits up and massages her temples, trying to ease the headache. Something falls to the futon she woke up on. It's one of her earrings. The other appears to be gone, probably knocked off or pulled off in the struggle. And there *was* a struggle. It's hazy, but she remembers lurching along the front of a deserted building, trying to hold onto consciousness long enough to get away, but Rodney grabbed her and pulled her back.

She looks at the little golden triangle – not real gold, of course, but a pretty thing – and tucks it under the futon. Partly because one earring is no good unless you're a pirate or a gay guy trying to look suave in a singles bar, but also because the three corners are sharp. It might come in handy.

There's a Porta-John in the corner of the cell, and like Jorge Castro, Cary Dressler, and Ellen Craslow before her (Stinky Steinman perhaps not so much), she knows what it means: someone intends for her to be here awhile. It's still hard for her to believe the someone is Professor Rodney Harris, retired biologist and nutritionist. It's easier to believe that Emily is his accomplice . . . or, more likely, he is hers. Because Emily's the Alpha dog in their relationship, and although Em extended herself to make a colleague of Bonnie, if not actually a friend, Bonnie never completely trusted her. Even in her brief time of employment, she tried to do everything right, because she had an idea Emily wasn't a woman you wanted to get crosswise with.

Bonnie examines the bars, home-welded but rock solid. There's a keypad — she can see it by leaning the side of her face against the bars — but there's a plastic cover over it and she can't get it off or even loosen it. Even if she could, happening on the right combination would be like getting all the Powerball numbers.

As did the previous inhabitants of this cell, she sees the camera lens peering down at her, but unlike her predecessors, she doesn't yell at it. She's a smart woman and knows that at some point someone will come. Most likely one of the Harrises. And are they going to apologize, say it's all been a terrible mistake? Unlikely.

Bonnie is very frightened.

There's an orange crate against the far wall with two bottles of Artesia water on it. Jorge Castro and Cary Dressler got Dasani, but Emily insisted on switching to Artesia, because Dasani is owned by Coca-Cola, and they are (according to her) sucking the upstate water table dry. Artesia is locally owned, which makes them more politically correct.

Bonnie opens one of the bottles, drinks half, and recaps it. Then she lifts the lid of the Porta-John and drops her pants. She can't do anything about the camera, so she lowers her head and covers her face as when as a small child she did something naughty, reasoning that if she couldn't see *them*, they couldn't see *her*. She finishes, drinks some more water, and sits on the futon.

With her thirst slaked, she actually feels — strange under the circumstances, but true — rested. She wouldn't go so far as to say refreshed, but rested. She tries to reason why they took her and can't get far. Sex would seem the most obvious motive, but they're *old*. Too old? Maybe not, and if it's sexual at their age, it's got to be something weird. Something that won't end well.

Could it be some kind of experimentation? One requiring human guinea pigs? She's heard around campus that Rodney Harris had a few screws loose — his screamy lectures about meat as the central pillar of nutrition are legendary — but can he be actually insane, like a mad scientist in a horror movie? If so, his laboratory must be somewhere else. What she's looking at is the kind of workshop where a retired oldster might putter around making bookcases or birdhouses. Or cell bars.

Bonnie turns her mind to who might figure out she's missing. Her mother is the most likely, but Penny won't realize something is wrong immediately; they're going through one of their cold snaps. Tom Higgins?

Forget about it, they've been quits for months, and besides, she's heard he's gone. Keisha might, but with the library barely running in low gear thanks to summer break and Covid, Keish might simply assume Bonnie is taking some time off. God knows she has plenty of sick days. Or suppose Keisha thinks Bonnie just decided to drop everything and leave town? Bonnie has talked about wanting to go west, young woman, go west, maybe to San Francisco or Carmel-by-the-Sea, but that's just so much blue-sky talk, and Keisha knows it.

Doesn't she?

A door opens at the top of the basement stairs. Bonnie goes to the bars of the cell. Rodney Harris comes down. Slowly, as if he might break. Emily usually brings the tray the first time, but today her sciatica is so bad that she's lying in bed with her Therma-Brace cinched around her back. Much good that will do; it's quack medicine at best. Pain pills, with their relentless destruction of the brain's synapses, are even worse.

Roddy thawed and stewed most of what remains of Peter Steinman and was able to make her a kind of heart-and-lung porridge sprinkled with bonemeal. It may help some, but not a lot. Human flesh that's been frozen and thawed seems to have little efficacy, and what Em really needs is fresh liver. But the Steinman boy's was harvested long since. Supplies always run out, and the benefits they get from their livestock simply don't last as long as they used to. He hasn't said as much to Emily, but he's sure she knows. She's not a scientist, but she's not dumb.

He stops a safe distance from the cell, drops to one knee, and sets the tray on the floor. When he straightens (with a wince; everything hurts this morning), Bonnie sees a purple bruise on his right cheekbone. It has spread up to his eye and almost down to his jaw. She has always been an even-tempered girl, largely exempt from the strongest emotions. She would have said only her mother could really get her goat, but the sight of that bruise makes her simultaneously furious and savagely happy.

I got you, didn't I? she thinks. *I got you good.*

'Why?' she asks.

Roddy says nothing. Emily has told him that is by far the best course, and she's right. You don't talk to a steer in a pen, and you certainly don't engage in a conversation with one. Why would you? The steer is merely food.

'What did I ever do to you, Professor Harris?'

Nothing at all, he thinks as he goes to get the broom leaning against the stairs.

Bonnie looks at the tray. There's a plastic go-cup lying on its side with a brown envelope tucked into its mouth, maybe some kind of insta-breakfast. The other thing on the tray is a slab of raw meat.

'Is that liver?'

No answer.

The broom is the wide kind that janitors use. He pushes the tray through a hinged flap in the bottom of the cell.

'I like liver,' Bonnie says, 'but with fried onions. And I prefer it cooked.'

He makes no reply, just goes back to the stairs and leans the broom against it. He starts back up.

'Professor?'

He turns to look at her, eyebrows raised.

'That's quite a bruise you've got there.'

He touches it and winces again. This also makes Bonnie happy.

'You know what? I wish I'd knocked your fucking crazy head right off your fucking neck.'

The unbruised side of his face reddens. He seems about to reply but restrains himself. He goes up the stairs and she hears the door close. No, not close; it slams. This also makes her happy.

She pulls the envelope from the go-cup. It's Ka'Chava. She's heard of it but never had any. She guesses she'll have some now. In spite of everything, she's hungry. Crazy but true. She tears off the top of the envelope, dumps it in the cup, and adds water from her other bottle. She stirs it with her finger, thinking the elderly dingbat could at least have provided a spoon. She tries it and finds it quite good.

Bonnie drinks half, then sets the go-cup on the closed lid of the Porta-John. She goes to the bars. Crazy or not, the old prof is a compulsive neatnik. The cement floor doesn't have a single spot of dirt on it. The wrenches are hung on pegs in descending order. So are the screwdrivers. Ditto the three saws – big, medium, and a small one Bonnie believes is called a keyhole saw. Pliers . . . chisels . . . rolls of tape . . . and . . .

Bonnie puts her hand over her mouth. She had been scared; now she's terrified. What she's looking at brings the reality of her situation home to her: she has been imprisoned like a rat in a cage and barring a miracle, she's not getting out alive.

Hanging like trophies on the pegboard next to the rolls of tape are her bike helmet and backpack.

July 27, 2021

1

Holly drives down Ridge Road to a two-hour parking zone, opens her window, and lights a cigarette. Then she calls the Harris residence. A man answers. Holly gives her name and occupation and asks if she could drop by and ask a few questions.

'What's this onguarding?'

'Pardon me?'

'I said what's this regarding, Miss—?'

Holly repeats her name and says she's interested in Cary Dressler. 'I've been working on a case where Mr Dressler's name came up. I went by the bowling alley where he worked—'

'Strike Em Out Lanes,' he says, sounding impatient.

'That's right. I'm trying to track him down. It has to do with a series of auto thefts. I can't go into the details, you understand, but I'd like to talk to him. I saw the picture of your bowling team with Mr Dressler in it, and I just thought you might have some idea where he got off to. I've already talked to Mr Clippard and Mr Welch, so since I'm nearby, I—'

'Dressler has been stealing cars?'

'I really can't go into that, Mr Harris. You *are* Mr Harris, aren't you?'

'*Professor* Harris. I suppose you can come by, but don't plan on staying long. I haven't seen young Mr Dressler in years and I'm quite busy.'

'Thank y—'

But Harris is gone.

2

Roddy puts his phone down and turns to Emily. Her sciatica has relented a bit and she no longer needs the wheelchair, but she's using her cane, her hair needs combing, and Roddy has an unkind thought: *She looks like the old witch in a fairy tale.*

'She's coming,' he says, 'but not about the Dahl girl. It's Dressler she's interested in. *She* says.'

'You don't believe that, do you?'

'Not necessarily, but it makes a degree of sense. She claims to be investigating a series of car things.' He pauses. '*Thefts*, car thefts. It could be. I doubt very much if private detectives work just one case at a time. It wouldn't be payable.' Is that the right word? Roddy decides it is.

'She's got separate cases involving two of the people we've taken? That would be a very large coincidence, wouldn't it?'

'They happen. And why would investigating Bonnie Dahl lead Gibson to the bowling alley? That elf-girl was no bowler.'

'Her name is Gibney. Holly Gibney. Perhaps I should talk to her when she comes.'

Roddy shakes his head. 'You didn't know Dressler. I did. It's me she wants to talk to, and I'll handle it.'

'Will you?' She gives him a searching look. 'You said *onguarding* instead of *regarding*. You . . . I don't exactly know how to say this, my love, but . . .'

'I've slipped a cog. There. I've said it for you. Did you think I wasn't aware? I am, and I'll make allowances.' He touches her cheek.

She presses her hand over his and smiles. 'I'll be watching from upstairs.'

'I know you will. I love you, muffin.'

'I love you, too,' she says, and makes her slow way to the stairs. Her ascent will be even slower, and painful, but she has no intention of having a chairlift installed, like the one in the house of the old bitch down the street. Em can hardly believe Olivia is still alive. And she stole that girl, who appeared to have some talent.

Especially for a black person. For a *negress*.

Emily likes that word.

3

Holly mounts the Harris porch and rings the bell. The door is opened by a tall slim man wearing dad jeans, mocs, and a polo shirt with the Bell College logo on the breast. His eyes are bright and intelligent, but beginning to sink in their sockets. His hair is white, but far from the luxuriant growth Hugh Clippard sports; pink scalp peeks through the comb-strokes. There's the ghost of a bruise on one cheek.

'Ms Gibney,' he says. 'Come into the living room. And you can take off the mask. There's no Clover here. Assuming there is such a thing, which I doubt.'

'Have you been vaccinated?'

He frowns at her. 'My wife and I observe healthy protocols.'

That's answer enough for Holly; she says she'll be more comfortable with her mask on. She wishes she'd worn a pair of her disposable gloves as well, but doesn't want to take them out of her pockets now. Harris is obviously cocked and locked on the subject of Covid. She doesn't want to set him off.

'As you wish.'

Holly follows him down the hall into a big wood-paneled room lit by electric sconces. The drapes are pulled to keep out the strong late-afternoon sun. Central air conditioning whispers. Somewhere light classical music is playing very quietly.

'I'm going to be a bad host and not ask you to sit,' Harris says. 'I'm writing a lengthy response to a rather stupid and badly researched article in *The Quarterly Journal of Nutrition*, and I don't want to lose the thread of my argument. Also, my wife is suffering one of her migraines, so I'd ask you to keep your voice low.'

'I'm sorry,' says Holly, who rarely raises her voice even when she's angry.

'Besides, my hearing is excellent.'

That much is true, Em thinks. She's in the spare bedroom, watching them on her laptop. A teacup-sized camera is hidden behind knick-knacks on the mantel. Emily's most immediate concern is that Rodney will give something away. He's still sharp most of the time, but as the day grows late, he has a tendency to misspeak and grow forgetful. She knows this is common in those who are suffering the onset of Alzheimer's or dementia – the syndrome is called sundowning – but she refuses to believe that can be true of the man she loves. Still, a seed of doubt has been planted. God forbid it should grow.

Holly tells Harris the car-theft story, which she has refined on the way over – like the little girl in the Saki story, romance at short notice is her specialty. She should have used the story with Clippard and Welch, but it came to her too late. She certainly plans to use it when she talks to Ernie Coggins, who interests her the most: still bowling and still married. The wife probably not suffering from sciatica, but it's possible, it's possible.

4

Barbara goes down to their father's old office. Jerome's computer is now on the desk, with papers piled on both sides of it. She assumes the thick stack on the right is the manuscript of his book. She sits down and thumbs through it to the last page: 359. *Jerome wrote all of this*, she marvels, and thinks of her own book of poems, which will run to perhaps a hundred and ten pages, mostly white space . . . assuming it's published at all. Olivia assures her it will be, but Barbara still finds it hard to believe. Poems not about 'the Black experience,' but about coping with horror. *Although sometimes there may not be that much difference*, she thinks, and gives a short laugh.

The orange flash drive is where Jerome said it would be. She turns on the computer, types in Jerome's password (#shizzle#), and waits for it to boot up. The wallpaper is a picture of Jerome and Barbara kneeling on either side of their dog Odell, who has now gone to wherever good dogs go.

She plugs in the drive. There are drafts of his book numbered 1, 2, and 3. There's correspondence. And a file labeled PIX. Barbara opens it and looks at a few photos of their notorious great-grandfather, always dressed to the nines and always wearing a derby hat slightly cocked to the right. *Signifying*, she thinks. There are also photos of an all-Black nightclub where dressed-to-the-nines patrons are jitterbugging (or maybe Lindy Hopping) while the band is knocking it out. She finds the one of the Biograph Theater, and then one of John Dillinger himself, lying on a mortuary slab. *Oough*, as Holly would say. Barbara closes the PIX file, drags it to an email addressed to her brother, and sends it off with a whoosh.

To the left of the computer is a litter of notes, the one on top reading *Call Mara abt promo*. The ones directly underneath appear to be about Chicago, Indianapolis, and Detroit in the thirties, each with many references to books about those places during Prohibition and the Depression. *Hope you're not overdoing it, J*, Barbara thinks.

Beneath the notes is a MapQuest printout of Deerfield Park and the surrounding area. Curious, Barbara picks it up. It has nothing to do with Jerome's book and everything to do with Holly's current case. There are three red dots with Jerome's neat printing below each of them.

Bonnie D, July 1 2021 is on the east side of the park, across from the overgrown few acres known as the Thickets.

The dot for *Ellen C, November 2018* is on the Bell College campus, placed directly on top of the Memorial Union, home of the Belfry. Barbara and some of her friends sometimes go there for burgers after using the Reynolds Library. The Reynolds reference room is good, and the computer room is awesome.

The last red dot is for *Peter S, Late November 2018*. Barbara also knows this location: it's the Dairy Whip, considered *déclassé* by high school students, but a favorite hangout of the younger fry.

One of them could have been me, she thinks.

Her chore in here is done. She shuts down the computer and gets up to leave. Then she sits down again and picks up the MapQuest printout. There's a coffee mug filled with pens on the desk. She takes the red one Jerome must have used to mark the map. She makes another dot on Ridge Road, across from Olivia Kingsbury's house. *Because that's where she saw him the night she was thinking about the poem she says was her last good one.*

Beneath the dot she prints: *Jorge Castro, October 2012*. Even as she does it, she feels she's being silly.

Probably Castro just said 'Fuck this stupid English Department' and left. Also 'Fuck Emily Harris and her unsuccessfully disguised homophobia, too.'

But with Castro added to Jerome's map, she sees something interesting and a tiny bit disturbing. The dots almost seem to circle the park. It's true that Bonnie's came a bit sooner than the others, summer instead of fall, but didn't Barbara see somewhere – maybe on that Netflix show *Mindhunter* – that homicidal maniacs have a tendency to wait a shorter and shorter time between their kills? Like drug addicts shooting up at ever more frequent intervals?

Ellen C and Peter S don't fit the pattern; they came close together. Maybe because the killer didn't get whatever he wanted from one of them? Because he or she didn't fully turn on the killer's bloodlight?

You're giving yourself the creeps, Barbara thinks. *Seeing monsters – like Chet Ondowsky – where there's really nothing but shadows.*

Still, she probably should pass on the information about Jorge Castro. She picks up her phone to call Holly, and it rings in her hand. It's Marie Duchamp. Olivia is in Kiner Memorial with a-fib. This time it's serious. Barbara forgets about calling Holly and hurries downstairs, telling her mother that she needs to use the car. When Tanya asks why, Barbara says a friend is in the hospital and she'll explain later. She has good news, but that must also wait until later.

'Is it a scholarship? Did you get a scholarship?'

'No, it's something else.'

'All right, dear,' Tanya says. 'Drive carefully.' It's her mantra.

5

Holly asks Rodney Harris if he has any idea where Cary Dressler may be now. Did he talk about plans to leave the city? Did he sometimes (this is a fresh bit of embroidery) appear to have large amounts of cash?

'I know he had a drug habit,' she confides. 'Thieves often do.'

'He seemed like a nice enough fellow,' Harris says. He's staring into space, a slight frown creasing his brow. Picture of a man trying to remember something that will help her. 'Didn't know him well but I knew he used drugs. Only *cannabis sativa*, so he said, but there may have been other ones . . .?'

His raised eyebrows invite Holly to confide, but she only smiles.

'Certainly cannabis is a known gateway for stronger substances,' he goes on in a pontifical tone. 'Not always, but it *is* habituating, and impairs cognitive development. It also causes adverse structural changes to the hippocampus, the temperature lobe's center of learning and memory. This is well known.'

Upstairs, Em winces. *Temporal lobe, dear . . . and don't get carried away. Please.*

Gibney doesn't appear to notice and it's as if Roddy has heard Em. 'Pardon the lecture, Ms Gibson. I will now climb down from my hobby horse.'

Holly laughs politely. She touches one of the gloves in her pocket and wishes again she could put them on. She doesn't want Professor Harris to think she's Howard Hughes, but the idea that everything she touches could be crawling with Covid-19 or the new Delta variant won't go away. Meanwhile Harris continues.

'Some of the other members of my team used to go out back with Dressler and "blow the joint," as they say. So did some of the women.'

'The Hot Witches?'

Harris's frown deepens. 'Yes, them. And others. One guesses they *fancied* him. But as I may have said, I didn't really know him. He was friendly enough, and he sometimes subbed in for a wounded warrior, so to speak, but we were mere acquaintances. I had no idea of his cash situation and I'm afraid I have no idea where he may have gone.'

Leave it there, love, Emily thinks. *See her to the door.*

Roddy takes Holly's elbow and does just that. 'Now I'm afraid I must return to my labors.'

'I totally understand,' Holly says. 'It was a long shot at best.' She reaches into her bag and gives him her card, careful not to touch his fingers. 'If you think of anything that might help, please give me a call.'

When they reach the door, Emily switches to the hall camera. Roddy asks, 'May I ask how you plan to proceed?'

Don't, Emily thinks. *Oh, don't, Roddy. There may be quicksand if you go there.*

But the woman – who seems too innocuous for Emily to be *too* worried – tells Roddy she really can't talk about it, and offers her elbow. With a smile that says he must suffer fools, Roddy touches it with his own.

'Thank you very much for your time, Mr Harris.'

'Not at all, Ms . . . what was your name again?'

'Gibney.'

'Enjoy the rest of your day, Ms Gibney, and I wish you success.'

6

As soon as Holly hears the front door close behind her, while she's still on the walk, she's reaching deep in her pocket for the hand sanitizer underneath the nitrile glove she wishes she'd worn. Forgetting her mask with the Dairy Whip boys was bad, but at least they were outside; her conversation with Rodney Harris happened in a room where the central air conditioning could waft the virus that had killed her mother anywhere, including into her nose and thus down to her smoke-polluted lungs.

You're being silly and hypochondriacal, she thinks, but that is the voice of her mother, who died of the fracking virus.

She finds what she was looking for, a little bottle of Germ-X, and pulls it out of her pocket. She squirts a dollop into her palm and rubs both hands vigorously, thinking that the sharp smell of alcohol, which used to terrify her as a child because it meant a shot was coming, is now the smell of comfort and conditional safety.

Upstairs, Emily is watching this and smiling. Not much can amuse her these days, given the constant pain in her back and down her leg, but seeing that mousy little bitch frantically dry-washing her hands? *That's* funny.

July 3, 2021

1

The Harrises' latest 'guest' doesn't eat the raw liver, and she tries to ration what remains of her water, but eventually both bottles are empty. She swirls her finger around the go-cup, getting the last of the Ka'Chava, but that only makes her thirstier. She's hungry, too.

Bonnie tries to remember what she last ate. A tuna-and-egg sandwich, wasn't it? Bought in the Belfry and eaten outside on one of the benches. She would give anything to have that sandwich back right now, not to mention the bottle of Diet Pepsi she bought at the Jet Mart. She would chug the whole sixteen ounces. Only there is no Diet Pepsi, and no phone. Only her helmet and backpack (looking like it's been emptied), hanging on the wall with the tools.

The raw liver starts to look good to her even after God knows how many hours at room temperature, so she hooks up the flap in the bottom of the cell and pushes it out, giving the tray a final shove with her tented fingers so it will be beyond her reach. *Get thee behind me, Satan*, she thinks, and swallows. She can hear the dry click in her throat and thinks that the liver must still be full of liquid. She can imagine it running down her throat, cooling it. Knowing the salt content would only add to her thirst doesn't help much. She goes back to the futon and lies down, but she keeps looking at the dish with the liver on it. After awhile she drifts into a thin, dream-haunted doze.

Eventually Rodney Harris comes back and she wakes up. He's wearing pajamas with firetrucks on them, plus robe and slippers, so Bonnie wrongly assumes it's evening. She further assumes that it's now been a day since they drugged and kidnapped her. The longest and most terrible day of her life, partly because she doesn't know what the hell is going on but mostly because all she's had for the last twenty-four hours are two bottles of water and a cup of Ka'Chava.

'I want some water,' she says, trying not to croak. 'Please.'

He takes the broom and slides the tray back through the flap. 'Eat your liver. Then you can have water.'

'It's raw and been sitting out all day! All last night, too . . . I guess. Is it the third? It is, isn't it?'

He doesn't answer that, but from his pocket he takes a bottle of Artesia water and holds it up. Bonnie doesn't want to give him the satisfaction of licking her lips but can't help it. After its day at room temperature the piece of liver looks like it's melting.

'Eat it. All of it. Then I'll give you the water.'

Bonnie decides she was half-right. It's not sex, but it is some kind of weird experiment. She's heard people at the college talk about how Professor Harris is a little bit gaga on the subject of what he calls 'perfect nutritional balance,' and ignored it as the usual bullshit – this professor is eccentric, that professor is obsessive-compulsive, the other prof picks his nose, there's a video of it on TikTok, check it out, it's hilarious. Now she wishes she'd listened. He's not just gaga, he's over-the-moon crazy. She thinks eating a piece of liver *tartare* is the least of her problems. She has to get out of here. She has to escape. And that means being smart and not giving in to panic. Her life depends on it.

This time she's able to restrain herself from licking her lips. She goes to one knee and pushes the tray back through the slot. 'Bring me a fresh piece and I'll eat it. *With* water, though. To wash it down.'

He looks offended. 'I assure you that liver isn't . . . isn't . . .' He struggles for what he wants to say, jaw moving from side to side. 'Isn't *microbially damaged*. In fact, like many other cuts of meat, calf's liver is *best* at room temperature. Have you never heard of aged steak?'

'It's turning *gray*!'

'You're being troublesome, Ms Dahl. And you are in no position to make deals.'

Bonnie grasps her head as if it hurts. Which it does, because of hunger and thirst. Not to mention fear. 'I'm trying to meet you halfway, is all. You have some reason for what you're doing, I guess—'

'I most certainly *do!*' he cries, his voice rising.

'—and I'm agreeing to do what you want, *but not that piece.* I won't!'

He turns and stomps back up the stairs, pausing only once to glare at her over his shoulder.

Bonnie swallows, and listens to the dry click in her throat. *I sound like a cricket,* she thinks. *One dying of thirst.*

2

Emily is in the kitchen. Her face is drawn with pain, and she looks her age. More than her age, actually. Roddy is shocked. For it to come to this after all they've done to hold senescence at bay! It's not fair that their special meals, so loaded with life-extending goodness, should wear off so quickly. It was three years between Castro and Dressler, and three years (give or take) between Dressler and the Steinman boy. Now they have Bonnie Dahl, and it's not only been less than three years but the symptoms of old age (he thinks of them as symptoms) have been creeping up for months.

'Is she eating it?'

'No. She says she will if I give her a fresh piece. We have one, of course, after the Chaslum girl it seemed prudent to keep an extra on hand—'

'Craslow, Craslow!' Em corrects him in a nagging voice that's utterly unlike her . . . at least when it's just the two of them and she's not in agony. 'Give it to her! I can't bear this pain!'

'Just a little longer,' he soothes. 'I want her thirstier. Thirst makes livestock amenable.' He brightens. 'And she may yet eat that one. She pushed it through the slot, but I noticed that this time she left it in reach.'

Emily has been standing but now she sits down with a wince and a gasp. The cords on her neck stand out. 'All right. If it must be, it must be.' She hesitates. 'Roddy, is this diet of ours really doing anything? It hasn't been our imaginations all along? Some sort of psychosomatic cure that's in our minds rather than our bodies?'

'When your migraines cease, is that psychosomatic?'

'No . . . at least I don't think—'

'And your sciatica! Your arthritis . . . and mine! Do you think I like this?' He holds up his hands. The knuckles are swollen, and he can straighten his fingers only with an effort. 'Do you think I like searching for words I know perfectly well? Or going into my office and realizing I don't know what I came in *for*? You've seen the results for yourself!'

'It used to last longer,' Emily whispers. 'That's all I'm saying. If she eats the liver tonight . . . the piece that's down there now or the one in the refrigerator . . . then tomorrow?'

Roddy knows that forty-eight hours would be better, and ninety-six before harvest is optimum, but the Dahl girl is young and the awakening of her own liver should happen quickly, speeding vital nutrients to every part of her body with every beat of her healthy young heart. They know this from the Steinman boy.

Besides, he can't stand to see his wife suffer.

'Tomorrow night,' he says. 'Assuming she eats.'

'Assuming,' Emily says. She's thinking of the intransigent bitch. The intransigent *vegan* bitch.

After all these years, Roddy can read her mind. 'She's not like the Black girl. She more or less agreed to eat if I gave her water—'

'More or less,' Em says, and sighs.

Roddy doesn't seem to hear her. He's staring off into the distance in a way she worries about more and more. It's like he's come unplugged. At last he says, 'But I must be careful. She hasn't asked enough questions. In fact, she's hardly asked any. Like Chaslow. There's been no begging and no screaming. Also like Chaslow. It wouldn't do to slip up.'

'Then don't,' Emily says. She takes his hand. 'I'm depending on you. And it's *Craslow*.'

He gives her a smile. 'We won't celebrate July Fourth this year, dear heart, but on the sixth . . .' His smile widens. 'On the sixth we feast.'

3

Roddy returns to the basement at ten o'clock that night, after assisting Emily back up the stairs. Now she's in bed, where she'll lie wakeful and in pain for most of the night, managing an hour or two of thin and unsatisfying sleep. If that. He assures himself that her questioning of the sacramental meals is caused not by rational thinking but by her pain, but it still bothers him.

He's holding the backup slab of liver on a plate, having seen from the video feed that Dahl has continued to refuse the first one. He wishes they had more time, both for her body's nutrients to awaken and because it's not good to give in to a prisoner's demands, but Emily can't wait for long. Soon she'll be insisting that he take her to a doctor for pain pills, and those things are death in a bottle.

He sets the plate down and tells Dahl to push out the plastic Ka'Chava go-cup. Dahl does it without asking why. She really is too much like the Chesley woman for his taste. There's a watchfulness about her that he doesn't like and will not trust.

From his robe pocket he takes a bottle of Artesia and pours some – not much – into the cup. Then he takes the broom and begins pushing the cup toward her. He has to be careful not to tip it over. The last thing he wants is for this bitter little comedy to turn into a farce. She lifts the flap and reaches out. 'Just hand it to me, Professor.'

The surest sign that he's slipping is that he almost does it. Then he chuckles and says, 'I think not.'

When the cup is close enough, she grabs it and chugs it. Two gulps is all it takes.

'Eat your liver and I'll give you the rest. Refuse and you won't see me again until tomorrow night.' An empty threat, but Dahl doesn't know that.

'You promise you'll give me the rest of the water?'

'Hand to heart. Assuming you don't vomit. And if you vomit into the Porta-Potty after I'm gone, Em will see it. Then we'll have trouble.'

'Professor, I'm already in trouble. Wouldn't you agree?'

She worries him more and more. Scares him a little, too. Ridiculous, but there it is. Instead of answering, he uses the broom to push in the liver. Dahl doesn't hesitate. She picks it up, sinks her teeth into the raw flesh, and tears off a bite. She chews.

He looks at the tiny droplets of blood on her lower lip with fascination. On July fifth, he will roll those lips in unbleached flour and fry them in a small skillet, perhaps with mushrooms and onions. Lips are fine sources of collagen, and hers will do wonders for his knees and elbows, even his creaky jaw. In the end this worrisome girl is going to be worth the trouble. She is going to donate some of her youth.

She takes another bite, chews, swallows. 'Not terrible,' she says. 'It's got a thicker taste than sauteed liver. Dense, somehow. Are you enjoying watching me eat, asshole?'

Roddy doesn't reply, but the answer is yes.

'I'm not getting out of this, am I? There's no sense saying I'll never tell a soul, and all that, is there?'

Roddy is prepared for this. He widens his eyes in surprise. 'Of course you will. This is a government research project. There'll be certain tests and of course you *will* have to sign a nondisclosure form, but once you've done that—'

He's interrupted by her laughter, which is both humorous and hysterical. 'If I believe that, you've got a bridge you want to sell me, I suppose. In Brooklyn, gently used. Just give me the fucking water when I finish this.'

At last her voice trembles, and her eyes take on the shine of tears. Roddy is relieved.

'Keep your promise.'

July 27, 2021

1

Holly returns to her former parking spot in the two-hour zone and smokes a cigarette with the door open and her feet on the pavement. It comes to her that there's something exceptionally perverse about taking all the proper precautions against Covid and then filling her lungs with this carcinogenic crap.

I have to stop, she thinks. *I really do. Just not today.*

The Golden Oldies bowling team is probably a bust. It's hard for her to remember now why she ever thought it would lead to something. Was it just because Cary Dressler also visited the Jet Mart Bonnie used on a regular basis? Well, Dressler's also gone, leaving his moped behind, but those are pretty thin connections. It certainly doesn't seem to her that Roddy Harris is a likely candidate for the Red Bank Predator (if there even is such a person). She doesn't know if Harris's wife suffers from sciatica as well as migraines – finding out might be possible, although Holly doesn't think it's a priority – but it's pretty obvious Harris has got his own problems. *Onguarding* for *regarding*, *Clover* for *Covid*, *temperature lobe* for *temporal lobe*, forgetting her name. There's also the way he simply stopped a couple of times, frowning and looking into space. It doesn't necessarily mean he's suffering the onset of Alzheimer's disease, but the age is right. Also . . .

'That's the way it started with Uncle Henry,' she says.

But since she's started running the Oldies down, she might as well finish the job. She snuffs her cigarette in her portable ashtray and heads for the turnpike. Ernie Coggins lives in Upriver, which is only four exits away. A quick run. But now that Uncle Henry has come into her mind, she can't stop thinking about him. When was the last time she visited? In the spring, wasn't it? Yes. Her mother nagged her into it – *guilt-tripped* her into it – last April, before Charlotte got sick.

Holly gets to the Upriver exit, slows, then changes her mind and continues north toward Covington, location of both her mother's house and the Rolling Hills Elder Care Center, where Uncle Henry is now living (if you want to call it that). It's also where another member of the Golden Oldies bowling team is living, so she can get two for the price of one. Of course Victor Anderson may not be any more *compos mentis* than her uncle; according to Hugh Clippard, Anderson suffered a stroke, and if he's in long-term care, he's probably not in recovery mode. Holly can check him off her list, though, and talk to Ernie Coggins tomorrow, when she's fresh. Plus, turnpike driving soothes her, and when Holly's in a tranquil state of mind, things sometimes occur to her.

But the whole thing is starting to feel like a wild goose-chase.

Her phone lights up three times on the four-hour drive to the same Days Inn where she stayed three nights before. She doesn't answer even though her car is Bluetooth-equipped. One call is from Jerome. One is from Pete Huntley. The third is from Penny Dahl, who undoubtedly wants an update. And deserves one.

2

By the time she gets to Covington, Holly's stomach is growling. She enters the Burger King drive-thru and orders without hesitation when her turn comes. She has favorites at all the fast food franchises. At Burger King it's always a Big Fish, a Hershey's Pie, and a Coke. As she approaches the payment window, she reaches into her left pocket for one of her emoji gloves and only finds the bottle of Germ-X. She grabs a Kleenex out of the center console and uses that to offer her money and take her change. The girl in the window gives her a pitying look. Holly finds a glove in her right pocket and puts it on just in time to drive up to the second window and take her food. She has no idea what happened to the missing glove and doesn't care. There's a whole box of them in the trunk, courtesy of Barbara Robinson.

She checks in at the motel and has to laugh at herself when she realizes that she has once again arrived without luggage. She could make another trip to Dollar General but decides against it, telling herself the stock market won't crash if she wears the same undies two days in a row. There's no point in going to the Elder Care Center tonight, either; visiting hours end at seven PM.

She eats slowly, enjoying her fish sandwich, enjoying the Hershey's Pie even more. There's nothing like empty calories, she sometimes thinks, when you're feeling confused and unsure of what to do next.

Oh, you know perfectly well what to do next, she thinks, and calls Penny Dahl. Who asks if she's made any progress.

'I don't know,' Holly says. This is, as Uncle Henry used to say, the God's honest.

'Either you have or you haven't!'

Holly doesn't want to tell Penny that her daughter might have become the latest victim of a serial killer. It may come to that – in her heart Holly is convinced it *will* come to that – but while she's still unsure it would be too cruel.

'I'm going to give you a full report, but I want another twenty-four hours. Are you all right with that?'

'No, I'm not *all right with that*! If you've found something, I have a right to know. I'm *paying* you, for Christ's sake!'

Holly says, 'Let me put it another way, Penny. Can you *live* with that?'

'I should fire you,' Penny grumbles.

'That's your prerogative,' Holly says, 'but an end-of-case report would still take me twenty-four hours to prepare. I'm chasing a couple of things.'

'Promising things?'

'I'm not sure.' She would like to say something more hopeful and can't.

There's silence. Then Penny says, 'I expect to hear from you by nine tomorrow night, or I *will* fire you.'

'Fair enough. It's just that right now I don't have my—'

Ducks in a row is how she means to finish, but Penny ends the call before she can.

3

Next, Holly calls Jerome. Before she can even say hello, he asks if she's talked to Barbara.

'No – should I?'

'Well, she's got some pretty amazing news, but I want her to tell you. Spoiler alert, she's also been writing, and just happens to be in the running for a literary prize with big bucks attached. Twenty-five K.'

'Are you kidding me?'

'I'm not. And don't you tell Mom and Dad. She may not have told them yet. But that's not why I called. I finally figured out what was bugging me about that van. The one in the security footage from the store?'

'What was it?'

'The body is too high. It's not jacked like one of those monster trucks, but it's noticeable – two or three feet more than normal. I looked online and the only vans like that are custom jobs for people with disabilities. The chassis gets raised to allow for a wheelchair ramp.'

4

Holly calls Pete from beside the ice machine, where she's having a smoke. He has come to the same conclusion about the van as Jerome, only he calls that kind of vehicle 'a crip wagon.' Holly winces, thanks him, and asks him how he's doing. He says he's like the guy in that Chicago song, feeling stronger every day. It crosses her mind that he's trying to convince himself.

She puts out her cigarette and sits on the stairs to think. Now she has one almost-concrete thing to tell Penny tomorrow night: it seems more and more likely that Bonnie was taken by someone pretending to be disabled. Maybe all of them were. Or maybe not just pretending? Holly thinks of something Imani said: *Poor old lady looked like she was in pain. She said she wasn't, but I know sciatica when I see it.*

She wishes now she had gotten eyes on Emily Harris. She should check at the college to see if anyone knows anything about her physical condition, and will be sure to get a good look at Ernie Coggins's wife when she talks to him tomorrow.

Back in her room, she lies on the bed and calls Barbara. Her call goes straight to voicemail. Holly asks for a callback before ten thirty, when she'll shut off her phone, say her evening prayer, and go to sleep. Then she calls Jerome back. 'I can't get Barbara, and my curiosity is killing me. Tell me what's going on.'

'It's really Barbara's news, Holly . . .'

'Pretty please? With sugar on it? *Vanilla* sugar?'

'Okay, but only if you promise to act surprised when Barb tells you.'

'I promise.'

So Jerome tells Holly how Barbara has been writing poetry in secret for a long time and met with Olivia Kingsbury—

'Olivia Kingsbury?' Holly exclaims, sitting up straight. 'Holy frijoles!'

'You know her, I take it.'

'Not personally, but my God, Jerome, she's one of America's greatest poets! I'm amazed that Barbara got up the courage to approach her, but good for her!'

'Barb's never been short on guts.'

'When I was a teenager trying to write my own poems, I read everything of Kingsbury's I could get my hands on! I didn't know she was still alive!'

'Almost a hundred, Barb says. Anyway, this Kingsbury checked out Barbara's poetry and agreed to mentor her. I don't know how long that went on, but the end result was Barb got put up for this prize, the Penworth or something—'

'The *Penley* Prize,' Holly says. She's awestruck and delighted for her friend, who has done all of this and managed to keep it a dead secret.

'Yeah, that sounds right. But don't bother asking what I've been up to, Hollyberry, my hundred thousand dollars and all. Not to mention my glitzy weekend in Montauk coming up. You wouldn't want to hear about the party where Spielberg might show up, or any of that boring old stuff.'

Holly does, of course, and they talk for almost half an hour. He tells her about his lunch at the Blarney Stone, the advance check handover, discussions about his book's launch and plans for promotion, plus a possible interview with *The American Historical Review*, a prospect that excites and terrifies him in equal measure.

When they have exhausted what he calls Jerome's Excellent New York Adventure, he asks her to update him on the case. She does, finishing by confessing that her investigation of the bowling team is probably a one-way trip down a blind alley. Jerome disagrees.

'Valid line of investigation, Hol. Dressler worked there. He was *targeted*. I think they all were. No, I'm sure.'

'Maybe,' Holly says, 'but I doubt if it was by an elderly bowler. The one I'm seeing tomorrow is actually a stroke victim. I guess I was hoping one of them is protecting a younger relative or friend. Protecting or enabling.'

The truth is, she's still hoping that. She has less than a day before she needs to bring her client up to date, and she'd like to have something concrete to tell Penny. That isn't the most important thing, though. She wants something concrete to tell *herself*.

5

While Holly is talking to Jerome, Barbara Robinson is sitting with Marie Duchamp in a waiting room at Kiner Memorial. What they're waiting to find out is whether or not the docs have been able to regulate Olivia's heartbeat. They are also waiting – although neither of them say it – to find out if the old poet is still alive.

Barbara calls home and gets her father. She tells Jim that she's in the hospital, waiting to get news about an old friend. A *very* old friend named Olivia Kingsbury. That's bad, but there's also good news. She tells him to call Jerome and he'll explain everything, but now she and Olivia's caregiver are expecting to hear from the doctor about Olivia's condition at any time.

'Are you all right, honey?' Jim asks.

The answer is no, but she says yes. He asks when she'll be home. Barbara says she doesn't know, repeats that she's fine, and ends the call. To pass the time, she checks her voicemails. She has one from Holly but doesn't want to talk to her friend yet. She didn't even want to talk to her dad. She's trying to concentrate all her psychic force on keeping Olivia alive. Undoubtedly stupid, but who knows? There really are more things in heaven and earth than most people believe, Hamlet was right about that. Barbara has seen some of them for herself.

She also has a text from Holly, and to this she replies, sending off a brief two-word response just as Olivia's doctor comes in and approaches them. One look at his face tells Barbara and Marie that the news is bad.

6

While Barbara is reading Holly's text and sending off her brief reply, Emily Harris is standing at the bedroom window and looking down at Ridge Road. When Roddy comes in she turns to him, crosses the room (slowly but steadily, only limping a little), and gives him a hug.

'Someone's feeling better,' Roddy says.

She smiles. 'Little by slowly, my dear. Little by slowly. The detective woman didn't seem exactly prepossessing, did she? With her mask and her prissy little questions?'

'She did not.'

'But we must keep an eye out for her. I tend to think you're right, that she may be investigating Dressler and Dahl as separate cases for separate clients, but I still find it hard to believe. And if she was here partly because of the Dahl girl and didn't say so, it's because she suspects something.'

They walk to the window together and look out at the nighttime street. Rodney Harris is thinking that if what they have done – what they are *doing* – comes out, they would be branded as crazy. His academic reputation, built up over decades, would come crashing down.

Emily, the far more practical member of their partnership, is still thinking about Bonnie Dahl. Something else is nagging at her, but she ignores it.

'What could the Gibney woman find out? Not much. Maybe nothing. Dahl did some secretarial work for me after Christmas, but only for a short time, and I paid cash. I asked her to keep quiet about it for that reason. Reminded her that it was undeclared income.'

'Before Christmas, too,' Roddy says. 'As a . . . you know . . .'

'As an elf, yes. For the party. But there were at least a dozen elves, all paid in cash, and they were forbidden to post about it on social media.'

Roddy snorts. 'You might as well tell the wind not to blow.'

Em admits that this is true, young people post everything, including photographs of their private parts, but she knows Bonnie Dahl never posted about her job as a Christmas elf. Not on Facebook, Instagram, or her Twitter feed. Emily has checked, but that's not all. 'She knew the secretarial job was in the offing, and she didn't want to lose it.'

'She may have told her mother.'

It's Em's turn to snort. 'Not that one, she thought her mother was a meddling bitch, and the boyfriend is out of the picture. The Gibney woman doesn't know about our relationship – our *brief* relationship – with the Dahl girl. At least she didn't this afternoon. Did you see how afraid she was to touch you? What a mouse!' Emily laughs, then winces and clutches the small of her back.

'My poor honey,' Rodney says. 'What about a little fresh cream for your ouchies?'

She gives him a grateful smile. 'That would be good. And Roddy? Do you still have Thing One?'

'Yes.'

'Carry it. Just in case. Don't forget!' He forgets so much these days.

'I'll carry it and I won't forget. Do you still have Thing Two?'

'Yes.' She kisses him. 'Now help me off with my nightgown.'

7

Bill Hodges told Holly once that a case was like an egg.

This was near the end of his life, when he was in a lot of pain and on a lot of medication. He was ordinarily a practical man – a cop first, last, and always – but when he was high on the morph, he had a tendency to speak in metaphors. Sitting at his bedside, Holly listened carefully. She wanted everything he could teach her. Every last thing.

'Most cases are fragile, the way eggs are fragile. Why? Because most criminals are dopes. When it comes to doing dirt, even the ones who are smart are dopes. Otherwise they wouldn't do dirt in the first place. So you treat a case like an egg. You crack it, you beat it, you put it in a pan with some butter. Then you make yourself a nice little omelet.'

Holly's case starts to crack in her Days Inn room as she's kneeling by her bed and saying her prayers.

July 4, 2021

1

Rodney Harris is the chef of the family, which is good because Emily is still suffering severe sciatic pain. When he asked her to rate it on the universal pain scale of one to ten, she told him it was currently standing at a twelve. And she looks it, with her eyes deeply sunken and her skin stretched so taut over her cheekbones that it shines. He tells her to just hang on, their current prisoner ate all of the liver last night and held it down. He says Emily's relief will come soon.

Tonight Chef Harris is making his famous garlic-butter lamb chops. Accompanying them will be fresh green beans garnished with bacon bits. The smell is wonderful and he's sure the Dahl girl is getting it, because the basement door is open and he's set a fan on the counter to blow across the top of the cast iron skillet where the lamb chops are sauteing.

He goes to the fridge and takes out the bottle of Diet Pepsi which was Bonnie's final purchase. It's nice and cold. He takes it down the stairs, going slow and holding onto the railing. His hips aren't as bad as poor Em's sciatica, but they're bad enough. And his sense of balance just isn't what it used to be. He thinks the cause may be some slight atrophy in the middle ear. That will also be better soon.

Dahl is standing at the bars of the cell. Her blond hair is clumpy and has lost most of its shine. Her face is haggard and pale. 'Where have you been?' she croaks, as if she's in charge and he's the butler. 'I've been down here all day!'

Roddy thinks that's a nonsensical thing to say – where else would she have been all day? – but he smiles. 'I've been rather busy. Writing a reply to a stupid article.'

He's always writing replies to stupid articles, and it's always like shouting into the void. Yet what can one do but soldier on? In any case he doubts if Bonnie Dahl cares much about *his* problems just now. Which is understandable. God knows when she last ate before the liver. She's hungry and terribly thirsty. He could tell her that her problems will soon be over, but he doubts if it would comfort her.

'Dinner is almost ready. Not liver this time, but—'

'Lamb,' she says. 'I can smell it and it's driving me crazy. I think you *want* me to smell it. If you mean to kill me, why don't you just do it and stop the torture?'

'It's not my intention to torture you.' This is true. He doesn't care one way or the other. She's *livestock*, for heaven's sake. 'Look what I brought you. Slake your thirst, cleanse your palette, and I'll bring you something much nicer than raw liver.'

The hell he will. Dahl is meant to die with a pure liver and an empty stomach. He puts the bottle of Diet Pepsi down and uses the broom to roll it carefully through the flap at the bottom of the cell. She bends, grabs it, and looks at it with greed and suspicion.

'Still sealed just as it came from the store,' Roddy says. 'See for yourself. I would have brought you one with sugar – for the energy, you know – but we don't keep soda in the house.'

Bonnie twists the cap, breaking the seal, and drinks. She doesn't notice the dot of glue sealing the minute hole where the hypodermic went in, and she's chugged over half the sixteen-ounce bottle before she stops and looks at him. 'This doesn't taste right.'

'Drink it all. Then I'll bring you lamb chops and green be—'

She flings the bottle through the bars and misses him by inches. Even only half-full, that would have left a bruise as nasty as the one she's already inflicted on him.

'What was in it? What did you give me?'

He doesn't answer. She's had nothing to eat except for the pound of liver yesterday, and nothing to drink today at all. Even though it's in solution instead of injected, the Valium, a big dose, hits her fast. Her knees begin to buckle after only three minutes of quite amazing profanity. She holds herself up by the bars, the considerable muscles in her arms bulging.

'Why?' she manages. '*Why?*'

'Because I love my wife.' He pauses, then adds, 'And myself, of course. I love myself. Pleasant dreams, Bonnie.'

She finally goes all the way down. Or so it seems. It would be prudent to be very careful with this one; she's young and he's old.

Give her some time.

2

Upstairs in their bedroom, Emily is curled on her side with one leg – the one with the inflamed sciatic nerve – bent to her stomach and the other outstretched. It's the only position that gives her any relief at all.

'She's out,' Rodney says.

'Are you sure? You must be very sure!'

From his pocket he takes a hypodermic needle. 'I intend to add some of this. Better safe than sorry.'

'But don't spoil her!' Emily reaches out to him. 'Don't spoil the meat! Don't spoil her *liver*! I need it, Roddy! I need it!'

'I know,' he says. 'Be strong, my love. It won't be long now.'

3

Going down the basement stairs, Roddy hears big sloppy snores. He judges them not to be the snores of someone faking sleep. Still, care must be taken. He pushes the handle of the broom through the flap and pokes her. No reaction. Again, harder. Still no reaction. He bends, hypodermic in one hand, and pushes the other through the flap. He takes her fingers and pulls her hand out. She grasps him by the wrist . . . but weakly. Then her fingers relax.

Take no chances with this one, he thinks, and injects her wrist. Just half the contents of the hypo. Then he waits.

Five minutes later he punches the code on the cell door, thinking that if she can put up a fight after a double dose of sedative, she's Supergirl. He would still like Emily to be standing by with the gun, but she's currently not capable of getting down the basement stairs. It would be nice to have an elevator, but they've never even discussed it. How would they explain the cell at the end of the basement to the workmen? Or the woodchipper?

There's no problem. Bonnie Dahl isn't Supergirl; she's out cold. Roddy takes her arms and drags her across the basement to the small door beside his racked wall of tools. Inside the next room, a fifty-gallon plastic bag hangs limp from the end of the woodchipper's ejector hose. In the middle of the room is an operating table. There are more tools in here, but these are of a lab and surgical variety.

The last part of this operation – the operation before the operation, so to speak – is the most difficult: getting the unconscious young woman on the table. Roddy manages to lift her one hundred and forty pounds, back creaking and hips screaming. For one terrifying moment he thinks he's going to drop her. Then he thinks of Em, lying in their bed with one leg drawn up, her face stamped with insupportable pain, and with a final effort he rolls Dahl onto the table. She almost tumbles off the other side, which would be a horrible joke. He grabs her hair in one hand and her thigh in the other and pulls her back. She gives a furry, guttural moan and a word that might be *mom*. He thinks how often they call for their mothers at the end, even if the mother in question is a bad one. The Steinman boy certainly did. Although the Steinman boy only became necessary because they didn't understand how crazily devoted Ellen Craslow was to her stupid vegan diet.

Roddy bends over, panting and hoping he won't have a cardiac event. *We should have a lift in* here, he thinks. It's true, but they could explain the livestock cage to lift installers no more than they could explain it to elevator installers. When his heartbeat finally slows, he clamps her wrists and her ankles. Then he sets out the pans for her organs, takes a scalpel, and begins cutting off her clothes.

July 27, 2021

1

Holly has reached the point in her prayers where she's telling God she still misses Bill Hodges when the universe throws her another rope.

Her phone starts playing its little tune. She doesn't recognize the number and almost rejects the call, thinking it will be some guy from India who wants her to extend her car's warranty or has an offer for a can't-miss Covid cure, but she's on a case – *chasing* the case – and so she takes it, prepared to hit end the minute the pitch starts.

'Hello? Is this Holly? Holly Gibney?'

'It is. Who's this?'

'Randy?' Like he's not completely sure of his own identity. 'Randy Holsten? You came around asking about Tom? And his girlfriend, that Bonnie?'

'That's right.'

'You told me to call if I remembered anything, remember?'

Holly doesn't think Randy is drunk, but she guesses he's had a few. 'I did. And have you?'

'Have I what?'

Patience, she thinks. 'Thought of anything, Randy.'

'Yeah, but it probably doesn't mean anything. I was at this party, right? New Year's Eve party, and I was pretty drunk—'

'So you said.'

'And I was in the kitchen because that's where the beer was, and this Bonnie came out and we talked a little. I don't think she was drunk, exactly, but she'd had a few, doing the zig-zag walk, if you

know what I mean. I did most of the talking, I always do when I'm
in the bag, and she mostly just listened. I think maybe she came out
to get away from Tom, did I tell you that?'

'You did.'

'But she said one thing I remembered. I didn't when we talked at
Starbucks, but I did after. Almost didn't call you, but then I thought
what the hell.'

'What was it?'

'I asked her what she did over the Christmas break and she said she
was an elf. I go *what*? And she says I was a Christmas elf. Doesn't
mean anything, right?'

Holly channels *The Empire Strikes Back*. 'Everything means something,
it does.'

Randy cracks up. 'Yoda! Beautiful! You rock, Holly. Hey, if you
ever want to go out and grab a burger and a pitcher sometime—'

Holly thanks him, says she'll take it under consideration, and extracts
herself from the call. She finishes her prayer on autopilot.

An elf. She said she was a Christmas elf. It's probably not important,
but as Yoda might also say: *Interesting, it is.*

Penny might know what Bonnie was talking about, but Holly doesn't
want to talk to Penny again until she has to. What she wants, now
that she's wide awake, is a cigarette. She dresses and goes down to the
ice machine. On the way she has an idea. After she lights up she looks
in her contacts for Lakeisha Stone and calls.

'If this is another church donation pitch—'

'It's not. It's Holly Gibney, Keisha. Can I ask you a quick question?'

'Sure, if it will help you find Bonnie. I mean, you haven't, have
you?'

Holly, who is ever more sure that Bonnie is no longer alive, says,
'Not yet. Did she ever say anything to you about being . . . this will
probably sound crazy . . . a Christmas elf?'

Keisha laughs. 'It ain't crazy a bit, girlfriend. She *was* a Christmas
elf. If Santa's elves dress up like Santa, that is, with the beard and the
red hat. But she *did* have elf shoes, cute green ones with curly toes.
Scored em at the Goodwill, she said. Why would you ask that?'

'Was it at a mall? A seasonal thing?'

'No, for a Christmas party. The party was on Zoom because of

Covid, but the elves – I don't know how many besides Bonnie, maybe
a dozen – went around to the party people with snacks and sixpacks
of beer. Or maybe some of them got champagne. Faculty, you know
– they gotta represent.'

Holly can feel something warm working up her back from the base
of her spine to the nape of her neck. There's still nothing real here,
but she's rarely had a stronger intuition.

'Whose party was it, do you know?'

'These old retired professors. He was Life Sciences, she's English.
The Harrises.'

2

Holly lights another cigarette and walks around the Days Inn parking
lot, too deep in her own thoughts to bother policing up the butt of
her last one. She just steps on it and keeps walking, head down, brow
furrowed. She's having trouble keeping up with her own suppositions
and has to remind herself that they're *only* suppositions. Bill talked
about how a case was like an egg. He also talked about Blue Chevrolet
Syndrome: as soon as you bought a blue Chevrolet, you saw blue
Chevies everywhere.

Supposition, she keeps telling herself as she lights yet another cigarette.
Not fact, only supposition. True enough.

But.

Cary Dressler worked at the Strike Em Out Lanes; Roddy Harris,
aka Small Ball, bowled at the Strike Em Out. Not only that, Cary
sometimes bowled on Roddy's team. Bonnie Dahl worked for the
Harrises over Christmas, although – slow down, girl! – it was only a
one-night gig. As for Ellen Craslow—

She calls Keisha back. 'Me again. I'm sorry to bother you if you
were getting ready for bed.'

Keisha laughs. 'Not me, I like to read late when the house is quiet.
What's up, pussycat?'

'Do you know if Bonnie had any further association with the Harrises?
After the Christmas party gig, I mean.'

'Actually, yeah. Bonnie worked for the Mrs Professor for awhile
early this year, writing thank-you letters and putting her contacts in

order. Shit like that. Showed her some computer stuff, too, although she thought Mrs Professor knew a little more about computer stuff than she let on.' Keisha hesitated. 'She said that maybe the old lady had a little bit of a letch for her. Why do you ask?'

'I'm just trying to trace her contacts and what she was doing between the end of 2020 and when she disappeared,' Holly says. This is only a kissing cousin to the truth. 'Can I ask you one more question, not about Bonnie but about the other woman you mentioned? Ellen Craslow?'

'Sure.'

'You said you guys used to talk with her in the Belfry, but didn't you say she also worked in the Life Sciences building?'

'Yes. It's right next door to the Union. Does it matter?'

'Probably not.' But maybe it does. Rodney Harris might still have an office in Life Sciences. College profs never really retire, do they? Even if he doesn't, he could have had one when Ellen went missing.

3

Holly is out of cigarettes, but there's a 7-Eleven adjacent to the motel. She's walking there along the service road when her phone lights up again. It's Tanya Robinson. Holly says hello and sits on a bench outside the convenience store. Dew has fallen and the seat of her pants gets wet. Ordinarily, this would bother her a great deal, since she doesn't have another pair. Now she barely notices.

'I wanted to fill you in on Barbara,' Tanya says.

Holly sits up straight. 'Is she all right?'

'She's fine. Did she tell you her news? I'm thinking she's had so much going on today that she hasn't had time.'

Holly pauses briefly, but if Tanya knows, it's probably all right to say she does. 'She didn't, but Jerome did. It's wonderful. In poetry circles the Penley Prize is a pretty big deal.'

Tanya laughs. 'Now I've got *two* writers in the family! It's hard to believe. My own grandfather could hardly read at all. As for Jim's grandfather . . . well, you know about him.'

Holly does. The notorious Chicago gangster Alton Robinson, subject of Jerome's soon-to-be-published book.

'Barbara has been meeting with a local poet named Olivia Kingsbury—'

'I know who she is,' Holly says. She doesn't bother to tell Tanya that Kingsbury is a lot more than a local poet. 'Jerome says she's been mentoring Barbara.'

'For months now, and today is the first I learned of it. I suppose she felt like she'd be accused of copying her brother if she told, which is ridiculous. But that's Barbara. Anyway, the two of them have become very close, and today Ms Kingsbury had to go to the hospital. A-fib. You know what that is?'

'Yes. It's too bad, but at her age things go wrong. Olivia Kingsbury is close to a hundred.'

'They got her stabilized, but the poor old thing has cancer – she's had it for years, Barbara said, but now it's spread to her lungs and brain. She said some more, but it was hard to make out because she was crying.'

'I'm so sorry.'

'She asked me to call all her friends. She's going back to Ms Kingsbury's house with the old lady's caregiver, who's as broken up as Barbie is. The two of them are going to spend the night, and I guess tomorrow they'll bring Ms Kingsbury home. The old lady told them she doesn't want to die in the hospital, and I don't blame her.'

'That's very grown-up of Barbara,' Holly says.

'She's a good girl. A *responsible* girl.' Tanya is crying a little herself now. 'She plans to stay there the rest of the week and over the weekend, but it may not be that long. Barbara said Ms Kingsbury made it clear that if the a-fib starts again, she doesn't want to go back to the hospital.'

'Understood.' Holly is thinking of her mother, who did die in the hospital. Alone. 'Give Barbara all my love. And about the Penley Prize – congratulate her on making the shortlist of the shortlist.'

'I will, Holly, but I don't think she cares about any of that just now. I offered to go over and Barbara said no. I think she and Marie – that's the caregiver's name – want to be left alone with Ms Kingsbury. She doesn't seem to have anyone else. She's outlived them all.'

4

The subtext of Tanya's call is that Barbara will be out of touch while attending to Kingsbury during her friend and mentor's final illness, but when Holly gets back to her room with two fresh packs of cigarettes in the pockets of her cargo pants, she calls Barbara anyway. Straight to voicemail. She says Tanya filled her in, and if Barbara needs anything she only has to call. She says she's sorry bad news came so close on the heels of the good.

'I love you,' Holly finishes.

She gets undressed, brushes her teeth with her finger and a little motel soap (*oough*), and goes to bed. She lies on her back, looking up into the dark. Her mind won't turn off and she's afraid she's in for a sleepless night. She remembers she has a few melatonin rattling around in the bottom of her bag and takes one with a sip of water. Then she checks her phone for text messages.

Tonight there's just one, and it's from Barbara. Only two words. Holly sits on the bed, reading them over and over. That heat is working its way up her spine again. The text she sent Barbara, along with the picture of Cary Dressler and the Golden Oldies bowling team, was brief: *Do you remember this guy?*

Barbara's reply, almost certainly sent from Kiner, judging by the time-stamp, is even briefer: *Which one?*

July 5, 2021

1

'I believe you'll be able to assist me tonight,' Roddy says as he enters the bedroom.

Emily bares her teeth in a pained smile. The hamburger he's brought her — rare, as she likes it — is still on the night table. She has managed only a single bite. 'I don't think I'll even be able to get out of bed tonight, let alone assist you. You'll have to do it yourself. This pain . . . beyond belief.'

He's holding a tray with a napkin on it. Now he lifts it, showing her a goblet filled with white, lardlike stuff streaked with red filaments. Beside it is a spoon. 'I've been saving it.'

This isn't true. The fact is he forgot all about it. He found it in the freezer while he was rooting around for one of those Stouffer's entrees he likes for lunch. He heated the suet pudding in the oven, very gently. Microwaving kills most nutrients, it's a known fact. No wonder so many Americans are so unhealthy; that kind of cooking should be banned by law.

Emily's sunken eyes brighten with greed. She stretches out a hand. 'Give it to me! You should have given it to me yesterday, you cruel man!'

'I didn't need you yesterday. Tonight I do. Half inside and half outside, Em. You know the drill. Half and half.'

He gives her the goblet and the spoon. Peter Steinman wasn't a particularly fatty child, but what he did give up when rendered was edible gold. His wife begins to eat quickly – *gobbling from the goblet,*

Roddy thinks. A drool of fat containing a few hairlike strands of tendon rolls down her chin. Roddy scoops it up deftly and tucks it back into her mouth. She sucks his finger, a thing that once upon a time would have turned the noodle in his pants into a railspike, but no more, and there's nothing that can be done about that. Viagra and the other erectile dysfunction drugs aren't just bad for the brain; they speed up the clock of the chromosomes. You lose six months of life for every Viagra-assisted act of intercourse. It's a proven fact, although the drug companies of course suppress it.

He snatches the goblet back from her before she can eat all of it. He almost drops it – what a tragedy that would be – but saves it before it can roll off the bed and shatter on the floor. 'Turn over. I'll raise your nightgown.'

'I can do it.' She does, revealing her wrinkled thighs and scrawny buttocks. He begins smoothing the remains of the fat and tendon on her left cheek and down her inner thigh, where that pesky nerve is sending out its high voltage. She gives a little moan.

'Better?'

'I think . . . yes, better. Oh God, it is.'

He gets every last bit from the goblet and continues to spread and knead. Soon the shine of the fat is almost gone as it sinks in, soothing that nasty red nerve and putting it back to sleep.

No, not to sleep, he thinks, *only a doze. Real relief will begin later, with the girl's liver. And then nourishing soups, stews, filets, and cutlets.*

There are little white crescents of fat under his nails. He licks and gnaws them clean, then pulls her nightgown back down. 'Now rest. Sleep, if you can. Get ready for tonight.'

He kisses the sweaty hollow of her temple.

2

Shortly before eleven that night, Bonnie Dahl wakes to find herself lying naked on a table in a small, brightly lit room. Her wrists and ankles are clamped. Rodney and Emily Harris are watching her. Both are wearing elbow-length gloves and long rubber aprons.

'Peekaboo,' Roddy says, 'I see you.'

Bonnie's head is still muzzy. She could almost believe this is a dream, the worst nightmare ever, but knows it isn't. She raises her head. It feels as heavy as a concrete block, but she manages. She sees they have drawn on her in Sharpie. It's like a kind of weird map.

'Are you going to rape me after all?' Her mouth is dry. The words are husky.

'No, dear,' Emily says. Her hair hangs in clumps around a face so pale and hollow-cheeked that it's little more than a skull. Her eyes glitter. Her mouth is a crimped line of pain. 'We're going to eat you.'

Bonnie begins to scream.

July 28, 2021

1

Emily stands at the bedroom window in the hour before dawn, looking out at Ridge Road, empty save for moonlight. Behind her, Rodney is sleeping with his mouth open, breathing in great rasping snores. The sound is mildly annoying, but Emily envies him his rest just the same. She woke at quarter past three and there will be no more sleep for her tonight. Because she knows what was nagging at her.

She should have known as soon as Gibney called with that cock-and-bull story about Dressler being suspected of car theft. It was so obvious. Why hadn't she? At first she wondered if she was beginning to lose her mind the way Rodney is losing his. (In this small hour she can admit that's the truth.) But she knows it isn't so. Her mind is as sharp as ever. It's just that some things are so big, so goddamned *obvious*, that you ignore them. Like an ugly, oversized piece of furniture that you get used to and just walk around. Until you run into it face first, that is.

Or until you have a dream about a certain black vegan bitch.

And I knew, Em thinks. *I must have. I told him separate cases involving two of the people we've taken would be a very large coincidence. He shrugged it off. Said coincidences happen, and I accepted that.*

Accepted *it! God, how stupid!*

Not once had she remembered – at least not then – that Gibney, using her LaurenBacallFan alias, had sent out queries to the Craslows she had found on Twitter. Em supposes that Dahl and Dressler really could be a coincidence. But Dahl, Dressler, and Craslow?

No.

Emily turns from the window and makes her slow way into their bathroom with one hand pressing into the small of her throbbing back. Standing on tiptoe (it hurts!), she reaches the top of the medicine cabinet and finds a dusty brown bottle with no label. Inside it are two green pills. These are their final escape hatch, should they be needed. Em can still hope they won't be. She goes back into the bedroom and looks down at her snoring, open-mouthed husband. She thinks, *He looks so old.*

She lies down and puts the little brown bottle under her pillow. She'll tell him what she now knows, and should have known earlier, in the morning. For now let the old dear sleep.

Emily lies on her back, staring up into the dark.

2

The melatonin worked. Holly wakes up feeling like a new woman. She showers and dresses, then checks her phone. She's set it to DO NOT DISTURB, and she sees that she got a call from Pete Huntley at quarter past one in the morning. There's a voicemail, but it's not Pete. It's his daughter, calling on Pete's phone.

'Hey, Holly, this is Shauna. Dad's in the hospital. He had a relapse. Goddam Covid won't let him go.'

He said he was feeling stronger every day, Holly thinks. *Like the Chicago song.*

'He tried to take a bag of trash down to the garbage chute. Fainted in the hall. Mrs Lothrop found him and called 911. I've been with him all night. No heart attack, no goddam ventilator, thank Christ for that. He seems better this morning, but I guess he might be one of those goddam long haulers. They're going to run some tests and then send him home. They need the room. This fucking shit's everywhere. You better take care of yourse—' That's where the message ends.

Holly feels like throwing her phone across the room. It is, as Shauna Huntley might say, a goddam bad way to start a goddam day. She remembers Althea Haverty at the bowling alley talking about fake flu and looking at Holly's offered elbow with mild contempt. Saying *no offense, but I don't do that.* Holly doesn't wish her in the hospital with an oxygen mask clamped over her fat Covid-denying face, but—

Actually she does.

3

Holly drives through Burger King for breakfast, wearing a fresh pair of gloves to pay at one window and pick up her food at the next. She eats in her room, checks out, then sets off for Rolling Hills Elder Care. She gets there still too early for visiting hours, so she parks, opens her door, and smokes a cigarette. She texts Barbara, asking what she meant by *which one*. She gets no reply, didn't expect one, doesn't really need one. Barb must have recognized Rodney Harris as well as Cary Dressler. Holly is very curious about how she met Professor Harris. One thing she knows for sure is that the idea of Barbara anywhere near Harris makes her uneasy.

She googles Professor Rodney Harris and gets all sorts of information, including pictures of a younger version with dark hair and only a few lines and wrinkles. She googles Professor Emily Harris and gets another info-drop, confirming what Keisha said. Bonnie knew Emily Harris. *Worked* for Emily Harris, in fact.

Rodney knew Cary Dressler. Didn't smoke dope with him, but did bowl with him when the Golden Oldies needed a sub.

Rodney *could* have known Ellen Craslow. Could have chatted her up, in fact; they worked in the same building and according to Keisha Stone, the woman was not averse to conversation.

She texts Barbara again, this time being more specific: *Is it Rodney Harris you recognized? Have you met him? I know you're busy but let me know when you can.*

She checks her watch and sees that it's nine AM. Visiting hours have officially begun. She doesn't expect to get anything new from Victor Anderson (if she gets anything at all), and she knows damn well she won't get anything from Uncle Henry, but she's here now, so she might as well go ahead. She can be done by ten, check in with Pete, then get on the road back to the city. Will she stop to talk with Ernie Coggins? She might, but she's leaning against.

All signs point to the Harrises.

4

Holly goes to the front desk and states who she wants to visit. The woman on desk duty, Mrs Norman, checks her computer and makes a brief call. She says Henry Sirois is currently having a sponge bath and getting his hair clipped. Victor Anderson is in the sunroom, and although he's alert and aware, he's very hard to understand. If Holly would like to wait a bit, his wife usually comes in shortly after visiting hours begin, and she understands him perfectly.

'Evelyn is a jewel,' Mrs Norman says.

Holly agrees to wait for Anderson's wife, because she's had an idea. It's probably a bad one, but it's the only one she has. Her partner is in the hospital, Jerome is in New York, and Barbara is occupied with her dying friend. Even if she were not, Holly wouldn't ask for her help. Not after Chet Ondowsky.

She boots up her iPad and looks at pictures of 93 Ridge Road, both on Zillow (where the Zestimate is $1.7 million) and on Google Street View. She's seen the house; what she wants now is a look at the garage, but she's disappointed. The driveway dips down and she can only see the roof. Enlarging the picture doesn't help. Too bad.

A slim woman comes in – white slacks, white lowtop sneakers, white hair in a fashionable pixie cut – and approaches Mrs Norman. They speak, and Mrs Norman points to where Holly is sitting. Holly gets up, introduces herself, and holds her elbow out. Mrs Anderson – Evelyn – gives it a tap and asks how she can help.

'I'd like to ask your husband a few questions. A very few, if it won't tire him out. I'm investigating the disappearance of someone who used to work at the Strike Em Out Lanes – Cary Dressler. I understand Mr Anderson sometimes bowled with him. Mrs Norman said you could . . . well . . .'

'Translate?' Mrs Anderson says with a smile. 'Yes, I can do that. I never met Mr Dressler, but I know who he is. Vic said he was an excellent bowler, and a nice fellow. Called him a *mensch*.' She lowers her voice to a whisper. 'I think they sometimes went out back to smoke pot.'

'So I've heard,' Holly whispers back.

'Do you suspect . . . gasp . . . *foul play*?' Evelyn is still smiling behind her mask.

Holly, who suspects exactly that, says she's only trying to find out where he went.

'Well, come on,' Evelyn Anderson says cheerfully. 'I doubt if he can

help you, but his mind is as clear as ever and it will do him good to
see a new face.'

5

In the sunroom, a few old people are eating late breakfasts or having
it fed to them. An episode of *Mayberry R.F.D.* is on the big-screen TV,
laugh-track cackling away. Victor Anderson is sitting in a wheelchair
that's turned away from the TV so he can look out at the lawn, where
a man on a riding lawnmower is cutting the grass. Anderson is actually
two men, Holly sees, built like a longshoreman from shoulders to waist,
broad shoulders and thick chest. Below those are pipestem legs ending
in bare feet that are blotched with eczema. Anderson has an N95 mask,
but it's pulled down around his neck.

Evelyn says, 'Hi there, handsome, want a date?'

He looks around, and Holly sees half of his face is drawn down in
a stressful grimace that shows his teeth on the left side. The right side
of his face tries to smile. He says, 'Hi . . . yooful.'

Evelyn ruffles his iron gray hair and kisses his cheek. 'I brought you
company. This lady is Holly Gibney. She wants to ask you a few questions about your bowling career. Is that okay?'

He gives a downward jerk of his head that might be a nod and says
something interrogatory.

'He wants to know what it's about.'

'Cary Dressler,' Holly says. 'Do you remember him?'

Anderson says something and gestures with his gnarly right hand.
The left lies dead on the arm of his chair, palm upturned.

'He says he can hear you, he's not deaf.'

Holly reddens. 'Sorry.'

'It's okay. I'd pull up his mask, but then I wouldn't understand him,
either. He *has* been vaxxed. Everyone here has.' She lowers her voice.
'A couple of the nurses and one of the aides refused, and they've been
let go.'

Holly taps her upper arm. 'Me too.'

'You remember Mr Dressler, don't you, Vic? You called him a
mensch.'

'*Meh*,' Anderson agrees, and makes his one-sided smile again. Holly thinks there was a time, and not so long ago, when he must have looked like Lee J. Cobb in *On the Waterfront* or *12 Angry Men*. Handsome and strong.

'Excuse me one minute,' Evelyn says, and leaves them. On the TV, Aunt Bea has just said something funny, and the laugh-track erupts in hilarity.

Holly draws up a chair. 'So you do remember Cary, Mr Anderson?'

'Yef.'

'And you remember Rodney Harris, right?'

'Oddy! All-all! Oore!'

Evelyn comes back. She has a small bottle of Cetaphil. 'He says sure. I don't know what all-all means.'

'I do,' Holly says. 'Small Ball, right?'

Anderson does another of his jerky nods. 'All-all, ight!'

His wife kisses him again, on the temple this time, then drops to her knees and begins rubbing cream into his scaly feet. There is a matter-of-fact kindness to this that makes Holly feel both glad and like crying. 'Answer Ms Gibney's questions, Vic, and then we'll have a nice little visit. Would you like some yogurt?'

'Oore!'

'All I'm really curious about, Mr Anderson, is how well Professor Harris knew Cary. I guess not very well, right?'

Anderson makes a chewing motion on the side of his face that still works, as if trying to wake the other side up. Then he talks. Holly can only get a few words and phrases, but Evelyn gets everything.

'He's saying that Roddy and Cary were good buddies.'

'Ooo-duddies!' Anderson agrees, and then goes on. Evelyn continues to work the cream into his feet as she listens. She smiles a couple of times and once laughs out loud, a sound Holly finds much more natural than the TV laugh-track.

'The prof didn't go out with the others to smoke, but sometimes he'd buy Cary a beer after the game. Vic says the prof encouraged Cary to talk about himself because—'

'No one else ever did,' Holly says. She got that part. To Vic she says, 'Let me be sure I understand, and then I'll let you get to your yogurt. You'd say they were good friends?'

Anderson gives his jerky half-nod. 'Yef.'

'Did they drink beer together at the bowling alley? The Bowlaroo, or whatever it's called?'

'Nef' or. Elly's.'

'Next door at Nelly's,' Evelyn says, and caps the lotion. 'Do you need anything else, Ms Gibney? He tires easily these days.'

'Holly.' A woman who kneels to rub lotion into her husband's feet can call her by her first name anytime. 'Please call me Holly. And no, that was it.'

'Why the interest in Professor Harris?' Evelyn asks . . . and wrinkles her nose a little. It's just a small tell, but Holly sees it.

'Did you know him?'

'Not really, but after the tournaments were over there was always a meal at someone's house. You know, like a celebration, win or lose. With Vic's team it was mostly lose.'

Anderson gives a rusty chuckle and his jerky nod.

'Anyway, when it was our turn we had a barbecue in our backyard, and the prof basically took over the grill. He said . . . actually *said* . . . that I was doing the burgers all wrong. Cooking the nutrients out of them, or something. I was polite about it, let him take over, but I thought it was very rude. Also . . .'

'*Aw!*' Anderson interjects. His grin is simultaneously awful and charming. '*Aff-aw!*'

'That's right,' Evelyn says. 'They were half-raw. I couldn't eat mine. Why *are* you so interested in Professor Harris? I thought it was Cary you were investigating.'

Holly puts on her best perplexed expression. 'It is, but I keep thinking if I talk to enough members of the bowling team, I'll find a thread I can pick up and follow. I've already talked to Mr Welch and Mr Clippard.'

'Oowee,' Anderson says. 'Oo-dole Oowee-a-Cli!'

'Good old Hughie the Clip,' Evelyn says absently.

'Yes, I got that. Vic, did Professor Harris drive a van?'

Anderson does that chewing thing again as he mulls this over. Then he says, 'Oobayoo.'

'I didn't get that, hon,' Evelyn says.

Holly did. 'He says it was a Subaru.'

6

At the desk she tells Mrs Norman she'll be back to see her uncle shortly, but she forgot something in the car. This is a lie. What she wants is a cigarette. And she needs to think.

She smokes in her usual position – driver's door open, head down, feet on the pavement, freebasing nicotine before going back inside to see Uncle Henry, who somehow missed Covid and continues to exist in what must be a twilight world of perplexity. Or maybe even perplexity is gone. He still has occasional brief periods of awareness, but these have grown farther and farther apart. His brain, once so adept at names and numbers and addresses – not to mention at hiding money from his niece – is now your basic carrier wave that gives an occasional blip.

She's glad she came to see Vic Anderson, partly because it cheered her to see such long-term affection between a husband and wife, but mostly because it casts a fascinating light on Rodney Harris. He drives a Subaru instead of a disability van – no big surprise, since he's obviously not disabled – but to Holly he looks more and more like someone who might be covering for the Red Bank Predator. Or abetting him.

According to Professor Harris, he and Cary Dressler were mere acquaintances. According to Vic Anderson, they sometimes had beers together at the bar next door – hops and grains apparently not defiling Harris's ideas of nutrition the way that marijuana did. Anderson said Harris encouraged Dressler to talk about himself 'because no one else ever did.'

Just a kindly old professor drawing out a lonely young man? Possible, but if so, why had Harris lied about it? The idea that Rodney Harris had a letch for Dressler, just as Keisha said Harris's wife might have had a letch for Bonnie, occurs to Holly, but she dismisses it. The possibility that Harris was information-gathering seems more likely.

Harris isn't killing people, not at his age, and the idea that his wife is helping him do it is ridiculous, so if what Holly is thinking is true, they *must* be covering for someone. She needs to check and find out if they have children, but right now she has to bite the bullet and see the human vegetable who still looks like her uncle.

But as she gets up, something else occurs to her. Holly doesn't like Facebook and only goes on it once in awhile under her own name so her account won't molder, but she goes there often as LaurenBacallFan. She does so now, and visits Penny Dahl's page. She should have gone there sooner, and isn't entirely surprised to see her own name. She is described as 'noted local detective Holly Gibney.' She hates the word *detective*, she's an *investigator*. And she should have told Penny not to post her name but didn't think of it.

She wonders if Professor Harris knows she's also investigating Bonnie Dahl's disappearance. If he has been, in other words, one step ahead of her.

'If he is, I just caught up,' Holly says, and goes back into Rolling Hills Elder Care to visit her uncle.

7

A new millionaire walks into an old folks' home suite, Holly thinks after giving a token knock on the door, which is already ajar. Some of the rooms in the Rolling Hills facility are single-occupancy; the majority are doubles, because it saves walking for the hard-working nurses, orderlies, and on-call doctors. (And doubtless maximizes profit.) There are also four two-room suites, and Uncle Henry has one of those. If the thought of how Henry Sirois, retired accountant, could afford such pricey digs has ever crossed Holly's mind (she can't remember if it ever did), she supposes she must have thought he had been a saving soul, just in case his old age should come to this.

Now she knows better.

Henry is sitting in his living room, dressed in a checked shirt and bluejeans that bag on a skinny body that used to be plump. His hair is freshly clipped and his face is smooth from a morning shave. Morning sun shines on his chin, which is wet with drool. There's some sort of a protein drink with a straw in it on the table beside him. An orderly she passed in the hall asked Holly if she would like to help him with it and Holly said she'd be happy to. The TV is on, tuned to a game show hosted by Allen Ludden, who went to his reward long ago.

Looking around at the sparse but very nice furnishings, including a king bed with hospital rails in the second room, Holly feels a dull and hopeless anger that is very unlike her. She was a deeply depressed teenager and still suffers bouts of depression, and she can be angry, but lacking Holly hope? Not her style. At least usually. Today, though, in this room, circumstances are different.

Esau sold his future for a bowl of lentil stew, she thinks. *I didn't sell mine for anything. They stole it . . . or tried. That's why I'm angry. And the two who did it are beyond my reach and reproach, although this one is still breathing. That's why I'm hopeless. I think.*

'How are you today, Uncle Henry?' she asks, pulling a chair up beside him. On TV, contestants are trying to guess *humiliate* and not having much luck. Holly could certainly help them there.

Henry turns his head to look at her and she can hear the tendons in his neck creak like rusty hinges. 'Janey,' he says, and turns his gaze back to the TV.

'No, I'm Holly.'

'Will you bring in the dog? I hear her barking.'

'Have some of this.'

She lifts the protein shake, which is in a capped plastic cup that won't shatter or spill if he knocks it on the floor. Without taking his eyes off the television, he closes his wrinkled lips around the straw and sucks. Holly has read up on Alzheimer's and knows that some things stay. Men and women who can't remember their own names can still ride a bike. Men and women who can't find their way home can still sing Broadway show tunes. Men and women who have learned to suck liquid from a straw as children can still do it even in their dotage, when all else is gone. Certain facts stay, as well.

'Who was the fifth President of the United States, Uncle Henry? Do you remember?'

'James Monroe,' Henry says, without hesitation and without taking his eyes from the TV.

'And who is President now?'

'Nixon. Nixy-Babes.' He chuckles. Protein shake runs down his chin. Holly wipes it away before it can dapple his shirt.

'Why did you do it, Uncle Henry?' But that isn't the right question – not that she expects an answer; the question is what you'd call rhetorical. 'Let me put it another way. Why did you *let* her do it?'

'Won't that dog ever shut up?'

She can't shut up the dog – if there ever was one it was in the long-ago – but she can shut up the TV. She uses the controller to do it.

'She didn't want me to succeed, did she? She didn't want me to have a life of my own.'

Uncle Henry turns toward her, mouth agape. 'Janey?'

'And you *let her*!'

Henry raises a hand to his face and wipes his mouth. 'Let *who*? Do *what*? Janey, why are you *shouting*?'

'*My mother!*' Holly shouts. Sometimes you can get through to him if you shout, and right now she wants to. She needs to. '*Fucking Charlotte Gibney!*'

'Charlie?'

What's the point? There is no point. *A new millionaire walks into a bar and discovers there is no point.* Holly wipes her eyes with her sleeve.

The door opens and the orderly who asked if Holly would help her uncle with his protein shake looks in disapprovingly. 'Is everything all right in here?'

'Yes,' Holly says. 'I was raising my voice so he'd hear me. He's a little deaf, you know.'

The orderly closes the door. Uncle Henry is staring at Holly. No, *gaping* at her, his expression one of deep puzzlement. He is a brainless old man in a two-room suite and here he will stay, drinking protein shakes and watching old game shows until he dies. She will come because it's her duty to come, and he will call her Janey — because Janey was his favorite — until he dies.

'She never even left a note,' Holly says, but not to him. He is out of reach. 'Felt no need to explain herself, let alone apologize. That's how she was. How she always was.'

'James Monroe,' says Uncle Henry, 'served from 1817 to 1825. Died in 1831. On the Fourth of July. Where is that fucking drink? It tastes like shit but I'm dry as an old cowchip.'

Holly raises the cup and Uncle Henry battens on the straw. He sucks until it crackles. When she puts the cup down the straw stays in his mouth. It makes him look like a clown. She pulls it out and says she has to go. She's ashamed of her pointless outburst. She raises the remote to turn the TV back on, but he puts his gnarled and liver-spotted hand over hers.

'Holly,' he says.

'Yes,' she says, surprised, and looks into his face. His eyes are clear. As clear as they ever get these days, anyway.

'Nobody could stand against Charlie. She always got her way.'

Not with me, Holly thinks. *I escaped. Thanks to Bill and only by the skin of my teeth, but I did.* 'You came out of the fog just to tell me *that*?'

No reply. She gives him a kiss and tells him again that she has to go.

'Get the man, Janey,' he says. 'The one who comes. Tell him I need him. I think I might have pissed myself.'

8

Barbara is in Olivia's living room, replying to Holly's text, when Marie calls down from the head of the stairs. 'I think you should come up, honey. She wants us both. I think . . . I think she might be going.'

Barbara sends the text off unfinished and runs upstairs. Olivia Kingsbury – graduate of Bryn Mawr, a poet whose work spans almost eighty years, shortlisted for the National Book Award, twice bruited for the Nobel, once on the front page of the *New York Times* (at the head of a peace march and carrying one side of a banner reading U.S. OUT OF VIETNAM NOW), longtime teacher at Bell College of Arts and Sciences, mentor to Barbara Robinson – is indeed going. Marie stands on one side of her bed, Barbara on the other. They each hold one of the old poet's hands. There are no last words. Olivia looks at Marie. She looks at Barbara. She smiles. She dies. A world of words dies with her.

9

On her way back to the city, Holly stops at a Wawa for gas. After she fills the tank, she drives to the far side of the parking lot and has a cigarette in her usual try-not-to-pollute-the-car position – door open, elbows on knees, feet on the pavement. She checks her phone and sees she's got a text from Barbara. To *which one* Holly has sent *What do you mean?* followed by a more exact request: *Is it Rodney Harris you recognized? Have you met him? I know you're busy but let me know when you can.*

The reply: *Went to Emily Harris for an intro, didn't dare cold-call on Olivia. Prof Harris was washing his car. We just said hi. BTW I added Jorge Castro to J's MapQuest. Probably not impor*

That's where the text ends. Holly supposes Barbara sent it off unfinished by mistake, then got busy doing something else. Holly's done that herself. She remembers Jerome telling her he marked the various disappearances on a MapQuest printout, but who is Jorge Castro?

She calls Barbara to find out. On the coffee table in Olivia Kingsbury's living room, Barbara's iPhone gives out a low phone-on-silent buzzing and then falls still. Holly starts to leave a message, then changes her mind. She locks her car and goes into the little Wawa restaurant (really just a jumped-up snack bar), where there's free WiFi. She buys a hamburger that's already grown old in its foil bag, adds a Coke, and sits down with her iPad. She plugs in Jorge Castro's name and gets a whole slew of hits, including an auto parts millionaire and a baseball player. She thinks the most likely Castro is the novelist and yes, that one has a connection to the college on the hill. Below Castro's Wikipedia entry is an article from *The BellRinger*, the college newspaper. She taps on the link, nibbling at her burger without really tasting it – not that there's much to taste. The store's WiFi is slow but gets there eventually. There's a big headline, so Holly guesses it was on page one of the issue published on October 29th of 2012.

CELEBRATED NOVELIST LEAVES SUDDENLY

By Kirk Ellway

Award-winning scribe Jorge Castro, author of such novels as *Catalepsy* and *The Forgotten City*, has suddenly and unexpectedly decamped from his position as writer-in-residence at the world-famous Bell College fiction workshop. He was two months into his fourth semester at Bell, and a great favorite of his students.

'I just don't know what I'm going to do without him,' said Brittany Angleton, who has just sold her first fantasy novel (werewolves!) to Crofter's Press. She added that he had promised to line-edit her work in progress. Jeremy Brock said, 'He was the best writing teacher I ever had.' Other students talked about his kindness and sense of humor. One member of the program who did not wish to be named agreed with that, but added, 'If your work was bad, he'd put it out of its misery.'

Fred Martin, who lived with Castro, said the two of them had had several discussions lately about their future, but added, 'They weren't arguments. I would never call them that. I had too much love and respect for Jorge and he for me for us to ever argue. They were discussions about the future, a full and frank exchange of views. I wanted to leave at the end of the fall semester. Jorge wanted to stay until the end of the year, perhaps even join the faculty.'

However, the discussions may have been closer to arguments than Mr Martin is willing to admit. A source in the police department told the *Ringer* that Castro left a note saying 'I've had all I can take.' When asked about that, Mr Martin said, 'It's ridiculous! If he felt that way, why would he have wanted to stay? And where did he go? I've heard nothing. I was the one who wanted to leave. I got very tired of the midwestern homophobia.'

In the spring semester Castro was part of an effort to save the Poetry Workshop, an effort that eventually failed. One English Department faculty member who wishes not to be named said, 'Jorge was very eloquent, but he accepted the final decision with good grace. Had he stayed and joined the faculty, I think he would have re-introduced the issue. He said noted poet (and retired faculty member) Olivia Kingsbury was on his side, and would be happy to speak to the department faculty if the subject could be raised again.'

When asked exactly when Castro left, Mr Martin admitted he didn't know, because he had moved out.

There's more, including a photo of Jorge Castro teaching and another that must be an author photo from the back jacket of one of his books. Holly thinks he's quite handsome. Not quite as good-looking as Antonio Banderas (a personal favorite), but in the same neighborhood.

She doesn't believe the article she's just read would come close to passing muster on a big city newspaper, even with the dire straits the print media has fallen into; it has a kind of undergraduate nudge-nudge, wink-wink feel that makes her think of *Inside View* or one of the *New York Post* gossip columns. But it's informative. Oh yes. That heat is going up her spine again. She thinks it's no wonder that Barbara added Castro to Jerome's map.

Olivia Kingsbury must have told her about him. And it fits, doesn't it? Even the notes fit. Castro: 'I've had all I can take.' Bonnie Dahl: 'I've had enough.' If those two disappearances weren't nine years apart . . .

Yes, and if the police weren't short-staffed because of Covid; if they weren't afraid that one of the current Black Lives Matter protests might spiral into violence; if there had ever been a single *body*, something besides a moped and a bike and a *skateboard* . . .

'And if pigs could fly, poop would rain all around us,' Holly mutters.

Jorge Castro in 2012, Cary Dressler in 2015, Ellen Craslow and Peter Steinman in 2018, Bonnie Dahl in 2021. All three years apart, give or take, except for Ellen and Peter. Maybe one of those two had authentically run away, but wasn't it also possible that something had gone wrong with one of them? Wasn't what the Predator wanted? But what *did* he want? Serial killers who had a sexual motive usually stuck to either men (Gacy, Dahmer) or women (Bundy, Rader, et al.). The Red Bank Predator took both . . . including one male child.

Why?

Holly thinks there's someone who can give her the answer: Professor Rodney Harris, aka Small Ball and Mr Meat. That nickname makes her think of Jeffrey Dahmer again, but that's too ridiculous to believe.

Holly tosses her half-eaten burger in the trash, takes her soda, and leaves.

10

It's Barbara's idea, and Marie agrees instantly. If, that is, they can get Rosalyn Burkhart on board. She's the head of the English Department.

The two women are out back on Olivia's patio, drinking sodas and waiting for the Crossman Funeral Home hack to come and take away the old poet's earthly remains. There is no question about any of the arrangements; Olivia left complete instructions with Marie after her last bout of a-fib, right down to the music she wanted played (Flogging Molly's 'If Ever I Leave This World Alive' at the start; 'Spirit in the Sky,' by Norman Greenbaum at the end). What she didn't specify was a memorial reading on the Bell College quad, and that's what Barbara suggested.

When Rosalyn hears that Olivia has passed, she bursts into tears. They have Marie's phone on speaker, and that makes them both cry. When the tears end, Barbara tells Professor Burkhart her idea, and the department head gets on board immediately.

'If it's outdoors we can gather,' she says. 'We can even make masks optional if people agree to stand six feet apart. We'll read her poems, is that the idea?'

'Yes,' Marie says. 'She has plenty of author copies. I'll bring them and we can hand them out.'

'Sunset's around quarter of nine this time of year,' Rosalyn says. 'We can gather on the quad at say . . . eight?'

Barbara and Marie share a glance and say yes together.

'I'll start making calls,' Rosalyn says. 'Will you do the same, Ms Duchamp?'

'Absolutely. We may duplicate a few, but that's okay.'

Barbara says, 'I'm going to the funeral home when Olivia goes. I want to spend some time in their chapel, just to think.' A new idea strikes her. 'And maybe I can get candles? We could light them at the reading?'

'Wonderful idea,' Rosalyn says. 'Are you the promising young poet Olivia talked about? You are, aren't you?'

'I guess I am,' Barbara says, 'but all I can think about now is her. I loved her so much.'

'We all did,' Rosalyn says, then gives a teary laugh. 'With the possible exception of Emmy Harris, that is. Join us when you can, Barbara. My office is in Terrell Hall. I assume we're all vaccinated?'

Barbara follows the hearse to the funeral home. She sits in the chapel, thinking about Olivia. She thinks *this is the way birds stitch the sky closed at sunset* and that makes her cry again. She asks Mr Greer, the funeral director, about candles. He gives her two boxes of them. She says they'll take up a collection at Olivia's memorial to pay for them. Mr Greer says that will not be necessary. She drives to the Bell campus and joins Rosalyn and Marie. Others come. They go outside, where there are tears and laughter and stories. The names of favorite poems are exchanged. More calls are made and more people join. Boxed wine makes an appearance. Toasts are given. Barbara feels the almost indescribable comfort of like minds and wishes she were one of these people who think stories and poems are as important as stocks and bonds. Then she thinks, *But I am.* She thinks, *Thank God for you, Olivia.*

The afternoon passes. In Olivia Kingsbury's living room, Barbara's phone sits on the coffee table, forgotten.

11

At three o'clock that afternoon Holly sits in her office, looking at her framed photo of Bill Hodges. She wishes he were here now. With no backup she can count on – unless she wants to call Izzy Jaynes, which she most assuredly does *not* want to do – Holly is on her own.

She goes to the window and looks out on Frederick Street. It always helps to speak her thoughts aloud, so that's what she does.

'I'm not surprised that the police didn't realize what was happening. This guy has been extremely smart as he goes about his business.'

And why wouldn't he be? she thinks.

'And why wouldn't he be? If I'm right, an extremely smart professor of biology has been helping him, getting background information before and planting false trails – at least in some cases – after. His wife is probably also helping him and she's smart, too. There are no bodies, they've been disposed of somehow, and the victims have absolutely nothing in common. I have no idea what the Predator's motive might be, or why the Harrises are aiding and abetting, but the very fact . . .'

She stops, frowning, thinking how she wants to say this (*sometimes thinking is knowing*, Bill used to say). Then she goes on, speaking to the window. Speaking to herself.

'The very fact that the victims are so different actually spotlights the *method*. Because in every case . . . except the Steinman boy, and I tend to think more and more that he was a victim of opportunity . . . *in every case* the Harrises are there in the background. Rodney bowled with Dressler. Craslow worked in the building where I'm sure Rodney has or had an office. Bonnie was one of their Christmas elves. And now this guy Jorge Castro. Emily Harris was his colleague in the Bell English Department. I think the Harrises are in this up to their necks. Are they using a disability van? Is one of them playing crippled quail?'

There's nothing she can prove, not one single fracking thing, but there may be one thing she *can* do. It would be the equivalent of giving a potential witness a sixpack of photographs to see if the wit can pick out the doer.

She searches her iPad, locates what she wants, then finds Imani McGuire's number in her notes and gives her a call. After re-introducing herself, Holly asks if she has Internet on her phone.

'Of course I do,' Immi says, sounding amused. 'Doesn't everybody?'

'Okay, go to the Bell College site. Can you do that?'

'Wait . . . gotta put you on speaker . . . okay, got it.'

'Select *YEAR*. It's on the pull-down menu.'

'Yup. Which year? They go all the way back to 1965.'

Holly has already picked one out and is looking at it on her tablet. '2010.'

'All right.' Immi sounds interested. 'What next?'

'Go to English Department Faculty. You should see pictures, some men and some women.'

'Yes, okay, I'm there.'

Holly is biting her lips. Here comes the big one. 'Do you see the woman who cleaned out Ellen's trailer?'

Imani doesn't keep her in suspense. 'Goddam! It's her. Younger, but I'm almost positive.'

A defense lawyer would tear a big hole in that *almost* in court, but they're not in court now.

'It says her name is Emily Harris.'

'Yes,' Holly says, and does a little dance in front of the window looking out on Frederick Street. 'Thank you.'

'What was a college professor doing cleaning out El's trailer?'

'That's a good question, isn't it?'

12

Holly writes a preliminary report, setting out everything that she's discovered, partly through her own investigations and partly because the universe threw her a couple of ropes. She likes to think (but doesn't quite believe) there's a kind of providence at work in matters of right and wrong, blind but powerful, like that statue of Lady Justice holding out her scales. That there's a force in the affairs of men and women standing on the side of the weak and unsuspecting, and against evil. It may be too late for Bonnie and the others, but if there are no future victims, that's a win.

She likes to think of herself as one of the good guys. Smoking aside, of course.

The report is slow work, full of suppositions, and it's late afternoon by the time it's done. She considers who she should send it to. Not Penny; that needs to be an in-person debriefing, not bad news – *terrible* news – that comes in an email filled with stilted phrases like *Investigator Gibney ascertained* and *According to Jet Mart store clerk Herrera*. Ordinarily she would send a copy to her partner's agency address, but Pete is in the hospital and she doesn't want to trouble him with her current case . . . which he advised her against taking in the first place.

Except that's bullshit.

She doesn't want to send it to him or anyone, at least not yet. Holly has come a long way from the shy introvert Bill Hodges met lurking outside a funeral home all those years ago, but that woman still lives inside her and always will. That woman is terrified of being wrong and still believes she is wrong as often as she's right. It's a quantum advance from the woman who thought she was *always* wrong, but the insecurity remains. At sixty and seventy – at eighty, if she lives that long, which she probably won't if she keeps smoking – she will still be getting up from her bed three or four nights a week to make sure she turned off the stove burners and locked the doors, even though she knows very well that she's done those things. If a case is like an egg, she is, too. One with a fragile shell. She is still afraid of being laughed at. Still afraid of being called Jibba-Jibba. This is what she carries.

I need to see the van, if it's there. Then *I can be sure.*

Yes. Getting a look at the van, plus Immi McGuire's identification of Emily Harris as the woman who cleaned out Ellen Craslow's trailer, will be enough to satisfy her. Then she can tell Bonnie's mother everything tonight at nine. She can give Penny the choice of having her continue the investigation, or the two of them going to Isabelle Jaynes of the city police. Holly will recommend the latter, because Izzy can have the Harrises brought in for questioning. According to their Wikipedia entries they are childless, but you can't trust everything you read on Wiki. What she believes – no, what she *knows* – is that these two old people are protecting *somebody*.

She doesn't try to fool herself into believing that the Harrises are harmless just because they're in their eighties; almost any human or animal will fight when cornered, old or not. But Rodney Harris no longer bowls because of his bad hips, and according to Imani, his wife suffers from sciatica. Holly thinks she's a match for them. Assuming she takes care. Of course if they catch her snooping around their garage they could report her to the police . . . but if the disability van is in their garage, and a potential mine of DNA evidence, would they?

Holly realizes she's been sitting in front of her preliminary report for almost forty-five minutes, going over and over her options like a gerbil on an exercise wheel. Bill would say it's time to shit or git. She saves her report and sends it to nobody. If something should happen to her – unlikely, but possible – Pete will find it. Or Jerome, when he comes back from his great adventure.

She opens the wall safe and takes out the .38 Smith & Wesson. It's a Victory model that was Bill's, and his father's before him. Now it's Holly's. When Bill was on the cops, his service weapon was a Glock automatic, but he preferred the S&W. Because, he said, a revolver never jams. There's also a box of shells in the safe. She loads the gun, leaving the chamber under the hammer empty as per Bill's instructions, and closes the cylinder. She drops the gun into her shoulder bag.

There's something else of Bill's in the safe, something she's taught herself to use with Pete's help. She takes out a flat alligator-skin case, nine inches by three, its surface rubbed smooth. She puts it in her bag with the gun (not to mention her few cosmetics, her ChapStick, her Kleenex, her little flashlight, her small can of pepper spray, her Bic lighter, and a fresh pack of cigarettes).

She asks Siri what time the sun sets, and Siri – accommodating and knowledgeable as ever, she even knows jokes – tells her it will be at 8:48 PM. She can't wait that long if she wants to get a good picture of the hoped-for van, but she thinks dusk is a good time for dirty work. The Harrises will probably be in their living room, watching either a movie or the Olympic Games going on in Tokyo. Holly hates to wait, but since she has to, she decides to go home and kill time there.

On the way out of the office she thinks of an ad she's seen on TV. Teenagers are running from a guy who looks like Leatherface. One suggests hiding in the attic. Another in the basement. The third says,

'Why can't we just get in the running car?' and points to it. The fourth, her boyfriend, says, 'Are you crazy? Let's hide behind the chainsaws.' So they do. The announcer intones, 'When you're in a horror movie, you make poor decisions.' Holly isn't in a horror movie, though, and she tells herself she isn't making a poor decision. She has her spray, and if she needs it, she has Bill's gun.

In her deepest heart, she knows better . . . but she also knows she needs to *see.*

13

At home, Holly makes something to eat and can't eat it. She calls Jerome and he picks up at once, sounding euphoric. 'Guess where I am!'

'On top of the Empire State Building.'

'No.'

'Times Square.'

'No.'

'Staten Island Ferry?'

He makes a buzzer sound.

'I give up, Jerome.'

'Central Park! It's beautiful! I could walk for miles in this place and see something new everywhere. It's even got an overgrown part like the Thickets in Deerfield Park, only it's called the Ramble!'

'Well, don't get mugged.'

'No, I can always do that when I come home.' He laughs.

'You sound happy.'

'I am. It's been an authentically good day. I'm happy for me, I'm happy for Barbara, and Mom and Dad are happy for both of us.'

'Of course they are,' Holly says. She isn't going to tell him that Barbara's friend and mentor died; that's not her news to pass on, and why bring him down? 'I'm also happy for you, Jerome. Just don't spoil it by calling me Hollyberry.'

'Wouldn't think of it. What's going on in the case?'

A thought blips across her mind: *This is my chance to get in the running car instead of hiding behind the chainsaws.* But the part of her mind that insists on checking the stove burners, the part that can never forget she left *A Day No Pigs Would Die* on the bus, whispers *not now, not yet.*

'Well,' she says, 'Barbara may have run across another one.'

She tells him about Jorge Castro. After that the conversation turns to his book and his hopes for it. They talk awhile longer, then Holly lets Jerome go to continue his magical mystery tour of Central Park. She realizes she hasn't told him about the sudden upgrade in her personal worth, either. Not him or anyone else. In a way, it's like not talking about the possibility of the van. In both cases there's a little too much baggage to unpack, at least now.

14

Barbara and Marie brought author copies of Olivia's twelve books, including a few of the hefty *Collected Poems*, but it turns out to be unnecessary. Most of the people gathering on the quad in the shade of the iconic bell tower bring their own. Many are dog-eared and battered. One is held together by rubber bands. Some are also carrying pictures of Olivia at various stages of her life (the most common is the one of her and Humphrey Bogart standing in front of the Trevi Fountain). Some bring flowers. One is wearing a tee-shirt, surely specially made for the occasion, reading simply OK LIVES.

Frankie's Dog Wagon shows up and does a brisk business in soft drinks and foot-longs. Barbara doesn't know if that was Rosalyn's idea or if Frankie showed up on his own. For all Barbara knows, Frankie is a fan of Olivia's work. That wouldn't surprise her. This evening nothing would surprise her. She has never felt so simultaneously sad, happy, and proud.

By six thirty there have to be over a hundred people on the quad, and more are coming. No one is waiting for the candles to be lit at dusk; a young man with a Mohawk mounts a stepstool and begins reading 'The Foal in the Wilderness' through a bullhorn. People gather around to listen, munching dogs, drinking sodas, munching fries and onion rings, drinking beer and wine.

Marie loops an arm around Barbara's shoulders. 'Isn't this wonderful? Wouldn't she have loved it?'

Barbara thinks back to her first meeting with the old poet, Olivia patting her enormous fur coat and saying *Fo, fo, faux fur*. She starts crying and hugs Marie. 'She would have loved it so much.'

Mohawk Boy gives way to a girl with a snake tattooed around one upper arm. The girl raises the bullhorn and begins reading 'I Was Taller When Young.'

Barbara listens. She's had a little wine, but her head has never felt clearer. *No more to drink*, she thinks. *You have to remember this. You have to remember it all your life.* As Tattoo Girl gives way to a skinny bespectacled guy who looks like a grad student, she remembers that she's left her cell phone at Olivia's house. Ordinarily she goes nowhere without it, but tonight she doesn't want it. What she wants is a hotdog with lots of mustard. And poetry. She wants to fill herself up with it.

15

While Barbara and Marie are handing out copies of Olivia's books to the few who don't have them, Roddy Harris is walking in Deerfield Park, as he often does in the late afternoon or early evening. It limbers up his sore hips — they're sorer than they should be after weeks of partaking of fresh comestibles courtesy of the Christmas elf — but there's another reason, as well. He doesn't like to admit it, but it's becoming harder and harder to hold onto things. To not lose the plot, as the saying is. Walking helps. It aerates the brain.

In the last weeks Roddy has eaten half a dozen dessert parfaits containing a mixture of ice cream, blueberries, and elf brains, but it's still harder and harder to stay mentally sharp. This is both bewildering and infuriating. All his research insists that consuming a diet rich in human brain tissue has positive and immediate benefits for the consumer. When male chimpanzees steal and kill the offspring of mothers unwise enough to leave their babies unguarded, they always eat the brains first. The reason might not be clear to them, but it is to researchers; the brains of primates contain fatty acids that are crucial for neurological development and neurological health. Fatty acids (and the human brain is sixty per cent fat) aren't manufactured by the body, so if they are being lost — as his are — they must be replaced. It's quite simple, and for the last nine years it's worked. Stated in simple terms that he would never dare put in a monograph or articulate in a lecture, eating healthy human brain tissue, especially the brain of a young person, cures Alzheimer's.

Or so he's believed . . . but what if he's wrong?

No, no, *no!*

He refuses to believe his years of research are in any way incorrect, but what if he is excreting neurological fats faster than he can take them in? What if he is quite literally pissing his brains out? The idea is ludicrous, of course, and yet he can no longer remember his zip code. He thinks he takes a size nine shoe, but can't be positive; maybe it's an eight. He would have to check the insole to be sure. The other day he had to struggle to remember his own middle name!

Mostly, he's been able to hide this erosion. Emily sees it, of course, but not even Emily has realized the extent of it. Thank God he's not teaching anymore, and thank God he's got Emily to edit and proofread his letters to the various academic journals he subscribes to.

A great deal of the time he's as sharp and on-point as ever. Sometimes he thinks of himself as a passenger in a plane flying over a clear land-scape at low altitude. Then the plane goes into a cloud, and everything is gray. You hold onto your armrests and wait out the bumps. When questions are asked, you smile and look wise instead of answering. Then the plane flies out of the cloud, the landscape is clear again, and all the facts are at your fingertips!

His walks in the park are soothing because he doesn't have to worry about saying the wrong thing or asking the wrong question, like the name of a person you've known for the last thirty years. In the park he doesn't have to be constantly on guard. He can stop trying so damn hard. He sometimes walks for miles, nibbling at the little balls of deep-fried human meat he keeps in his pocket, savoring the porky taste and the crunch (he still has all his own teeth, a thing he's damn proud of).

One path leads to another, then to a third and fourth. Sometimes he sits on a bench and looks at birds he can no longer name . . . and when he's by himself, he no longer *has* to name them. Because after all, a bird by any other name would still be a bird, Shakespeare was right about that. On occasion he's even rented one of the brightly colored little boats lined up on the dock of Deerfield Pond and pedaled across it, enjoying the still water and the peace of not caring if he's in the cloud or out of it.

Of course there was one occasion when he couldn't remember how to get home, or what his house number was. He *could* remember the name of their street, though, and when he asked a groundskeeper to kindly point him in the direction of Ridge Road, the man did so as if it were a matter of course. Probably it was. Deerfield is a big park and people got turned around all the time.

Emily is suffering her own problems. Since the Christmas elf, with her bonanza of fatty tissue, her sciatica is better, but these days it never leaves her entirely alone. There was a time – after Castro, after Dressler – when he watched her tango across the living room, arms outstretched to embrace an invisible partner. They'd even had sex, especially after Castro, but no more. Not in . . . three years? Four? When *was* Castro?

It's wrong for her to feel that way, all wrong. Human meat contains macro- and micronutrients that are available in such abundance in no other flesh. Only genus *suidae* even comes close – warthogs, boars, your common barnyard pig. Human muscle and bone marrow cure arthritis and sciatica; the Spanish physician Arnold of Villanova knew that in the thirteenth century. Pope Innocent VIII ate the powdered brains of young boys and drank their blood. In medieval England, the flesh of hanged prisoners was considered a delicacy.

But Em is fading. He knows her as well as she knows him, and he sees it.

As if thinking about her has summoned her, his phone plays a bit of 'Copacabana,' Emily's ringtone.

Gather yourself, he thinks. *Gather yourself and be sharp. Be* there.

'Hello, my love, what's up?'

'There's good news and bad news,' she says. 'Which do you want first?'

'The good, of course. You know I like dessert before vegetables.'

'The good news is that the old bitch who stole my protégé has finally popped her clogs.'

His circuits are firing well just now and it only takes him a second to respond. 'You're speaking of Olivia Kingsbury.'

'None other.' Em gives a short and humorless laugh. 'Can you imagine how tough she'd be? Like pemmican!'

'You speak metaphorically, of course,' Roddy says. He's ahead of her this once, aware that they are talking on their cells, and cell phone calls may be intercepted.

'Of course, of course,' Em says. 'Ding-dong, the bitch is dead. Where are you, lovey? In the park?'

'Yes.' He sits down on a bench. In the distance he can hear children in the playground, but not many, from the sound of them; it's dinnertime.

'When will you be home?'

'Oh . . . in a bit. Did you say there was bad news?'

'Unfortunately. Do you remember the woman who came to see us about Dressler?'

'Yes.' He has only the vaguest recollection.

'I think she has suspicions that we've been involved in . . . you know.'

'Absolutely.' He has no idea what she's talking about. The plane is entering another cloudbank.

'We should talk, because this may be serious. Be back before dark, all right? I'm making elf sandwiches. Lots of mustard, the way you like it.'

'Sounds good.' It does, but only in an academic sort of way; not so long ago the thought of a sandwich made with thin-shaved slices of human meat (so tender!) would have made him ravenous. 'I'll just walk a little more. Work up an appetite.'

'Okay, honey. Don't forget.'

Roddy puts his phone back in his pocket and looks around. Where, exactly, is he? Then he sees the statue of Thomas Edison holding up a lightbulb and knows he's near the pond. Good! He always enjoys looking at the pond.

The woman who came to see us about Dressler.

Okay, now he remembers. A little mouse too frightened to take off her mask. One of the elbow-tappers. What could they possibly have to fear from her?

Thanks to earplugs coated with human fat – he wears them at night – his ears are as good as his teeth, and he can hear the faint sound of someone at the college huckstering through an amplification system. He has no idea what can be going on up there with the college shut down for the summer, not to mention all the ridiculous scaremongering about what Emily calls the New Flu, but maybe it has to do with that Black lad who was killed resisting the police. Whatever it is has nothing to do with him.

Roddy Harris, PhD in biology, renowned nutritionist, aka Mr Meat, walks on.

16

Uncle Henry used to say Holly would be early for everything, and it's true. She makes it halfway through the evening news, David Muir spieling on about Covid, Covid, and more Covid, and then she can wait no longer. She leaves her apartment and drives across town with the evening light, still strong, slanting in through her windshield and making her squint even with the sun visor down. She cuts through the campus and hears something happening on the quad – words she can't make out blaring through a mic or a bullhorn – and assumes it's a BLM rally.

She cruises down the long curving street past the Victorians on one side and the park on the other, obeying the 25 MPH speed limit and being careful not to slow as she passes the Harris home. But she gives it a good look. No sign of life, which doesn't mean anything. They *may* have gone out to dinner, but given the country's current situation – Covid, Covid, and more Covid – Holly doubts it. They're probably watching television or eating in, maybe both at the same time. She can't see if the garage has two bays because of that damn sloping driveway, but she can see its roof, and it certainly looks big enough for two vehicles.

She also scopes out the house next door, the one with the FOR SALE sign out front and a lawn that needs watering. *Real estate agent should take care of that*, Holly thinks, and wonders if the agent might by chance be George Rafferty. The sign doesn't say. It's not the agent or the lawn she's interested in, anyway. It's the privacy hedge running the length of the vacant property. All the way past the Harris garage.

Holly continues down the hill and pulls in at the curb a little way up from the playground. There's a parking lot there (the very one from which Jorge Castro was taken, in fact), and there are plenty of empty spaces, but she wants to smoke while she waits and she doesn't want little kids watching her indulge her nasty habit. She opens her door, swings her legs out, and lights up.

Twenty past seven. She takes her phone out of her pocket, thinks about calling Isabelle Jaynes, and puts it away again. She needs to see if that van is in the Harrises' garage. If it isn't, Holly will tell Penny she's against going to the police – no proof, only a few circumstantial path-crossings that could be dismissed by the Harrises (or their lawyer) as coincidence – but if there's even a faint chance that Bonnie is still alive, Penny will almost certainly opt for the cops. That will tip off the Harrises that they've been pegged, and they will pass that news on to whoever they're protecting. That person, that *predator*, will then likely disappear.

The van. If the van is there, all will be well.

Most of the little kids have left the playground now. A trio of teenagers, two boys and a girl, are goofing on the little roundabout, the boys pushing, the girl riding with her arms lifted and her hair flying back. Holly supposes they will be joined by others. Whatever is happening at the college on the hill holds no interest for townie boys and girls.

She checks her watch again. 7:30. She can't wait too long if she wants to get a good picture of the van, always supposing there is one, but there's still too much daylight. Holly decides to wait until quarter of eight. Let the shadows draw a little longer. But it's hard. Waiting has never been her forte, and surely if she's careful, she could—

No. Wait. Bill's voice.

The teenagers at the roundabout are joined by a few others and they stroll off into the park. They might be bound for the Thickets. They might even be bound for Drive-In Rock. Holly lights another cigarette and smokes with her door open and her feet on the pavement. She smokes slowly, but even so it's only seven-forty by the time she finishes. She decides she can wait no longer. She puts the cigarette out in her portable ashtray and puts the tin (currently choked with butts, she really has to stop . . . or at least cut down) in the center console. She takes out a Columbus Clippers gimme cap and pulls it down on her forehead. She locks her car and starts up the sidewalk toward the empty house next to the Harrises'.

17

Provisional clarity returns and Roddy thinks: *What if the woman who's got Em worried knows about the Black girl?* He can't remember the Black girl's name – possibly Evelyn – but he knows she was a vegan, and troublesome. Did Em say something about Twitter? Someone checking out that Black girl on Twitter?

Leaving the pond behind, he walks slowly along a wide gravel path that comes out near the playground. He sits on a bench to rest his hips before climbing the hill to his house, but also to avoid any interaction with the teenagers who are playing on a merry-go-round meant only for little kids.

Across the street, maybe forty or so yards up from the playground parking lot, a woman is sitting with her car door open, smoking a cigarette. Although she only looks vaguely familiar, there's nothing vague about the alarm bells that start going off in Roddy's head. Something's wrong about her. Very wrong.

He can still clear his mind when he absolutely has to, and he makes that effort now. The woman is sitting with her elbows on her thighs, her head lowered, raising one hand occasionally to take a puff on her cancer stick. When she finishes, she puts it out in a little tin, maybe a Sucrets box, and sits up straight. He thinks he knew even before that, because she's wearing the same cargo pants she had on when she came to the house, or a pair just like them. But when he sees her face, he's sure. It's the elbow-tapper who came asking about Cary Dressler. The woman who is also investigating Bonnie Dahl, although she never said so.

She has suspicions, Emily said.

This may be serious, Emily said.

Roddy thinks she's right.

He takes his phone out of his pocket and calls home. Across the street, the woman puts on a hat, pulling it down low against the evening sun (or to hide her eyes). She locks her car. It flashes its lights. She walks away. In his hand the phone rings once . . . twice . . . three times.

'Come on,' Roddy whispers. 'Come on, come *on*.'

Emily picks up. 'If you're calling to say that *now* you're hungry—'

'I'm not.' Across the street, the elbow-tapper is heading up the hill. 'That woman is coming, Molly Givens or whatever her name is, and I don't think she's coming to ask more questions, or she wouldn't have parked down the street. I think she's snoop—'

But Emily is gone.

Roddy puts his phone back into his left front pocket and pats the righthand one, hoping he has what he wants. He usually carries it when he's walking by himself, sometimes there are dangerous people in the park. It's there. He gets up from the bench and crosses the street. The woman is walking fast (especially for a smoker) and his bad hips mean he can't keep up, but it may still be all right as long as she doesn't look back.

How much does she know? he asks himself. *Does she know about the vegan girl, Evelyn or Eleanor or whatever her name was?*

If she knows about her as well as Cary and the Dahl girl, it . . . it . . .

'It could spoil everything,' he whispers to himself.

18

Emily hurries into the downstairs office. It hurts to hurry but she hurries anyway, making little whimpering sounds and pressing the fingers of both hands into the lumbar region of her back, as if to hold it together. The most excruciating pain of the sciatica passed after they ate the Dahl girl's liver – Roddy gave her the lion's share and she gobbled it half-raw – but it hasn't gone away entirely, as it did after Castro and Dressler. She dreads future pain if it returns full force, but right now there's this inquisitive bitch to deal with, not Molly Givens but Holly Gibney.

How much does she know?

Em decides she doesn't care. With Ellen Craslow added to the equation, she knows enough. Roddy may have gotten her name wrong, but he's right about one thing: you don't park your car a quarter of a mile down the street if you're just coming to ask questions. You only park a quarter of a mile down the street if you want to pry into other people's business.

They have a state-of-the-art alarm system that covers the entire perimeter of the house and grounds. It doesn't call the police unless it's not been shut off sixty minutes after it's first tripped. When it was installed, burglars and home invaders weren't their primary concern, although of course they never said that. Em turns on the alarm, sets it to HOUSE ONLY, then turns on all ten of their cameras, which Roddy installed himself in a happier time when he could be trusted to do such things. They cover the kitchen, the living room, the basement (of course), the front of the house, the sides, the back, and the garage.

Emily sits down to watch. She tells herself they've come too far to turn back now.

19

Holly approaches the vacant house at 91 Ridge Road. She takes a quick glance ahead of her and to the far side of the street. She sees no one, and with no hesitation, because she who hesitates is lost, veers onto the dying lawn and walks up the left side of the house, putting the bulk of it between her and 93 next door on the right.

Behind the house she crosses a flagstone patio toward the hedge dividing this yard from the Harrises'. She steps briskly, without slowing. She's in it now, and a colder version of Holly takes over. It's the same one that threw all those loathsome china figurines into the fireplace of her mother's house. She walks slowly down the hedge. Thanks to the hot, dry summer and the lack of any lawn and grounds mainten-ance, at least since the previous owners moved out, Holly finds several thin places. The best is opposite what she guesses is the Harrises' kitchen, but she doesn't want that one. The worst is opposite the garage, which figures, but that's still the one she means to use. At least she's wearing long sleeves and long pants.

She bends and peers through the hedge at the garage. It's a side view and she *still* can't see if it's a one- or two-car garage, but she does see something interesting. There's only one window, and it's entirely black. It might be a shade, but Holly thinks it might also have been painted over on the inside.

'Who does *that*?' she murmurs, but the answer seems obvious: someone with something to hide.

Holly turns her back, hugs her shoulder bag against her breasts, and pushes through the hedge. She emerges with nothing worse than a few scratches on the nape of her neck. She looks around. There are a couple of plastic garbage cans and a recycling bin beneath the garage's eave. To her right she can see the driveway leading back to the street and the roof of a passing car.

She walks to the one window and yes, it's been blinded with matte black paint. She goes around to the rear and finds what she was hoping to find — a back door. She expects it to be locked and it is. She takes the alligator-skin case out of her bag and opens it. Inside, lined up like surgical instruments, are Bill Hodges's lockpicks. She examines the lock. It's a Yale, so she takes out the hook pick and slides it in at the top of the keyway — very gently, so as not to disturb any of the locking pins. The second pick goes in beneath it. Holly twists the second pick to the right until it binds. Then she's able to trip the top pin with the hook pick . . . she hears it retract . . . and the second pin . . . and . . .

Is there a third? If so, it hasn't engaged. It's an old lock, so it's possible there isn't. Slowly, her upper teeth pressed into her lower lip almost hard enough to make it bleed, she rotates the hook pick and pushes. There's an audible click and for a moment she's afraid she's lost one of the pins and will have to start over. Then the door comes ajar, pushed by the pressure of the two picks.

Holly lets out her breath and puts the picks back into the case. She drops the case into her bag, which is now hung around her neck. She straightens and takes her phone from her pocket.

Be there, she thinks. *Please be there.*

20

Emily can't wait for Roddy; for all she knows, his slippery mind has skated him off in some other direction entirely. Three concrete steps lead down from the kitchen door to the Harris patio. She sits on the lowest, then lies down. The concrete riser biting into her back is painful, but she can't think about that now. She cocks one of her legs to the side and puts one arm behind her, at what she hopes will look like an awkward angle. God knows it feels awkward. Does she look like an old lady who's just taken a serious fall? One who needs help badly?

I better, she thinks. *I just better.*

21

The van is there, and Holly doesn't even have to check if it's been customized with a chassis-lift to allow for a ramp to emerge. Above the rear bumper is a Wisconsin license plate with the wheelchair symbol that means this is a duly accredited vehicle for people with disabilities. The light coming in the back door is fading but more than adequate. She raises her iPhone and snaps three pictures. She thinks the plate alone will be enough to get a police investigation started.

She knows it's time to go, *past* time, but she wants more. She shoots a quick glance over her shoulder – no one there – and approaches the back of the van. The windows have been darkened, but when she puts her forehead against one and cups her hands to the sides of her face, she can see inside.

She can see a wheelchair.

This is how they do it, she thinks with a burst of triumph. *This is how they get their targets to stop. Then whoever they're working with – the real bad guy – pops out of the van and does the rest.*

She really has to stop pressing her luck. She takes three more snaps of the wheelchair, backs out of the garage, and pulls the door shut. She turns toward the hedge, meaning to go back the way she came, and that's when a weak voice cries, 'Help! Will somebody help me? I've fallen and it hurts terribly!'

Holly isn't convinced. Not even close. Partly because it's awfully convenient, but mostly because her own mother has played the same *oh the pain is so bad* card when she wanted Holly to stay around . . . or, lacking that, to leave feeling so guilty that she'd come back sooner. For a long time it worked. *And when it stopped working*, Holly thinks, *she and Uncle Henry ran a con on me.*

'Help! Please, someone help me!'

Holly almost backs through the hedge anyway, leaving the woman – Emily Harris for sure – to emote on her own, then changes her mind. She walks to the end of the garage and peers around it. The woman is sprawled on the steps, one leg cocked, one arm bent behind her. Her housedress is rucked up to mid-thigh. She's skinny and pale and frail and certainly looks in pain. Holly decides to put on a little performance of her own. *We'll be like Bette Davis and Joan Crawford in* What Ever Happened to Baby Jane, she thinks. *And if her husband comes out, so much the better.*

'Oh my God!' she says, approaching the downed woman. 'What happened?'

'I slipped,' the woman says. The tremble in her voice is good, but

Holly thinks the sob of pain that follows is strictly summer stock. 'Please help me. Can you straighten my leg? I don't think it's broken, but—'

'Maybe you need a wheelchair,' Holly says sympathetically. 'There's one in your van, isn't there?'

Harris's eyes flicker a little at that, then she gives a groan. Holly thinks it's not entirely fake. This woman is in pain, all right, but she's also desperate.

Holly bends down, one hand deep in her bag. Not gripping Bill's .38 but touching its short barrel. 'How many have you taken, Professor Harris? I know about four for sure, and I think there might be another one, a writer. And who have you taken them *for*? That's what I really want to—'

Emily brings her hand out from behind her back. In it is a Vipertek VTS-989, known in the Harris household as Thing One. It throws 300 volts, but Holly doesn't give her a chance to trigger it. From the moment she saw Emily Harris so artfully posed on the patio steps, she hasn't trusted the hand behind the woman's back. She pulls Bill's revolver from her bag by the barrel and in one smooth motion slams the butt against Emily's wrist. Thing One goes clattering across the decorative bricks unfired.

'*Ow!*' Emily shrieks. This shriek is entirely authentic. '*You broke my wrist, you bitch!*'

'Tasers are illegal in this state,' Holly says, bending to pick it up, 'but I think that will be the least of your worries when—'

She sees the woman's eyes shift and starts to turn, but it's too late. The electrodes of a Vipertek are sharp enough to penetrate three layers of clothes, even if the top one is a winter parka, and Holly is wearing nothing but a cotton shirt. The electrodes of Thing Two penetrate it and her bra's backstrap with no problem. Holly goes on her toes, throws her arms into the air like a football ref signaling the kick is good, then collapses to the bricks.

'Thank God the cavalry has arrived,' Emily says. 'Help me up. That nosy cunt broke my wrist.'

He does so, and as she looks down at Holly, Em actually laughs. Just a shaky chuckle, but real enough. 'It made me forget all about my back for a moment, there's that. I'll want a poultice, and perhaps one of your special tisanes. Is she dead? Please tell me she's not dead. We have to find out how much she knows, and if she's told anyone yet.'

Roddy kneels and puts his fingers on Holly's neck. 'Pulse is thready, but it's there. She'll be back with us in an hour or two.'

'No she won't,' Emily says, 'because you're going to give her an injection. Not Valium, either. Ketamine.' She puts her good hand in the small of her back and stretches. 'I think my back is actually better. Maybe I should have tried cement-step therapy before this. We'll find out what we need to know, then kill her.'

'This may be the end,' Roddy says. His lips are trembling, his eyes wet. 'Thank God we've got the pills—'

Yes. They do. Emily has brought them downstairs. Just in case.

'Maybe, maybe not. Never say die, my love; never say die. In any case, her days of snooping are done.' She deals Holly a vicious kick in the ribs. 'This is what you get for sticking your nose in where it doesn't belong, bitch.' And to Roddy: 'Get a blanket. We'll have to drag her. If she breaks a leg when we slide her down the stairs to the basement, too bad. She won't suffer for long.'

22

At nine o'clock that night Penny Dahl is sitting on the front porch of her neat little Cape Cod in the suburb of Upriver, about twelve miles north of the city center. It's been another hot day, but it's cooling off now and it's pleasant out here. A few fireflies — not as many as when Penny was a girl — stitch random patterns above the lawn. Her phone is in her lap. She expects it to ring at any moment with the promised call from her investigator.

By nine fifteen, when the call still hasn't come, Penny is irritated. When it hasn't come at nine thirty, she's simmering. She's *paying* this woman, and more than she can afford. Herbert, her ex, has agreed to chip in, which lightens the burden, but still — money is money, and an appointment is an appointment.

At nine forty she calls Holly's number and gets voicemail. It's short and to the point: 'You've reached Holly Gibney. I can't come to the phone now. Please leave a brief message and a callback number.'

'This is Penny. You were supposed to update me at nine. Call me back *immediately*.'

She ends the call. She watches the fireflies. She has always had a short fuse – both Herbert Dahl and Bonnie would testify to that – and by ten o'clock she's not just simmering, she's boiling. She calls Holly again and waits for the beep. When it comes, she says, 'I'm going to wait until ten thirty, then I'm going to bed and you can consider yourself terminated.' But that bloodless word doesn't adequately express her anger. *'Fired.'* She pushes the end button extra hard, as if *that* would help.

Ten thirty arrives. Then quarter of eleven. Penny realizes that she's getting dew-damp. She calls one more time and gets another helping of voicemail. 'This is Penny, your employer. *Former* employer. You're fired.' She starts to end the call, then thinks of something else. 'And I want my money back! You're useless!'

She stalks into the house, flings her phone onto the living room sofa, and goes into the bathroom to brush her teeth. She sees herself in the mirror – too thin, too pale, looking ten years older than her age. No, make it fifteen. Her daughter is missing, maybe dead, and her crack investigator is probably out somewhere, drinking in a bar.

She's crying when she undresses and goes to bed. No, not drinking in a bar. Some people undoubtedly are, but not that mousy little broad, with her careful masking and oh-so-current elbow-bumps. She's probably home watching television with her phone off.

'Forgot all about me,' Penny says into the dark. She has never felt so alone in her life. 'Stupid bitch. Fuck her.'

She closes her eyes.

July 29, 2021

1

At some point that night, Holly has a strange dream. She's in a cage behind crisscrossed bars that make many squares. Sitting on a kitchen chair and looking in at her is an old man. She can't see him very well because her vision keeps doubling on her, but he appears to be covered in fire engines. 'Did you know,' he says, 'that there are 2,600 calories in the human liver? Some are fat-cals, but most, almost all, are pure protein. This wonderful organ . . .'

The Fire Engine Man continues his lecture – now something about the thighs – but she doesn't want to listen. It's a terrible dream, worse than the ones about her mother, and she has the worst headache of her life.

Holly closes her eyes and drifts back into darkness.

2

Penny is so mad she can't sleep. She only thrashes around in the bed until it's a total mess. But by three o'clock that morning, her rage at Holly has morphed into nagging disquiet. Her daughter is gone, as if she stepped on one of the world's many hidden trapdoors and vanished from sight. What if the same thing has happened to Holly?

While her anger was burning hot she called Holly useless, but she hadn't *seemed* useless. On the contrary, she'd seemed very competent, and her track record – Penny had done her due diligence – bore that out. Sometimes, though, even competent people made mistakes. Stepped on one of those hidden trapdoors and boom, down they went.

Penny gets up, retrieves her phone, and tries Holly again. Voicemail again. She's reminded of how her unease grew when she kept trying Bonnie and getting *her* voicemail. She can tell herself that this isn't the same, there's a reasonable explanation, it's only been six hours since the missed appointment, but at three in the morning the mind fills up with unpleasant shadows and some of them have teeth. She wishes she had a personal number for Holly's partner as well as the one listed on the website, but she doesn't. Only Holly's personal and the Finders Keepers office number. So she's out of luck, isn't she? Besides, who leaves their phone on active duty at such an ungodly hour?

Lots of people, she thinks. *The parents of teenagers . . . people on the night shift . . . maybe even private investigators.*

She has an idea and goes to the Finders Keepers website. The partner's name and office phone number are there, also a list of services and the hours when the office is open: 9 AM to 4 PM, just like Penny's bank. At the bottom of the web page is *After hours call 225 521 6283* and below that, in red: *If you feel you are in immediate danger, call 911 RIGHT NOW.*

Penny has no intention of calling 911; they'd laugh at her. If anyone answered at all, that is. But the after-hours number is almost certainly an answering service. She calls it. The woman who picks up sounds sleepy and has an intermittent cough. Penny pictures someone who's working a job that can be done from home, even when sick.

'This is Braden Answering Service, which client do you wish to reach?'

'Finders Keepers. My name is Penelope Dahl. I need to speak to one of the partners. His name is Peter Huntley. It could be urgent.' She decides that isn't strong enough. 'I mean it is. It is urgent.'

'Ma'am, I'm not allowed to give out private num—'

'But you must have them, don't you? For emergencies?'

The answering service woman doesn't reply. Unless a coughing fit is a reply.

'I've been calling Holly Gibney, she's the other partner. Calling and calling. She doesn't answer. *Her* private number is 440 771 8218. You can check that. But I don't have *his*. I need a little help here. Please.'

The answering service woman coughs. There's a ruffle of pages. *Checking her protocols,* Penny thinks. Then the woman says, 'Leave me your number and I'll give it to him. Or more likely leave it on his voicemail. It's three thirty in the morning, you know.'

'I do know. Tell him to call Penelope Dahl. Penny. My number is—'

'I have that on my screen.' The woman is coughing again.

'Thank you. So much. And ma'am? Take care of yourself.'

When twenty minutes pass with no callback from Huntley (she didn't really expect one), Penny returns to bed with her phone beside her. She drifts off to sleep. She dreams her daughter comes home. Penny hugs her and says she will never interfere in her daughter's life again. The phone stays quiet.

3

Holly doesn't regain consciousness, she rises back to it and into a world of pain. She's only had one hangover in her life – the result of a badly spent New Year's Eve she doesn't like to think about – but it was mild compared to this. Her brain feels like a blood-soaked sponge in a bone cage. Her bottom is throbbing. It's as if a bunch of wasps, the new kind they call murder wasps, sank their poison-filled stingers into her back and the nape of her neck. Her ribs on the right side hurt so badly that it's hard to draw each breath. Eyes still closed, she presses there gently. It makes the pain worse, but they seem intact.

She opens her eyes to see where she is and a bolt of pain goes through her head even though the lights in the Harris basement are low. She lifts her shirt on the right side. That makes the wasp stings hurt worse than ever and another bolt of pain goes through her head, but she gets a good look – better than she wants to – at a huge bruise, mostly purple but black just below her bra.

She kicked me. After I was out, that bitch kicked me.

On the heels of that: *Which bitch?*

Emily Harris. That *bitch.*

She's in a cage. Crisscrossed bars form squares. Beyond them is a cement-floored basement with a large steel box at the far end. It's standing in what looks like a workshop area. Above the cage, the lens of a camera peers down. There's a kitchen chair in front of the cage, so the Fire Engine Man wasn't a dream after all. He was sitting right there.

She's lying on a futon. There's a blue plastic potty squatting in one corner. She's able to get to her feet (slowly, slowly) by grasping the bars and pulling herself up by her left hand. She tries to add her right, but the ache in her ribs is too much. The effort of standing makes her headache worse, but standing takes some of the pressure off her bruised ribs. Now she's aware that she's fiercely, fiercely thirsty. She feels like she could drink a gallon of water without stopping.

She takes shuffling baby steps toward the potty, lifts the lid, and sees nothing inside, not even water laced with that blue disinfectant that looks like antifreeze or windshield washer fluid. The potty is as dry as her mouth and throat.

Her memory of what happened is blurry at best, but she has to get it back. Has to get her *wits* back. Holly has a good idea that she's going to die in this cage where others have died before her, probably at the hands of the Red Bank Predator, but if she doesn't get her wits back, she'll die for sure. Her bag is gone. Her phone is gone. Bill's gun is gone. No one knows she's here. Her wits are all she has.

4

Roddy Harris is sitting on the front porch, wearing slippers and a robe over blue pajamas covered with red firetrucks. Emily gave them to him for his birthday years ago as a joke, but he likes them. They remind him of his childhood, when he loved to watch the firetrucks go by.

He has been sitting on the porch since sunrise, drinking coffee from his tall Starbucks travel mug and waiting for the police. Now it's nine thirty on this Thursday morning and there's been nothing but the usual traffic. This isn't a guarantee that no one knows where the woman has gone, but it's a step in the right direction. Roddy believes that if noon comes and goes with no police, they can begin to assume that Miss Nosy Girl hasn't been missed. At least not yet.

Her address, an apartment building on the east side, was on her driver's license. Because poor Emmy's back wasn't up to walking down the hill to where Nosy Girl's car was parked, Roddy did it. By then it was dark. He drove it up to their house, where Em took over. Roddy followed her in their Subaru to Nosy Girl's building. A button on the visor lifted the gate to the underground parking garage. Em parked (in this hot midsummer there were plenty of vacancies) and limped back up the ramp to the Subaru. She insisted on driving home, although she could only use one hand effectively. Probably because she was afraid Roddy wouldn't remember the way, which was ridiculous. He'd had a few Elf Bites after they got Nosy Girl downstairs and into the cell – so had Em – and he was clear, very clear. Not quite so clear this morning, but clear enough. Like Holly, he understood this would be a very bad time to lose his wits.

Emily joins him. She's wearing an Ace bandage wound tight around her wrist. It's swollen and throbs like hell. The Gibney woman tried her best to break it but didn't quite succeed. 'She's awake. We need to talk to her.'

'Both of us?'

'That would be best.'

'All right, dear.'

They go into the house. On the kitchen counter in a white dish are the two green pills: cyanide, the poison with which Joseph and Magda Goebbels killed their six children in the *Führerbunker*. Roddy scoops them up and puts them in his pocket. He has no intention of leaving their final means of escape in the kitchen while they are in the basement.

Emily takes a bottle of Artesia water from the refrigerator. There is no raw calves' liver in there. There is no need for any. They want nothing to do with Nosy Girl's smoke-polluted carcass, didn't even have to discuss it.

Emily gives Roddy her thin smile. 'Let's see what she has to say for herself, shall we?'

'Be careful on the stairs, dear,' Roddy says. 'Mind your back.'

Em replies that she'll be fine, but hands the bottle of water to Roddy so she can grip the railing with her good hand, and she goes down very slowly, a step at a time. *Like an old woman*, Roddy mourns. *If we get out of this somehow, I suppose we'll have to take another one, and soon.*

Risk or no risk, he can't bear to see her suffer.

5

Holly watches them descend. They move with glassy care, and she's once again amazed that they have taken her prisoner. That old ad comes to mind. She should have gone to the running car after all instead of hiding behind the chainsaws.

'I wouldn't believe you'd have much to smile about in your current situation, Ms Gibney, but apparently you do.' Emily has both hands at the small of her back. 'Would you like to share?'

Never answer a suspect's questions, Bill used to say. *They answer yours.*

'Hello again, Professor Harris,' she says, looking past Emily . . . who, by her expression, does not enjoy being looked past. 'You came up behind me, didn't you? With your own Taser.'

'I did,' Roddy says, and rather proudly.

'Were you here last night? I seem to remember your pajamas.'

'I was.'

Emily's eyes widen and Holly thinks, *You didn't know that, did you?*

Em turns to her husband and takes the water. 'I think that's enough, dear. Let me ask the questions.'

Holly has an idea there will only be one question before they slam the big door and turn out all the lights, and she would like to postpone it. She has remembered something else from last night, and it fits with the undergraduate nickname for this man. Fits perfectly. Were she free and talking with friends about the case in bright daylight she would have considered the idea absurd, but in this basement – thirsty, in severe pain, a prisoner – it makes perfect sense.

'Is he eating them? Is that why you take them?'

They exchange a puzzled look that can be nothing but authentic. Then Emily bursts into surprisingly girlish laughter. After a moment, Roddy joins her. As they laugh they share the particular telepathic look that is the sole property of a couple that's been together for many decades. Roddy gives a slight nod – *tell her, why not* – and Emily turns to Holly.

'There is no he, dear, only we. *We* eat them.'

6

While Holly is discovering that she's been locked in a cage by a pair of elderly cannibals, Penny Dahl is in the shower with her hair full of shampoo. Her phone rings. She steps out onto the bathmat and plucks it off the clothes hamper while soapy water runs down her neck and back. She checks the number. Holly? No.

'Hello?'

It isn't a man who replies but a woman, and she doesn't bother with hello. 'Why did you call in the middle of the night? What's the big emergency?'

'Who is this? I asked for a callback from Peter Hun—'

'It's his daughter. Dad's in the hospital. He has Covid. I'm on his phone. What do you want?'

'I was in the shower. Can I rinse off and call you back?'

The woman gives a longsuffering sigh. 'Sure, fine.'

'My screen says unknown number. Can you—'

The woman gives her the number and Penny writes it in the steam on the bathroom mirror, repeating it over and over to herself for good measure as she turns the shower back on and sticks her head under it. It's a half-assed rinse job, but she can finish later. She wraps herself in a towel and calls back.

'This is Shauna. What's your deal, Ms Dahl?'

Penny tells her that Holly was investigating the disappearance of her daughter and was supposed to call to report her progress at nine last night. There was no call, and since then, including this morning, Penny gets only voicemail.

'I don't know what I can do for y—'

A male voice interrupts her. 'Give it to me.'

'Dad, no. The doctor said—'

'Give me the damn phone.'

Shauna says, 'If you set back his recovery—'

Then she's gone. A man coughs into Penny's ear, reminding her of the woman from the answering service. 'This is Pete,' he says. 'I apologize for my daughter. She's in full protect-the-old-guy mode.'

Faintly: 'Oh my fuck, *really*?'

'Start over, please.'

Penny goes through it again. This time she finishes by saying, 'Maybe it's nothing, but since my daughter disappeared, anyone not showing up makes me crazy.'

'Maybe nothing, maybe something,' Pete says. 'Holly's always on time. It's a thing with her. I want—' He coughs dryly. 'I want to give you Jerome Robinson's number. He works with us sometimes. He . . . well, shit. I forgot. Jerome is in New York. You can try him if you want, but his sister Barbara might be a better bet. I'm pretty sure she and Jerome both have keys to Holly's apartment. I have one, too, but I'm—' More coughing. 'I'm in Kiner. Another day, they tell me, then more quarantining at home. Shauna, too. I guess I could send a nurse down with the key.'

Penny is in the kitchen now, and dripping on the floor. She grabs a pen from beside the day planner. 'I hope it won't come to that. Give me those numbers.'

He does. Penny jots them down. Shauna recaptures the phone, says an unceremonious 'G'bye,' and then Penny is on her own again.

She tries both numbers, the one for Barbara first since she's in town. She gets voicemail from both. She leaves messages, then goes back into the bathroom to finish her shower. It's the second time this month that she's had the feeling that something is wrong, and the first time she was right.

Holly's always on time. It's a thing with her.

7

'You *eat* them,' Holly echoes.

There *is* no Red Bank Predator. It should be impossible to believe, but it's not. Only two old college professors living in a neat Victorian home near a prestigious college.

Roddy steps forward eagerly, almost within grabbing distance. Emily pulls him back by his robe, wincing as she does it. Roddy doesn't seem to notice.

'All mammals are cannibals,' he says, 'but only *homo sapiens* has a silly taboo about it, one that flies in the face of all known medical facts.'

'Roddy—'

He ignores her. He's dying to expound. To explain. They have never done that with any of their other captures, but this isn't livestock; he doesn't have to worry about her adrenals flooding her flesh before they are ready to slaughter.

'That taboo is less than three hundred years old, and even now many tribes – *long-lived* tribes, I might add – enjoy the benefits of human flesh.'

'Roddy, this isn't the time—'

'Do you know how many calories are contained in the body of an adult human being of average weight? *One hundred and twenty-six thousand!*' His voice has begun to rise to the screamy pitch many of his nutrition and biology classes would have recognized in days of yore. 'Healthy human flesh and blood cures *epilepsy*, it cures *amyotrophic lateral sclerosis*, it cures *sciatica*! Healthy human fat cures *otosclerosis*, the main cause of *deafness*, and drops of warm liquid fat in the eyes spontaneously heals *macular*—'

'Roddy, *enough!*'

He gives her a stubborn look. 'Human flesh ensures *longevity*. Look at us, if you have any doubts. Late eighties, yet hale and healthy!'

Holly wonders if he's having a kind of Alzheimer's-induced dream, or if he's just batpoop out of his mind. Maybe it's both. She just saw the way they came downstairs, step by careful, hesitating step. Like human Ming vases.

'Let's get to the point,' Emily says. 'Who have you told? Who knows you're here?'

Holly doesn't reply.

Emily gives her scimitar smile. 'Sorry, I misspoke. *Nobody* knows you're here, at least at the present time, or they would have come looking for you.'

'The police,' Roddy amplifies. 'Five-O. The po-po.' He actually makes a *rurr-rurr-rurr* sound and twirls one bunched and crooked finger in the air.

'Excuse my husband,' Emily says. 'He's upset and it makes him garrulous. I'm also upset, but it makes me curious. Who *will* know you're here?'

Holly doesn't reply.

Emily holds up the bottle of water. 'You must be thirsty.'

Holly doesn't reply.

'Tell me who you've told . . . assuming you've told anyone. Maybe you haven't. The fact that no one has come looking for you suggests that, and quite strongly.'

Holly doesn't reply.

'Let's go,' she tells Roddy. 'What we have here is a stubborn bitch.'

'You don't understand,' Roddy says to Holly. 'No one would understand.'

'Shall we give her a few hours to think it over, my love?'

'Yes,' Roddy says. There's been a vacancy about him, but now it clears, at least a little. 'Unless someone comes. Then we won't need her input, will we?'

'No,' Emily says, 'in that case we would not.'

'I'm going to die no matter what I do or don't tell you,' Holly says. 'Aren't I?'

'Not necessarily,' Emily says. 'I think you have no proof. I think you came here to *get* proof. You took pictures of our van with your phone, but your phone is gone. Without proof, we could perhaps let you go.'

As if this cage doesn't exist, Holly thinks.

'On the other hand . . .' She raises her arm, showing the Ace bandage. 'You hurt me.'

Holly thinks of lifting her shirt and showing the bruise. Of saying, *I think we're even on that score.* She doesn't. What she says is, 'Maybe you have something for that.'

'Already applied,' Roddy says briskly. 'A poultice of fat.'

From Bonnie Dahl, Holly thinks, and that is when the absolute truth of it hits her and she sags back a little.

Emily holds up the water. 'Tell me what I want to know and I'll give this to you.'

Holly says nothing.

'All right,' Emily says, with sadness that's utterly unconvincing, 'the truth is you're almost certainly going to die. But do you want to die thirsty?'

Holly, who can't believe she isn't dead already, makes no reply.

'Come on, Roddy,' Emily says, leading him back toward the stairs. Roddy goes with her docilely. 'She needs some time to think about it.'

'Yes. But not too much.'

'No, not too much. She must be *terribly* thirsty.'

They go up the stairs as carefully as they went down them. *Fall,* Holly urges. *Fall! Stumble and fall and break your fracking necks!*

But neither of them falls. The door between the world upstairs and this basement dungeon closes. Holly is left alone with her throbbing head, her other aches, and her thirst.

8

It's busy, that nine o'clock hour, both on Ridge Road and several other places. It's the nine o'clock hour when Emily calls Roddy in from the porch to talk to Holly in the basement. It's the hour when Penny Dahl speaks to Shauna and Pete Huntley, then leaves voicemails on the phones of Jerome and Barbara Robinson.

It's also the nine o'clock hour when Barbara comes downstairs from the guest room in Olivia's house, where she's spent the night. She's wearing shorts and a top loaned to her by Marie Duchamp. They're not quite the same size, but close enough. Barbara can't remember the last time she slept so late. She's not hungover, possibly because Marie told her to take two Tylenol before going to bed — a sure cure, she said, unless you really took a bath in the stuff — but possibly because she switched to sparkling water when a bunch of them, led by department head Rosalyn Burkhart, went to the Green Door Pub. Which, Rosalyn said, had been Olivia's watering hole of choice before giving up booze in her seventies, after her first bout of a-fib.

Like most teenagers, the first thing Barbara does is make a beeline for her phone. She sees it's down to 26 per cent power, and she left her charger at home. She also sees she has a missed call and a voicemail that must have come in just as she was dressing. She thinks it will be one of those nuisance VMs telling her she can update her car's warranty (as if she had one), but it's not. It's from Penny Dahl, Holly's client.

Barbara listens to it with growing concern. Her first thought is an accident. Her friend lives alone, and accidents sometimes happen to such people. They can slip in the shower or on the stairs. They can fall asleep with a lit cigarette (Barbara has known for some time that Holly's smoking again). Or they can be assaulted in a parking garage, like the one under Holly's building. Only robbed if lucky, beaten or raped if not.

As Marie comes downstairs – more slowly, because Marie did *not* switch to sparkling water last night – Barbara calls Holly. She gets a recorded message telling her Holly's mailbox is full.

Barbara doesn't like that.

'I have to go and check on someone,' she tells Marie. 'A friend.'

Marie, still wearing last night's clothes and suffering a bad case of bed head, asks if she'd like a cup of coffee first.

'Maybe later,' Barbara says. She likes this less and less. It isn't just accidents she's thinking about now, it's Holly's current case. She grabs her bag, drops her phone into it, and leaves in her mother's car.

9

Roddy on the porch again. Emily joins him. He's staring vacantly into the street. *He comes and goes,* Emily thinks. *One day he'll go and not come back.*

She has no doubt that Gibney would eventually tell them what they want – *need* – to know, but Em doesn't think they can afford to wait. That means she has to think for both of them. She doesn't want to swallow cyanide, although she will if she has to; better suicide than seeing their names spattered across every newspaper and cable news outlet, not just in America but around the world. Her reputation, built up so carefully over the years, will fall to ruins. Roddy's, too. *The College Cannibals,* she thinks. *That's what they'll call us.*

Better cyanide than that. Absolutely. But if there's a chance, she wants to take it. And if they have to stop what they've been doing, would that really be so terrible? More and more she wonders if they've just been fooling themselves all along. She knows a two-word phrase from her own reading on the subject of nutrition and miracle cures. It's a phrase that's already occurred to the battered and thirsty woman in their basement.

Meanwhile, time is ticking, and maybe – just maybe – they won't have to wait for Gibney to talk.

'Roddy.'

'Mmm?' Looking out at the street.

'Roddy, look at me.' She snaps her fingers in front of his eyes. 'Pay attention.'

He turns to her. 'How is your back, dear one?'

'Better. A little bit.' It's true. Probably a six on the universal pain scale today. 'I have to do something. You need to stay here, but *don't go downstairs*. If the police come and they don't have a search warrant, send them away and call me. Are you following this?'

'Yes.' He looks like he is, but she doesn't trust that.

'Repeat it back to me.'

He does. Perfectly.

'If they do have a warrant, let them in. Then call me and take one of those pills. Do you remember where you put them?'

'Of course.' He gives her an impatient look. 'They are in my pocket.'

'Good. Give me one.' And because of his alarmed look (he's such a dear): 'Just in case.'

He smiles at that and singsongs, 'Where are you going, my little one, little one?'

'It doesn't matter. Don't concern yourself. I'll be back by noon at the latest.'

'All right. Here is your pill. Be careful with it.'

She kisses the corner of his mouth, then gives him an impulsive hug to boot. She loves him, and she realizes that this mess is really *her* mess. If not for her, Roddy would have just gone on fulminating, spending his retirement writing responses in his various journals (journals he sometimes throws across the room in disgust). Certainly he never would have published anything about the benefits of eating human flesh; he was smart enough (*then*) to know what such ideas would do to his reputation. 'They'd call me Modest Proposal Harris,' he grumbled once. (He'd read the Jonathan Swift essay at her urging.) It was she who had moved him – *them* – from the theoretical to the practical, and she had the perfect test case: the spic who had dared cross her about the Poetry Workshop. Eating that queerboy's supposedly talented brains had been a pleasure.

And it did help, she tells herself. *It really did. It helped both of us.*

Holly's purse is on the living room coffee table, along with the hat she'd been wearing. Emily jams the hat on her own head and roots through the purse, past all the jumble of Holly's on-the-move life (including masks and cigarettes – the ironic juxtaposition doesn't escape Emily), and comes up with what looks like an entry card of some sort. She pockets it. The woman's gun, the one she hurt Em's wrist with, is on the mantel.

Gibney's phone is long gone, but Emily made sure to comb through it before removing the SIM card and then putting it in the microwave for good measure. Access was easy enough; all Em had to do was apply the unconscious woman's fingerprint to the screen, and once again, when opening location services in the privacy settings. She saw the last two places Gibney visited before coming here were her office and her home. Emily doesn't dare go back to the apartment building in broad daylight, but she thinks the office is a better bet, because the troublesome woman actually spent quite a bit of time there.

Gibney has (soon it will be *had*) a partner named Pete Huntley, but when Emily finds Huntley on Facebook, she discovers a wonderfully fortuitous thing. He doesn't post much himself, but the comments and messages tell Emily all she needs to know: he's got Covid. He was at home, and now he's in the hospital. The last comment, posted only an hour ago, is from someone named Isabelle Jaynes and reads, *Tomorrow you'll be back home and on your feet in a week or two! Get Well, you Grumpy Old . . .* and then an emoji of a bear.

If Gibney is working for the elf's mother, she may have taken time to write a report. If so, and if that's the only artifact – other than Gibney herself, and she'll soon be nothing but wet clumps in a plastic disposal bag – and if Emily can get the hard copy . . . or delete it from Gibney's computer . . .

It's a long shot, but one well worth taking. Meanwhile, their prisoner will be getting thirstier and more willing to talk. *Maybe even craving a cigarette*, Emily thinks, and smiles. This is a desperate situation, but she's never felt more alive. And at least it's taken her mind off her back. She starts to leave, then rethinks that. She takes an Elf Parfait from the refrigerator – gray, with red swirls – and gobbles it.

Tasty!

The thing about human flesh, she's discovered, is that you start off curious. Then you get to liking it. Eventually you get to love it, and one day you can't get enough.

Instead of going out the kitchen door to get to the garage, she takes

the long way around so she can speak to Roddy again. 'Repeat what
I told you.'

He does. Letter-perfect.

'Don't go down there, Roddy. That's the most important thing. Not
until I get back.'

'Buddy system,' he says.

'That's right, buddy system.' And she walks down the driveway to
get the Subaru.

10

Besides her thirst, her pounding headache, and more other pains than
she cares to count, Holly is scared. She's been close to death on other
occasions, but never any closer than this. She understands they're going
to kill her no matter what, and it won't be long. As they say in the
old film noir movies Holly is so fond of, *she knows too much.*

She's not entirely sure what the big metal box is on the far side of
the basement but suspects it might be a woodchipper. The hose goes
through the wall and into whatever is on the other side of the small
door in the workshop area. *That's how they get rid of them*, she thinks.
Whatever's left of them. God only knows how they'd got their disposal
unit down here.

She looks at the pegboard on the far wall and sees two items there
that aren't tools. One is a bike helmet. Next to it is a backpack. Holly's
knees weaken at the sight of them, and she sits down on the futon,
gasping a little at the pain in her ribs. The futon moves a little. She
sees the edge of something beneath it. She lifts the futon to see what
it is.

11

Barbara has a key to Holly's apartment but no gate-opener, so she parks
on the street, goes down the ramp, and ducks under the bar. Right
away she sees something she doesn't like. Holly's car is there, but it's
parked close to the ramp, and both of Holly's assigned spaces – one
for her, one for a guest – are much further in. And another thing: the
left front tire is over the yellow line and intruding on the next parking

space. Holly would never park that way. She'd take one look, then get back in her car and make the adjustment.

Maybe she was in a hurry.

Maybe so, but her own spaces are closer to the elevator and the stairs. It's the stairs Barbara takes, because you need a swipe card for the elevator and she doesn't have one. She goes up at a trot, more anxious than ever. On Holly's floor she uses her key, opens the door, and pokes her head in.

'Holly? Are you here?'

No answer. Barbara checks the place quickly, almost running from room to room. Everything is in its place and everything is neat as a pin – bed made, kitchen counters free of crumbs and spills, bathroom spotless. The only thing Barbara notices is the lingering smell of cigarette smoke, and even that's faint. There are aromatherapy candles in every room, and the only ashtray is in the dish drainer, clean as a whistle. It looks good. Fine, in fact.

But the car.

The car bothers her. In the wrong space, and sloppily parked.

Her phone rings. It's Jerome. 'Did you track her down?'

'No. I'm in her apartment now. I don't like it, J.' She tells him about the car, thinking he'll dismiss it, but Jerome doesn't like it, either.

'Huh. Look in the little basket by the front door. She always drops her keys there when she comes in. I've seen her do it a thousand times.'

Barbara looks. There's a spare key to Holly's Prius there, but not her keyring. Not her swipe card for the elevator, either. 'They're probably in that big shoulder bag of hers.'

'Maybe, but why is her car there and she's not?'

'She took the bus?' Barbara says doubtfully.

'They're not running a regular schedule because of Covid. I found that out when I tried to take one to the airport. I had to Uber.'

'Poor you,' she says, but it's a bad attempt at their usual amiable raillery.

'I have a bad feeling about this, Ba. I think I'm going to come home.'

'Jerome, no!'

'Jerome yes. I'll see what I can get for a flight. If she turns up before I get on a plane, call me or shoot me a text.'

'What about your glitzy weekend in Montauk? You might get a chance to meet Spielberg!'

'I didn't like his last two movies, anyway. She seemed fine when I talked to her yesterday, but . . .' He trails off, but goes on before she can speak: 'It might be the case. The Dahl woman left me a message, too. She sounded really worried. Hols could have run across the wrong person investigating Bonnie's disappearance. And the others. Now there's this guy Castro from nine or ten years ago, add him to the list.'

'Maybe. I don't know.' All Barbara knows for sure is that Holly would never have parked that way. It's sloppy, and sloppy is one thing Holly isn't.

'Have you tried calling the office?'

'Yes. On the way over. Voicemail.'

'Maybe you should go there. Make sure she isn't . . . I don't know.' But Barbara knows. *Make sure she isn't dead.*

'We're probably jumping at shadows, J. There might be a perfectly reasonable explanation for this, and you'll be flying home for nothing.'

'Check the office. Just, if you find her before I get on a plane, let me know.'

She leaves and hurries back down the stairs.

12

As Barbara is talking to her brother in Holly's empty apartment, Rodney Harris is on his porch, planning the letter he will write to *Gut*, an important journal dedicated to gastroenterology and hepatology. In the latest issue, Roddy has read a perfectly absurd paper by George Hawkins, about the relationship he claims to have discovered between the pylorus and Crohn's disease. Hawkins – a PhD, no less! – has totally misrepresented papers written by Myron DeLong and . . . and that other fellow, whose name Roddy can't recall at the moment. Hawkins's conclusions are thus completely wrong.

Roddy munches from his supply of deep-fried Elf Balls, relishing the crunch as he bites down. *My response will destroy him*, he thinks contentedly.

He recalls that they have a prisoner in the basement. He can't remember her name, but he does remember the look of horror on her face when Em told her how they had managed to keep the worst depredations of old age at bay. The idea of knocking down her foolish prejudices one by one pleases him almost as much as writing the letter to *Gut* that will knock down Professor George Hawkins's flimsy house of cards. He has forgotten Emily's command to stay out of the basement. Even if he had recalled it, he would have dismissed it as foolish. The woman is in a *cage*, for God's sake!

He gets up and goes into the house, tossing another Elf Ball into his mouth as he does. They have a wonderfully clarifying effect.

13

Holly creaks to her feet as Harris descends to the basement. She's wondering if this is it, how it ends. He comes to the foot of the stairs and just stands there for a moment. Off in his own universe. He's still wearing his robe and pajamas. He takes something brown and round from the pocket of his robe and tosses it into his mouth. Holly doesn't want to believe it's a piece of Penny Dahl's daughter, but suspects it is. Her left hand is a fist, squeezing and releasing in time with the pulsing ache in her head, short nails digging into her palm.

'Is that what I think it is?'

He gives her a conspiratorial smile but says nothing.

'Are they good for pain? Because I hurt all over.'

'Yes, they have an analgesic effect,' he says, and pops another. 'Quite amazing. Several popes knew of the beneficial effects. The Vatican keeps it quiet, but *there are records*!'

'Could I . . . could you give me one?' The idea of eating a piece of Penny Dahl's daughter makes her feel almost nauseated enough to throw up, but she tries to look both pleading and hopeful.

He smiles, pulls one of the little brown balls from the pocket of his robe, and starts toward her. Then he stops and shakes a finger at her like an indulgent parent who has caught his three-year-old drawing crayon pictures on the wallpaper. 'Aah-aah-aah,' he says. 'Perhaps not, Miss . . . what was your name?'

'Holly. Holly Gibney.'

Roddy glances at the broom they use to push food and water through the flap, then shakes his head. He starts to put the brown ball back into his pocket, then changes his mind and tosses it into his mouth.

'If you don't want to help me, what did you come down for, Mr Harris?'

'*Professor* Harris.'

'I'm sorry. Professor. Did you want to talk?'

He just stands there, looking off into space. Holly would like to wring his scrawny neck, but he's still at the foot of the stairs, twenty or twenty-five feet away. She wishes her arms were that long.

He turns to go back up, then remembers why he came down and turns to her again. 'Let's talk liver. The human liver that has been *awakened*. Shall we?'

'All right.' She doesn't know how she can entice him to come closer, but as long as he doesn't go upstairs – or if his wife, whose brains appear to be in better working order, doesn't come down – something may occur to her. 'How do you wake up a liver, Professor?'

'By eating *another* liver, of course.' He gives her a look that asks how she can be so stupid. 'Calves' liver is best, but I suspect pigs' liver would be almost as good. We've never tried it. Because of the prions. Also, if it's not broke—'

'Don't fix it,' Holly finishes. Her head is pounding so fiercely it makes her feel like her eyeballs are pulsing, and her thirst is enormous, but she gives him her best *I'm eager to learn* smile. Her hand squeezes and releases, squeezes and releases.

'Correct! Absolutely correct! What's not broken need not be fixed. It's axiomatic! I suspect *human* liver would be best of all, but to feed a person fresh human liver from *another* person, the problem would be . . . obviously . . . would be . . .' He frowns into space.

'That you'd need *two* prisoners,' Holly says.

'Yes! *Yes!* Obvious! Axiomatic! But the liver . . . what was I saying?'

'Awakened,' Holly says. 'Possibly . . . made ready?'

'Exactly. The liver is the grail. The true holy grail. A *sacrament*. Did you know the human liver contains all nine essential amino acids? That it's especially high in lysine?'

'Which prevents cold sores,' says Holly, who is prone to them.

'That's the *least* of its attributes!' Harris's voice is rising in pitch. Soon it will reach the ranting near scream that disturbed some students so much that they dropped his classes. 'Lysine cures *anxiety*! Lysine heals *wounds*! The liver is a lysine *treasure chest*! It also revitalizes the thymus gland, which creates T-cells! And Covid? *Covid?*' He laughs, and even that is a near scream. 'Those who are fortunate enough to eat of the human liver, most particularly the *awakened* human liver, those fortunate ones *laugh* at Covid, as I and my wife do! Oh, and iron! Human liver is richer in iron than the livers of calves . . . sheep . . . pigs . . . deer . . . woodchucks . . . you name it. There is more iron in a human liver than in the liver of a blue whale, and a blue whale weighs *one hundred and sixty-five tons*! Iron wards off fatigue and improves circulation, *especially in the BRAAIIIN*!' Roddy taps his temple, where a node of small veins is pulsing.

Holly thinks, *I am speaking to an authentic mad scientist.* Only of course she's not speaking; she's listening. Nor is Rodney Harris lecturing. Not anymore. He's hollering at an invisible audience of unbelievers.

'*Ounces, MERE OUNCES, of human liver contain seven hundred per cent of EVERY VITAMIN needed for the creation of red cell formation and cell METABOLISM! Look at my skin, my good elf, just look at it!*'

Roddy grasps one hollow wrinkled cheek and palpates it like a dentist preparing to inject Novocain into a patient's gum. '*Smooth! Smooth as the fabled BABY'S BOTTOM! And that's just the LIVER!*' He pauses to catch his breath. 'As for the consumption of *brain tissue*—'

'All bullshit,' Holly says. It just pops out. She has no plan, no strategy. She's just had enough. Thoughts of humoring him have gone straight out the window.

He stares at her, wide-eyed. He has been speaking to that invisible audience, *swaying* them, and some callow undergraduate with nothing but high school biology as a foundation has had the temerity to challenge him. 'What? *What* do you say?'

'I call bullshit,' Holly replies. She's holding the crossbars loosely in her right hand, the left fisted above her right breast, her face pressed into one of the squares, staring at him. Her care not to use vulgarities, learned at her mother's knee, has also gone out the window. 'This is medicine-show crap, right up there with copper bracelets and magic crystals. Smooth skin? Have you looked in a mirror lately, Professor? You're as wrinkled as an unmade bed.'

'Shut up!' His cheeks are glowing dull red. That snarl of veins in his temple is pulsing faster, faster. 'Shut up, you . . . you *twerp!*'

They're going to kill me, but I'm going to tell this man a few basic truths before they do.

'As for improved brain function . . . you're suffering Alzheimer's, Professor, and not just early-onset. You can't remember my name, and in a few months, maybe only a few weeks, you won't be able to remember your own, either.'

'Shut up! Shut up! You're an ignorant know-nothing!'

He takes a step toward her. This is exactly what Holly was hoping for when she asked him to share one of his horrid brown balls of flesh, but now she barely notices. In her rage — at him, at his wife, at her current hopeless situation — she has even forgotten her thirst.

'You *think* you're better. Your wife thinks *she's* better. Maybe for awhile you even *were* better. It happens. You're not the only one who reads the science magazines. It's called—'

'Stop! It's a lie! It's a FILTHY FUCKING LIE!'

He doesn't want her to say what he knows might be true, but she intends to. She'll have to be quiet when she's dead, but she's not dead yet.

14

As Holly is informing Rodney Harris that he's not the only one who reads the science magazines, Emily is entering the Frederick Building. She finds the idea of masks ridiculous but she's happy to be wearing one now, and Holly's gimme cap is pulled down so the visor shades her eyes. She goes to the building directory and checks it. Finders Keepers is on the fifth floor, along with the offices of Furniture Imports, Inc., and David & Daughter, Forensic Accountants.

Emily steps into the elevator and pushes 5. When she gets out, she makes sure the hall is empty and limps down to the door with FINDERS KEEPERS INVESTIGATIVE AGENCY on it. Since she has Holly's keys, she's happy to find the door locked. It means no receptionist on duty. If there had been, she would have put on a vague old woman act and said she must have gotten off on the wrong floor, so sorry. She begins going through Holly's keys, trying ones that look like they

might fit, hoping no one comes out of Furniture Imports or David &
Daughter to use the loo.

The third key fits. She lets herself into a waiting area. Air conditioning whooshes softly. She checks the computer on the small desk,
hoping it's only asleep, but no joy. She opens the door to the right
and peeps into what must be the male partner's office, judging by the
framed sports pages on the wall. The one headlined CLEVELAND
WINS WORLD'S SERIES (*bad grammar there*, she thinks) is probably
real, but not BROWNS WIN SUPERBOWL!

The other office is Gibney's. She hurries to Holly's computer and
pushes a random key, hoping to wake it up if it's asleep. This one is,
but it wants a password to unlock any possible treasures within. She
tries several, including HollyGibney, hollygibney, FindersKeepers, finderskeepers, LaurenBacallFan, and password. None of them work. She
looks on the desk, which is neat, orderly, and bare except for a notepad.
On the top sheet are doodles of flowers and a few jottings. There is
the name *Imani*, which means nothing to Emily, but *Elm Grove Trailer
Park* does; Emily went there to clear out enough things from the
Craslow bitch's trailer to make it appear she was gone. Em doesn't like
that, but what's printed below it she likes even less: *BellRinger* and
J. Castro and *2012*.

How can the bitch have found out so *much*?

Em tears this sheet off, and the one beneath it for good measure. She
balls them up and puts them in her pocket. She checks the desk drawers
one by one, hoping for a written report. She doesn't find one, and
admits that even finding one wouldn't have eased her mind unless it was
written in longhand. Nor does she find a slip of paper with Holly's
password written on it, and a wave of angry despair rolls through her.

We should have had an exit plan beyond cyanide pills, she thinks. *Why
didn't we?*

The answer seems obvious: because they're old, and old people can't
run very far or very fast.

*Maybe there's no report. Maybe the stupid woman was too unsure of her
conclusions to write one or tell anyone.*

Emily decides it's the best she can hope for. She'll go home. Roddy
will shoot the Gibney bitch as he did the Craslow bitch. They'll run
her through the Morbark, pulverizing her bones and liquifying the rest

of her, including her nicotine-poisoned liver. Then out into the lake in the *Marie Cather*, where they'll stop above the deepest part and drop the remains of Holly Gibney over the side in a plastic disposal bag. After that they will continue hoping for the best. What else is there? Suicide, of course, but Emily still hopes it won't come to that.

She finds the wall safe, predictably hidden behind a picture of a mountain meadow. She tries the handle, expecting nothing, and nothing is what she gets. She gives the combo a disgusted spin, rehangs the picture, and turns off the computer. She decides the notepad is a little out of place, so she squares it up. Then she retreats the way she came, wiping everything she touched, starting with the computer keyboard. She finishes with the knob of the office door, after putting on her mask and peering through the spyhole to make sure the coast is clear. She is halfway down the hall before she remembers she forgot to re-lock the door. She goes back and does it, once more taking care to wipe away her fingerprints.

In the elevator she pulls the brim of the gimme cap down. She encounters only one person in the lobby and with her head lowered sees only jeans and sneakers as Barbara Robinson passes her on her way to the elevator. It's time to go home and tie up at least one troublesome loose end.

As she pushes open the door to the street, a particularly vicious bolt of pain strikes the small of her back. Emily stands on the sidewalk, grimacing, waiting for it to let up. It does, at least a little, and she thanks God (who of course doesn't exist) for the Elf Parfait she ate before leaving the house. She crosses Frederick Street to her car, limping more severely than ever.

The phrase that Holly is screaming at her husband at that very moment comes into her mind and she rejects it.

15

'*IT'S CALLED THE PLACEBO EFFECT, you half brain-dead idi—*'

He rushes at her, screaming at her to shut up, the placebo effect doesn't exist, it's nothing but the manipulation of statistics by a cadre of lazy, pseudoscientific—

She grabs him the second he comes within reach. Again, there's no thought, not even a shred of advance planning; she simply shoots her right arm through the bars and curls it around his neck. It hurts her bruised ribs, but in her adrenaline-fired state she barely notices.

He tries to jerk free and almost makes it. Holly redoubles her grip and yanks him against the bars. His bathrobe is sliding off, revealing his ridiculous firetruck pajamas.

'Let me go!' Choking, almost gurgling the words. *'Let me go!'*

Holly remembers what she has in her left hand. What she's been squeezing so tightly it's cut into her palm. It's a triangular earring, the mate of the one she found in the weeds next to the abandoned auto body shop. She shoves that hand through the bars and, holding the earring tightly between her thumb and forefinger, runs one of its three golden points across Harris's scrawny throat in a semicircle from one jaw to the other. She expects nothing, just does it. For most of that ten-inch semicircle, the point barely cuts the skin; a paper cut might go deeper and draw more blood. Then it catches on a bulging tendon and digs deeper. Roddy helps by jerking his head to the side, trying to get clear of whatever she's cutting him with. The earring slices through his jugular vein and Holly takes first one faceful of warm blood and then another as his heart pumps it at her. It's in her eyes and it burns.

Roddy gives a convulsive jerk and breaks her grip. He staggers toward the stairs with the back of his bathrobe hanging almost to his waist and the rest of it dragging on the floor. He puts his hand to his neck. Blood jets through his fingers. He blunders into the broom that's propped there and stumbles over it. His head hits the stair-rail and he goes to his knees. The spurts of blood continue, but they're starting to weaken. He uses the rail to gain his feet and turns to her. His eyes are wide. He reaches out and makes a guttural sound that could be anything, but Holly thinks it might be his wife's name. The bathrobe slips all the way off. It makes her think of a snake shedding its skin. He takes two steps toward her, waving his arms, then goes down on his face. The front of his skull thuds on the concrete. His fingers twitch. He tries to raise his head and can't. Blood trickles across the concrete.

Holly is frozen with shock and amazement. Her arms are still sticking out through two of the squares made by the crisscrossing bars. The earring is still in her left hand, which is now wearing a wet red glove.

At first the only thought in her mind is Lady Macbeth's question: who would have thought the old man had so much blood in him?

Then another one surfaces: *Where is his wife?*

She takes one step backward, then two, then trips over her own foot and sits down hard on the futon. She cries out in the pain of her bruised and outraged ribs. The earring drops from her hand.

She waits for Emily.

16

Barbara barely glances at the woman who passes her in the lobby of the Frederick Building. She's thinking of *Deduction, Please*, a series of children's detective books that Jerome read as a kid and then passed on to her. She doesn't know if her and J's fascination with Holly's chosen field (his especially) originated in those books, but it might have.

There were thirty or forty mysteries in each *Deduction, Please*, each only two or three pages long. They featured a sleuth with the unlikely name of Dutch Spyglass. Dutch would come to the scene of the crime, observe, talk to a few people, and then solve the mystery (usually robbery, sometimes arson or a clonk on the head, never murder). Dutch always concluded the same way: 'All the clues are there! The solution is in your grasp! Deduction, please?' Jerome was able to solve the cases some of the time, Barbara almost never . . . although when she turned to the back of the book and read the case summary, it always seemed obvious.

As she goes up in the elevator, she thinks the disappearances Holly has been investigating are like those mini-mysteries she puzzled over when she was nine or ten. Nastier, more sinister, but essentially the same. *All the clues are there, the solution is in your grasp.* Barbara almost thinks that's true. She wishes she could turn to the back of the book and read the solution, but there *is* no book. Only her missing friend.

She goes down the hall and opens the door to Finders Keepers with her key. 'Holly?'

No answer, but Barbara has the queerest sensation that either someone is here or has been not long ago. It's not a smell, just a feeling that the air has been disturbed recently.

'Anyone?'

Nothing. She takes a quick look into Pete's office. She even checks the coat closet. Then she goes to the door of Holly's office. She pauses there for a moment, her hand on the knob, afraid she's going to find Holly dead in her chair, eyes open and glazed. She forces herself to open the door, telling herself she won't see Holly but if she does she mustn't scream.

Holly's not there, but Barbara's sense of a recent presence doesn't go away. She looks at Holly's desk and sees nothing but a blank pad, the one she uses when she's doodling, taking notes, or both. It's neatly centered, and that's Holly all the way. Barbara pushes a key on the computer's keypad and frowns when nothing happens. Holly almost never turns her computer off, just lets it go to sleep. She says she hates even a short wait while it boots up.

Barbara turns it on and when the starter screen appears, she uses the notebook app on her phone to find the password that opens all the office computers: Qxtt4#%ck. She types it in. Nothing happens except for the quick annoying shake that means the Mac has rejected the password. She tries again in case she's entered it wrong. Same result. She frowns, then barks a small exasperated laugh as she gets it. The password changes automatically every six months, a security feature that means Qxtt4#%ck became obsolete on July first. Holly has neglected to give her the new one, and Barbara – busy with her own affairs – has forgotten to ask. Jerome may have it, but she's guessing he doesn't. He's also been busy with his own affairs.

Deduction, please?

Barbara has none. She gets up, starts to leave, then, almost on a whim, takes down the Turner landscape print on the wall. The company safe is behind it. And although it's shut and locked, Barbara sees something that adds to her disquiet. When Holly uses the safe, she always resets the combination dial to zero. It's one of her little compulsions. Pete wouldn't bother if he used the safe, but Pete's been out almost all month.

She tries the handle. Locked. She doesn't know the combination, so she can't check to see if anything has been taken. What she can do is reset the dial to zero, put back the painting, and call her brother.

17

Emily parks in the driveway and gets out of the Subaru a little too fast. Another bolt of pain goes through her back. It's becoming harder and harder to believe they're holding back the tide of senescence, a thing they've taken as an article of faith since dining on Jorge Castro.

Not faith, she insists. *Science. The science is there. These are just nerve spasms brought on by tension. They'll pass, and once they do I'll continue my recovery.*

She goes up the front steps, palms pressed into the lumbar area at the base of her spine. Roddy is no longer on the porch; nothing there but a half-empty coffee cup and his notebook. She looks down at it and is distressed to see his formerly neat handwriting has begun to sprawl and shake. Nor has he kept to the notebook's blue lines. His sentences go up and down as if he'd written them on the *Marie Cather* in a heavy swell.

She expects to find him in the living room or in the downstairs office, but he's in neither, and when she goes into the kitchen she sees the basement door is standing open. Emily feels a sinking in the pit of her stomach. She goes to the door. 'Roddy?'

It's the woman who answers. The wretched snooping woman. 'He's down here, Professor, and I think he's given his last lecture.'

18

Jerome tells Barbara he won't be flying home after all. There was a flight scheduled at 12:40 PM, but when he called to book a seat, he was told it has been canceled because of Covid. The pilot and three members of the cabin crew had tested positive.

'I'm going to try and rent a car. It's just shy of five hundred miles. I can be home by midnight. Earlier, if the traffic isn't too bad.'

'Are you sure you're old enough to rent one?' She hopes he is. She wants him with her, wants him bad.

'As of my birthday two months ago, I am. I can even get a discount with my Authors Guild card. Crazy, huh?'

'You want to know what's crazy? I think someone's been in the office. I'm here now.' She tells him about how she had to turn the computer on instead of just waking it up with a keystroke, and how the combination dial was set in the 70s instead of at zero. 'Do you have her password? The one that kicked in at the start of the month?'

'Gee, no. Haven't been there at all. My book, you know.'

Barbara knows. 'She might have turned her computer off, I've told her they suck power even when they're asleep, but forgetting to set the combo dial to zero? You know Holly.'

'But why would anyone go there?' Jerome asks, then answers his own question. 'Maybe someone's worried about what she's been finding out. Wants to know if she's written a report, or talked to her client. Barb, you have to phone the Dahl woman. Tell her to be careful.'

'I don't know her num . . .' Barbara thinks of the message Penny Dahl left. Her number will be in Barbara's contacts. 'Never mind, yes I do. I'm more worried about Holly than I am about Bonnie Dahl's mother.'

'Right there with you, sis. What about the police? Isabelle Jaynes?'

'What am I supposed to say? That she parked her car in the wrong space with a tire on the yellow line and forgot to turn the wall safe dial back to zero so call out the National Guard?'

'Yeah. Yeah, I see your point. But Izzy's sort of a friend. Do you want me to call her?'

'No, I'll do it. But before I do, tell me everything you know about the case.'

'I already—'

'You did, but I was wrapped up in my own shit, so tell me again. Because I feel like I almost know. I just can't . . . I'm so upset . . . just go through it again. Please.'

So he does.

19

Emily comes halfway down the stairs and stops when she sees her husband lying facedown in a spreading pool of blood. 'What happened?' she screams. '*What happened?*'

'I cut his throat,' Holly says. She's standing against the cement wall at the far side of the cell, next to the potty. She feels remarkably calm. 'Would you like to hear a joke I made up?'

Emily bolts down the final six or eight risers. A mistake. She trips on the last one and loses her balance. She puts out her hands to break her fall, and Holly hears the snap as a bone in her left arm – old and brittle – fractures. This time it's a shriek instead of a scream, not of horror but of pain. She crawls to Roddy and turns his head. The blood from his cut throat has begun to coagulate, and there's a sticky ripping sound as his cheek pulls free of it.

'A new millionaire walks into a bar and orders a mai-tai . . .'

'*What did you do? WHAT DID YOU DO TO RODDY?*'

'Weren't you listening? Cut his fracking throat.' Holly bends and picks up the golden earring. 'With this. It was Bonnie's. If there was ever a case of revenge from beyond the grave, I'd say this is it.'

Emily gets up . . . too fast. Not a scream or a shriek this time, but a howl of agony as her back goes nuclear. And her left arm is hanging crookedly.

Broke at the elbow, Holly thinks. *Good.*

'Oh my *God*! Oh my *dear God*! *HOW IT HURTS!*'

'I only wish you'd split your crazy evil skull,' Holly tells her. She raises the earring. It glitters under the fluorescents. 'Come over here, Professor. Let me put you out of your misery, which looks to be considerable. Maybe it's not too late to catch up with your husband on his way to hell.'

Emily is bent over, haglike. Her hair, which she put up in a neat bun that morning, is coming loose and hanging around her face. Holly thinks it adds to her overall witchy-woman vibe. She wonders if the calm she feels means she's lost her mind. She thinks not, because she's perfectly clear on one thing: if Emily Harris can get back up to the first floor – and then back down – Holly is going to die.

At least I got one of them, she thinks, and then flashes on Bogie saying *We'll always have Paris.*

Emily takes shuffling baby steps to the stairs. She grasps the rail. She looks back once, not at Holly but at her husband, lying dead on the floor. Then – very slowly, pulling herself along – she begins to climb. She's breathing in harsh gasps.

Holly calls after her. 'A new millionaire walks into a bar and orders a mai-tai. Fall and break your neck, you bitch, *fall!*'

But Emily doesn't.

20

Barbara thinks there may be a solution to the mystery of Holly's disappearance in the back of the book after all. If, that is, you think of Penny Dahl as the back of the book. There's a MISSING WOMAN flier on a streetlight pole next to the Frederick Building's parking lot. It's been faded by three weeks of weather and part of it is flapping in the hot late-morning breeze, but Barbara can still see the girl's smiling face.

Dead, she thinks. *That girl is dead. Please God, Holly's not dead, too.*

She calls Penny Dahl's number. As the phone rings, she looks at the picture of the smiling blond woman on the poster. Not much older than Barbara herself.

Be there, Mrs Dahl. Answer your damn phone.

Penny does, sounding breathless. 'Hello?'

'This is Barbara Robinson, Mrs Dahl.'

'Did you get my message? Have you found her? Is she all right?'

Barbara doesn't know if she's talking about Bonnie or Holly. In either case, the answer is the same. 'Still missing. I know you and Holly were supposed to talk last night. Did she send you a report instead? Have you checked your email?'

'I did, and there was nothing.'

'Would you check again?'

Penny Dahl tells her to hold on. Barbara stands looking at the picture of this woman's missing daughter as she does. Blond all-American cheerleader type, every white boy's dream. She waits, with sweat rolling down her cheeks. She keeps remembering the combination dial. *Sorry, wrong number*, she thinks.

Penny comes back. 'No. Nothing.'

So if there's a report, it's probably locked inside the Finders Keepers computer system. Barbara thanks Penny and calls Pete Huntley. He answers himself, having hectored his daughter into giving up custody of his phone.

'Pete, it's Barbara, and before you ask, she's still gone.' She tells him about the un-Hollylike parking job at the apartment building and the combination dial oddity. Then she asks the big question: does he have the company computers' password, which was automatically reset on July first?

She has to wait through a coughing fit before he can answer. 'Hell, no. Holly takes care of all that stuff.'

'Are you *sure* she didn't give it to you?'

'Yes. I would have written it down if she did. And before you ask, I don't have the combo to the safe, either. She gave it to me a few months back, and that I did write down, but I lost the paper I wrote it on. I never use it, anyway. Sorry, kiddo.'

Barbara is disappointed but not surprised. She thanks him, ends the call, and stands staring at the smiling blond on the MISSING poster. The heat has mastered her antiperspirant and sweat is now trickling down from her armpits. She doubts if there's a hard copy in the safe, anyway. Holly is particular about keeping it all in 'the box' – which is what she calls her computer – until she's sure the case is over. She hates having to reprint after making changes or additions; it's another of her tics. If she did write a report and filed it to the cloud, it's going to stay there until an IT guy – one with high-powered skills – can open the Finders Keepers computers, and by then it may be too late. Will *probably* be too late.

Jerome said she should call Isabelle Jaynes and Barbara said she would, but to what purpose? Holly has been missing for less than twenty-four hours. There's no blood or sign of a struggle in her apartment or her office. She can't even ask Izzy to put out a BOLO alert on Holly's car, because it's in Holly's apartment building garage. Just parked in the wrong space, and people do that all the time.

Not Holly. She wouldn't.

Barbara decides to go home. Her parents won't be there, and she doesn't want to upset them with this at work. What she wants is Jerome, and when she gets to the house, she calls him. The message she gets says he can't answer because he's driving. Barbara tells herself that's good, but it doesn't feel good. Nothing does.

21

Maybe she'll collapse upstairs, Holly thinks. *Broken arm, bad back . . . it could happen.* But she doesn't believe it will.

She waits, and just as she's beginning to hope, a shoe appears. Then another. Then the hem of the crazy lady's skirt. She comes down slowly, one step at a time, panting and holding tightly to the stair-rail with her right hand. Her left dangles. Her face is so pale it could be the face of a corpse. Tucked into the waistband of her skirt is a gun. Although Holly can only see the butt, she'd know that gun anywhere. Emily intends to kill her with Bill Hodges's .38.

'You bitch,' Emily rasps. She has reached the foot of the stairs. 'Your snooping has ruined everything.'

'It was ruined long before I came on the scene.' Holly backs up slowly until she can back no more. She even raises her hands, much good that will do. 'It was the placebo effect all along, Emily. Expectation aids body chemistry. I'm a little bit of a hypochondriac, so I know. And I've seen the numbers. Scientists have known about the placebo effect for years. I'm sure that in his heart, your husband did, as well.'

If Holly hoped to provoke the sort of rage that caused this woman's husband to act so rashly, she's disappointed. If she hoped Emily might shoot herself in the stomach while taking the .38 out of her waistband, she's similarly disappointed. In truth, Holly isn't aware of feeling anything at all, but her senses are sharply – almost supernaturally – attuned. She sees everything, hears everything, right down to the slight rattle in Emily Harris's throat as she draws each quick breath. Holly wonders if everyone, at least those who see death coming for them, experiences this divinely sharp focus, the brain's last attempt to take in everything before everything is taken away.

Emily is looking down at her husband. 'Alas, poor Roddy,' she says. 'I knew him well.'

'Listen to you,' Holly says, her back to the wall, her hands splayed against the concrete. 'A cannibal quoting Shakespeare. That deserves a place in the Guinness Book of—'

'Shut up. *Shut up!*'

Holly has no intention of shutting up. She has been a meek mouse too much of her life. Her mother: *Speak when spoken to.* Uncle Henry: *Children should be seen and not heard.* Well, frack them. No, *fuck* them. In a matter of seconds this woman is going to shut her up forever, but as with Roddy, she means to have her say first.

'I've been trying to tell you a joke I made up. A new millionaire walks into a bar, and—'

'Shut up!'

Emily raises the gun and fires. Although it's a revolver of relatively small caliber, the report is deafening in the basement. A spark jumps from one of the home-welded bars (Roddy found a video on YouTube and followed it with excellent results). Holly sees a chip fly upward from the cement wall above the blue plastic potty. She thinks, *I didn't even have time to duck.*

'—and asks for a mai—'

'Shut up!'

Holly slides along the wall to the left just as Emily fires again. There's no spark this time; the slug goes through one of the squares and makes a penny-sized hole in the concrete where Holly was standing a second before. The gun wavers in Emily's hand and Holly thinks, *She's a lefty, and that's the arm she broke. She's shooting with her dumb hand.*

'And asks for a mai-tai. Are you with me so far? This is pretty good, at least *I* think so. The bartender goes to make it and the woman hears a voice say "Congratulations, Holly! You deserve—"'

Emily starts forward, wanting to get close, but catches a foot in Roddy's bathrobe and falls again. One knee comes down on the late professor's butt. The other knee lands on the concrete. Her body twists at the waist, she cries out in pain, and the gun goes off. This bullet goes into the back of Roddy's head. Not that he feels it.

Stay down, Holly thinks. *Stay down. STAY DOWN!*

But Emily rises, although the pain makes her scream and she can't manage to get fully upright. Holly doesn't think she looks like a witch anymore; now she looks like the Hunchback of Notre Dame. Her eyes are bulging. There are white curds at the corners of her mouth and Holly doesn't want to consider what the woman may have eaten, telling herself she needed the strength, before coming back down to end Holly with her mentor's gun. Which she now raises.

'Come on,' Holly says. 'Show me what you can do.'

She slides to the left along the wall, ducking at the same time, feeling as fragile as one of her mother's china figurines. This time she's a little late and Emily is a little lucky. Holly feels a burning streak across her right arm above the elbow. Holly also knows her Shakespeare and thinks of *Hamlet*: *a hit, a very palpable hit.* But only a graze. It doesn't hurt much, at least not yet.

'So this voice says "Congratulations, Holly! You deserve every fracking cent of that money." But when she looks around, no one is there. Then she hears a voice on the *other* side say—'

'*Shut up, shut up, SHUT UP!*'

Just before Emily fires again, Holly drops to her knees. She hears the *hzzzz* of the bullet passing just over her head, close enough to part her hair. For all she knows it *did* part her hair.

'Sorry, Professor,' Holly says, getting up. 'Pistols are only good at close range.' She can feel blood soaking the sleeve of her shirt. It's warm, and warmth is good. Warmth is life. 'And you're shooting with the wrong hand, too. Let's end this. I'll make it easy for you. Just let me finish my joke.'

She walks to the front of the cell and pushes her face into one of the squares. Bars press against her cheeks and the bars are cold. 'So this *other* voice says, "You're looking especially pretty tonight, Holly." But when she looks, still no one there! The bartender comes back with the drink, and—'

Emily lurches forward. She presses the short barrel of Bill's pistol against Holly's forehead and pulls the trigger. There's a dry click as the hammer falls on the chamber Holly has left empty, as Bill taught her . . . because revolvers, unlike the Glock that was his service weapon, have no safeties.

There is just long enough for Emily to register surprise before Holly shoots her hands through the bars, seizes Emily's head, and twists it to the left with all her strength. Holly heard a snap when the old woman's arm broke. What she hears this time is a muffled *crack*. Emily's knees buckle. Her head slides out of Holly's grip as she goes down, leaving Holly with nothing but a few gray hairs in her left hand. They feel nasty, like cobwebs, and she wipes them away on her shirt. She hears herself breathing in great gasps, and the world tries to swim away from her. She can't let that happen, so she slaps herself across the face. Blood flies from her wounded arm. Droplets spatter on the bars of the cage.

Emily has ended up in a kind of squat, legs beneath her but twisted in opposite directions from the knees down, her face resting against the cage. One of the bars has pulled her nose up into a pig's snout. Like her legs, her open eyes appear to be staring in different directions. Holly drops to her knees, raises the feeding-flap, and gets the gun. It's empty but can still be useful. If Emily is still alive (Holly doubts it), if she moves at all, Holly intends to beat her fracking head in.

There is no movement. Holly counts aloud to sixty. Still on her knees, she reaches through one of the lower squares and presses her fingers into the side of Emily's neck. The boneless way the woman's head rolls over onto her shoulder tells Holly all she needs to know (what she knew already), but she keeps her fingers there for another sixty count. She feels nothing. Not even a few final erratic beats of a dying heart.

Holly gets up, still breathing in those great gasps, but she can't keep her feet. She sits down heavily on the futon. She's alive. She can't believe it. She does believe it. The pain in her ribs convinces her. The burn in her arm convinces her. And her thirst convinces her. She feels that she could drink all five of the Great Lakes dry.

They are both dead. She cut the throat of one, broke the neck of the other. And here she sits in a cage no one knows about. Someone will come eventually, but how long before that happens? And how long can a human being go without water? She doesn't know. She can't even remember the last time she had a drink.

She slides up the sleeve of her shirt, hissing with pain as the cloth passes over the wound. She sees it was a little more than a graze, after all. The skin is split two inches above her right elbow, and she can look into the meat of her arm. The bone isn't visible, and she supposes that's good, but the wound is bleeding freely. She knows blood-loss will also contribute to her thirst, which is raging now and will soon be . . . what? What's beyond raging? She can't think of the word any more than she can think of how many days a person can go without water.

I killed them both from inside this cage. That *should go in the Guinness Book of World Records.*

Holly works her way out of her shirt. It's a slow operation, and painful, but she finally manages. She ties it around the gunshot wound – another slow operation – and knots it with her teeth. Then she leans back against the concrete wall and begins to wait.

'A new millionaire walks into a bar,' she croaks, 'and orders a mai-tai. While the bartender is making it, she hears someone say, "You deserve that money, Holly. Every fracking cent." She looks and there's nobody there. *Then* she hears a voice on her *other* side say, "You killed them both from inside the cage, you're in the Guinness Book of World Records, way to go, you're a star."'

Has Emily moved? Surely not. Surely her imagination. Holly knows she should shut up, talking will only make her thirstier, but she needs to finish the fracking joke, even if her only audience is a couple of dead old people.

'The bartender comes back and she says, "I keep hearing voices saying these nice things, what's up with that?" And the bartender says . . . he says . . .'

She passes out.

22

While Holly is losing consciousness (and just before the punchline, too), Barbara is at home, in the office that's now Jerome's. She's looking at the MapQuest printout with the red dots on it marking the various disappearances. Which now includes the one she herself made to mark Jorge Castro, who went missing in the fall of 2012. Barbara put that dot on Ridge Road across from Olivia's house. *Did I tell you I saw him shortly before he disappeared?* Olivia said that. *Running. He always ran at night, to the park and back again. Even in the rain, and it was raining that night.* And something else: *I certainly never saw him again.*

Barbara traces a route from the Bell campus down Ridge Road to the park. To the playground in the park. What if it was there? There's a parking lot, and if there was a van, like the one in the security footage of Bonnie in the store . . .

Something nibbles at her. Something about the van? About Ridge Road? Both? She doesn't know, although she's sure Dutch Spyglass would.

Her phone rings. It's Jerome. He asks her for an update. She tells him about the calls she made and the one she hasn't made, to Izzy Jaynes. He tells her she was probably right to skip that one. He says he's making good time, already in New Jersey, but he doesn't want to exceed the speed limit by more than five miles an hour. Barbara doesn't have to ask him why; he's driving while Black. He doesn't even want to risk talking on his cell while on the road. He pulled into a rest area to call her, and he wants to get going again.

Before he can end the call, Barbara blurts out her worst fear. 'What if she's dead, J?'

There's a pause. She can hear turnpike traffic. Then he says, 'She's not. I'd feel it if she was. Gotta go, Ba. I'll be home by eleven.'

'I'm going to lie down,' Barbara says. 'Maybe something will come to me. I feel like I know more than I think I know. Did you ever have that feeling?'

'Quite often.'

Barbara goes into her room and stretches out on her bed. She doesn't expect to sleep, but maybe she can clear her mind. She closes her eyes. She thinks about Olivia and Olivia's many stories. She remembers asking the old poet about the famous picture of her and Bogart in front of the Trevi Fountain. In particular about her wide-eyed, almost startled smile. Olivia saying, *If I looked startled it's because he had his hand on my ass.*

Barbara falls asleep.

23

Holly is in the sunroom of Rolling Hills Elder Care. It's empty except for her mother and her uncle. They are sitting at one of the tables, watching a bowling match on the big-screen television and drinking tall glasses of iced tea.

'Can I have some?' Holly croaks. 'I'm thirsty.'

They look around. They salute her with those tall glasses and drink. There are lemon wedges stuck in the rims of the glasses, which are beaded with condensation. Holly thinks of how much she would like to stick out her tongue to lick those little drops of condensate from the sides of their glasses. She'd lick them all the way to the top, suck the lemon wedges, then drain them both.

'You couldn't handle that much money,' Uncle Henry says, and sips. 'We did it for your own good.'

'You're fragile,' Charlotte says, and takes her own sip. So delicate! How can she not just guzzle? Holly would guzzle both glasses, if only they would give them to her.

Charlotte holds hers out to Holly. 'You can have it.'

Uncle Henry holds his out. 'You can have this one, too.'

And together, chanting like children: 'As soon as you agree to stop all this dangerous foolishness and come home.'

Holly claws her way out of this dream. Reality is the cage in the Harris basement. Her ribs still hurt and the wound in her arm feels like somebody drenched it with lighter fluid and set it on fire, but those pains are subservient to her thirst, which is unrelenting. At least the gash from the bullet seems to have stopped bleeding; what's on her makeshift bandage is brown instead of red. She thinks pulling the shirt off the wound is going to hurt a great deal, but that's nothing she has to worry about now.

She gets to her feet and goes to the bars. The body of Rodney Harris lies near the stairs. Emily has fallen out of her final slumped-over crouch and lies on her side. She must have left the door to the kitchen open because flies have gathered, sampling Roddy's spilled blood. There's plenty to sample.

Holly thinks, *I would sell my soul for a glass of beer . . . and I don't even like beer.*

She thinks of how her dream ended, that childlike chant: *As soon as you agree to stop all this dangerous foolishness and come home.*

She assures herself that someone will come. Someone *has* to come. The question is what kind of shape she'll be in when that happens. Or if she'll be alive at all. Yet even now, hurting all over, with two bodies outside the cage in which she is locked, raging with thirst . . .

'I regret nothing,' she croaks. '*Nothing.*'

Well, one thing. Hiding behind the chainsaws was a big mistake.

Holly thinks, *I need to learn to trust myself more. Will have to work on that.*

24

Barbara is also dreaming. She bursts into the living room of Olivia Kingsbury's house on Ridge Road to find Olivia in her accustomed chair, reading a book – it's Adrienne Rich's *Diving into the Wreck* – and eating a small sandwich. There's a cup of steaming tea on the table beside her.

'I thought you were dead!' Barbara cries. 'They told me you were dead!'

'Nonsense,' Olivia says, putting her book down. 'I fully intend to celebrate my hundredth. Did I tell you about the time Jorge Castro spoke up at the meeting to decide the fate of the Poetry Workshop? Emily never lost that smile of hers, but her eyes—'

Barbara's cell phone trills and the dream falls apart. It was wonderful while it lasted because in it Olivia was alive, but a dream was all it was. She grabs her phone and sees her mother's smiling photo on the screen. She also sees the time: 4:03 PM. Jerome must be in Pennsylvania by now.

'Hey . . .' She has to clear her throat. 'Hey, Mom.'

'Were you napping?'

'I just meant to lie down, but I guess I fell asleep. I dreamed Olivia was still alive.'

'Oh, honey. I'm so sorry. I had dreams like that after your Gramma Annie died. I was always sorry to wake up.'

'Yeah. Like that.' Barbara scruffs a hand through her hair and thinks about what dream-Olivia was saying when the phone woke her. Like her passing thought about the van in the security footage, it seems it might be important. *Dutch would know*, she thinks. *Dutch would have this shit all figured out.*

'—Holly?'

'What?'

'I asked if you've located Holly yet. Or if she's been back in touch.'

'No, huh-uh, not yet.' She still has no intention of telling Tanya about her fears. Maybe after J gets back, but not until.

'She's probably upstate, taking care of her mother's affairs.' Tanya lowers her voice. 'I'd never say it to Holly, but Charlotte Gibney didn't die of Covid, she died of stupidity.'

Barbara has to smile at that. 'I think Holly knows, Mom.'

'I called to tell you I'm meeting your dad for dinner. At a fancy-schmancy restaurant.'

'Nice!' Barbara says. 'Which one?'

Tanya tells her, but Barbara hardly hears. She feels like a stroke of lightning has gone off in her head.

Which one?

'—the actual date.'

'Okay, right.'

Tanya laughs. 'Did you even hear me? I said it's an early anniversary dinner because he has to be away on the actual date. There's money for takeout if you want it, just check the kitchen draw—'

'Have a good time, Mom. I have to go. Love you.'

'Love you, t—'

But Barbara ends the call and scrolls back through her texts to and from Holly. Here it is: *Which one?*

Barbara asked that because she knew *two* of the men in the picture Holly sent her. One was Cary Dressler, the dishy young guy all the girls in her PE class were crushing on. The other was Professor Harris. She saw him washing his car when she went to Emily Harris, hoping for an introduction to Olivia Kingsbury. On that warm winter day both of the Harris garage bays were open, and in the other one there had been a van. Had he seen her looking at it, and made haste to close the garage door? To hide it?

Bullshit. You're making that up.

Maybe, but now she knows what Olivia was about to say when her mother's call woke her up. She knows because Olivia actually said it: *Em never lost that smile of hers, but her eyes . . . her eyes looked like she wanted to kill him.*

Jorge Castro, the first of the disappearances.

'You're crazy,' Barbara whispers to herself. 'Just because *he* knew Cary Dressler . . . and *she* knew Castro . . . and didn't like him . . .'

Did I tell you I saw him shortly before he disappeared?

'You're crazy,' Barbara repeats. 'They're *old.*'

But . . . Bonnie Dahl. The *last* of the disappearances. Could it be . . .?

She hurries into Jerome's office, powers up his computer, and googles what she wants. Then she calls Marie Duchamp.

'Do you remember the time Olivia told us about the Harrises' Christmas party? How they sent Santas around to hand out snacks and beer?'

'Oh yes,' Marie says, and laughs. 'Only they were supposed to be Santa's *elves.* Olivia thought it was a perfect example of Emily Harris – she meant to keep her Christmas party streak alive, come hell, high water, or Covid. We ate the snacks, drank the beer – Livvie had two cans, against my strong advice – but skipped the Zoom.'

'She said a blond girl delivered to your place. A pretty blond Santa.'

'Right . . .' Marie sounds disappointingly vague.

'Would you recognize her if I sent you a picture?'

'They were *Santa* outfits, Barb, complete with snowy white fake beards.'

'Oh.' Barbara deflates. 'Fuck. Well, thanks anyw—'

'No, wait a second. Our elf was cold from riding her bike, so Olivia gave her a teensy knock of booze. I remember because Olivia said, "You can have the whiskey if you take off your whiskers." And she did. Pretty girl. Looked like she was having fun. I guess I might recognize her, at that.'

'Let me send you the picture. Stay on the line.'

Bonnie's Facebook and Instagram pages are very much alive, thanks to her mother, and Barbara sends Marie the picture of Bonnie on her bike, wearing a strappy top and white shorts.

'Did you get it?' *It can't be her. It just can't be.*

'Yes, and that's her. That was our Christmas elf. Why?'

'Thanks, Marie.'

Barbara hangs up, feeling numb. Professor Harris knowing Cary might mean nothing, and Emily Harris knowing and not liking Jorge Castro also might mean nothing. But Bonnie makes three. And if you add in the van . . .

She almost calls Jerome, then stops. He'll want to speed up, then he might get pulled over. Like every Black person in the city, Barbara is very aware of what happened to Maleek Dutton when *he* got pulled over.

What to do?

The answer seems obvious – go to 93 Ridge Road and see if Holly's there. If not, find out if they know where she is. Maybe the Harrises don't have anything to do with the disappearances, Barbara can't think of any reason why they would, old people aren't serial killers, but she's sure of one thing: Holly knew what Barbara knows, and *she* would have gone there.

Barbara isn't afraid of Roddy and Emily, but there may be someone else involved. Which means taking precautions. She goes to her closet, stands on tiptoe, and moves aside Oingo and Boingo, stuffed bears that used to reside on her bed. She no longer needs them beside her at night to keep her safe from the boogeymonster, but she can't get rid of them. They are treasured relics.

Behind them is a Nike shoebox. She takes it down and opens it. She couldn't ask Holly for a gun after the affair of Chet Ondowsky, she would have refused and suggested counseling, so she asked Pete instead, after swearing him to secrecy. He gave her a purse-sized .22 automatic with no argument, and when she offered to pay him for it, he shook his head. 'Just don't shoot yourself with it, Cookie, and don't shoot anyone else.' He thought that over and added, 'Unless they deserve it.'

Barbara doesn't expect to shoot anyone this afternoon, but threatening isn't out of the question. She needs to know where Holly is. If the Harrises deny knowledge, and she thinks they're lying . . . yes, threatening might be in order. Even if it means jail time.

Barbara thinks, *I wouldn't be the first poet to go to jail.*

On the way out she snags an Indians cap from the basket by the front door, puts it on, and stops dead in her tracks. She thinks of Holly's computer being off instead of asleep. She thinks of the combination lock not set to zero. And then she remembers a woman she passed in the lobby of the Frederick Building, going out as Barbara was going in. The woman was limping, she remembers that. And wearing a billed cap similar to the one Barbara has just put on. The woman's head was lowered, allowing Barbara to read what was on the front of it: Columbus Clippers.

She doesn't know if that woman was Emily Harris, but Barbara knows Holly also had a Clippers hat. There are plenty of people in the city wearing Indians lids, and plenty of people wearing Cardinals lids, and quite a few wearing Royals lids. But Clippers hats? Not many. Was that woman, who might or might not have been Emily Harris, on the fifth floor? Did she perhaps have Holly's keys as well as her hat? Did she turn off the computer after powering it up? Spin the safe's combination dial? Unlikely, but . . .

But.

It gnaws at Barbara enough for her to decide she doesn't want either of the Harrises to see her coming until she's at their door and ready to hit them with her question: *Where is she? Where's Holly?*

25

She rides her ten-speed to Ridge Road and chains it to the bike rack in the parking lot adjacent to the park playground. She checks her watch and sees it's ten past five. Barbara walks up the hill past Olivia's house. She has always liked Holly's no-nonsense, unsexy cargo pants, so ordered a pair for herself. She's wearing them now. The .22 is in one of the flap pockets, her phone in the other.

She decides a reconnaissance pass wouldn't be a bad idea. She tugs down the brim of her cap, lowers her head, and strolls slowly past 93, as if on her way to the college at the top of the hill. She shoots a quick glance to her left and sees something odd: the Harrises' front door is standing ajar. No one is on the porch, but there's a table with a large travel mug on it. Even a quick glance is enough for Barbara to recognize the Starbucks logo.

She goes as far as 109, then turns and walks back. This time when she lowers her head she spots something in the gutter that she knows well. It's a nitrile glove covered with various emojis. She *should* know it; she gave a box of those gloves to Holly herself, as a joke present.

Barbara calls Pete Huntley, praying that he will answer. He does.

'Hey, Cookie, did you locate her ye—'

'Listen to me, Pete, okay? This is probably nothing and I'm probably going to call you back in five minutes, but if I don't, call Isabelle Jaynes and tell her to send police to 93 Ridge Road. Tell her to come, too. Have you got that?'

'Why? What happened? Is this about Holly?'

'Tell me the address. Repeat it.'

'93 Ridge Road. But don't do anything stu—'

'Five minutes. If I don't call back, call Ms Jaynes and send Five-O.'

She slips her phone back into her left front pocket and takes the gun out of her right pocket. Is it loaded? She never checked, but she remembers Pete telling her that an unloaded gun isn't very useful if you wake up and find a prowler in your house. It feels heavy enough to be loaded.

She goes up the porch steps, puts the gun behind her back, and rings the bell. With the door ajar she hears its double tone quite clearly, but no one comes. She rings again. 'Hello? Anyone home? Professor Harris? Emily?'

She hears something, very faint. It could be a voice; it could be someone's radio playing loud through an open window on the next block. Barbara knocks, and her fist pushes the door wider. She's looking down the wood-paneled front hall. Gloomy. Did she think that on her previous visit? She can't remember. What she does remember is that it smelled stuffy, somehow. And the tea was awful.

'Hello, is anyone home?'

Yes, she hears a voice, all right. Very faint. No way to tell what it's saying, or possibly shouting. Barbara hesitates on the porch, thinking *Come into my parlor, said the spider to the fly.*

She peeks behind the door. Sees no one hiding there. Biting her lip, sweat trickling down the back of her neck, the little automatic now held stiffly at her side but with her finger outside the trigger guard as Pete instructed her, Barbara ventures down the hall to the living room.

'Hello? *Hello?*'

Now she hears the voice better. It's still muffled, and hoarse, but she thinks it's Holly. She could be wrong about that, but there's no doubt about what it's saying: '*Help! Help me!*'

Barbara runs into the kitchen and sees a door on the far side of the refrigerator standing open. There's a padlock hanging from the hasp. She sees steps leading down to a basement and something at the bottom. She tells herself it can't be what it looks like, already knowing it is.

'Holly? *Holly!*'

'Down here!' Her voice is a broken croak. '*Down here!*'

Barbara goes halfway down the stairs and stops. It's a body, all right. The male Professor Harris is sprawled on the floor in a puddle of drying blood. His wife is slumped at the foot of some sort of cage. In it, standing at the crisscrossed bars with a bloody shirt wrapped around her arm, is Holly Gibney. Her hair is plastered to her cheeks. There are smears of blood on her face. Because she's taken off her shirt to use as a bandage, Barbara can see a bruise, grotesquely large, spreading up her side like ink.

When Holly recognizes who it is, she begins to cry. 'Barbara,' she manages in her cracked voice. 'Barbara, oh thank God. I can't believe it's you.'

Barbara looks around. 'Where is he, Holly? Where's the guy who killed them? Is he still in the house?'

'There's no guy,' Holly croaks. 'No Red Bank Predator. *I* killed them. Barbara, get me some water. Please. I'm—' She puts her hands to her throat and makes a horrible grating sound. '*Please.*'

'All right. Yes.' Her phone is trilling and trilling. That will be Pete. Or maybe Isabelle Jaynes. 'As long as you're sure no one is going to jump me.'

'No,' Holly says. 'It was all them.' And shocks Barbara by dry-spitting on Emily Harris's slumped corpse.

Barbara turns to go back upstairs and get water. That's the priority; she doesn't need to take any calls just now because Pete will send the police and the police need to come, oh God they need to come as fast as possible.

'*Barbara!*' It's a shriek with splinters in it. Holly sounds like she's either lost her mind or is on the verge. '*Get it from the sink! Don't look in the refrigerator! DON'T LOOK IN THE REFRIGERATOR!*'

Barbara runs up the stairs and into the kitchen. She has no idea what's happened here. Her mind is frozen on just one thought: water. There are cabinets on either side of the sink. Barbara puts her gun on the counter and opens one. Plates. She opens another and sees glasses. She fills one, starts back to the basement door, then changes her mind and fills another. Carrying a glass in each hand, she goes back down the stairs. There's a corona of blood around Professor Harris and she sidles past it.

She stops in front of Emily's body and stretches to pass one of the glasses through the bars. Holly seizes it, spilling some, and chugs the rest down in big gulps. She tosses it behind her onto the futon and holds out her hand through one of the squares. 'More.' Her voice is clearer now.

Barbara gives her the other glass. Holly drinks half of it. 'Good,' she says. 'So fracking good.'

'I told Pete to send police if I didn't call him back. And the lady detective. How do I let you out, Holly?'

Holly points to the keypad but shakes her head. 'I don't know the numbers. Barbara . . .' She stops and swipes at her face. 'How did you . . . never mind, that's for later. Go upstairs. Meet them.'

'All right. I'll call Pete again and tell him—'

'Did I see a gun? Do you have a gun?'

'Yes. Pete—'

'Don't have it when the police come. Remember the Dutton boy.'

'But what—'

'Later, Barbara. And thank you. Thank you so much.'

Barbara goes back to the stairs, again being careful to skirt the gore that has spread around Rodney Harris. She looks back once and sees Holly drinking the rest of the second glass. She's holding onto the bars with her other hand, as if to keep from collapsing.

What happened here? What the fuck *happened?*

In the kitchen she can hear sirens, still faint. She sees her .22 on the counter and thinks of Holly telling her *don't have it when the police come, remember the Dutton boy*. She picks it up and puts it in the breadbox, on top of a package of English muffins.

Before leaving the kitchen, she can't resist opening the fridge and peeking inside. She's prepared for anything but sees nothing that warranted Holly's warning. There's skim milk, some eggs and butter, yogurt, veggies, a Tupperware box containing what looks like cranberry jelly, and a few packages of red meat in Saran wrap. Maybe steak. Also six or eight parfait dessert glasses filled with what's probably vanilla pudding with swirls of strawberry. Looks tasty.

She closes the refrigerator and goes back outside.

26

A city police cruiser pulls up to the curb, siren unwinding to silence. There's an unmarked sedan behind it, following so close it almost hits the cruiser's bumper. Mindful of what Holly said and her own Black skin, Barbara stands on the top step of the porch with her hands held out from her sides, palms turned to show they're empty.

Two uniform cops come up the walk. The one in the lead nevertheless has his hand on the butt of his Glock. 'What's going on here?' he asks. 'What's the big emergency?'

The other one, older, asks, 'Are you high, sweetheart?'

Before Barbara has to dignify that with an answer – she will realize later the question wasn't entirely stupid or racist; she was clearly in shock — the door of the unmarked car slams and Isabelle Jaynes is hurrying across the lawn. She's wearing jeans and a plain white tee. Her police badge is slung around her neck and she's got her own Glock on one hip.

'Stand back,' she tells the cops. 'I know this young lady. Barbara, right? Jerome's sister.'

'Yes,' Barbara says. 'Holly's in the basement. Locked in a cage. The old professors who live here are dead, and . . . and . . .' She begins to cry.

'Take it easy.' Izzy puts an arm around Barbara's shaking shoulders. 'They're dead, I get that . . . and what?'

'And Holly says she killed them.'

27

Holly hears footsteps and voices overhead, then sees feet. She remembers Emily descending those stairs, coming to kill her with Bill's gun, and shudders. She'll see those old lady shoes in her dreams. But these aren't shoes, they're suede boots. Above them are bluejeans instead of a dress. They stop when the owner of the jeans sees the bodies. Isabelle comes the rest of the way down the stairs slowly, gun drawn. She sees Holly standing behind the crisscrossed bars, her face smeared with blood and a bloody shirt tied around her arm. There's more drying on her chest above the cups of her bra.

'What the fuck happened here, Holly? How badly are you hurt?'

'Some of the blood is mine, but most of it's his,' she says, and points a trembling finger at the dead man in the fire engine pajamas. 'I can tell you everything once you get me out of here, but how am I going to tell *her*?' She puts her forehead against the bars.

Izzy comes forward and takes one of Holly's hands. It's cold. The two cops are on the stairs now, gawking at the bodies. Barbara, standing above them in the doorway, can hear more sirens approaching.

Izzy: 'Tell who, Holly? Tell who what?'

'Penny Dahl,' Holly says, crying harder than ever. 'How am I ever going to tell her what happened to her daughter? How am I going to tell *any* of them?'

28

By six o'clock, Ridge Road is lined with police cars, two crime scene vans, the county coroner's station wagon, and an ambulance with its doors open and two EMTs waiting. There's also a red panel truck with Upsala County Fire Department painted in gold on the side. Most of the residents of the street have come out to watch the show. Barbara Robinson has been sent out of the house but has been allowed to stay on the lawn. Ordered to, actually. She has called Jerome and Pete, telling them both that Holly has been hurt, but Barbara thinks – hopes – not too badly. The important thing is she's safe. Barbara doesn't tell them Holly is still locked up in the Harrises' basement; that would lead to questions for which she has no answers. At least not yet. She thought of calling her parents, and didn't. There will be time to talk to them later. For now, let them have their anniversary dinner.

There's a horrified murmur from the crowd of residents across the street as two bodies, bagged and on stretchers, are carried out. Another county truck comes slowly down Ridge Road and parks in the middle of the street to receive them.

Barbara's phone rings. It's Jerome. She sits down on the grass to take the call. She can cry. With Jerome that's okay.

29

Twenty minutes later Holly is crouched in the far corner of the cell across from the Porta-Potty. Her legs are drawn up and she has buried her face in her arms. A man in a welder's mask is cutting through the bars, and the long room is filled with coruscating light. Izzy Jaynes is at the other end of the basement, where she first examines the wood-chipper and then yells to one of the crime scene techs. She points to Bonnie's bike helmet and backpack and tells him to bag both.

A steel bar clatters to the concrete floor. Then another. Izzy walks up to the FD guy running the cutting torch, keeping one arm up to shield her eyes. 'How much longer?'

'I think we can get her out in another ten minutes. Maybe twenty. Someone did a hell of a job putting this thing together.'

Izzy goes back to the workshop part of the basement and tries the door there. It's locked. She motions to one of the bigger cops – there are half a dozen blues down here now, basically just milling around. 'You better bust that,' she says. 'I'm pretty sure I heard someone inside.'

He grins. 'You got it, boss.'

He hits the door with his shoulder, and it gives way immediately. He stumbles inside. Izzy follows and finds a light switch beside the door. Overhead fluorescents come on, a lot of them. The two of them stand, stunned.

'What the fuck is *that*?' the widebody asks.

Izzy knows, even if it's hard to believe what her eyes are reporting. 'I'd say it's an operating table.'

'And the bag?' He's pointing to the big green sack hanging down from the end of the hose. It's distended into a teardrop shape by what's inside. Stuff Izzy doesn't want to think about, let alone see.

'Leave it for the forensics guys and the ME,' she says, and thinks of Holly saying *How am I ever going to tell her what happened to her daughter?*

30

Forty minutes later Holly emerges onto the Harrises' porch, supported by an EMT on one side and Izzy Jaynes on the other, but mostly walking under her own power. Barbara gets up, runs to her, hugs her, and turns to Izzy. 'I want to go with her to the hospital.'

Instead of refusing, Izzy says they'll both go.

Holly wants to walk to the waiting ambulance, but EMTs insist on a stretcher before she can descend the porch steps. Now there are news vans as well as all the official vehicles, but they are being kept at the top and bottom of the hill, behind police tape. There's even a helicopter circling overhead.

Holly is hoisted into the ambulance. One of the EMTs shoots her up with something. She tries to protest, but he says it will help with the pain. Izzy sits on one side of the secured stretcher, Barbara on the other.

'Wipe my face, please,' Holly says. 'The blood is drying to a crack-glaze.'

Izzy shakes her head. 'No can do. Not until you've been photographed and we've got swabs.'

The ambulance pulls out, siren yelling. Barbara holds on as it takes the corner at the bottom of the hill.

'That's a woodchipper in the basement,' Izzy says. 'My father had one at his cabin upstate, but a lot smaller.'

'Yes. I saw it. Can I have a drink? Please?'

'There's a cooler with Gatorade in it,' one of the EMTs calls back.

'Oh God, please,' Holly says.

Barbara finds the cooler, opens a bottle of orange Gatorade, and puts it in Holly's outstretched hand. Holly's eyes look up at them from above her bloody cheeks as she drinks.

She looks like she's wearing warpaint, Barbara thinks. *And I guess that's okay, because she's been in a war.*

'The chipper's outflow goes to a bag in that little . . .' Izzy pauses. She was about to say *operating room,* but that's not right. '. . . that little torture chamber. Is the stuff inside what I think it is? Because it stinks.'

Holly nods. 'They must not have had a chance to get rid of the . . . the leftovers this time. I don't know how they did that with the others, but my guess is the lake. You'll figure it out.'

'And the rest of her?'

'Check the refrigerator.'

Barbara thinks of the wrapped cuts of meat. She thinks of the parfait glasses. And feels like screaming.

'I have to tell you something,' Holly says to Izzy and Barbara. Whatever the EMT has given her is working. The pain in her arm and her ribs hasn't gone away, but it's receding. She thinks of the therapist she saw when she was younger. 'I need to *share* something.'

Izzy takes her hand and gives it a squeeze. 'Save it. I'll need to hear everything, but right now you just need to take it easy.'

'It's not about the case. I made up a joke and I've never had a chance to tell anyone. I tried to tell the woman . . . Emily . . . before she could shoot me, but then things got . . . complicated.'

'Go on,' Barbara says, and takes Holly's hand. 'Tell it now.'

'A new millionaire . . . me, actually, long story . . . walks into a bar and orders a mai-tai. When the bartender goes to make it, she hears a voice saying "You deserve that money, Holly. Every cent." She looks around and sees no one. She's the only customer at the bar. Then she hears a voice on the other side. It says, "You look very pretty tonight, Holly." The bartender comes back and she says, "I keep hearing voices saying nice things about me, but when I look, no one's there." And the bartender says—'

The EMT who gave her the shot looks back at her. He's grinning. 'He says "We charge for the drinks, but the nuts are complimentary."'

Holly's mouth drops open. 'You *know* it?'

'God, yes,' the EMT says. 'That's an old one. You must've heard it somewhere and just forgot.'

Holly begins to laugh.

31

In a treatment room at Kiner, Holly is swabbed for DNA and photographed. Barbara gently wipes her face clean afterward. The resident on duty in the ER examines the bullet-wound and pronounces it 'basically superficial.' He says if it had gone deeper and shattered the bone, that would be a different deal. Izzy gives her two thumbs up.

The doctor pulls off the shirt she's used as a bandage, which starts the bleeding again. He cleans the wound, probes for shrapnel (there is none), then packs it. He says there's no need for staples or sutures (a relief) and wraps it tightly. He says she'll need a sling, but one of the nurses will take care of that. Also a course of antibiotics. Meanwhile, he's got an ICU full of Covid patients to deal with, most of them unvaccinated.

'I got you a room here,' Izzy says, then smiles. 'Actually that's a lie. The Chief of Police got it.'

'Other people need it more.' The floaty feeling from the injection started to go away when the doc pulled the shirt out of the coagulating blood in the arm wound – *rrrip* – and by the time he'd finished disinfecting and probing, it was entirely gone.

'You're staying,' Izzy says flatly. 'Gunshot wound observation is mandatory in this town. Twenty-four hours. Be grateful they're not stashing you in a hallway or the cafeteria. There are plenty of people in both places, coughing their lungs out. A nurse will give you some more pain med. Or a good-looking intern, if you're lucky. Get a good night's sleep. We'll start debriefing you on this shitshow tomorrow. You'll be doing a lot of talking.'

Holly turns to Barbara. 'Give me your phone, Barb. I have to call Penny.'

Barbara starts to get it out of her pocket, but Izzy holds up a hand like a traffic cop. 'Absolutely not. You don't even know for sure that Bonnie Dahl is dead.'

'I know,' Holly said. 'You do, too. You saw her bike helmet.'

'Yes, and her name is on the flap of the pack.'

'There was an earring, too,' Holly says. 'It's in the cell where they locked me up.'

'We'll find it. They may have found it already. A six-man forensics crew is going over that basement as we speak, and a team from the FBI is on its way. After the basement, we'll go through the whole house. Fine-tooth comb stuff.'

'It's a gold triangle,' Holly says. 'Sharp points. I found the other one outside the abandoned shop where they kidnapped her. The one in the cell was under the futon. Bonnie must have left it there. I used it to cut Professor Harris's throat.'

And closes her eyes.

July 30, 2021

1

At ten o'clock, Holly is rolled into Kiner Memorial's ninth-floor conference room in a wheelchair. She doesn't need it, but it's hospital protocol; she has another eight hours of blood-pressure and temp checks before she'll be released. Waiting for her are Izzy, Izzy's partner, George Washburn, the plump-cheeked District Attorney, and a sharp-dressed man of about fifty who introduces himself as Herbert Beale of the FBI. Holly assumes he's there because of the kidnapping aspect, even though there's no Interstate angle. Bill Hodges told her once that the Feebs always like getting involved in high-profile cases, especially when they're winding down. *Gluttons for TV time*, he said. Barbara, Jerome, and Pete Huntley are also attending, by Zoom. Holly insisted.

The plump-cheeked man rises and approaches Holly with his hand outstretched. 'I'm Albert Tantleff, the Upsala County District Attorney.' Holly offers him her good elbow instead of her hand. Smiling indulgently, as if at a child, he bumps her elbow with his own. 'I believe we can dispense with the masks, since we've all been vaccinated and the air circulation in here seems very good.'

'I prefer to keep mine on,' Holly says. It's a hospital, after all, and hospitals are full of sick people.

'As you like.' He gives her another smile of the indulgent variety and returns to his seat. 'Detective Jaynes, your show.'

Izzy – also wearing her mask, perhaps in deference to the guest of honor – powers up her iPad and shows Holly a photograph of a bloodstained earring in a plastic evidence bag. 'Can you confirm that this is the earring you used to cut Rodney Harris's throat?'

Agent Beale leans forward over his folded hands. His eyes are as cold and blue as ice chips, but there's a faint smile on his mouth. Possibly of admiration.

'Yes,' Holly says. She knows what she must say next, thanks to Pete. 'I acted in self-defense, being in fear for my life.' Thinking, *I also hated that crazy piece of poop.*

'So stipulated,' DA Tantleff says.

'Do you have the other earring?' Izzy asks.

'I do. In the top drawer of my desk at the office. I could show you a picture of it, only the Harrises took my phone after they tased me. But Penny has one, I emailed it to her. Has anyone talked to her yet?'

Barbara says, 'I did. I called her.'

Tantleff whips around to look at the screen at the head of the conference table. No indulgent smile now. 'You were not authorized to do that, Ms Robinson.'

'Probably not, but I did it anyway,' Barbara says. Holly feels like applauding. 'She was so worried about Holly. I told her she was all right. I didn't tell her anything else.'

'What about the refrigerator?' Holly asks. 'Were there . . .' She trails off, either not sure how to finish or not willing to.

'There were many cuts of meat, both in their fridge and in the freezer,' Izzy says. 'There's no doubt they're human. There are still patches of skin on some of them.'

'Oh my God.' That's Jerome, who's sitting with Barbara in his writing room. 'Oh my fucking God, *really?*'

'Really,' Izzy says. 'They're being DNA tested as we speak, this went right to the head of the line. There were also seven tall dessert-type glasses which the county coroner says probably contain human brain tissue as well as dura mater and bits of tendon.' She pauses. 'Plus what he believes to be whipped cream.'

Silence. *That's right, give them time to digest it,* Holly thinks, and clamps a hand to her mask to keep from bursting into gales of horri-fied laughter.

'Are you all right, Ms Gibney?' Izzy's partner asks.

'Fine.'

Izzy continues. 'We also found meat sticks – you know, like Slim Jims or Jack Link's – which may or may not be human, and a large Tupperware container of small meatballs. Any or all of these items may once have been a part of Bonnie Rae Dahl. The DNA will tell us. The Harrises also had a small auxiliary freezer in their pantry. There's a lot of meat in there, too. Most of it looks like ordinary steaks, chops, bacon, and chicken. At the very bottom, however . . .' On her iPad she shows them the picture of a frozen roast. 'We don't know what this is for sure, or where it came from, but it's sure not a leg of lamb.'

'Jesus Christ,' Tantleff says, 'and I have no one to prosecute.' He shoots an almost accusatory look at Holly. 'You killed them both.'

From the conference room TV screen, Pete Huntley speaks up. To Holly he looks better, but he also looks like he's lost a fair amount of weight. Maybe thirty pounds. Holly thinks it would be good for him if he keeps it off, but she guesses he won't, human nature being what it is. 'What's wrong with you, Tant? They were cannibals! They probably wouldn't have had time to eat her, but they sure as fuck would have killed her.'

'I didn't mean—'

Izzy's phone rings and this time Tantleff's accusing glance is directed at her. 'I thought we agreed all phones would be silenced while we—'

'I'm sorry, but I really have to take this. It's Dana Aaronson with the forensics team. I asked him to call if they found anything particularly . . . Hello? Dana? What have you got?'

She listens, looking vaguely sick. The way Holly herself felt in the middle of the night, when she finally had to ring her call button, even though she knew how busy the nursing staff was. The nurse who came soothed her through the worst of the panic attack, then gave her a Valium from her own private stash.

Izzy ends the call. 'Dana's team has found over a dozen unmarked jars in the Harris bathroom. He thinks . . .' She clears her throat. 'There's really no way to say this except to say it. He thinks they may have been using human fat as a kind of lotion. Perhaps hoping to soothe their various aches and pains.'

'They thought it worked,' Holly says. *And for all I know, maybe it did. At least for awhile. Human nature being what it is.*

'Tell us everything, Holly,' Izzy says. 'Start to finish.'

Holly does, starting with Penny's first call. It takes over an hour. She only has one case of the shakes – when talking about how, as Emily was trying to put a bullet in her, she felt like a china figurine. She has to stop then to get control of herself. Izzy's partner, Washburn, asks her if she wants a break. Holly says no, she wants to finish, and she does.

'I knew the gun was empty after five, Bill told me I mustn't ever load the chamber under the hammer. She put the muzzle in the middle of my forehead. I let her because I wanted to see the expression on her face when she pulled the trigger and nothing happened. Her surprise was quite gratifying. Once I saw it, I reached through the bars, grabbed her head, and broke her fracking neck.'

It's Pete who breaks the silence, with one word. '*Good.*'

Tantleff clears his throat. 'According to you, there were at least four victims. Five, if you count Ortega.'

'*Castro*,' Barbara says, sounding indignant. 'Jorge Castro. I found Freddy Martin's Facebook page. He was Castro's partner, and he was convinced—'

'You have no standing in this case,' Tantleff says, 'so I'm asking you, with all due respect, to butt out.'

'*You* butt out,' Holly says. 'Let her talk.'

Tantleff huffs but doesn't protest. Barbara goes on.

'Mr Martin has been convinced all along that Mr Castro was murdered. He says Castro had relatives in Dayton, in Nogales, El Paso, and Mexico City. He's never gotten in touch with any of them and Martin says he would have.'

'He was their first,' Holly says. 'I'm sure of it. But speaking of relatives, what about those of the others?' She thinks Ellen Craslow's Georgia kin won't care much one way or the other, but Imani at the trailer park will want to know. Bonnie's father will want to know as well as her mother. But it's Vera Steinman she thinks of mostly, a woman who now has every excuse to drink and pill herself to death.

'No one's been informed,' George Washburn says. 'Not yet.' He nods at Tantleff. 'It's his case, in tandem with the Chief of Police.'

Tantleff heaves a longsuffering sigh. 'We'll give the investigation teams as much time as we can, but we can't count on keeping this contained for very long. Someone will talk. There's a press conference in my near future that I don't look forward to.'

'But you'll tell next-of-kin first,' Holly says. Almost insists.

Izzy answers before Tantleff can. 'Of course. Starting with Penny Dahl.'

Jerome speaks up, and Holly thinks he may also be thinking of Peter Steinman's mother. 'Can you at least keep the cannibalism part out of it?'

Izzy Jaynes puts her hands to her temples, as if trying to suppress a headache. 'No. There'll be a private grand jury, but this will come out anyway. It's too explosive to be kept secret. The relatives need to know before they see it in *Inside* fucking *View*.'

The meeting ends shortly thereafter. Holly is exhausted. She goes back to her rare-as-hen's-teeth private room, closes the door, gets into bed, and cries herself to sleep. She dreams of Emily Harris putting the barrel of Bill's pistol to her forehead and saying, 'I loaded the last chamber, you nosy bitch. The joke's on you.'

2

A nurse – not the one who gave her the Valium – wakes her at quarter past two that afternoon and says, 'Detective Jaynes called the nurses' station. She says she needs you.' She hands Holly a cell phone and a disinfecting wipe.

'I'm in the hospital chapel,' Izzy says. 'Can you come down?'

Holly wheelchairs to the elevator. On the second floor she follows the signs to Kiner's nondenominational chapel. It's empty except for Izzy, who is sitting in a front row pew. Held loosely in one hand is a set of rosary beads.

Holly stops next to her. 'You told Penny?'

'Roger that.' Izzy's eyes are red and puffy.

'I'm guessing it didn't go so well?'

Izzy turns and gives Holly a look of such unhappiness that Holly can barely stand to look back. But she does. She has to, because Izzy did the dirty job Holly should have done herself. 'How the fuck do you *think* it went?'

Holly says nothing, and after a few seconds Izzy takes Holly's hand. 'This case has taught me a lesson, Gibney. Just when you think you've seen the worst human beings have to offer, you find out you're wrong.

There's no end to evil. I took Stella Randolph with me. I knew I needed help with this one, and she's the department's mental health counselor. She talks to cops after officer-involved shootings. Other stuff, too.'

'You told Penny that Bonnie was dead, and—?'

'And then I told her *why* Bonnie was dead. What they did to her. I tried to be euphemistic . . . I think that's the word . . . but she knew what I was talking about. Or what I was trying *not* to talk about. She just sat there for a moment with her hands clasped in her lap, looking at me. Like a woman attending a really interesting lecture. Then she started screaming. Stella tried to hug her and Dahl pushed her away so hard that Stella tripped over a hassock and fell on the floor. Dahl started to claw at her face. Didn't break the skin – she would've if her nails had been longer – but left big red marks all down her cheeks. I wrapped her up in a bearhug to stop her doing that, but she went on screaming. At last she calmed down a little, or maybe she was just exhausted, but I'll remember that screaming for the rest of my life. It's one thing to bring somebody news of a death, I must have done it two dozen times, but the rest of it . . . Holly, do you think they were conscious when they were killed?'

'I don't know.' *And don't want to.* 'Did she say anything about . . . me?'

'Yes. That she never wants to see you again.'

3

There's a double row of houses that look deserted in the blaring afternoon sun. No one is moving on the cracked sidewalks. Jerome thinks Sycamore Street (where there are no sycamores) looks like a movie set that's been used but not struck yet. Vera Steinman's old Chevy is in the same place as when he last visited, with its bumper sticker reading WHAT WOULD SCOOBY DO? Jerome wishes *he* knew what to do, or what to say.

Maybe, he thinks, *she won't be home.* The car suggests she is, but for all he knows, the car no longer runs and Peter Steinman's deep-dish drunk of a mother may have no license to drive.

I should get out of here, he thinks. *Just get away while I still have a chance.*

He knocks on the door instead. He's sure of one thing: assuming she doesn't just slam the door on him, he must look her straight in the face and tell the best, most sincere lie of his life.

The door opens. Vera hasn't dressed up for him because she didn't know he was coming, but she looks perfectly okay in her white slacks and shell top. She looks sober, too . . . but of course she looked sober the last time he was here.

'Oh my. It's Jerome, right?'

'Yes. Jerome Robinson.'

'I don't remember much about the last time you were here, but I remember the doctor saying "That kid saved your life."'

He doesn't offer his elbow but puts out his hand. She shakes it firmly.

'I see by your face that you're not here with good news, Jerome.'

'No, ma'am. I'm not. I came because I didn't want you to hear it from anyone else.'

'Because we have a connection, don't we?' She sounds perfectly calm, but her face is waxy pale. 'Like it or not, we do.'

'Yes, ma'am, I guess that's true.'

'No bad news on the stoop. Come in. And call me Vera, for God's sake.'

He comes in. She closes the door. The air conditioner is still laboring. The living room is still a bit shabby but neat and clean.

'In case you're wondering, I'm sober. I don't know how long that will last, but I have resumed going to meetings. Three so far. And I went to my sponsor, prepared to grovel. I found it wasn't necessary, which was a great relief. Is he dead? Is Peter dead?'

'Yes. I'm very, very sorry, Vera.'

'Was it about sex? Some twisted sex thing?'

'No.'

'Who killed him?'

'An old couple. Rodney and Emily Harris. They killed four others that we know of. You'll be informed by the police. You can tell them I was here first. Say I wanted to be the one, because . . . well . . .'

'Because you saved my life. Because we have that connection.' Still perfectly calm, but her eyes have filled with tears. 'Yes. Yes. Yes.'

She reaches behind herself, finds the arm of the chair in front of the television, and sits down. Only it's more of a fall.

Jerome kneels in front of her like a suitor about to propose marriage. He takes her hands, which are dead cold. None of this was planned, he's just winging it. Did she say they had a connection? It's true. He knows that much. He feels that much. His voice is steady, and thank God for that.

'The Harrises were insane. Stuff will come out about what they did, bad stuff, but you need to know one thing.' It's time for the lie, and it might not even *be* a lie, because he doesn't know. 'It was quick. Whatever happened to his body . . . whatever they did . . . happened afterward. He was gone by then.'

'To wherever we go.'

'Yes. To wherever we go.'

'He didn't suffer?'

'No.'

Her hands tighten on his. 'Do you swear to that?'

'Yes.'

'May your mother die and go to hell if you're lying?'

'Yes.'

'How do you know?'

'Pathologist's report.'

Her hands loosen. 'I need a drink.'

'I'm sure you do, but don't take one. Honor your son.'

Vera gives a shaky laugh. 'Honor my *son*? Do you hear yourself?'

'Yes. I hear myself.'

'I need to call my sponsor. Will you stay with me until she comes?'

'Yes,' Jerome says. And he does.

August 4, 2021

Holly is at home watching a Netflix comedy without really seeing it, just marking time until she can take another pain pill (or she may double-dip), when her buzzer goes. It's Isabelle Jaynes, and she has company: Herbert Beale and another FBI man named Curtis Rogan. Rogan, a profiler who specializes in serial killers, flew in with the FBI team.

Izzy asks Holly if she's seen that day's paper. Holly read the headline on her iPad – **WERE THEY CANNIBALS**? – and that's enough for her. 'I guess the DA will have to have that press conference now.'

'He and Chief Murphy are set for noon. The coverage won't just be local, either. I have to believe Randall Murphy is thanking his lucky stars that he was still in Minneapolis when all of them except Bonnie Dahl were taken. The reason we're here is because of what our forensics guys and the FBI team found in the Harris bedroom closet.'

'What?' Thinking, *what now?*

'Diaries,' Herbert Beale says. 'Hers. She started keeping them in October of 2012, shortly before the murder of Jorge Luis Castro. Agent Rogan here has been studying them.'

'I've got a long way to go,' Rogan says. 'There's over a thousand pages.' He's a soft-spoken man with short, thinning hair and rimless spectacles. 'Fascinating stuff.'

'*Terrifying* stuff,' Izzy says. 'I've read enough to say that while they were both crazy, she was the crazier of the two. By far.'

'I think further study will bear that out,' Rogan says. 'I don't believe

Rodney Harris would have done much more than . . . what's the word? Fume, perhaps? He wouldn't have done much more than fume at how hidebound his colleagues were and how irrational the taboo was against eating human flesh.'

'She talked him into the first one, didn't she?' Holly says. 'She pitched him on using Castro as a way for her husband to go from the theoretical to the practical. Conception to execution. Because she disliked Castro.'

'*Disliked?*' Izzy says, and laughs. 'Oh, Holly, you have no idea. She *hated* him. And not just him – she had plenty of hate to go around. Beneath that well-groomed and pleasantly authoritative surface, Emily Harris was a balls-to-the-wall psychotic. Let me show you an example of the Ms Hyde that was underneath Professor Jekyll.'

She turns her iPad to Holly. On the screen is a photo of a diary page. Written over and over again, like a bad child who has to write *I will not throw spitballs in class*, is this: *I HATE THAT SPIC I HATE THAT FUCKING SPIC I HATE THAT FAGGOT SPIC I HATE THAT BUTT-PUNCHING FAGGOT SPIC . . .* and so on.

'Four more pages of just that,' Izzy says.

Rogan says, 'In these diaries is an Emily Harris who never attended the English Department meetings. And I'm just getting started.'

'Here's another one,' Izzy says. She swipes to a new photo. On this page of her diary, Emily has written the n-word over and over, in big, screaming capitals. There are other pejoratives, as well.

'We're thinking she kept her hate-diaries even from her husband,' Herbert Beale says, 'but we'll never know for sure unless she says so in here.'

'This stuff is gold,' Rogan says.

'I'd use another word for it,' Holly says.

'I mean from a psychological standpoint. One thing seems clear. She participated in the . . . the *ingestion* of Mr Castro to please her husband. He insisted on it. But she speaks of it as a miracle cure for her back and for her husband's arthritis. There were other imagined benefits, as well, including increased brainpower. Some of this stuff is like high-cable infomercials in hell. Eventually, though, the effects began to wear off.'

'So they did it again,' Holly says flatly. 'And again.'

'They should have been caught after Castro,' Izzy says. 'And if not after him, after Dressler. The wheelchair ploy was clever enough, and they did some background work, but their attempts to clean up afterward were strictly slipshod.'

'They were old,' Holly says quietly. 'No one expects old people to be serial killers. Let alone cannibals.'

Izzy says, 'If not for you, Holly, they'd probably still be living in that house and eating their hellish meals. "Oh," people would say, "he's a little dotty and she's a little crotchety, but they're basically all right."'

'Barbara figured it out quicker than I did.'

'Some truth to that, but you did the spadework.'

'And her friend helped,' Holly says. 'Olivia Kingsbury. The old poet. I think she was the one who tied it together for Barbara.'

Beale looks at Rogan and gives him a nod. They stand up. 'You're going to be besieged by the press, Ms Gibney.'

'It won't be the first time.' Then, with no idea she's going to say it until the words pop out of her mouth: 'The nuts are complimentary.'

Beale and Rogan look puzzled, but Izzy laughs and Holly joins her. It feels good to laugh. Damn good.

August 18, 2021

There's a balcony outside Holly's apartment, just big enough for two chairs and a small table. At eleven o'clock on this Wednesday morning she's sitting out there, having a cup of coffee. She'd like to have a cigarette to go with it, but the urge is fading. It's been over three weeks since her last one, and with God's grace there will never be another. It's a warm morning, but not oppressive; the heatwave that blanketed the city for most of July and the first two weeks of August seems to have broken.

Ordinarily Holly would be in the office at this hour, dressed in one of her many pantsuits and wearing light makeup, but this morning – and most other mornings since her enforced twenty-four-hour stay in Kiner – she's in her pajamas and slippers. According to the answering machine and the website, the office is closed for staff vacations and will re-open on September 6th. In truth, Holly's not sure Finders Keepers will ever re-open.

Pete, fully recovered, is visiting his son and daughter-in-law in Saginaw. He'll be back at the end of the month, but has started to talk about full retirement. He has his pension from the PD, and after twenty-five years on the job it's a good one. If that's his decision, Holly will be happy to add a very decent severance package. If she decides to sell the business (which she could, and for a good price), it will be more than decent.

As for herself, she is a new millionaire who can afford a mai-tai in any of the city's priciest watering holes. In fact, she could *buy* a pricey watering hole, if she desired. Which she doesn't. The thought of retiring and living on the money her mother and uncle hid from her has occurred to her frequently in the weeks following her time in the Harrises' basement cage.

She has told herself she's still too young to retire, and it's probably true. She has told herself that she wouldn't know what to do with herself, and that's probably also true. But she keeps thinking of what Izzy Jaynes said that day in the chapel, after telling Penny Dahl that, euphemisms aside, her daughter had not only been killed, she had been eaten. The best parts of her, at least; the rest finished up as red paste and bone fragments in a plastic bag at the end of a woodchipper's hose.

Just when you think you've seen the worst human beings have to offer, you find out you're wrong, Izzy said. Then added the kicker: *There's no end to evil.*

Holly supposes she already knew that, and better than Izzy. The outsider masquerading as Terry Maitland was evil. So was the one masquerading as Chet Ondowsky. The same was true of Brady Hartsfield, who found a way to go on doing dirt (Bill's phrase) even after he should have been rendered harmless. Rendered that way by Holly herself.

But Roddy and Emily Harris were worse.

Why? Because there was nothing supernatural about them. Because you couldn't say their evil came from outside, and comfort yourself with the idea that if there were malign outside forces, there were probably good ones, as well. The Harrises' evil was both prosaic and outlandish, like a crazy mother putting her baby in a microwave oven because he won't stop crying, or a child of twelve going on a shooting rampage and killing half a dozen of his classmates.

Holly isn't sure she wants to revisit a world capable of holding people like Rodney. Or like Emily, who was even worse: more calculating and at the same time much, much crazier.

Some things have come clear, partly as a result of Emily's diaries. They now understand why the Steinman boy came so close on the heels of Ellen Craslow. Ellen was a vegan and refused to eat the liver (referred to in the diaries as THG, standing for the holy grail). She went on refusing even when she was dying of thirst. In the end, none of the others held out. Holly wasn't sure she could have, but Ellen did, and God bless her for it. Rodney ended up shooting her like a recalcitrant steer. Following Ellen's death, Emily filled pages with vituperative rage; *jungle bunny lesbo cunt* was the least of it.

They even know the fake name Emily used at the trailer park: Dickinson, as in Emily.

Holly had to keep reminding herself that the woman who wrote all those vile things had been a respected faculty member, a winner of awards, a patron of the Reynolds Library, and an influential member of the English Department even after her retirement. In 2004 she had received a plaque announcing her as the city's Woman of the Year. There was a banquet at which Emily spoke of women's empowerment.

Izzy had told her something else: the gun Roddy used to shoot Ellen Craslow was a Ruger Security-9, with an extended fifteen-round clip. If Emily had gotten that one instead of Bill's revolver, she would have had ten more chances to finish Holly . . . who could only have dodged for so long in that cage.

'But it was upstairs,' Izzy said, 'and she had a broken arm as well as a bad back. Lucky for you.'

Yes, lucky for her. Lucky Holly Gibney, who had not only survived but was now a millionaire. She could close up shop and move on to another phase of her life. One where people like the Harrises would only be cable news fodder, which could be muted or turned off in favor of a romcom.

She hears her phone ring – her personal, not the office line. The office line had rung a lot in the wake of Holly's new – or renewed – celebrity, but now the calls have thankfully tapered off. She gets up and goes into her office, carrying her coffee cup. The photo on her phone's screen is Barbara Robinson.

'Hi, Barbara. How's it going?'

Silence, but Holly can hear Barbara's breathing, and feels a stab of alarm. 'Barb? Are you okay?'

'Yes . . . yes. Just stunned. Mom and Dad aren't here, and Jerome—'

'In New York again, I know.'

'So I called you. I had to call somebody.'

'What happened?'

'I won.'

'Won what?'

'The Penley. The Penley Prize. Random House is going to publish *Stitching the Sky Closed.*' Now that Barbara has passed on her news, she begins to cry. 'I'm going to dedicate it to Olivia. God, I wish she were alive to know.'

'Barbara, that's so wonderful. There's a cash award, too, right?'

'Twenty-five thousand dollars. But it will be the advance against royalties, that's what the email I got said, and poetry books never sell many copies.'

'Don't tell that to Amanda Gorman,' Holly says.

Barbara laughs even though she's still crying. 'Not the same thing. Her poems, like the one she read at the Inauguration, are optimistic. Mine are . . . well . . .'

'Different,' Holly says.

Barbara has given her some of them to read, and Holly knows them for what they are: a kind of coping mechanism. An effort for Barbara to reconcile her good and generous heart with the horror she experienced in an elevator the previous year. The horror of Chet Ondowsky. Not to mention the horror of finding her friend in a cage with her face smeared in blood and two dead bodies nearby.

Holly has seen more, experienced more – she was, after all, *in* that cage – and has no poetry as a safety valve; the best she ever managed was (let's face it) pretty bad. But she *has* started enjoying horror movies again, and those harmless scares might be a start. She knows some people would consider that perverse, but it really isn't.

'You have to call Jerome,' Holly says. 'First Jerome, then your folks.'

'Yes, right away. But I'm glad I talked to you first.'

'I'm pleased that you did.' More than pleased, actually.

'Do you know anything more? About . . . the business?'

That's what Barbara calls it these days: *the business.*

'No. If you're talking about their . . . I don't know . . . their *descent*, we may never know it all. It's good we were able to stop them when we did—'

'*You*,' Barbara says. '*You* stopped them.'

Holly knows there were a lot of people involved, from Keisha Stone to Emilio Herrera at the Jet Mart, but doesn't say so.

'In the end, it's probably pretty prosaic,' she says. 'They stepped over a line, that's all, which made it easier the next time. And the placebo effect played a part. His mind was crumbling, and in a way, hers was, too. They would have been caught eventually, but probably not before they did it again. Maybe more than once. Serial killers start to speed up, and it was happening to them. Let's just say all's well that ends well . . . as well as could be, maybe.'

It would certainly be nice to think so, she thinks.

'I'd rather talk about your big prize. Are you the youngest ever to win it?'

'Yes, by six years! The letter said they found my essay refreshing. Can you believe that shit?'

'Yes. Barb, I can believe it. And I'm so happy for you. Now go on and make the rest of your calls.'

'I will. I love you, Holly.'

'I love you, too,' Holly says. 'So much.'

She puts the phone back on its charger and heads to the kitchen to refresh her coffee. Before she can get there, the office line starts ringing. She hasn't answered that one since the end of July, just let the phone robot pick up, or the service. Most of the calls have been requests for interviews, several from tabloids with big money attached. She listens to the messages but has answered none of them. She doesn't need their money.

Now she stands by her desk, looking at the office phone. Five rings and it will go to the robot. It's already on number three.

Just when you think you've seen the worst human beings have to offer, Holly thinks, and *There's no end to evil.*

This is the call, she thinks. *This is the one I've been waiting for.*

She can pick it up and go on with the business of investigating. That means touching evil, of which there is no end. Or she can let it go to voicemail, and if she does that, she's not just blue-skying the idea of retirement; she really means to pull the pin and live on her riches.

Four rings.

She asks herself what Bill Hodges would do. But there's a more important question – what would Bill want *her* to do?

Halfway through the fifth ring, she picks up the phone.

'Hello, this is Holly Gibney. How can I help?'

August 14, 2021–June 2, 2022

Author's Note

Although *Holly* closely follows the events of the short novel *If It Bleeds* in the collection of the same name, Constant Readers and students of current events may notice there's at least one very large continuity lapse. Although Covid plays a big part in *Holly* – in fact, several story points depend on it – there's no mention of the pandemic in *If It Bleeds*, even though December of 2020, the time period in which *Bleeds* is set, was a terrible month for this disease in America, with at least 65,000 reported deaths.

The reason is simple: when I wrote *If It Bleeds* in 2019, Covid wasn't on the radar. I hate it when real events screw with my fiction, but that happens from time to time. I'd change *If It Bleeds* if I could, but that would entail rewriting the entire story, and as we used to say in my marathon Hearts games back in college, if it's laid, it's played. I just wanted you to know I'm aware of the glitch.

A considerable portion of the American population – not a majority, I'm relieved to say – are anti-vaccination. These folks may think the Covid through-line in *Holly* is preachy (the term for this sort of fiction, which I sort of love, is 'soapboxing'). That's not the case. I think fiction is most believable when it coexists with real-world events, real-world individuals, even brand names. Holly's mother has died of Covid, and Holly herself is a bit of a hypochondriac. It seemed natural to me that she would hold strong opinions about Covid and take every precaution (cigarettes excepted). It's true that my opinions match hers on the subject, but I like to think that if I had chosen an anti-vaccination character as either my protagonist or as an important supporting character, I would give a fair representation of those views.

Which brings me to Rodney Harris. He's a fine example of a character whose views most certainly don't match my own. Every fact and historical anecdote about cannibalism that Roddy presents happens to be true. It's his conclusions that are false. The idea that eating human liver can cure Alzheimer's, for example, is utter bullshit. Not that one can blame Rodney for cherry-picking his data; the man is clearly crazy as a loon. And now that I think of it, that comparison is an insult to loons.

My research, as always, was done by the wonderful Robin Furth. She gave me a complete tutorial on cannibalism, but that was just where her contributions started. She also went back to the *Mr Mercedes* trilogy and created a complete timeline for Holly Gibney. That necessitated quite a bit of rewriting on my part, but it also saved me from any number of howlers. I think I did an okay job, with one exception: Uncle Henry apparently had kids, who have been excluded from this narrative. Robin is my Goddess of Research. Please give her the credit for the stuff that's right. For the stuff that's wrong, I get the blame.

For help with Latin (mine is rusty), I need to thank Tim Ingram and Peter Jones of Classics for All, a charity that supports the teaching of many classical subjects. Find them on Facebook or with Google.

My longtime agent and friend, Charles 'Chuck' Verrill, died early in 2022. The loss I felt at his passing was in some measure alleviated by the speed with which his longtime business partner, Liz Darhansoff, stepped in to handle the book- and story-related matters so I could go on making shit up, which is what I do best. In spite of her own deep grief, Liz never missed a beat. I'd be lost without her, and that goes for her sterling associates in the agency, Michele Mortimer and Eric Amling. Big thanks.

Chris Lotts is my foreign rights man, and is chiefly responsible for getting my books known around the world. He's also a great guy.

Rand Holston, also a great guy, fields requests for movie and TV rights. I've known him for over forty years and consider him one of my friends as well as a business partner.

Nan Graham edited the book. Her suggested changes almost always worked, and her suggested cuts – although painful – picked the story up whenever it lagged or went off on a tangent. They say the devil is in the details, but when it comes to *my* details, Nan has always been an angel. It's nice to have such a pro on my team.

Thanks to Molly, aka the Thing of Evil, who always keeps me amused when my spirits sag.

Most thanks of all to my wife, the novelist Tabitha King, who supports me in every way. I couldn't ask for a better life's companion. It was Tabby who talked me through the short section of this book that was hardest for me to write: Jerome's final conversation with Vera Steinman. I love you, kiddo.

One final thing before I let you go. I had to write this book to write one scene, which I saw clearly in my mind: Holly attending her mother's Zoom funeral. I didn't have a story to go with it, which was unfortunate, but I kept my feelers out because I've loved Holly from the first and wanted to be with her again. Then one day I read a newspaper story about an honor killing. I didn't think that could be my story, but I loved the headline, which was something like this: EVERYONE THOUGHT THEY WERE A SWEET OLD COUPLE UNTIL THE BODIES BEGAN TURNING UP IN THE BACKYARD.

Killer old folks, I thought. *That's my story*. I wrote it, and now you've read it. I hope you enjoyed it. And, as always, thank you for coming to another dark place with me.

Stephen King